Sugar and spice and everything sexy make the perfect recipe for romance in this brand-new series by Peggy Jaeger. Look for exclusive recipes in each book!

Kandy Laine built her wildly popular food empire the old-fashioned way—starting with the basic ingredients of her grandmother's recipes and flavoring it all with her particular brand of sweet spice. From her cookbooks to her hit TV show, Kandy is a kitchen queen—and suddenly someone is determined to poison her cup. With odd accidents and threatening messages piling up, strong-willed Kandy can't protest when her team hires someone to keep her safe—but she can't deny that the man for the job looks delicious. . .

Josh Keane is a private investigator, not a bodyguard. But with one eyeful of Kandy's ebony curls and dimpled smile, he's signing on to uncover who's cooking up trouble for the gorgeous chef. As the attraction between them starts to simmer, it's not easy to keep his mind on the job, but when the strange distractions turn to true danger, he'll stop at nothing to keep Kandy safe—and show her that a future together is on the menu. . .

Books by Peggy Jaeger

Will Cook for Love
Cooking with Kandy

Published by Kensington Publishing Corporation

Cooking with Kandy

Will Cook for Love

Peggy Jaeger

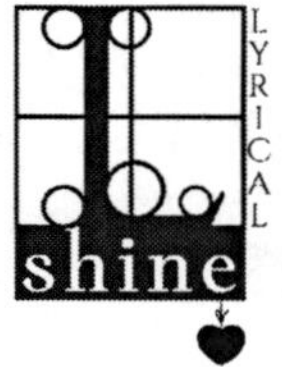

LYRICAL SHINE
Kensington Publishing Corp.
www.kensingtonbooks.com

Lyrical Press books are published by
Kensington Publishing Corp.
119 West 40th Street
New York, NY 10018

All Kensington titles, imprints, and distributed lines are available at special quantity discounts for bulk purchases for sales promotion, premiums, fund-raising, and educational or institutional use.

Special book excerpts or customized printings can also be created to fit specific needs. For details, write or phone the office of the Kensington Special Sales Manager:
Kensington Publishing Corp.
119 West 40th Street
New York, NY 10018
Attn. Special Sales Department. Phone: 1-800-221-2647.

First Electronic Edition: April 2017
eISBN-13: 978-1-5161-0107-8
eISBN-10: 1-5161-0107-3

First Print Edition: April 2017
ISBN-13: 978-1-5161-0110-8
ISBN-10: 1-5161-0110-3

Printed in the United States of America

For Kathleen Phillips.

Sister-in-law. Matron of honor. Godmother to my baby girl. Sister, wife, daughter, friend, nurse. You are so many things to so many people, but to me, you are simply my sister from another mother. I'm so glad you are part of my life. . .

This one's for you.

Acknowledgements

No book writes itself. From thought to page to publication, it takes a group of well-meaning, dedicated, and involved people to get that story told and have it be the best it can be, so there are a few people who need a shoutout from me for helping to get *Cooking with Kandy* into the hands of readers.

First and foremost, Erin Jaeger for being my first—and the most loved—of my editors and readers. Your mastery of the written and spoken word is a delight to experience and I am so happy you are part of "my team."

To the lovely, talented, and kind women of the New Hampshire chapter of RWA, your acceptance of me and all my quirks has given me the courage to find my writing voice and to pursue my lifelong dream with no regrets or worries about failure. You are truly friends and comrades in my arms.

A huge thank you to Steven Zacharius and the staff of Kensington/Lyrical for putting my dream into reality.

Last and by no means at all least, my Kensington Editor Esi Sogah for believing in me, for having infinitesimal patience, and for always being there when I had a question or concern. Your insights, suggestions, and guidance have made this daunting process of publication so much easier to navigate through. You are a kindred spirit in your love of the performing arts and I so enjoy living vicariously through your theater attendance!

Thank you all,
Peggy

Chapter One

"Hold on to your forks, folks, because today I'm making one of Grandma Sophie's to-die-for layer cakes, guaranteed to make your sweet tooth tingle." Kandy Laine aimed a wide, dimpled grin at the television camera.

The moment her sexy, heart-stopping smile flashed, Josh Keane knew he was in trouble.

Serious trouble.

He stood on the sidelines of the studio kitchen set, where he'd been instructed to wait, visitor badge secured to his jacket, and watched the hostess of EBC's most popular food show, *Cooking with Kandy*, film her season premiere.

"She'd discovered the benefit of adding pudding to the batter to increase the cake's moisture content decades before any of the big commercial baking companies did," Kandy told the camera.

Josh ran a hand through his thick, black hair and blew out a breath. From his concealed vantage point behind the studio equipment, he was impressed by the practiced ease with which she moved around the set kitchen, talking nonstop, explaining the details of the recipe she was preparing without the use of cue cards or even a glance at the teleprompter.

A little kick of awareness ricocheted through his midsection every time she glanced up, looked into the camera, and spoke. It was as intimate as if she were speaking to him and no one else.

Kandy lifted the baking tins from the cooling rack and turned them upside down to deliver two perfect cake rounds. "Perfection," she said, adding with a chuckle, "Grandma sure knew what she was talking about."

After reading the bio her assistant had faxed to him the night before, Josh had gone to bed, his dreams filled with visions of a tiny cherub-faced angel soaring around a kitchen.

One look at Kandy Laine in the flesh knocked that ethereal vision to hell.

At five-foot-nine in flats, most of it was leg packed into second-skin jeans. Jet-black curls tumbled down the middle of her back, secured from her face by a flaming red headband.

And that *face*.

Heart-shaped, its peak descended almost to the middle of a smooth, flawless forehead. Arched eyebrows and thick eyelashes framed her eyes, the outer corners tipped upward at a slight angle, their color a blue that rivaled a pale sky.

"Make sure you don't overbeat the frosting," Kandy instructed in a throaty voice made for seduction. "If you do, you'll break it down and your cake will have a flat, metallic taste. Another of Grandma's helpful hints," she added with a wink and a devilish grin.

When her dimples emerged, that little kick tackled his insides again.

Maybe he should just forget this whole thing. Leave now while no one was looking.

"Mr. Keane?"

Josh took a deep breath and turned to the serious-faced blonde in wire-framed glasses who'd appeared next to him.

"I'm Stacy Peters. Max's daughter? I'm the one who contacted you."

Josh extended his hand to her outstretched one.

"You got my fax?"

He nodded. "I read through it last night. I've got to tell you, Miss Peters, bodyguard's not my usual gig. Investigations are more my speed."

"I realize that, but my dad told me how you and your partner helped his firm with a securities investigation last spring. He's a very good judge of character and he claims you're the best at what you do, so please, hear me out?"

Resigned, Josh swept his gaze back to the set. The hostess was busy assembling the now-cooled cake.

"Come with me. I'll explain everything." She led him from the back of the studio set down a long hallway, and into a room.

"This is my office."

He opened the bottom button on his jacket and sat in the cushioned chair she indicated. The room was large, windowless, and crammed with books and furniture.

"First, I'll be honest." She sat behind a desk cluttered with paper, various magazines, and two computer monitors. "Kandy is totally opposed to the idea of a bodyguard."

Great. "Won't make the job easy."

"I know, but she's just being stubborn. She doesn't believe there's anything to be concerned about."

"And you do?"

She nodded. "Kandy's just too obstinate to accept it. She refuses to think someone is out to harm her. Her exact words on the subject are 'why would anyone?'"

Josh leaned back in the chair and crossed one leg over the other. "She doesn't feel there's a problem, then?"

"I think she doesn't want to *believe* there is, which is different. But unusual things have happened and I'm worried."

"Why don't you start at the beginning, take me through everything, so I can get a better picture of your concerns."

Stacy leaned forward, elbows resting on her desk. "Two months ago we were on a working vacation in Los Angeles."

"Who's 'we'?"

"Kandy, myself, Reva—her agent—and Gemma, one of Kandy's sisters." She ticked the names off on her fingers. "We had car trouble one night while on the way to dinner. Kandy was driving, which she does almost like a NASCAR pro. The brakes gave out when we came around a curve. The car picked up speed and, by the grace of God and Kandy's skills, we managed not to crash. But it was a scary few minutes."

"Did you have the car inspected?"

"Yes. The brake line had a nick. Not all the way through, but enough so the stress of driving caused the fluid to leach out."

"Was there a police investigation?"

"Minimal. Since the car was a rental, the cops just cited the company for poorly maintaining it."

He shrugged. "Sounds negligent, but plausible."

"Kandy thought so, too. The next thing happened when we got home. Kandy went back to her condo and found the door unlocked."

"Didn't she think that was unusual?"

"Well, yeah, but after the fact she told me she thought the housekeeper might have forgotten to lock up when she left."

"Doesn't say a lot for the housekeeper," Josh said. "Was anything missing?"

"Not missing, no." She pushed her glasses up higher on her nose. "But there was something wrong. At first Kandy didn't realize it. She was so beat from the trip and the time difference that she just crashed. The next morning, she discovered her home answering machine had been unplugged from the wall. Kandy is old-fashioned in some ways and the answering machine was Grandma's, so she uses it for family members to leave her messages instead of on her cell. Then, when it was time to get dressed, she noticed something was off in her closet."

"Off, how?"

Stacy sighed and swiped at her bangs. "You have to know Kandy to understand this. She's the most organized and meticulous person on the planet. She can tell you down to the penny how much is in her checking account. She knows what's missing from her pantry when she needs to shop, and she never uses a list. All of her shoes are lined up according to color and heel height."

Josh whistled. "Sounds obsessive."

"Being obsessive's gotten her where she is. Anyway, some of the things in her closet weren't in the places they should have been. Spring blouses in the fall section, skirts with pants, things out of order. Nothing major, just items out of place."

"How did she explain it?"

"Well, again, she thought the housekeeper might have riffled through them. But she couldn't come up with a reason why."

"Did she confront the woman?"

"No," she said, lips pressed tightly together. Josh could feel her displeasure from across the room. "Kandy refused to. Claimed she probably did it herself. Blamed it on the stress of the television season starting and the new book coming out at the same time."

"So she brushed it off." Josh thought for a moment. "Does anyone aside from the housekeeper have a key?"

"I do."

"Where do you keep it?"

She opened the bottom drawer of her desk and took out a key chain with a number of keys. Holding it up, she jiggled it a few times and said, "Everyone in my family has at one time or another given me a spare key to something. Houses, cars, condos. I keep them here in case of an emergency, or if someone ever forgets theirs. I don't even know which one belongs to which person."

Josh grinned. "You're the responsible one in the family, aren't you?"

She didn't return the smile. Instead, she threw the keys back into the drawer and pushed it closed.

"I wanted to confront the housekeeper, but Kandy wouldn't let me. Then, her wallet went missing."

"Stolen?"

"I thought so. Kandy assumed—again–she'd misplaced it."

"Did she file a theft report?"

"She didn't want to, but I forced her hand. We had to change all her credit cards, pin numbers, etc." She sat back and blew out a breath. "What a hassle it was. A few days later, the wallet showed up in her office closet."

"So she *had* misplaced it."

Stacy stared at him.

"Except you don't think so, do you?" he added.

"No. Kandy is methodical, like I said, and it takes a lot to distract her, so I find it hard to imagine she took her wallet out and put it in her closet without thinking."

Josh nodded. "Were there any charges on the credit cards when it went missing?"

"No."

"If it had been stolen you'd expect there would be."

Stacy took a breath then said, "I know. Anyway, the latest thing to happen is the reason I felt we finally needed to take action. About a week ago, we were in preproduction for the season premiere. Kandy was going over some blocking with the director—"

"Blocking?" He leaned forward and rested his elbows on his knees, folding his hands together.

"It's when they decide where to put the cameras while Kandy's moving around the kitchen, so every shot is perfect."

"Got it."

"Cort Mason, our director, and Kandy were standing at the kitchen island, going over some of the directions, when a spotlight fell from the rafter column."

"Was anyone hurt?"

"No. Cort heard the cable snapping, and looked up just as the light started to disengage. He pushed them both out of the way. The light weighs more than two hundred pounds. They could have been crushed to death."

"What did you do about it?"

"Cort screamed about notifying the network; I wanted to call the police. But Kandy nixed both ideas without even a consideration."

"Why?"

"When we asked the studio set manager and the lighting grip, both said they hadn't checked the lights in a while, so we couldn't know for sure if it had been tampered with or had just started to give from weight and age."

"Is that common?"

She shrugged. "In the past the crew has found a loose-fitting light during an inspection. Like I said, they're not given a great deal of thought unless a bulb burns out. When they did look at the connection after the fall, nothing seemed out of the ordinary. No cut lines or frayed wires."

Josh sat back and considered what she'd told him.

"So, to be clear, you don't think these are just arbitrary accidents or coincidences. You think someone is bothering her, intentionally trying to harm her?"

Stacy gnawed on her bottom lip again and nodded. "Yes."

"I have to ask, why? To what end would harming and harassing her serve?"

"I wish I knew. We could have been hurt if the car had crashed, and Kandy could have been severely injured if it weren't for Cort's quick thinking."

"But the clothes, the wallet," Josh said, "those seem more petty than harmful."

"I agree, it's weird. But I have this nagging thought something isn't right, and it makes me think she needs protecting."

"And I still disagree."

They both turned at the sound of the voice.

Standing in the open doorway, arms crossed at her chest, Kandy Laine regarded them with a look of annoyance. From twenty feet away and under harsh studio lights, she'd been beautiful. Up close and in person she was magnificent. Even with the thick theatrical makeup, her face was luminous.

"How long have you been standing there?" Stacy asked.

"Long enough." She came into the room, her hand extended. "I'm Kandy Laine."

He rose from the chair. "Josh Keane."

Years of practiced professionalism stopped him from showing any outward reaction when their hands met. But on the inside, it was like being targeted with a stun gun—quick, intense, heart-stopping. Raw, primal energy filtered through her long fingers into his.

One of her eyebrows arched a bit higher as she regarded him.

"Well, Mr. Keane, my cousin here seems to think I'm in need of your services. What, exactly, are they?"

He couldn't tell if she was serious or amused.

"I run a private investigations company along with a partner. We do corporate research, background checks, insurance fraud detection, things of that nature. Plus, I do a small amount of protection work when I find an assignment to my liking."

He watched her face as amusement won. Kandy's lips curled back and a bark of laughter jumped from her. The hearty, caustic sound was a stark contrast to the lovely woman standing before him.

"So I'm an assignment, am I?" Her grin lit the room in all four corners.

"Kandy," Stacy said. "Sit down and let's talk about this. Please."

Josh held a mental breath while she decided to stay or march out. He was pleased when she plopped down on the leather couch across from the desk.

Stacy rose, came around the desk, and sat next to her cousin. "Kan, I know you're against this, but you can't just keep disregarding the strange things that have been happening to you."

"Every one of them is explainable—"

Stacy raised her hand. "No. You just *wish* they were. Now, I asked Mr. Keane to come down here today to discuss the possibility of looking into these incidents. We need answers."

Kandy stared at her cousin for a few seconds and then turned her gaze to Josh.

He sensed the battle playing in her mind. From what he'd read in her bio coupled with the in-depth Internet search he'd done before coming to the studio, this was a woman used to calling the shots. To relinquish some control couldn't be an easy feat for her, by any means.

A moment later she sighed, and said, "Oh all right. If it will get you off my back and let me get back to my show, then fine. I'll go along with looking into everything, even though I think it's a huge waste of time. But I don't need a bodyguard. I won't have my life disrupted with someone following me around every second of the day."

"You don't have a choice in the matter," Stacy said.

"What?"

Stacy's gaze shot to Josh and then back to Kandy's irritated face. "Part of the package with hiring Mr. Keane is he'll provide protection for you until I'm satisfied it's not needed."

"Stacy, I will not live with someone constantly monitoring me." She jumped up from the couch, her voice rising like her body.

"You have to," Stacy said, keeping her tone calm and even. "When I told Reva what happened with the light fixture, she had her phone in her hand, ready to call the network. But we realized the bosses would have hired outside people to investigate and I knew you'd hate that even more, so we didn't. This way, with Mr. Keane working for us, you can have one-on-one protection from someone who'll be looking out for your best interest and not the network's."

"Stacy, I can't allow this—"

"If I may," Josh said.

Kandy's gaze held barely suppressed fury as she turned toward him. Her lips flattened and grew tight; he had to give her kudos for her self-control.

She gave him a curt nod. "Go ahead."

Josh had dealt with resistant clients before and measured his response. "What Miss Peters says makes a great deal of sense. I can understand you value your privacy, and I assure you, I'd be as unobtrusive as possible if I was with you. You could live your life as you usually do, no restrictions. Unless, of course, I found a need for them." When he saw the anger leap back across her face, he raised a hand. "Let me finish. You could go where you want. Do what you want. I'd be shadowing you, not limiting you. Nothing would have to change. It would be my job to see you'd maintain as normal a life as possible."

"My life isn't what anyone would term *normal*." She'd reined in her anger, her voice once again seductively low and calm. "I'm on the go from the minute I wake up, working fourteen-to sixteen-hour days most of the time. I have a national book tour starting in two weeks, plus I'm filming the new season. There are public appearances and television interview spots I'm scheduled to do. Go, go, go, all day, every day. You should know what you'd be setting yourself up for."

Josh relaxed for the first time since meeting her. "Don't worry about me. I'm used to working long hours, and I can take whatever schedule is thrown at me."

The embers banked in her eyes, replaced by what looked like a challenge. "It might be interesting to see if that's true, Mr. Keane."

"Josh is fine."

She nodded again. "Look. I came down to talk to you about tomorrow's schedule, but I've got to get back to the set now. We have another segment to shoot before we call it a day."

When she stood, Josh did as well. With a quick drag of her gaze from his feet to his head, she cocked an exquisite eyebrow, her lips pulling back in a question. "I have a hard time believing you could ever be unobtrusive."

Josh rocked back on his heels and shoved his hands in his pants pockets. "You'd be surprised."

A reluctant grin danced on her face.

After she left, Stacy let out a relieved sigh. "For a second I thought she'd pull rank on me and yank the plug on this whole idea."

"Would she?"

She shook her head. "Maybe, but probably not. Kandy's a maverick in heels when it comes to business." Softness moved into her eyes and voice. "But she's a total mush when it comes to family. She may not be concerned, but she doesn't want to see anyone else worried. Acquiescing like she did is typical. She'll do anything to make sure everyone is happy." She ran a hand through her hair.

"I have a few questions," Josh said.

"Okay."

"Has she been getting any negative fan mail lately?"

"Our cousin, Tricia Walters, is in charge of all the correspondence concerning Kandy, but she hasn't mentioned anything worrisome or out of the ordinary."

"How about on social media? Threatening tweets, something like that?"

"No. None."

"What about in her personal life?"

"Like what, for instance?"

"Is there a man in the picture?"

Stacy ran her tongue over her front teeth. "At present, no. But she was dating a guy a few months back who turned out to be a real piece of work."

"How so?"

"He was using her to make connections in the business."

"An actor?"

"No. He wanted to produce...direct." She flipped her hand in the air again. "I forget which. He claimed he had a project the network bigwigs would love and he was using Kandy as an entrée to float his idea to them."

Josh nodded and slipped his hands into his trouser pockets again. "A player."

Stacy's grin was fast. For the first time, he saw the family resemblance in the dimples and the light in her eyes. "For lack of a better word, yes. When Kandy found out about it, she dumped him cold."

"How'd he take it?"

Shrugging, she said, "Not well. He'd show up on set when we were filming and demand to speak to her. He'd call her cell and the office phone a dozen times a day. After a few weeks, though, he stopped."

"Why, when he'd been so persistent?"

The light in her eyes grew brighter, laughter flowing across them. "I think I'll let Kandy tell you what finally brought the situation to a head."

"Okay, but I'll need his name and personal info."

"In all sincerity I don't think he's behind this. He doesn't have the intelligence."

"All the same, I need to know about him."

"Okay. I'll put everything together for you." She peered up at him through her glasses and he got the distinct impression he was being assessed.

"So," she said, "does this mean you're taking the job?"

Josh realized he'd made the decision the moment he'd met Kandy face-to-face.

"Yeah." He set his mouth in a determined line. "I'm taking the job."

Chapter Two

"That looked great," Cort Mason said, as he came around from behind a camera. "I think we're done for today, everybody."

"Come and get it," Kandy called.

Josh watched from the sidelines as the crew, like men starved for a lifetime, descended on the set kitchen and crowded around the marble-topped counter. For a few minutes Kandy doled out pieces of the cake she'd baked to anyone who wanted a taste.

While the workers dispersed, Cort tossed an affectionate arm around his star's shoulders. "We got a lot accomplished today."

"We have more to do tomorrow," she said. "I want the herb segment shot in the morning. The weather forecast is great up until noon. The morning sun should give us some excellent natural lighting."

"Okay." He took the slice of cake she offered him.

"Is this one of the perks of working for your show?" Josh asked, as he walked up to them and leaned his elbows on the counter.

"The best one," Cort said through a mouthful of cake. "I gained seven pounds the first season alone. I had to buy a treadmill for season two."

Kandy laughed and licked frosting off her fingers. "Would you like a piece?" she asked Josh.

The laugh, coupled with the innocent, provocative way her tongue laved across her fingers, struck him momentarily dumb.

"Don't say no," Cort warned. "You have no idea what you're missing if you do."

Josh tossed him a nod. "Two things I never pass up are cake and pie."

"Then stick around for tomorrow's show." The director rolled his eyes. "She's baking apple *and* pumpkin."

"Oh, I have a feeling he'll be here," Kandy said, a dry inflection in her voice.

Cort threw her a puzzled look.

"I'm Josh Keane." He extended his hand to the director.

"We haven't met before, have we?" Cort asked, his gaze scouring Josh's face.

"He's a…friend," Kandy explained before Josh could say anything.

Cort looked from Josh to his star. "Oh?"

"Yes, *oh,*" she replied.

Josh watched the interplay between director and star. Kandy's stance and direct gaze all but challenged the man to say something else. An undercurrent Josh didn't understand streamed between them.

Cort shook his head and put his empty plate down on the counter. "Okay. While I'd like nothing more than to stand around and chat, there's work to be done. Let's go see the magic we made today."

As the three of them proceeded down to the editing department, Cort threw a speculative glance at Josh but kept silent.

Josh took the time to study Kandy's director. At about fifty, his light brown hair was just starting to go gray at the temples. Trim, either from judicious use of the treadmill he'd mentioned or naturally, and a little below six feet, Kandy stood almost eye-to-eye with him.

But Josh noticed other things aside from the physical attributes of the man. The unconscious way Cort jiggled the keys in his pocket gave silent voice there were nerves jumping under his skin. The surreptitious glances Cort stole at Kandy every few seconds, his eyes flitting upward but his head remaining down, let Josh know the nerves were zeroed in on his star, and the investigator in Josh wondered why.

* * *

"Editing is the tedious part of the job," Kandy told him in the elevator. "Prepare to be bored."

Josh nodded. "Boredom is a state of mind."

"Brawn *and* brains," she said, eyebrows lifting, eyes widening in a mocking motion.

When his lips twisted into a full grin, Kandy grinned back.

Since her first view of him seated across from her cousin, his long legs splayed out in front of him, Kandy knew he would tower over her. No easy feat for most of the male population she came in contact with. When he'd stood, she found herself staring up into the greenest pair of eyes she'd ever seen. The color of moist grass, deep and verdant, they housed an intelligence and intensity she assumed perceived much more than the average man.

Kandy suspected this was a guy who set pulses racing on every woman he encountered. Shoulders that went on for yards tapered into a narrow waist and slim hips, clad in what she recognized as expensive trousers. The black crewneck shirt under his sports jacket mimicked the color of his hair.

All in all, a man a girl might lose her head over.

Not that she was interested in losing her head.

For twenty-eight years her life had been focused on one thing: cooking. All aspects of it, from the imaginative recipe conceptions, to the growing of her own special herbs and spices. From shopping to chopping and baking to braising. Every nuance of being able to create the perfect taste to tempt the senses.

Kandy's work ethic was intense, and since the launch and unprecedented success of her cooking show, she was busier than ever. She enjoyed the freedom her success provided, and appreciated the financial independence her prosperity had given her.

Lately, though, a feeling something was missing in her life—something important, even necessary—had started to seep through her system at odd times. Chalking it up to a ridiculous and busy schedule coupled with little sleep, she pushed it to the back of her mind.

"I don't like that shot." She pointed to the video monitor. "The cake doesn't look appetizing enough."

"Are you kidding?" Cort's face was a cloud of bewilderment. "My mouth is watering just looking at it."

Squinting at the image, she told the film editor, "Move ahead a few seconds, please. There. I think this shot should lead the segment, not the other one."

Cort viewed the two sections side by side. "You're right, Kan. The second one highlights the cake better. We'll cut into it from here."

She leaned back in her chair and crossed her arms over her chest. "What do you think?" She turned and asked Josh. "Better the second way or the first?"

"The second," he said without hesitation.

"Why?"

"Because you're right. The angle of the shot in the first makes the cake look flat and unappealing. In the second you get more a feel that when you cut into it and taste it, you'll be satisfied. It'll be a pleasurable experience."

Cort spun to stare at him, matching Kandy's bemused expression.

Josh shrugged. "You asked."

"You got all that from the second shot?" Cort said.

He nodded.

"You're not an artist, are you?"

Josh laughed. "Nope. I just like to eat. What's that saying? You taste first with your eyes?"

Cort glanced at Kandy, who met his gaze with a haughty grin.

"I hate it when you're right."

Her grin turned into a smirk. She looked over her shoulder at Josh and winked, her pulse missing a beat when a boyish grin came back at her.

The rest of the editing took up another hour. At five thirty Cort said, "What we've got so far is tight. With tomorrow's footage filming should be almost complete. Let's call it a day."

"Fine with me." Kandy stood and stretched. "I've got some stuff to finish up."

They parted outside the editing room.

Kandy strode toward the elevator bank, Josh in tow. When she turned and stopped without warning, he crashed into her and put his hands on her upper arms to steady them both.

At his touch, Kandy froze. The furnace of heat steeping through her sleeve from his fingertips sent a warm, lava-hot rush sluicing down her insides.

"Sorry," Josh mumbled. "You stopped."

"Yeah, I did." She took a step back, forcing him to let go of her arms. "Look, maybe we should get some things straight about this following-me-around stuff."

Josh folded his hands into his pants pockets. "Okay. Where were you heading?"

"My office."

Josh nodded. "Let's go."

They rode the elevator in silence.

"This is it," she said when the elevator stopped.

She went before him down the hallway and when she came to a closed, massive set of oak double doors, she kept moving, pushing through them effortlessly. The outer corridor was empty.

"Clock stops at five thirty," she told him, spying the way he glanced at the empty desks. "That's a rule I never break. No matter how busy we are, or what our deadline is, I make sure everyone up here is out by then."

"Why? I would think that long hours are the norm in this business."

"Everyone deserves free time, time with family, time to wind down. I won't have people working for me when they're exhausted, or thinking about the soccer game they're missing for their kid. No one's productive then. I like everyone to be rested, fresh, and on the ball. I realized early on it was the way to bring out the creative best in everyone."

"But you don't adhere to your own rules."

She leveled a gaze at him. "That's because I'm the boss. I thrive on deadlines and do some of my finest work when I'm exhausted."

The slow, perceptive grin that spread across his face made her stomach muscles giddy-up.

"I bet you give great holiday bonuses," he said, rocking back on his heels.

Because it was true, she smiled. "My office is in here." She pushed through another set of doors and preceded him in.

While he took in the surroundings, Kandy wondered if he saw the room the way she did. A corner office, it had full-length, floor-to-ceiling windows on three sides and an unobstructed view of Battery Park and the Statue of Liberty.

The interior design was her own and she'd gone for comfort and ease in the furnishings. Three couches circled one another in the center of the room, and in the middle sat an impressive glass table, currently covered with files, paper, magazines, and a few fabric swatches. A grandfather clock stood, unwound, against the far wall, the hour hand stuck at nine, the minute hand at twelve.

A large, cherrywood desk faced the windows, not the inner room, complete with two computers and a laptop. Two printers were on a pullout stand next to the desk.

"Interesting." Josh gazed around the room. "I assume the reason your desk faces this way is for the great view?"

"Why waste it by having my back to it?"

"What's up with the clock?"

She glanced over at it. "That's the exact time my first book went on sale."

"So what? Time stopped for you then?"

"No. The way I see it, my life started precisely at that moment."

His eyebrows rose. "Says a lot about what you expect and want out of life."

"Don't read too much into it," she said, unaccustomed embarrassment washing through her. Without even knowing her he'd hit her personality right on the head. "The clock also has sentimental value. It was Grandma's." Kandy moved to the couches. "Come on, have a seat. Let's talk specifics."

Josh sat opposite her and leaned back into the couch, crossing one long leg over the other.

"I'm going to say this once because I feel we should get it out of the way," she started. "I don't think I need a bodyguard, and I don't think anything that's happened recently can't be explained away. I find this whole situation of having someone follow every move I make unnerving. I'm not used to working this way. I don't want to have to stop every five minutes to explain where I'm going or who I'm going to be meeting with. I just go. I have too much to do in a day to worry about someone keeping up with me."

When he remained silent, she continued. "I'm willing to go along with the entire scheme until you prove there's really no reason for it, which I think you'll discover pretty quickly. But I won't be hampered in any way going about my day. Understand?"

He nodded again. "As I told you before, I'm not going to ask you to change anything you normally do. My presence is merely to try and prevent anything else from happening. With that in mind, though, I will need to know the particulars of your everyday routine. Where you're going, who you're meeting with, and how you're getting there. I'll need to know about any phone calls, or any unusual mail. I'll need to know about your personal life, but I won't interfere in it. Your cousin seems to believe you're in some kind of danger. It's my job to figure out if her suspicions are warranted. I'll need you to cooperate, but I promise, I won't intrude on your life in any way if I can possibly prevent it."

She stared at him for a moment, taking in his words. "What do you mean by 'personal life'?"

With an easygoing swipe of his hand through the air, he clarified. "Boyfriends, dinner dates, social engagements. I'll need to know who you're seeing so they can be checked out."

"You mean investigate them?"

"Yes."

"That's ridiculous! It's a terrible invasion of privacy."

"It's necessary."

After a few moments, Kandy blew out a large breath and crossed her arms again over her chest. "Well, it's moot anyway, because I'm not seeing anyone."

"You were until recently."

One eyebrow arched high on her forehead. "Stacy told you about Evan?"

"Just you were seeing someone and it ended. She didn't give me any particulars. She said you would."

"Fat chance," she muttered. "It's over. End of story."

"Just for a second, consider this." He eased forward, propping his elbows on his knees. "These strange things started happening after you broke up with the guy, didn't they?"

"I suppose," she said, considering.

"There could be a connection."

"Doubtful," she said. "Evan's severely lacking in brains. Trust me on this."

"I'm still going to check him out."

"Okay, fine. Do it if you have to. I don't care about him anyway." She rose and walked to the windows. The sun was still bright, an effect of the long summer day.

"Have you received any phone calls, e-mails, or texts that seemed strange or off?"

"You'll have to ask Tricia Walters about the social media stuff. She's in charge of all of that. I simply don't have the time to tweet and troll around on Facebook."

"Okay. Phone calls, then? Any hang-ups? Someone there but not talking? Anything like that?"

She sighed and rubbed her eyelids with the pads of her fingers.

"Kandy?"

She hadn't realized he'd moved until his image reflected in the glass window. The heat on her neck from his stare was warm and intense.

"About a week ago," she said after a few seconds. "It started about a week ago."

He touched her shoulders and rotated her around to face him. "Tell me."

For a moment she couldn't breathe. His eyes, she discovered, weren't solid green, but dotted with lighter flecks of gold and amber.

She licked her lips and said, "I was working here. Pretty late, like ten-ish. I think it was last Monday. The phone rang."

"Which phone?"

"The one on my desk. I picked it up, said hello, but no one answered. I thought it was a telemarketer, you know? When you pick up there's silence until the computer alerts the caller there's someone on the line, and then they connect? But I held on for about ten seconds. Nothing. Just silence. I could hear...something...in the background. After saying hello about ten times, I hung up."

"Was it the only call?"

"That night. The next one came the following morning, when I was getting ready to leave."

"At home?"

Her black curls bounced when she nodded. "My condo, here in the city."

"Landline or cell?"

"Land," she said. "It was about five thirty. I'd just finished my workout, was about to take a shower. The phone rang. At that hour you always think it's bad news. Someone died or something."

He nodded. "Was anyone on the other end?"

"Yes."

"Do you know who it was?" he prompted.

She shook her head. "The person screamed one word and then hung up." Remembering the sound and her shock at the word, she rubbed her hands up and down her arms.

"What word?"

She looked up into his eyes, wondering what he would think when she told him. "*Whore.*"

Kandy moved from the window to a small refrigerator. She took out a bottle of water, drank, and then recapped it.

"Anything else?" he asked, watching her, his expression flat and unreadable.

Somehow, it felt better telling him than keeping it to herself. "Yesterday. I was just leaving the studio. I did a quick stop back here before meeting with my agent uptown."

"And?"

She sighed. Taking the headband off, she massaged her temples, then scraped her hands through the sides of her hair. "My phone message light was blinking. When I accessed the messages there were two. One was from my sister Abby reminding me about another sister's birthday party this weekend."

When she didn't continue, he moved toward her. "And the other?"

She crossed her arms over her chest and turned back to the window. "It was a woman, I think. The voice was hushed, like someone trying to disguise it. She whispered 'All whores go to hell when they die. You will, too.'"

"You didn't save the message, did you?"

Kandy turned, walked back to her desk, and pressed two buttons on the phone. After a signal beep, the message replayed.

It had been hard to listen to yesterday when she was alone. It was more embarrassing than difficult to have Josh listen to it now.

"I agree with you," he told her when it ended. "It does sound like a woman."

"Thought I'd find you guys here." Stacy came into the office, interrupting them, a stack of papers in her hand.

"We were just finishing up." Kandy planted a quick smile on her face, not wanting her cousin to know what they'd been discussing for the past several minutes.

"I've got the list you asked for." Stacy handed Josh a stack of papers.

"What list?" Kandy asked.

"Just compiling info," he told her calmly. "Background stuff."

Because she was suddenly tired, she didn't pursue it.

"Okay, well, if that's everything, I need to get home and change. The party is in less than two hours."

"Party?" Josh asked.

It was Stacy who answered. "At the Waldorf. To promote the new cookbook. Snazzy event sponsored by the publisher. Black tie."

"You mean tuxedo?"

Kandy smiled genuinely for the first time since coming into the office. He sounded alarmed—a thought that secretly charmed her. "Why? Don't own one?"

The half grin, half smirk he threw her made her toes curl.

"Oh, I own one. Just didn't know I'd be putting it on tonight. I'll have to swing by my place to get it."

"Feel free," Kandy said. She grabbed her purse and slung it across her shoulder. "We'll go over the next few days' scheduling tomorrow, Stace."

"Okay. See you in a few."

She left the office, Kandy close on her heels.

"Hold on a sec," Josh said, laying a restraining hand on her arm. "You don't seem to get this whole layout yet."

"What are you talking about?"

His strong hand against her skin was equal parts annoying and fascinating. To have both emotions warring inside her served only to aggravate her more.

"I go where you go," he told her in a tone she didn't think allowed for discussion.

"I get that." She rolled her eyes. "I don't like it, but I get it."

"The opposite holds, too. I've gotta stop by my place for a few things. You're coming with me."

"But I need to get home and—"

She watched his mouth instantly harden into a thin, tight line. "No arguments," he said.

Chapter Three

After leaving the office, they'd climbed into Kandy's waiting limo and stopped for a few minutes at Josh's apartment. Kandy tapped her feet in vexation as she waited in the foyer while Josh tossed his tuxedo and a few other sundries into an overnight bag.

It was a quick trip uptown to her Park Avenue condo despite the end of rush-hour traffic.

He wasn't surprised when the elevator stopped at the top floor. Just as in her office, the view from her living room was spectacular.

"You can put your things in the guest room," she told him, heading off to her own space.

When she emerged an hour later, his mouth went dry as dust despite the sparkling water he'd been drinking.

"Ready?" she asked, adjusting a two-carat diamond stud in one ear.

He gulped the last of his water and nodded.

She looked spectacular garbed in a super-short black, sleeveless sequined dress with four-inch dragon-lady killer heels. Her legs went on forever, all the way up to heaven and back, and made his mouth dry again just looking at them.

During the limo ride to the Waldorf, she filled him in on the guest list.

"Stacy will be there, so you'll see one familiar face. The Masons may or may not show. Cort wasn't sure his wife was up to it."

"Something wrong with her?"

Kandy sighed and shrugged. She didn't say any more on the matter, so he didn't push, but made a mental note to research the Masons further.

"You'll meet my agent, Reva Lowenstein. She's a real trip. Most of my family will be there, too."

"Stacy mentioned some of them work for you."

She nodded, the jewels in her earlobes twinkling in the dim light of the limo. "In one capacity or another."

"No problems with nepotism?"

A corner of her mouth quirked upward. "None. They wouldn't be working for me if they weren't good at what they do. My sister Gemma, for instance, is an amazing photographer. She does all the pictures for my books and my publicity shots. I don't trust anyone else."

"Who else?" he asked, needing to know as many of the players in her world as possible.

"Stacy's mom, my aunt Lucy." The smile dancing across her mouth turned wicked. "You'll like her. Everyone does. She's an unapologetic flirt and a fabulous stylist. The decor you see on set is her doing."

Josh remembered the homey, chic studio kitchen "She knows her stuff."

"A daytime Emmy for set design doesn't lie."

"Anyone else I should know about beforehand?"

"Not really. I'm sure they'll all find you and introduce themselves."

The wistfulness in her voice surprised him. "Why?"

When she turned, her expression could only be described as wry. Forehead slightly furrowed, one beautifully sculpted brow rising just a fraction, and the crooked way her mouth ambled into a laconic grin made his pulse pound.

She pierced him with a look that was at once challenging and worried. "You'll be arriving with me, which will be enough to send them all into a frenzy wanting to know who you are."

"What would you like me to tell them?"

"Leave it up in the air, I guess," she replied with a shrug. "Stacy most likely told Reva about you, because she tells her everything connected with me." She rolled her eyes. "So, unless they've talked to the others—which I doubt, since no one has called me—the rest of the family will be in the dark. I'd like to keep it that way."

"I agree," he told her. "The less people who know why I'm following you around, the easier it'll be to find out who's bothering you. You'd be amazed at the things people tell me, especially when they don't know what I do for a living."

Kandy considered him from across the limo. "No. I don't think I'd be amazed at all."

"We're here, Kandy," the driver announced.

In the elevator she was quick to say, "Just try not to hover, okay? I want to enjoy this party and not be worried something is going to happen, which I will be if you're all over me."

"Isn't that why I'm here, though? To prevent something from happening?"

"Just so we're clear: don't feel you have to cling to my side. Have a drink. Enjoy the food. Mingle. Got it?"

"Got it," he said, swallowing a chuckle.

When they entered the ballroom, a smattering of applause quickly blossomed into a full rolling thunder that had Kandy beaming.

A cadaver-thin woman made her way through the crowd at a swift and determined pace. Snow-white hair cut into a fashionable, swinging bob ending just below her square chin, framing gray eyes so light they seemed ice blue from a distance. Her lips were embalmed in a striking scarlet offsetting the paleness of her translucent skin. She had an unlit e-cigarette in one hand, a half-filled martini glass in the other.

When Josh moved to stand in front of her, Kandy sidestepped him and whispered, "Cool it. It's Reva."

"About time you showed." The woman lifted up to kiss Kandy's cheek.

"Had to make an entrance," she said.

Reva's slate-colored eyes widened and their calculating gleam turned hard and firm when she noticed Josh. "And you are?"

Josh put out his hand. The agent gripped her cigarette with her drink hand and extended the empty one toward him. He was surprised to feel the grip rival his own.

"Josh Keane, Ms. Lowenstein."

"Stacy's man." Her nod was quick and perfunctory. "I want to talk to you. In private."

"Oh for God's sake," Kandy said. "Don't go grilling him."

She turned to her client, a dazzling smile tripping across her scarlet lips. "But, babe, it's what I do best. Now, come and mingle. People have been waiting." She hooked an arm in Kandy's and led her off.

"Reva's a dynamo."

When he turned he found Stacy at his side.

"I got that impression," he told her. "She wants to talk to me. Privately."

"I'm not surprised. She's extremely protective of Kandy. She'll want to know everything you find out. Did you get a chance to read those papers I gave you?"

He nodded. "When Kandy was getting ready I gave them a once-over. A pretty extensive list of people has her private phone numbers."

Stacy sighed and took a sip of the drink in her hand. "She always wants to make sure anyone can get hold of her if they need to. Is it a problem?"

"It makes narrowing the field of possibilities a little tougher."

"Oh. I didn't think of that."

"Stacy, who is this handsome man and why haven't you introduced me yet?"

They both turned. Josh's eyes met the laughing blue ones of an attractive, middle-aged woman in a low-cut silk sheath matching the color of her eyes. That she was related to Kandy was evident. The height, the angle of the jaw, even the way her lips curved proved the genetic link.

"Mama," Stacy whispered, "behave."

"You must be Max's wife," Josh said, taking the woman's hand. "I'm Josh Keane. I know your husband through Latimer and Roberts," he added, naming the law firm they'd been introduced by.

The blue eyes narrowed and her gaze gamboled across his face. "I could shoot my husband for neglecting to ever mention you."

Good-natured flirting was an art, and Josh sensed this woman was a master. Relaxing, he said, "Oh, but I know all about you, Mrs. Peters."

She laughed, reminding Josh instantly of Kandy. "Let's hope not, for both our sakes. And it's Lucy."

Josh nodded.

"Now, then," she said, "just who, exactly, are you and why did you arrive with my niece?"

Stacy threw a quick silencing glance her way. "Mama, that's rude."

"I don't think it's rude at all, do you, Mr. Keane?"

"It's Josh, and no, I don't."

"Are you two an item?" Lucy asked, making Stacy blanch.

"In a way," he replied.

"What way? We're very protective of our Kandace Sophia."

Thinking back to his discussion with Kandy, he said easily, "Let's just say your niece and I have a mutual desire to be together right now."

He had to clamp his lips together to keep from laughing when her face lit up like a Broadway billboard.

"Oh, well, good for her. It's about time. After the last moron, you're more than an improvement."

"Mama," Stacy said, inveigling her way between them and taking her mother's arm in a not-too-soft grip, "can you find Aunt Trudi for me? I need to ask her a few things about next week's shooting schedule."

Lucy glanced over her shoulder. "I just saw her over by the bar. Can't it wait?"

"I'm afraid not. Would you?"

Lucy Peters looked from Josh to her daughter. With a theatrical sigh, she said, "All right, dear. I'll go tell her you're looking for her. I expect

I'll be seeing you again, Joshua."

With one last penetrating look at her daughter, Lucy flittered away.

Stacy blew out a slow breath.

"Kandy told me she didn't think anyone else in the family knew about your concerns," he said.

"She's right. There's no need to worry them all about this. Sorry my mom was so blunt. It's a family trait."

As the woman reached the bar, she threw one brief smile back over her shoulder, her gaze zeroing in on his. "Your mother's a very beautiful woman."

"Yeah, she is," Stacy said, a ghost of a grin on her face. "Personal style and good grooming are her muses. Kandy's hired most of the family in one capacity or another. My aunt Trudi is her secretary and keeper of the daily diary. In all honesty, she's more of an asset to me than to Kandy. She keeps me organized, knows where Kandy has to be, what's going on with her timetable and agenda. Our aunt Callie is Kandy's makeup artist. Aunt Callie's two daughters are research assistants and computer jocks. They keep the info rolling, answer e-mails, track interviews, get Kandy recipe info. Stuff like that."

"And her sister Gemma is her photographer."

"Yeah, and a great one in her own right. She works primarily for Kandy, but you've probably seen some of her commercial work. She did the ad campaign for Mistaire."

Josh nodded at the familiar perfume company name. "Kandy seems very loyal to your family."

Stacy nodded. "If it weren't for her, we wouldn't have the comfortable lifestyles we do. None of our parents were rich before she made it big. Since she has, she's taken most of us along for the ride."

Josh honed in on her words. "Most? Not all?"

Stacy bit her lower lip and looked up at him. "Not everyone in the family basks in Kandy's success."

"Anything I should know about those not happy with the situation?"

She was quick to disavow him of the thought. "No. No, really. I don't mean to give you the wrong impression. Sorry."

He wanted to ask more, but she begged off, saying she had to talk to her aunt.

Josh made his way to the bar, his eyes skimming the crowd for his client. Five-nine with four-inch heels, she wasn't hard to find.

Reclining back against a table, arms crossed in front of her, she was listening intently to a tall, gray-haired gentleman in an Armani suit.

Josh ordered bottled water, leaned a hip against the bar, and watched her.

Her eyes were focused on the man speaking and she nodded every few seconds at what he said. At one point though, Kandy turned her head, connected with Josh's gaze, and winked, a small playful smile crossing her lips. Just as quick she turned back to her companion, seemingly engrossed in what he was saying.

For a moment, Josh wondered if he'd imagined the look.

But he hadn't. That little eye motion—seductive, secretive, and oh so sexy—hadn't been his imagination. And what it did to his insides wasn't his imagination, either.

"You came with Kandy, didn't you?" a throaty voice asked, close to his ear.

Josh choked on the water, dribbling some of it down his chin. Swiping at it with the back of his hand, he looked over at Kandy's clone.

She was eye level with him, just as Kandy was in heels. The shape of the face, the color of the eyes, and the slight bend of the chin were Kandy's to a *T*. The one difference was the hair. Kandy's was a torrent of midnight black curls, so deep and shiny it almost shone blue. This woman's hair was shorter by about twelve inches, straight as a pin, but still a solid, lustrous ebony.

"Yes," he told her. "And you are?"

She extended her hand. "Gemma Laine."

"Photographer."

One sculpted, black eyebrow rose just as her sister's was wont to do.

"Kandy filled me in on a few of the people who'd be here. Plus." He nodded to the camera slung around her neck. From surveillance work he'd done in the past, he knew the price tag on the device and was impressed.

"You have me at a disadvantage," she said, still claiming his hand. "You know who I am, but..."

She let the sentence dangle, her eyes drilling right through him.

"Josh Keane." When he pulled back on his hand, she seemed reluctant to turn it over.

"And you are, what? Colleague? Friend? Fan?"

"You could say all three. Right now we're pretty much joined at the hip."

She let out a sigh that clearly communicated her disappointment. "Oh well. Good for her. I'll have a scotch and soda if you don't mind."

Josh gave the bartender the order and then considered Gemma. "You're younger than Kandy."

"Three years."

"Young to have such a first-class professional reputation."

Gemma thanked the bartender and downed a large portion of her drink before replying. "Long day," she explained.

"Must have been." The corners of his lips twitched.

"Anyway. I work for Kandy for three reasons. One, she's my sister and I love her to death. Two, she gave me my first camera when I was still in high school. Launched me into my career, a fact I will be eternally grateful for."

"And third?" he asked as she took another hit of the drink.

Gemma Laine stared straight into his face, a broad and devilish smile gleaming across it, identical to her older sister's. "The pay and perks are unbelievable."

"Perks?"

"Sure." She lifted one shoulder. "I get great media exposure with every book she writes, which in turn brings me more work. I get to go to fabulous parties like this one and hobnob with all the ritzy New York elite who fawn over sister dear. And I get to meet gorgeous men like you."

Before he could stop himself, Josh grinned. "I'm beginning to think flirting is a genetic trait in your family."

"Oh, you've met Aunt Lucy?"

His laugh was quick, loud, and full of pleasure. Several heads turned toward them.

"Yes, I have," he said, regaining his composure.

"She's nothing compared to my mother," Gemma said, rolling her eyes, a twin movement he'd noticed in her sister. "Better eat your Wheaties before you meet her."

From his left side, Kandy slid up to them and said, "Gemma, what family secrets are you divulging?"

"No secrets. Just facts. He's met Aunt Lucy. I was just preparing him for Mom."

"Oh God." Kandy leaned onto the bar, her head in her hands. "I forgot to tell you about my mother. Bartender, could I please have some champagne?"

While he went to pour it, she asked her sister, "Is she here yet?"

"I called before I came. She was still primping. That was an hour ago."

"Her timing's perfect as always." Kandy took the champagne glass and sipped. "Mmmm. Yummy. Okay, look. I'd better warn you." Kandy turned her attention to him. "My mother's not your typical middle-aged sedate matron."

Gemma snorted. "You got that right."

Kandy shushed her sister then turned back to Josh. "My parents were married for fourteen years, ten of which she was pregnant. We all lived with Grandma Sophie because my father wasn't what you'd call career-driven."

"Another understatement," Gemma said. "He was a bum."

"Gemma, please." Kandy's patience was clearly beginning to strain. To Josh, she added, "Okay, that's an apt description, I have to admit. He left when I was thirteen. Mom went a little psycho after he bolted."

"A little?" Gemma snapped. "Get real. She went full-fledged nuts."

Kandy chose to ignore her this time. "She'd been chained to him for all those years—since she was seventeen. Pregnant, changing diapers, and nursing for most of them. When he left, she felt she'd been pardoned from a death sentence. So, she went a little wild. Dyed her hair, lost a ton of weight, and started to explore her, well, her sexual identity."

When she blushed at her own depiction, Josh said, "She found herself. No longer wife and mother, but independent woman."

Nodding, Kandy smiled. "Perfect picture. Anyway, she's still on her path to discovery."

"What my sister is delicately trying to say is our mother gets off on the cougar-on-the-prowl role. Plays it to the hilt. Anything in pants is a target. So be warned and beware." Gemma tossed back her drink. Draining it, she banged the glass down on the bar. "I've gotta go mingle and take some pictures. Earn my keep. It was really nice meeting you. Really nice. Too bad you're Kandy's. You're way cuter then the last guy who, by the way, was an asshole."

With that, she meandered away from them.

Josh met Kandy's thoughtful gaze after he'd watched her sister go. "What? She's a cute kid," he said.

"And she knows it. Look," she said, her tone growing serious. "I'm a little uncomfortable with what people are asking me about you. What they're implying."

"Which is?"

"Well, they seem to think we're involved. You know. Together. *Dating.*"

For the first time since they'd met, Josh saw nerves in her. "Would you prefer they knew the real reason I'm with you?" he asked, lowering his voice for her ears only.

She took another sip of champagne and then looked up at him. "No, I don't."

He turned to face the wall, rested his arms on the bar, and snaked a foot into the bar rail. His body was close to hers, their shoulders almost touching.

"If you want to keep why I'm hanging around you a secret from everyone, I think it's the most plausible explanation. Let 'em think we're dating."

"You don't mind?"

He shook his head. "Part of the job. No harm done if people assume we're having an affair. Not to me, anyway."

"God, I hate that word. It sounds so seedy and torrid."

Josh's mind drifted for a moment, imagining just how hot and spicy an affair with Kandy Laine would be.

But despite how delicious it sounded, a steamy romance wasn't included in the contract. She was his client. His responsibility.

"If it's a means to an end, I can go along with it until this whole thing is resolved," he told her. "Can you?"

Worry filled her eyes. "I guess I'll have to. We know the truth at least," she added with a sigh.

Josh took the moment to ask a question. "Who was the man you were speaking to just now? About sixty, gray hair?"

After taking another sip of her champagne she said, "Harvey Little. My publisher. He's the one paying for all this decadence." She waved her hand toward the ballroom.

"Ever have any trouble with him? Professionally? Personally?"

Her eyes widened to the size of half dollars. "You've got to be kidding. Harvey Little? The sweetest man in publishing?"

"He's never made any overt moves on you, anything that might be misconstrued?"

"Never," she said, gulping champagne. "He's gay."

Josh turned back to the room and found the subject in question in close conversation with Reva. "You sure about that?"

Kandy followed his line of sight. "Yes. He's been in a committed relationship for more than twenty years. Besides"—she finished her drink—"he loves how much money my books bring in. If something happened to me, it would be like getting rid of the golden goose."

He couldn't decide if being thought of that way bothered her or not.

Out of the corner of his eye, he caught Cort Mason entering the room. The director was smoothing down his hair when he saw Kandy and made a beeline for the bar, adjusting his jacket as he did.

"Hello, doll." He bussed Kandy's proffered cheek. "Keane," he said, extending his hand. "How's this bash going?"

"Fine," she replied. "Where's Alyssa?"

"Terrible headache. Sends her regrets. Quite a crowd. Little's gone all out."

He ordered a drink and Josh couldn't help but notice how quickly he'd veered the subject away from his wife.

"Oh crap," Kandy said a second later. "Who let *him* in?"

Josh mimicked her stare and saw a thirtyish man in a well-fitted tuxedo enter the room. "Who's that?"

"The asshole I mentioned earlier." Gemma answered, coming up to them. "I saw him get off the elevator. Figured you could use some re-inforcements."

Kandy put an arm around her sister's shoulders. "Thanks, but I think I can handle Evan."

When she started to move toward the man, Josh put a gentle, restraining hand on her arm. "Joined at the hip, remember?"

She stopped, stared at him and then at the way his hand was snaked around her upper arm.

Without a word, she nodded.

"There you are. The woman of the hour."

Josh took in the measure of the man Kandy had been involved with. He was a little less than six foot and filled out the shoulders of the tuxedo well. His blond hair was streaked with auburn, cut straight and fashionably long, ending just at the collar of his jacket. Perfect, professionally white teeth gleamed at Kandy like high-beam headlights. Josh knew in an instant they were veneers, just as he knew the hair color was bottle-enhanced.

"Evan, what are you doing here?" Kandy asked.

"I came to wish you good luck with the book, of course."

Even his voice sounded fake. Evan Chandler was trying much too hard to hide the backwoods southern twang Josh recognized lurking beneath the well-toned vowels.

"I thought I made it clear I didn't want to ever see you again the last time you showed up without an invitation."

The steel in her voice warmed Josh's heart.

"Old news. All buried under the bridge now." His smile was dazzling and perfectly fake.

"You're mixing your metaphors, Evan. Please leave. This is a private party and you weren't invited."

The man's bonhomie shifted a tad, his smile losing some of its luster. "Still mad, Kandy? That's not like you."

"Oh, it's very like me, Evan. Once I'm lied to, I never give a second chance."

"And still just as high-handed, I see. Can't you just accept I want to wish you good luck?"

"*Bull.* You never do anything without an ulterior motive."

"So untrusting. Can't we just put the past away and be friends? I miss you."

When he stepped in closer, Josh countered the move and placed himself firmly in the way.

"She asked you to leave."

"Who the hell are you?"

The fire flaming in Chandler's eyes was comical. Josh took a step closer and was rewarded when Evan shifted backward.

"Who I am is none of your business. Now, do everyone a favor and get lost."

Flustered, Evan looked from one face to the other. "Kandy, I just want—"

"I don't care what you want. Leave. Now. And don't try to see me again." She turned and stalked away, Gemma at her heels.

"Kandy," Evan called after her as he took a step in her direction.

Josh barred his way. He had an inch or two and about fifty pounds on Chandler, and used every bit of it to his advantage.

"Look, I don't know who you are, but I need to speak with her, so get out of my way." Chandler put a hand up to shove Josh.

"Wrong move," Josh said, quiet as death. He wrapped his hand around Chandler's wrist and turned it sideways.

"Ow. Let go of me."

"I will just as soon as I'm convinced you're gone for good."

Quite a few inquiring gazes followed them as Josh led him from the ballroom and back to the bank of elevators.

"I'm gonna kick your ass," Evan shouted.

"I don't think so, pal." Josh shoved him onto a waiting elevator and let go of him with a snap of his hand. "Now, get lost."

He waited until the elevator doors shut, watching as Evan Chandler rubbed his wrist and glared.

Josh returned to the filled room and scanned it for Kandy.

"She's in the ladies' room with Gemma," Cort said, coming up and handing him a drink. "Here. Give her this. She'll need it. And by the way, good move with Chandler. I never liked him."

"Seems to be the general consensus." He took the proffered glass.

He made his way to the other side of the room, ignoring the stares and whispers of the crowd, found the lounge, and knocked. "Kandy? It's Josh. Can I come in?"

It was Gemma who answered. "Yes."

The sisters were seated in twin floral Queen Anne chairs, Gemma reclining back into hers, arms crossed over her chest. Kandy was opposite, head wrung in her hands.

"Cort thought you could use this," he said, handing her the champagne flute.

He'd expected tears, but was surprised to see Kandy's beautiful face pinch in a scowl, her eyes flaring with sweltering anger and venom when she looked up at him.

"Thanks." Kandy took the drink and downed half of it in one gulp.

When she wiped her lips with the back of her hand, the corners of Gemma's mouth lifted and she asked Josh, "What did you do to the turd?"

"Explained he needed to leave, put him in the elevator, and made sure he went down in it."

"Made him how?" Kandy asked.

"Little persuasion trick I know. His wrist's gonna be sore tomorrow. Maybe for the next few days."

"You *physically* removed him?" Gemma asked.

Josh almost laughed at the excitement in her voice. He shrugged. "Yeah. He was going to follow Kandy if I didn't."

"Please tell me you have unmarried, available brothers at home," Gemma said.

It hurt to keep the smile from his face, but he did. "Three, in fact."

"Are they all like you? No, scratch that." She sighed, the sound wistful. "I doubt there's anyone like you."

"If you mean are they all workaholics and career-driven, then no. They're not like me. But they *are* available."

"I'll keep it in mind." She glanced at her sister and said, "Well, looks like my work here is done. She's all yours now." She stood and kissed the top of Kandy's head. "Evan Chandler is an egotistical, phony prick. Remember that."

"How could I forget it?" Kandy grabbed her sister's hand and kissed the back of it. "Thanks."

When Gemma left, Josh took her empty chair. "You okay?"

She took a deep breath before saying, "Mad, but okay. I underestimated him."

"How so?"

"I didn't think he'd have the guts to crash my party. I thought he was too much of a wimp to risk it after our last encounter. Guess I was wrong."

She stood and crossed to the vanity. Peering at her reflection, she ran a lazy hand through her hair, fluffing the curls. She caught his gaze, watching her, in the mirror. "Aren't you going to ask me about it?"

He'd considered it. But the weary look in her eyes told him he was better off asking Stacy or Gemma. "No. If you want to talk, I'll listen. Otherwise, you've got a pretty fancy shindig going on out there." He cocked his thumb in the direction of the ballroom. "Maybe you want to get back and enjoy it. Bask in the adulation," he said with a good-natured grin.

She turned to him and her eyes softened. When her lips moved upward into a small, lazy smile, the dimples dancing, his legs went a little soft and he was thankful he was seated.

"Yeah," she said, moving to him. When he stood, she linked her arm in his. "Thanks. You're right. Let's go have a party."

He returned her smile, glad he could help.

"You're not so bad, Keane. This bodyguard thing might be fun after all."

It was a moment before he trusted himself to speak. "I aim to please."

Chapter Four

"There you are." Reva ran up to them when they came out of the lounge. "Harvey wants you. The press has arrived."

"Sell-my-soul time," Kandy told Josh. "I need to do this solo."

"Sure." He unwrapped her hand from his arm and squeezed it. "I'll be close."

She smiled at him and winked. "Where?" she asked Reva.

"Over by the faux fountain."

"Who?"

"The *Times*, *People*, *Food & Wine*, the *Post*, and *Gourmet*."

"Okay." She took a breath and smoothed her dress from waist to hem. With a huge, all-teeth smile she headed into the lion's den with her head held high. She ambled over to her publisher, wound her arm into his, and, after a quick peck to his cheek, greeted the press.

"What's the first printing on this one, Kandy?"

It was Little who answered. "Million and a half copies," he said. The pride in his voice was difficult to miss.

"You're still number one on our nonfiction list for your last cookbook," the *New York Times* reporter said.

"With a little luck, when the list is revised this week, I'll be one *and* two," Kandy said with glee.

"What's your next project?" the *Food and Wine* reporter asked.

"Well, we need to finish shooting the season premiere. Then we move on to the Thanksgiving special, and the Christmas one right after that. In fact," Kandy said, "you can ask my director all about it. Cort, come here."

Mason adjusted his jacket and moved through the throng to stand on the other side of Kandy. Linking her arm in his, she smiled again at the media. "You all know Cort Mason."

A few photographs were taken and questions asked and answered. Gemma moved about the group, shooting from different angles and perspectives.

Kandy answered all the mundane and predictable questions put to her. But her mind wasn't on the gaggle of reporters all wanting her attention. It was centered on the man standing close by. He looked totally at ease watching her, one shoulder relaxed against a column, hands folded in his tuxedo pants pockets. But she knew he was anything but. If she wasn't mistaken, his languid posture belied the coiled tension she'd sensed in him when he led her back to the ballroom. The hard muscled fortress of his arm pressed against her hand as she held on to it was tight and taut, like a spring ready to be released.

When she'd first set eyes on him that afternoon she'd thought him handsome in a rugged, visceral way. Now, resplendent in a sinfully well-fitted tuxedo, he looked film-star perfect, as if he'd just stepped out of a 1940s black-and-white romantic comedy.

All in all, he was just the kind of man she'd always fantasized about having in her life and knew in her soul she'd never get. Men like Josh Keane were married to their careers, much the same way she was. But where a woman would compromise, a man wouldn't. She'd learned it firsthand when she'd hit the fame wagon. Men *expected* the woman to be the one who'd make the time for the relationship to work while they pursued their goals and ambitions. The few relationships Kandy had been involved in had all ended the same way—except for Evan Chandler. *She'd* dumped him. The others had walked away when she'd been unwilling to make concessions in her professional life to satisfy their egotistical needs.

Would she ever find a man who'd be willing to put her desires ahead of his own? Experience had her doubting it.

After twenty minutes, Reva broke into the crowd and announced they were finished. With smiles and handshakes all around, she thanked each of them for coming, all the while ushering them from the room.

When they were gone, Josh pushed off the column and moved to her. "She's good at that," he said, nodding toward Reva.

"No one's better," she said. "You hungry?"

"I could eat. Why?"

She leaned in closer and, sotto voce, said, "I'll deny this to my death if you ever repeat it, but the food Harvey ordered isn't great and I'm starving. I'd like to slip away and get something more substantial."

"Isn't it a little rude to leave your own party?"

A grin spread across her face like wildfire. "Yeah, but I don't care. We all have to work in the morning. I've had enough smiling, mingling, and answering questions. I want to eat, have a hot bath, and jump into bed."

A heartbeat passed and she couldn't read what was written in his eyes as he stared at her.

Finally, he shook his head once, side to side, and said, "Okay. You're the boss."

"And don't you forget it," she replied. "Let's go."

Without speaking to anyone, they exited a back door of the ballroom.

"You're sure no one will be mad at you for leaving?" he asked as they rode the elevator down to the waiting limo.

She shrugged. "Mad? No. A little ticked off, maybe? Reva will be. So will Harvey. But they'll get over it. And there's always the possibility no one will notice we're gone."

Josh snorted. "Forget it. You'll be missed before we get to the car."

"Where to, Kandy?" the driver asked as he held the door for them.

"You like pizza?" she asked Josh.

"Isn't it a food group?"

Laughing, she told the driver to take them home.

"I thought we were going for pizza," Josh said.

"We are. The best in town."

* * *

Fifteen minutes later, Josh removed his tux jacket, undid his bow tie, and rolled up his sleeves. He watched as Kandy set the oven temperature and took out a large plastic bag from the refrigerator.

Her kitchen was a study in culinary artistry. The appliances were all state-of-the-art and top-of-the-line steel. Two double ovens, side by side, sat between a ceramic, deep-welled double sink on one side and a full eight-burner range complete with hood on the other. The refrigerator was massive, and, from what Josh could see, every shelf was fully stocked. A separate, two-door freezer was installed alongside, and an industrial dishwasher completed the operational side of the room.

Sage-colored marble countertops sparkled under recessed ceiling lights. A suspended steel rack dipped down from the ceiling providing easy access to several sparkling pots and pans. She'd done the walls in tiles of a muted green, the floor a cacophony of Moroccan-inspired curlicues. One entire wall was devoted to cabinets and closets, painted pure, bright white, their hardware matching the pattern on the floor. Josh guessed if he opened just one cabinet he'd find enough nonperishable items to feed half the building for a week.

"This dough needs a few minutes to soften up," Kandy said. "What do you like for toppings?"

He didn't even stop to think. "Mushrooms, pepperoni, ham. Pineapple's always good."

"A man after my own stomach," she said, reaching into the refrigerator again. "I've got all those, plus some sliced meatballs. Sound good?"

"Sounds like heaven."

"Here, you chop these." She handed him two large portobello mushrooms and a knife.

He let out a low whistle. "I know S.W.A.T. teams who don't have weapons as good as this." He held up the knife, inspected it, then carefully laid it down on the counter and moved to the sink to wash his hands.

"Only the best utensils." She kicked off her shoes and joined him.

Without the extra inches she came to just below his ear. She squirted liquid soap into her hands and rubbed them together, her long fingers lathering the soap into frothy bubbles as they scrubbed from palm to nail, back and forth, her skin growing slick and slippery with each movement, the bouquet of floral scents tickling his nose.

She grabbed a tea towel after rinsing her hands, while he said, "Your mother never showed tonight. After the buildup you and Gemma gave me, I was looking forward to meeting her."

Her lips twisted into a dry smirk. "Don't worry, you will. She likes to drop by the studio unannounced. I never get any work done when she does because the crew goes wild for her."

"You're kidding, right?"

She unwrapped the pizza dough and began shaping it into a ball.

From his perspective, Josh was enlightened about just how erotic food preparation could be. He watched Kandy knead and massage the dough in a strong, steady rhythm, her hands fisting and pulling, then uncurling and yanking it with each movement to form it into the shape she wanted.

"No, I'm not. You'll see for yourself," she said. "She's a tornado."

"Is that why she doesn't work for you?"

"What do you mean?" With a flick of her hands, she tossed the dough into the air. It spun and twirled a few times and landed perfectly back in her hands.

"You do that well."

"Practice. Answer my question."

While she continued to toss, he finished chopping the mushrooms. "I've seen for myself how much of your family works for you."

"*With.* Not for. We're all in this together."

"Okay, *with* then. Aunts, cousins, siblings. Most of your recipes come from your grandmother. But your mother isn't included in the mix. Makes me wonder why not."

She placed the shaped dough onto a stone pizza wheel.

"Easy," she told him, taking a quart jar of what he assumed was pizza sauce from the refrigerator. "She doesn't want to work. Period."

"She doesn't have a job?"

"Nope, doesn't need one."

He took a moment, considering her statement and then said, "You support her, don't you?" as she spread the sauce evenly over the dough with a wooden spoon.

Making concentric circles from the center outward, Kandy nodded, her attention on her task. "She deserves the luxury. She worked like a dog after my father left. We never saw her. She'd work, sleep, and on her days off, well, she'd be gone on her own."

"Finding herself," he said, watching her face for its reaction.

He was rewarded when she blushed.

"Yeah." Silently, she arranged the shredded cheese over the sauce. "Hand me the mushrooms."

"You're good at giving orders," he said, scooping them up and placing the pile in her outstretched hands.

When the heat of his skin came in contact with hers, Josh swore he saw a little flash of light ignite from the simple touch.

He wondered if she felt it, too, because she stood, rooted, her hands balanced under his as he opened them and dropped the mushrooms into her palms. Her eyes dilated and moistened as she gazed up at him.

"What else do you want me to do?" he asked.

She shook her head and he would have given anything to know what she was thinking.

"You can slice the pineapple," she told him in a voice that sounded like it needed air.

He nodded, rinsed the knife under the faucet, and did as she asked. This time he waited for her to break the silence.

Kandy spread the meatball slices across the cheese, then took the cut fruit and did the same, layering each item with precision.

When she appeared satisfied her creation was perfect, she lifted the pizza wheel, placed it in the oven, and set the timer.

Josh sat silent throughout her movements.

When she turned from the oven, she asked, "Want something to drink?"

"Bottled water, if you have it."

She took two from the refrigerator, gave one to him, and kept the other, then sat down opposite him.

They drank for a few moments in silence before Josh decided he'd put off asking the questions he needed to for long enough. Waiting for the pizza to cook offered him the perfect opportunity.

"I need to clarify a few things," he said as a way of introduction.

"About?"

"What I've been hired to do. Namely, find out who's been bothering you."

"Okay. Shoot."

He checked his mental list and placed certain items ahead of others. "First of all, a lot of people have your private phone numbers. Office, cell, home. Stacy gave me a list this afternoon; I was surprised it was so extensive."

Kandy took a pull from the bottle. "I always want it to be easy for people to get in touch with me. There are times when I'm out of the studio and the office for most of the day, either doing a location piece, touring, or at guest spots. It's just easier if I can be readily reached."

"That's going to make narrowing down the field more difficult. Don't get me wrong, it can be done. But for now, I'd like to give you another cell. One only I'll have access to."

"Why?"

"So you can reach me at any time, and vice versa. You can call from it, it can't be traced, the number's blocked to any incoming calls, so only I'll be able to get in touch with you."

"I don't see why, but okay. You have this phone?"

"In my bag. I'll show you how it works after we eat."

She nodded. "What else?"

"I have to ask personal questions. Intimate ones. I know you value your privacy," he added when she sat upright and squared her shoulders. "But in order to find out who's been bothering you, I need to know about you, your friends, your family. I need to look at everyone as a potential suspect. And I need to know about things in your life."

"Like what?"

"For starters, your breakup with Chandler."

Her sigh was long and deep. "You said you weren't going to grill me on him."

"I'm not, Kandy. I don't care who you sleep with, or have slept with. The private details of your relationship are just that: private. But I need to know what happened to rule him in or out as a suspect."

"It's not Evan," she said, hands flat on the table, staring at Josh.

"You can't know for certain. He surprised you once already by showing up tonight. You admitted you'd underestimated him. Maybe you have again."

She took another pull of water, and then frowned. "What do you want to know?"

"What caused the breakup?"

She stared at him for a moment, then lowered her eyes. "He was using me to try and promote his so-called production company. He called my sponsors and the network executives and tried to get appointments with them, using my name, so he could pitch a project he wanted developed for television."

"Did he tell you this?"

She shook her head. "Someone who knew what was going on behind my back told me."

"Who?"

He could practically hear her debating with herself about whether or not to tell him.

"Kandy, you have to trust me."

He watched her face as she made her decision. After a few tense seconds, she said, "Cort."

"What did he say?"

She finished her water and did a quick check of the oven timer. "I'd been seeing Evan for a while. He never once asked me to do any favors for him with regard to the network. I thought we…well, let's just say I thought we had a pretty decent relationship. He never complained when I had to work a funky schedule or a day's shooting changed our plans. However, one day Evan came to the studio when I was out at an interview and he wasn't looking for me. It seems he'd been waiting to get Cort alone to discuss his ideas, but never had the chance. *I* was always around."

Bitterness infused her words. The creep had hurt her, that was plain, and even if he wasn't responsible for harassing her, Josh promised punishment.

"Anyway. Cort put him off. Told him he wasn't the person to talk to. Evan was persistent and there was a bit of a blowup. I didn't notice anything different in how they acted toward each other, but about a week later Evan told me I should think about finding a new director, that Cort didn't have my best interests in mind. I told him he was wrong, but he wouldn't let it go. I asked if anything had happened between them and he denied it. So of course I went to Cort. Evan is such an egotist he never imagined I would doubt him."

"But to your credit, you did."

She shifted in her chair. "Cort's been with me since the beginning of the show. I trust him completely. He was reluctant to tell me what happened, but finally did. I asked around and found a few other people Evan had spoken to as well. Stacy was one of them."

"I'm surprised she didn't tell you."

Kandy shrugged.

"What did you do when you found out?"

The timer sounded and Kandy removed the pizza from the oven, putting it on top of the counter to cool. While she pulled dishes from one of the cabinets and utensils from the drawers, she continued.

"Confronted him. He denied it. I called him a liar. He called me some choice names I'd rather not repeat, and then I had him thrown out of my office by security. He called me every day for a week after that. Pleading. Whining. Apologizing. I found out he was following me when he showed up at a location shoot. I made my position crystal clear on our relationship, and it was the last time I saw him until tonight."

With a marble-handled cutting wheel, she divided the pizza into individual slices and filled his plate, then her own.

"What did you tell him then that was different from the other times?"

"It wasn't what I said, but what I did," she answered, biting into the delicious-smelling crust.

Josh took his own sample and groaned in pleasure. "God, Kandy, this is incredible."

Grinning, she said, "It's the sauce. Grandma's recipe."

"You could mass produce this and make a fortune." He polished off the first piece in four bites and she handed him another.

"I have enough on my plate right now, thanks. Besides, there are about a dozen or so recipes I've never revealed to anyone. I'm keeping them in my private collection."

"Why?"

She wiped her mouth with a napkin, and said, "It sounds corny, but to keep some of Grandma's secrets makes me feel close to her. It's like part of her is still with me. And only with me."

Josh nodded. "I can understand that. Now answer my question. What did you do to Chandler?"

She sighed and took another bite. After swallowing, she said, "We were at the Fulton Fish Market filming a show segment. During a shooting break Evan approached me, all conciliatory and amiable. I wanted to throw up. He was persistent, even grabbing me at one point to kiss me. I didn't really think about what I was doing. I saw the boning knife lying on the fish counter, grabbed it, and, well."

Josh was charmed when she blushed to the roots of her curly black hair.

"I aimed the knife at his crotch and told him if he didn't leave me alone I'd cut his balls off and give them to the fisherman for bait. It worked. He was so stunned, he left, babbling that I was crazy."

"It would work for me, too," Josh said, grimacing. "With any man."

She shrugged again and took a bite of her pizza. "That was it. End of story, until tonight."

"Okay. I have to tell you, he's pretty high on my list. Who else do you know who might have an ax to grind?"

Kandy rose and took two more waters from the refrigerator. Handing one to him, she said, "Personally? Or in business?"

"Both."

"Professional cooking's not the mild-mannered business you might think," she said after a minute. "I started young and rose fast. You don't make a lot of friends that way."

If she was bitter, he couldn't hear it in her voice.

"Professional jealousies?" he asked.

"A few. My cookbooks are always on the *New York Times* bestseller list, usually bumping someone down a few notches. I'd certainly be mad if it happened to me."

Josh made a mental note to ask Reva.

"What about on a personal level?"

Kandy scratched her nose with the flat of her hand and frowned. Sighing, she said, "My cousin Daniel isn't too happy with me these days."

"Does he work for you? I mean, *with* you?"

"He did. I had to fire him about a month ago."

"Why?"

She took a sip and said, "Daniel is Aunt Lucy's oldest, Stacy's big brother. He was one of the sound crew technicians. I started hearing some noise about problems with him from the other techs, but ignored them, figuring it was just personality differences, something petty like that."

"What changed your mind?"

"He started showing up to work late, not coming back from lunch, and a few times it was obvious he'd been drinking. I saw his behavior twice myself, so I confronted him. It didn't go well." She shook her head and her voice turned sad. "We wound up having a huge shouting match in the middle of the studio kitchen. Again, some choice names were thrown around. Aunt Lucy couldn't even calm him down. I fired him on the spot. Told him to pack up his gear and get out."

"Did he go without a fight?"

"Yeah. Angry. Pissed. But compliant. I haven't seen him since."

"Has your aunt or Stacy spoken with him about it?"

She shook her head. "If they have, they haven't mentioned it to me. I guess this weekend I'll find out if he's still mad."

"Why? What's this weekend?"

"My sister Eleanor's twenty-first birthday. I'm doing the food and hosting. Everyone in the family is invited."

"Where?"

"My weekend house in the Hamptons. We've been planning it for months."

"Who's we?"

"Gemma, and two of my other sisters, Belinda and Abby. They've done most of the planning. I'm furnishing the house and doing the eats."

"On top of everything else you're already doing?"

She rose and took her dish to the sink. Rinsing it, she sighed. "It's family, and that comes before everything. Besides, Eleanor deserves this party. Of all my sisters, she's the dearest and the sweetest. And the smartest. She just found out she's been accepted to Harvard Medical School in the fall."

Josh took his own dish to the sink and was prepared to wash it, but Kandy took it from him, rinsed it along with the other utensils she'd used, and put them all in the dishwasher.

"Look," she said, turning to him, one hand on her hip. "I've got some work to do before bed. Can we continue this inquisition in the morning?"

He nodded. "No problem."

She put the leftover pizza into a plastic storage container and into the refrigerator. When she turned out the kitchen light, he followed her through the hallway. Where the wings converged, they stopped.

"Everything you'll need is either in your bathroom or in one of the guest room closets. Feel free."

"Thanks. One more thing?"

Her brows lifted in a question.

"What's your morning routine? What time do you get up?"

The dimples in her chin deepened as a lazy grin spread slow and sumptuous across her lips. There was a tiny trace of pizza sauce still lining them and for a hot second he envisioned wiping it away.

And not with his fingertip.

"My daily workout is at four thirty," she said. "I leave for the studio at six."

He knew she was waiting for his reaction. It took a great deal of willpower not to blanch at the ungodly hour.

"You do it here, or go to a gym?" he asked, proud his voice sounded free of emotion.

"Here. The gym's down the hall, next to the guest bathroom. I'll try not to wake you."

"Thanks, but like I said before, where you go, I go. See you at four thirty."

He could tell she was trying to keep another grin from her lips.

"Okay."

Back in his room, Josh realized he hadn't given her the cell phone. He pulled it out of his duffel and went back toward her wing of the apartment.

He knocked even though the bedroom door was open, and walked in.

"Kandy? I forgot to give—"

She was standing next to the bed facing him, arms crossed in front of her chest. When she glanced up he saw fear drench her eyes. He quickly moved into the room and to her side. "What's wrong?"

She was shaking, her whole body trembling like a windblown leaf. Without thought, he pulled her into his arms.

"Kandy?"

She clung to him, her hands balling into his shirt. "My answering machine," she said, her voice vibrating with emotion.

She nodded toward the flickering light coming from the older-model device sitting on her bedside table.

"A message?"

She nodded and pressed her face into his chest.

"Sit down," he said, and gently guided her onto the bed. He plopped down next to her and threw an arm around her shoulder, knowing she needed the physical contact, the warmth.

He pressed the *Play* button on the machine.

"*You filthy whore! I want you dead!*"

She shuddered against him.

"Do you recognize the voice?" He pulled back, forcing her to look at him

He expected tears, but her eyes were dry, her pupils constricted.

He expected her to shout and vent. She was silent and mute as she leaned into him.

Her color was pale, her lips a frosty blue.

Shock.

"Kandy? Do you?" He gave her a tiny shake.

She blinked a few times and then stared straight at his face. "No. No, I don't."

"This is your private line? The one only for family?"

"Mostly, y-yes."

"What does that mean? Who else has the number?"

"Cort. Reva. A few…friends."

"Okay. I'm taking the tape out."

She didn't try to stop him.

"I'm unplugging this phone and I want you to turn your cell off, too."

Some of her color was returning.

"What if someone needs me? They won't have any way to get in touch with me."

"Too bad. You need privacy and peace. Sleep."

She gaped openmouthed at him and he was prepared for her to fight more about it.

"All right," she said after a few seconds. "All right. I can do without the phone for one night."

"Forget about working, too. Get ready for bed and just go to sleep. Shut down."

"I need to—"

"No arguments. You need to sleep more than you need to do anything else tonight. It'll all still be there in the morning."

She frowned at him and he was actually glad to see it. It told him she was coming out of the shock and back to herself.

"You're very bossy," she told him, repeating his words back at him.

"Come's with the job. Now go get ready for bed."

He was mildly surprised when she did.

Josh unplugged the phone along with the answering machine. He left her cell phone on the dresser in the charging dock but made sure it was turned off.

Walking back to his room, his mind was racing. He needed to find out who was behind this, and soon. Kandy, strong-willed though she appeared, was frightened and trying her best to hide it. Josh felt it in the way she'd clung to him. Wanting—needing—to be held, helped, and comforted. She hadn't brokered with him on leaving the phone in case of an emergency, she'd accepted it. Nor had she argued when he told her to forget about working.

Kandy was a woman used to giving orders, not following them blindly. He knew just how afraid she must really be to simply acquiesce to his commands.

Booting up his laptop, he plugged in a few security keys and was able to weave into the local usage track of the phone company's website to see if the call could be traced.

He typed in an access code and Kandy's unlisted home phone number.

Within a minute he knew the call had been made in Manhattan, but the number was untraceable.

Not a total loss. At least he knew the geographic origination.

A little while later Josh made his way back to Kandy's bedroom. The door was still ajar, the light inside off. He crept in, saw her huddled under the covers, and listened to her breathe for a few seconds. When he was satisfied she was out, he went back to his own room, prepared for a long, boring night of research.

Chapter Five

Kandy's feet pummeled the treadmill as she increased the pace through the mountain-climbing program.

She needed this run to clear her head. Last night's events had left her shaken and confused.

Shaken? Ha! Scared witless was more like it.

The phone message had been disturbing and frightening, sure, but the feel of Josh Keane's arms around her, warming her and giving comfort, had been overwhelming. The titanium-steel hardness of his chest when she'd buried her face into it had not only reassured, but aroused her.

Completely.

She couldn't remember ever being so turned on just by being held.

The feel of him, the actual sensation of his rock-hard body against hers as he held her, gently, was more powerful than any seductive touch could have been.

Josh kept pace with her on the adjoining treadmill. She had her iPod plugged in and ran to the beat of the music. Josh ran music-free, his rhythm steady as he tore through his own preprogrammed routine. Kandy glanced over to check his status to see he'd also selected a mountain run. His stride was much wider than hers, though, his pace almost double.

The ceiling-mounted television in front of them was on and cued to the early morning news. She tried to keep her gaze fixed on the screen, or in front of her, or anywhere that wasn't on him. Watching those powerful, muscle-laden calves and thighs go through their pace was almost too much to handle. Not to mention the way his T-shirt fit snugly across his ripped-to-godlike-perfection chest and those broad, corded arms, showing and defining all the toned muscle groups beneath it.

No, it was too much to watch.

He wouldn't be around forever to distract her like this. He'd find out what was going on and then be off to his next job, which was for the best. She had too much to do, too much that needed her undivided attention, to be sidetracked by this gorgeous man following her and watching her every move.

Kandy had no time to worry about things she couldn't control, like this supposed harasser. She'd tried ignoring the incidents away, tried to convince Stacy it was nothing. Now she had to contend with an outsider going through her friends' and family's personal business.

Josh claimed he wouldn't disturb her life in any way, but he already had just with his presence. In one day he'd insinuated himself into her home, her life. Even her head.

And she just wasn't sure how she felt about it.

The treadmill slowed to a walking pace.

"Almost done?" Josh asked.

Bathed in shiny sweat, his muscles glowed with definition. Each crevice where the sinew curved in his upper arms was pooled with dampness.

Kandy swallowed. "Five-minute cooldown."

"You doing any weights?" He pointed his chin to the equipment in a corner of the room.

He'd been running for more than forty-five minutes at a gallop pace and his breathing was still steady and calm. "No. I've got a six thirty meeting with the production crew I've got to prep for."

"Okay."

He continued his run while she finished the walk.

When the machine timed out, she grabbed a towel and slung it across her neck. She was sweating, but not nearly to the extent Josh was.

"I'll be ready to leave in a half hour," she told him.

He gave her a thumbs-up and kept running.

Josh was waiting in the kitchen for her when it was time to go.

She'd pulled her hair back into a high ponytail, her face naked. Before filming, she'd be made up for the camera and dressed in gardening togs. For now, she wore a pink jogging suit with matching designer sneakers, a black T-shirt under the lightweight jacket.

"You look comfortable," Josh said, a coffee mug in his hand.

"I'll dress for the camera at the studio," she told him, and filled a travel mug with coffee. "Did you sleep okay?"

"Shouldn't I be asking you that?"

"I slept fine," she told him. "I shut down completely once I turned the light out. Didn't wake up until the alarm went off this morning."

Josh nodded. "Good."

"So, did you?" she asked. "Sleep okay? Bed was okay?"

"Everything was fine, Kandy."

It was her turn to nod. She topped off the travel mug, turned and asked, "You want to take some of this with you?"

"Nope. One cup's my limit, thanks. So far, like everything else I've sampled, it's delicious."

"Thanks, but I can only take half the credit. I borrowed an old mix recipe of Grandma's and added a few spices."

"Again, if you packaged this stuff, you'd make a fortune."

Smiling at the compliment, she looked at her watch and said, "Time to go."

Once they were settled in the waiting limo, Josh asked, "Is this your normal daily routine? Leave this same time every day?"

"Pretty much." She dug into her briefcase and extracted some papers. "I'm usually at the office by six fifteen. The film crew arrives by eight, so by the time hair, makeup, dressing, and blocking are done, we shoot anytime after nine thirty."

"Weekends, too?"

"No. Weekends are a sacred cow. I won't film on those days unless it's unavoidable. The staff deserves time off."

"I got the impression your weekends were spent working."

"I usually do, either at the condo trying out new recipes or putting together ideas for upcoming shows. During the summer I drive out to the Hamptons house on Friday nights. Come back Sunday. Sometimes there's a function to go to on Saturday night, so I'll stick around in the city. This weekend I'll leave early Friday afternoon to start getting the food ready for the party. It'll be delivered that morning."

Josh nodded. "Someone's at your beach house to take the delivery?"

"A cleaning lady comes in every Thursday, even in the winter. That's been Gemma's Christmas present to me since I got the house."

"She gave you a cleaning lady for a present?"

She grinned. "Yeah. Otherwise I'd spend the first day dusting and vacuuming."

"Nice present. Agency hire?"

"No. Gemma found her on her own. She put an ad in the paper, asked some of her friends who have houses in the same town to recommend someone. She's a real asset, too. Greta. She's German, sixtyish, and smiles all the time. Hardly speaks any English."

"Stacy told me you have a housekeeper at your condo, too. I haven't seen her."

"And you won't. Not unless we're there during the day, which I almost never am. She comes in at nine, twice a week. She's very reliable and I've never had any trouble with her."

"Even when you thought she'd riffled through your closets?"

"Let me guess; Stacy again?"

"Yup. She told me you border on obsessive/compulsive, too, but I figured that one out for myself."

Just inside of insulted, in most part because it was true, Kandy frowned. "I'm not OCD. I'm just uber-focused."

"Call it whatever you want." He explained the incidents Stacy had already reported to him. "Is there anything else you can add, aside from last night's phone message?"

She'd tried to forget about that. The venom in the voice, the hatred in the words. "No."

"I'm meeting with your agent at the studio today, and Stacy's going to bring me to the kid in charge of your media stuff."

"Tricia Walters. She's my aunt Callie's oldest."

"Why aren't I surprised?"

When his mouth pulled into a grin, all teeth and boyish mirth, Kandy's pulse jumped. All of a sudden it was hot in the back of the limo, though the air conditioning was turned up high.

"I'm also doing background checks on all the people close to you. My partner is working on it back at the office."

The heat infusing her system turned to a block of ice.

"I can't allow that."

He put his hands up. "Hold on. I know you don't like it, but it's necessary."

"No, it's not. Whoever is bothering me isn't someone close to me. I know it. I feel it." She pounded on her chest, once, for emphasis.

Josh stared at her for a few moments, then said, "Think this through. The person responsible obviously *is* close to you or can get close to you without worrying about discovery. It's someone who knows you, knows your schedule, knows how to reach you anywhere, anytime. Someone you won't, *can't,* suspect."

To hear him put it in words so simple numbed her.

Her breath hissed out and her vision faded, all the blood rushing down to her toes.

Josh closed the distance between them in a heartbeat. The papers she'd removed from her bag scattered about in disarray.

Taking her hands with his, Josh worried the knuckles.

"Look, Kandy, I'm sorry to be so direct, but I need you to understand what you're dealing with. I know it hurts to think someone you know is behind this. But for your own safety, you need to accept it's probably true."

Kandy looked down at their coupled hands. She'd always thought hers were large for a woman, but right now, tucked into Josh's massive and powerful ones, for the first time in her life they felt small. Dainty. At twenty-eight the skin over them was still smooth and clear, but the sinew and muscles beneath them were strong and coarse, used to hard work and labor. Her nails were kept short so she could cook without worry of damaging an expensive manicure.

In comparison, Josh's hands were massive hulks of muscle and tanned flesh, the fingers long and solid, the nails short. A smattering of freckles peeked out from under his sleeve, his skin warm and smooth against hers.

She took a deep breath and let herself look at his face. Concern and kindness were grooved into the lines on his brow and in the downturn of his mouth.

"I understand." She swallowed, her gaze steady. "I don't like it one bit, and, for the record, I don't think it's true. But I understand. Just please be discreet. I don't want anyone hurt by this snooping."

He squeezed her hands and let them go. In an instant she felt empty and cold.

"Discretion's a job requirement. Don't worry. The only one who'll be hurt is the one making your life uncomfortable. I promise."

She believed him.

The car pulled up to the studio building, and she bent down to retrieve her fallen papers. Josh did as well.

Their faces were a breath apart, a fistful of paper between them.

Kandy stared into a green so intense she felt she could fall into it and be transported to a calm and serene meadow, bright with sunshine and hot with passion. His warm breath whispered against her cheek as they remained, bent, lost in each other's eyes. Her stomach careened through a small series of somersaults. All she needed to do was move a few inches and her lips would be on his.

That she considered shifting her position so she could capture them, flabbergasted her.

Without blinking, she sat back in one quick rush.

"Here." He handed her the pages he'd grabbed.

Was it her imagination, or wishful thinking, that his voice sounded a little gruff? A little tight?

The driver opened the car door and she was brought back to reality.

"Thanks." She shoved all the papers back into her briefcase, never once looking at them.

When they entered the lobby, Kandy greeted the security guard at the front desk before the duo went up in the elevator.

"I have a meeting with the production crew in a few minutes," she told him.

He nodded, his gaze zeroed in on the floor numbers as they ascended.

"There'll be breakfast, if you're hungry. It's prepared by the network caterers, so you'll get a sample of everything. It's usually a pretty extensive spread."

I'm babbling. Good, God. It's nerves. Just nerves.

When the doors opened, Josh followed her out and down to her office.

"I have to go over these papers," she told him as she settled down behind her desk.

"Go ahead. Pretend I'm not here," he said, and dropped onto one of her couches, cell phone in his hand.

"Impossible," she muttered.

The needed work got the better of her a moment later, and she was able to focus her attention on it.

But she never forgot he was in the room.

Fifteen minutes later a knock on the door propelled him to an upright position.

"It's just me," Stacy said, coming in. "Are you ready for the meeting?"

Rising, Kandy said, "Yeah. Everyone here?"

Stacy nodded. "Morning," she said with a smile to Josh.

He returned it. "You look fresh. Didn't make it a late night?"

"No. And speaking of." She turned her attention back to her cousin. "You left entirely too early."

Kandy shrugged. "I was tired. Plus, seeing Evan spoiled the whole thing for me."

"If you'd hung around ten minutes more you would have seen your mom."

Kandy kept walking. "So she showed up after all?"

"She sure did," Stacy said with a laugh. "I thought Harvey was going to need cardiac resuscitation after she sucked him into her web. Really, Kan, you missed a classic scene."

"Did Harvey survive?" Kandy asked, knowing how powerful a force her mother could be when in seduction mode.

"Yup. The last time I saw him, Reva managed to get him away from

Aunt Hannah and was offering him a napkin to wipe the sweat pouring off his head."

Kandy's mouth twisted at the description. "I'll call him today and make amends."

"Oh, you don't need to. I heard him tell Reva if he was straight he would have left with her in a heartbeat."

Kandy chuckled at the thought of her sex-kitten mother with her debonair publisher.

"I told you we should have stayed," Josh said. He held the door open to the conference room for both of them. "Sounds like we missed a good show."

As she walked passed him, she glanced up from under her lashes and said, "Don't worry. You'll get your chance to be seduced."

Chapter Six

Once everyone was seated, the production crew surrounding the table, Josh ambled over to the food prep area and filled a plate.

There were plenty of empty chairs at the conference table, but he chose to stand off to the sidelines and be as unobtrusive as possible, just as he'd promised.

With a hip settled against one of the window ledges, he watched Kandy interact with her team. A few of them tossed inquisitive glances his way, but no one questioned Kandy—or him—about his presence.

Kandy herself took no food, just a bottled water, while those around her had full, overflowing plates.

He wasn't surprised that she was a natural leader. Questions were asked succinctly and with a clarity that impressed him, and brokered no confusion or disorder in her answers. He saw her challenge some of her staff's views, compliment them on the presentation, and question several standards he had no clue about.

When the meeting ended he was much more cognizant of the roles involved in shooting a television show than he'd ever thought he would be.

"What's next?" he asked when everyone quit the room except Stacy, himself, and Kandy.

"Hair and makeup," Stacy answered. "Then we shoot."

"Today we're filming in the garden on the roof," Kandy said. "I'm doing a segment on homegrown herbs and spices."

"Homegrown on a midtown roof. Impressive."

"We think so," Stacy told him, before answering her cell phone.

While she spoke to the caller, Kandy and Josh continued on to the dressing room.

"Well, Joshua, we meet again," Lucy said when they entered.

Her perfume engulfed him, a wide smile, all teeth and scarlet lips, gracing her face.

"You must be the hunk my sister has been telling me about," Josh heard. When he turned he was met with the deepest pair of blue eyes he'd ever seen, surrounded by the face of a well-cared-for woman of about fifty.

"Aunt Callie, this is Josh," Kandy said, plopping down in the makeup chair. "He's a…a friend."

"Wish I had friends who looked like you," Callie Walters said, extending her hand to Josh.

"Are all the women in your family gorgeous, Kandy?" he asked. "Because I haven't met one so far who isn't."

Callie's smile grew even wider, as the pleasure of his compliment shone in her eyes. "I see Lucy didn't exaggerate. This one's a keeper," she told her niece.

From her seat, Kandy rolled her eyes. "Can we get started, please? The weather report is calling for rain."

"Certainly, dear," Callie said, throwing one last, flirtatious slant Josh's way.

Reva blew into the room just as Callie began rolling her niece's hair in curlers.

Josh glanced over what he assumed was her business attire, quite different from the outfit he'd seen her decked out in the night before. This morning her gray bob was pulled off her face by a black headband, allowing a full view of enormous, dropped pearls adorning her ears. Her form-fitting malachite green suit was cut perfectly to her small frame, the body-hugging skirt ending barely an inch above her knee. Jet-black three-inch pumps finished the look.

"Babe, mind if I steal Josh for a few minutes?"

Kandy stared into the makeup mirror at her. Reva's eyes widened a fraction in a silent question.

"Go ahead," she told her.

"You will come back?" Lucy said to him from the closet doorway as she pulled out clothing choices for her niece.

Josh knew it wasn't a question, so he just grinned back at her.

"I'm a little upset you whisked Kandy away so early last night," Reva told him as they walked down the hallway to Kandy's office.

He shrugged and dropped his hands into his pants pockets. "It was her call. I thought we should stay, but she'd had enough."

"Evan Chandler," Reva said, mouth turning downward into a scowl, disgust filling her voice. "I never liked him."

"That seems to be the general opinion of everyone I've met so far. Why would someone as smart and savvy as Kandy be involved with a guy like that?"

"He's a professional charmer. I'm sure he played on Kandy's good nature, for all it was worth. She hasn't been the most proliferative dater in all the years I've known her. In fact, Evan was the first man she spent any considerable time with. Have a seat." She waved at the couches, went to the refrigerator, and took out a bottled water.

Josh shook his head when she asked if he wanted one.

"What did you want to speak to me about? I don't want to leave Kandy for too long," he asked when she settled in across from him.

"A few things. First and foremost, I want to thank you for taking the job. Stacy said Kandy's been hard to convince something really is going on, and having you in the mix now makes me feel better about her safety."

Josh waited.

"I thought I'd be able to give you a little more background on what's happened that's made me so worried about her."

"Stacy's already filled me in."

"She doesn't know everything."

While Josh just stared at her, she took a long pull of water and continued. "The incident in LA was worrisome, I'll admit. At the time, though, I wasn't convinced anything other than stupidity on the rental agency's part was involved."

"When did your opinion change? With the lighting incident?"

She shook her head. "A little before, actually. I was in here with Kandy going over her book contract. We'd just finished the negotiations for the next one and were having a celebratory glass of champagne because I was able to get Harvey Little to double his first offer."

"And that's a good thing?"

"You bet your sweet ass it is. Kandy's contract for the book being released today was for 1.5 million. The next one is 3.5 million. And that doesn't even include the foreign rights."

Josh was stunned. "For a cookbook?"

"Not just any cookbook. A *Kandy Laine* cookbook. She's sold out every single first, second, and third printing within two months of publication on each one. It's why Harvey upped the first print run on *Sugar-Coated Kandy*. He's releasing over a million and a half copies of this one. You can't believe the amount of money she pulls in for him. They've never gone to paperback. And e-book cookbooks don't generally do well as a rule, but hers do."

"Amazing."

"No. Kandy," she said simply, with a nonchalant wave of her hand. "She's hit a niche with the public few celebrity chefs have ever come close to. She's got endorsement deals for pots and pans, kitchen gadgetry, and I've even got one company who wants to market some of her sauces. Everything Kandy has touched so far has turned to culinary gold. But I'm getting off subject."

She took another sip of water. "We were in here, celebrating, and Kandy slipped out for a few minutes. Her private line rang so I answered it. I've done it before. It's usually her mother calling or one of her sisters. They're all very close."

"But it wasn't this time?"

Reva shook her head. "At first I didn't think anyone was on the line. I didn't hear any background noise. After saying hello twice, I was set to hang up, but then this voice screamed into the wire and I just stood there, staggered."

"Man or woman?"

"After thinking about it, I feel it was a woman. The voice was shrill, not deep."

"What was said?"

Reva's hard gaze bore straight through him. Josh thought in that instant she looked like a lioness willing to pounce and protect her cub from danger. He'd never really understood the phrase *if looks could kill* until he saw Reva's expression.

"'Die, whore! Die.' It was screamed, twice. Then the call disconnected."

"What did you do?"

"Well, first I just stood there like an idiot with the phone in my hand, staring at it. I couldn't believe it, couldn't take it in. Then I thought it must be a crank call, or maybe even a really wrong number."

"Did you tell Kandy?"

She shook her head, the blond and white strands swaying. "I didn't bother. When she came back into the room I told her I'd just finished up a call to my office. She never suspected anything. It was only when I found out about everything else I put two and two together."

"She's been getting calls at home, too," he confided. "Along the same line as the one you intercepted."

He watched her eyes narrow into slits. "*Jesus.* Maybe we should notify the police. What if some wacko really is hell-bent on doing her harm?"

"If you think this through, you'll realize it's not some random wacko. It's someone she knows; she just doesn't want to believe it."

Reva stared across at him for a few moments. “You mean because the calls have been on her private unlisted lines, don’t you?”

“Yup. Plus, the lighting accident, and even her supposedly misplaced wallet. It makes me think it’s someone who’s able to get close enough to the studio without being suspected, like it’s a natural thing to be around her.”

“Oh God, she’ll never believe it’s someone close to her. Never.” She downed the remainder of the water, crushing the bottle and tossing it into the recycling basket under Kandy’s desk. “Wait a minute; she fired her cousin a few weeks ago. Did she tell you that?”

“Yeah. I’ve already started looking at him. I should know more by this afternoon.”

“My money’s still on Evan Chandler. He’s a creep and, I think, fully capable of terrorizing someone.”

“You’re the only one who’s admitted that so far. Why do you think it’s him? Playing devil’s advocate here,” he said. “Everyone else I’ve talked to, including Kandy, keeps telling me he’s not smart enough.”

“I disagree. I think he’s fully capable of being malicious and vindictive. You only got a glimpse of him yesterday. But I dealt with him for more than three months. He could be quite nasty when things didn’t go his way. He wanted Kandy, not only because he thought she’d introduce him to network executives, but because she looked good on his arm, which, in turn, made him look good. Evan is all about appearance.”

“I figured that one out for myself. He’s a superficial moron who thinks he’s a player.”

“Perfect description.”

“Is there anything else you can tell me?”

“I don’t think so.”

Josh thought for moment. “Stacy let it slip not everyone in Kandy’s family is happy with her success. Has she shut anyone out?”

“No, it’s not her who’s done the shutting out. You should be able to tell by now, even though you’ve known her only a short time, Kandy is a family-conscious woman. They mean everything to her and she tries to help them out as much as she can. Her grandmother instilled this deep sense of family loyalty in her from an early age. No matter what path Kandy would have taken in life I think she would have included her family in her success. But not everyone is receptive to her assistance.”

“Give me a name, Reva.”

He could see she was mentally weighing her options on how much to say. Finally, he guessed, she thought Kandy’s welfare was more important than potentially slandering someone.

"Her uncle Peter. Peter Czewski. He's the middle sibling in her mother's generation. The only male, which is probably at the heart of the whole matter." Her lips thinned and she crossed her arms over the front of her suit.

"What's the story?"

"I don't know it all. You'll have to talk to Kandy to get the full Monty. But the basic background is Peter claims to be a writer."

"Claims?"

"I've read his stuff. Kandy asked me to as a favor."

"And?"

"To put it bluntly, it sucks. He doesn't know basic grammar and sentence structure. I couldn't even follow the plotline in the four manuscripts he sent."

"So, what? He's jealous of Kandy's success?"

"It's more, I think. She offered him a job as a researcher for her first cookbook. He declined, saying the work was beneath him. Instead, he asked her to do him the favor of letting me see his work. The problem is his writing is pitiful."

"Did you tell him that?"

She nodded. "In the nicest, subtlest way I could."

Josh could figure out what happened next. "He didn't take it well, did he?"

"No. The worst part is, he blames Kandy. My guess is he thinks she somehow poisoned my opinion of him before I ever read his work just because he rejected her original offer."

"So he's someone else I need to speak to."

"I would. Definitely. Betrayal, perceived or actual, is always a good motive for vindictive behavior, right?"

"Yeah. Anyone else?"

She tapped her fingers on her chin and drew her thin brows together in thought. "No. That's it, since you know about the other incidents from Stacy."

"Okay. I'd better get back."

They both rose. "I'll walk with you," she said. "I have to speak to her about her book tour schedule."

When they arrived back at the makeup room, Josh was stunned at the transformation in Kandy. Gone was the ponytail, replaced by a sedate coif, where her curly hair was tamed and pulled off her face at the temples to ski down her back. The heavy studio makeup he'd seen her wear yesterday had been applied with a lighter hand today. She'd changed into a tight-fitting pair of washed denim overalls, with a baby blue long-sleeved Henley underneath.

"All done being grilled?" Kandy asked, the grin on her face playful.

"I'll have you know I do not grill," Reva replied from behind them in a voice dripping with acid.

"Yes, you do, and you know it." Kandy checked her reflection in the mirror.

"I think I'd like a chance to grill him," Lucy said. "What about you?" she asked her sister.

Josh swiped at his mouth to hide the grin lurking there.

Both women were studying him as if they'd like to devour him whole. They could be close to thirty years his senior, but his ego vaulted just looking at their assessing expressions.

"It might be fun," Lucy said, placing Kandy's discarded clothes on hangers.

"It would certainly be memorable," her sister added, rearranging the makeup pots she'd used on her niece.

"Down, girls," Kandy told her aunts. "Josh isn't used to such flagrant temptation, and I don't want him to be damaged so early in the game. Come on. I'll rescue you. You can ride up to the roof with me."

She snaked one hand around his arm and gave him a gentle tug.

"Kandy, I need to tell you something," Reva said.

"Ride with us."

Once they were out of the makeup room and away from the prying eyes of her aunts, Kandy removed her arm. "Sorry about those two," she said, her demeanor going from playful to serious.

"Are they always like that?" he asked, finally letting the grin he'd been holding back come to the surface.

Kandy rolled her beautifully made-up eyes. "For as long as I can remember. They get it from their dad, my grandfather. He was an outrageous flirt. Had all the ladies in Grandma's neighborhood at his beck and call."

"How'd she feel about it?"

Kandy got into the waiting elevator and punched in the roof access. She turned to him, crossed her arms in front of her, and said, "She loved it. Kept him out of her hair and out of her kitchen as much as possible. She actually used to encourage him to do favors for the widows in the area so he'd be gone for hours at a clip."

"She wasn't jealous?"

"Not a whit. Grandpa loved her to pieces. Couldn't imagine a life without her. He used to tell me his life started the day he met her. They were married three weeks later."

"As much as this touching trip down memory lane is moving me toward emotions not experienced in years," Reva said, "I need to go over something with you and get back to my office. I *do* have other clients, you know."

Kandy turned to her and said, "Shoot."

The elevators doors opened and the three of them stepped out.

While Reva spoke with Kandy, Josh took in the beauty surrounding them.

They were at the very top of the thirty-story building, the entire roof enclosed by a glass solarium at least twenty feet high. The magnificent natural lighting filtering through the glass made the need for the artificial studio lights redundant. The climate was temperate and comfortable, with just a hint of humidity. Six rows of long tables housed dozens of flowering pots; hanging baskets of numerous blooms and buds lined one part of the glass ceiling, dripping down toward the center of the room.

The fragrance that hit him was enticing, sensual, and beguiling. Much like the woman at his side.

"What do you think?" Kandy asked him once Reva left.

"It's the prettiest hothouse I've ever seen."

"It's not really a hothouse," she said, cocking her head. "More like a life-size terrarium."

"Did you plant all of these?" He swiped a hand across the area.

"Most. The herbs are mine. There are twenty-five varieties blooming right now. By month's end, it'll bump up to about forty. Come on. I'll take you on a tour."

She guided him around the spacious area, pointing out her favorite flowers, budding spices, and herbs. He wasn't surprised when she gave him the Latin names and origins of everything she indicated. He had a feeling Kandy made herself an expert on anything she attempted, be it cooking or gardening.

"Kandy? You ready?" the assistant director called from across the roof.

"Yup."

They moved in his direction, Josh noting Lucy and Callie had come to the roof as well.

"Don't be worried about them," Kandy said in a low voice. "They'll act professionally up here. No flirting. Honest."

"I was beginning to really enjoy it."

She stared up at him, her crystal blue eyes slitting. "I'll just bet you were. Typical male."

"Where's Cort?" she asked a moment later as Callie swiped some powder across her nose.

"He just phoned from downstairs. He'll be up in minute," the A.D. told her.

"You're good." Callie stepped back.

Together, Kandy and the A.D., whose name Josh learned from Lucy was Mark Begman, moved to the herb section of the solarium. They were going over Kandy's demonstration of how to gently pick an herb without harming its flavor. Josh watched the man move in front of her making a square shape of his two thumbs and index fingers.

"They really do that?" he asked Lucy. "I always thought it was just a gag."

"It helps him see the shot more clearly from the camera's perspective," Lucy said, all business and polish, no teasing banter.

Cort arrived a few seconds later, greeted everyone with a gruff "Morning," and moved over to Kandy and Mark. He spoke with them for a few moments before turning.

"Let's try to do this in one, two at the most, kids. The weather's gonna turn soon and I don't want to move to the artificial lights if we don't have to, okay? Places."

Cort moved next to the main camera, after making sure the other three were ready to go as well.

"All set, Kandy?"

She smiled and gave him a thumbs-up sign.

Cort nodded and Mark called, "Quiet! In five…four…three…"

He counted the last two on his fingers.

"There's nothing better than the aroma of homegrown herbs and spices added to your cooking. Especially if they're freshly picked from your own garden."

She continued her speech for three minutes, uninterrupted, flawless, and without the use of cue cards.

"Cut!" Cort called. "That was great, Kandy."

"I want to do another one."

"That one was perfect," Cort said. "I don't think—"

"I want to do another one."

There was steel in her voice, coupled with a hard, determined glare no one on the roof missed, including Josh.

Cort stared at her for a lengthy moment. Then, he nodded. "Again everyone. Time?"

In his opinion, Josh thought the first was as perfect as it could get. She never faltered with the second take, either.

When Cort stopped the action again, Callie jumped up from her seat and adjusted Kandy's hair, her makeup, and her clothing before the next take began.

When the filming restarted, Kandy bent over a flat of basil, explaining the different varieties of the herb and the ways it could be used to enhance food flavors.

"The best way to keep the flavor as rich and potent as possible," she told the camera, "is to very gently pinch the leaves at the point where they shoot from the stalk. Like this."

She put one hand on the base of the plant, the other on one of the leaves. With a gentle tug, she separated the leaf from its stem. A dollop of dirt shot up from the flat when she did.

"Cut!" Cort called. "What happened?"

"I tugged too hard. The dirt's all over the place." She started to swipe at the flat when her brow furrowed and her eyes squinted. "What is this?"

Josh moved in closer just as she yanked something long and slender from the dirt.

When she screamed and jumped back, he bolted to her side.

"What's wrong?" He pulled her shaking form into his arms. She was ghost white under the pancake makeup, her eyes wide with shock.

She folded into him, her gaze never moving from the dirt.

Josh tightened his grip when he felt the magnitude of her quaking. With a quick glance down at the table, he found the handle of a knife jutting up from the dirt. That didn't bother him half as much as what was pierced by the blade end, stuck, half hidden in the dirt.

A dead rat.

The knife was impaled through its chest. The rodent lay supine in the bed, its arms and legs curled inward in rigor. Its neck had been sliced clear through to the spine and hung by a tenuous, thin tendon, congealed blood circled around it.

In the next second Kandy's grip on his arm slackened as her eyes rolled upward and her head lolled back. Josh caught her right before she dropped to the ground.

Chapter Seven

Josh scooped her up in his arms and carried her from the scene and straight to her office, where they were met by a frantic Stacy.

"What happened?" she yelled, her eyes raking down her cousin's body. "Mark called me. Is she hurt? Should I get a doctor?"

"Calm down, Stacy, and lower your voice," Lucy told her in a tone only a mother could use effectively.

"Let's just get her settled," Callie said. "She'll be fine after a cup of tea."

Josh laid Kandy down on one of the couches, Lucy appearing with a knitted afghan to toss over her.

"Kandy?" Josh squatted next to her. "Look at me. You're in your office. You're okay."

Slowly, she nodded. "Why?" she asked, her blurry gaze trying to focus on his face. Her voice sounded faraway and hollow to her own ears.

"I'll find out. I promise."

Unable to stop them, tears slipped down her cheeks. Josh, in a move so tender it threatened to shatter her already coiled nerves, reached out and caught one with his finger as it slid downward. He gathered her close, moved up on the couch, and pulled her onto his lap.

The shaking came full force, rocking her body as she felt him soothe and snuggle, rubbing his hands up and down her back, whispering into her hair.

Behind them she heard the aunts tell Stacy what had happened on the roof, their voices muffled.

"Why does someone hate me so much?" she whispered. "Why?"

"Shush. Don't think about it. I'm here. Just lean on me."

He continued rocking her for a few minutes more, until Callie came over with a cup of tea.

"Drink this. You'll feel better after you do," her aunt said.

Kandy reached for the cup with trembling hands.

"Let me have it." Josh took it from Callie. To Kandy, he said, "You'll just spill it all over yourself. Take a few sips and settle down. Then I'll let you hold it."

He tipped it toward her lips, held it steady so she could drink.

She obeyed without debating. Her gaze stayed on his eyes as she drank the hot, strong liquid. For some reason she couldn't fathom, just staring at his steady, composed face helped to calm her nerves. A minute later her hands began to settle.

"Better?" he asked.

With a nod, she said, "I can sit up."

He let her, shifting so she leaned the long way across the couch, from one end almost to the other. As soon as she was out of his warm grasp, she folded her legs under and pulled the afghan completely over her body.

"Here." He handed her the cup. "Go slow."

Once again she did as he commanded.

"I'm okay," she said after a bit. Turning to her aunts and cousin, she added, "Sorry to be so much trouble."

All three of them protested at the same time.

"I'm gonna head back upstairs for a few minutes," Josh said. "You'll be okay here?"

"We'll stay with her," Stacy said. "She won't be alone."

He nodded, took one last look at her, and left.

The moment he exited the room they all started talking in a rush. Kandy blocked them out and sipped her tea, focusing instead on how it had felt to be held in Josh's strong, reassuring grip.

* * *

Josh stalked off the elevator and found the crew huddled behind the cameras, talking.

Cort was the first to notice him. He jumped from his chair and followed Josh to where the rat still lay.

"How is she?" he asked.

"Shaken, but coming out of it." Josh glanced over at the garden bed.

"No one touched it," the director told him. "Just as you ordered."

Josh nodded. "Good. I need a plastic bag, like one of those gallon baggies. Something that can be sealed, but big enough to fit this thing."

Cort called out for Mark and told him what was needed.

Josh's gaze swept around the set. He spotted a pair of discarded gardening gloves and donned them.

When Mark returned with the plastic bag complete with a zippered lock, Josh gingerly lifted the knife and the rat, supporting its dangling head, and placed them into the bag, sealing it. Mark had also brought a paper bag to camouflage the baggie's contents.

"What are you going to do with that thing?" Cort asked.

The director's color was even paler and more ashen than when Josh had first seen him barely fifteen minutes ago. His upper lip and brows were bathed in a fine sheet of oily sweat and he was jangling his keys in his pants pocket.

"You okay?" Josh asked.

"Fuck, no!" One hand swiped at his hair from temple to nape. "This is bloody upsetting."

"That's one word for it. To answer your question, I'm taking this to a friend of mine who works at the city's crime lab. He can see if there are any prints on the knife."

"Prints? *Fingerprints?* Why?"

"I think that's obvious, Mason."

It took him a second. Through squinting eyes, Cort asked, "Are you a cop?"

"No. I'm not."

Something in Cort's eyes shifted. He took a deep breath and asked, "Where's Kandy?"

"I left her with the aunts and Stacy."

"I gather the rest of the day is a wash," Cort said, shoulders slumping. "She won't want to go on. I know I wouldn't."

"I think it's a pretty safe bet."

With that, Josh left the roof, paper bag in hand. He stopped outside Kandy's office and placed the bag on the floor next to the door.

All four women were still in the room and had been joined by a scowling Gemma, who made a beeline for him. "What the hell is all this about?" she shouted.

"Gem, please," Kandy said from the couch. "Don't yell at him. It's not his fault."

"The hell it isn't," she countered. "Weren't you hired to protect her, keep her safe? You're doing a lousy job of it."

Josh's left eyebrow rose at her words. To Kandy he said, "I guess the secret's out."

"I told them," Stacy said. "Kandy wouldn't."

"That was her choice to make, not yours," he told her cousin.

"It's okay," Kandy said. Expelling a huge breath, she rubbed her eyes. "They were bound to find out anyway. Just promise me it stops here," she said, her gaze traveling from one to the next. "I don't want anyone else knowing."

"Not even Hannah?" Lucy asked.

"No!" Kandy cried. "Mom's the last person who should know. She'll just make everything worse than it already is." She tossed off the afghan and stood.

Josh moved in quickly when he saw she was a little unsteady on her feet.

"Take it easy." He placed a hand on her elbow.

"I'm okay. Really."

He had to admit she looked better than she had when he'd left her. Her color had returned and her eyes had lost their glazed, frozen stare.

"Stacy, call Cort." She came around her desk. "I want him to get ready to shoot the pie segment."

"You're not serious?" Stacy crossed to her cousin. "Kan, the last thing you need to worry about is work. Take the rest of the day off. Go home."

"I will not."

Josh's eyes widened at the heat in her voice.

"Nothing as stupid as this is going to make me stop production. We have a schedule to keep, a program to wrap, and I intend to do it. We have contracts to honor and I won't let anything delay the schedule."

She turned her attention to Josh. "I assume you'll be taking care of finding out who put that thing in my garden?"

He nodded. "On it."

"Fine." She glanced out the office window. "The light's already shifted, and the clouds are moving in fast, so we can forget about the roof shot now. But I want the pie one completed today. I'll go down to the studio and start prepping and baking as soon as the kitchen can be readied."

"Kandy—" Gemma began.

"No." She threw up a silencing hand. "I'm fine. I want to work. Stacy, notify Cort and the crew. I'll be ready in a half hour. Aunt Callie, I need to be fixed."

Callie's eyes traveled from niece to niece and then to Josh. His small nod was mimicked by one of her own. "Okay, sweetheart. Let's get you back to your dressing room and get you freshened up."

"Ladies, I'd like a word in private with Kandy first, please."

The aunts and a still visibly shaken Stacy exited the office.

"You, too," he told Gemma.

Arms crossed in front of her, a dour look on her face, she told him, "I don't get this whole thing. Shouldn't you be calling the police? Shouldn't *you* have from the start?" she asked, whirling to Kandy.

"Please, Gem, not now," Kandy said, massaging her temples.

"Yes, now. I want answers, damn it. This is your safety we're talking about."

"The police haven't been involved for a number of reasons," Josh said, interceding, "not the least of which is they're outsiders. It makes more sense to have me working on the inside, questioning, researching, and keeping an eye on Kandy. People are more willing to talk to someone they don't consider law enforcement."

Gemma stared at him for a few seconds, a suggestion of annoyance still hovering in her blue eyes. After a long moment her shoulders relaxed. "That makes some kind of stupid sense." With a sigh, she turned her attention back to her sister. "Why didn't you tell me?"

Kandy plopped down in her leather desk chair, leaned her arms on the desk, and linked her fingers. "I didn't believe there was a real problem," she said, "so I didn't want to worry anyone unnecessarily."

"That's just dumb. If all these things were happening to one of us, you'd be first in line trying to get to the bottom of it. You know it, too."

She nodded. "I can't argue with you there."

"So how come we're not allowed the same privilege of worrying about you?"

For an answer Kandy shook her head.

Her younger sister moved to the desk and bent down to eye level. "I love you, Kan. I just want you safe."

Kandy, eyes glistening, placed her palms on Gemma's cheeks. "I know you do. And that's why Josh is here. To keep me safe and find out who's doing all this. Let him do his job."

He didn't think Gemma looked all that convinced when she rose and said, "Okay. Fair enough."

Kandy's body relaxed. "Thanks."

Turning to him, Gemma raked her gaze down his body and then back up again. "Hindsight. When I really look at you, you look like a bodyguard."

"Private investigator."

She flipped a hand into the air. "Whatever. Just find out who's responsible for this."

"Bet on it."

She slung her bag over her shoulder and exited the office, saying, "Call me later," to her sister.

When they were alone, Josh moved to Kandy's side. "You okay?"

She slumped back in the chair and ran her hands through her hair. "Not really, but they all need to think I am."

He stared at her for a moment, admiring her honesty.

"Captain of the ship syndrome." He folded his hands in his pockets.

When she just gaped wide-eyed at him, he shrugged.

"In order to *keep* order, you need to keep your head; stay calm, maintain a cool attitude, even when it seems impossible to do so. That way, the ship stays afloat; everyone stays composed and focused."

She stared up at him, amazement on her face. "You continually surprise me."

"It's not hard to understand, Kandy. You run a multimillion-dollar business with your name, and your name alone, attached to it. If you falter, everyone else follows suit. If you stand tall, the line stays stable. It's one of the first precepts of running a successful business."

"Not only a business," she told him, leaning back in her chair, her arms folded across her midsection. "Grandma was always the calm in any storm. With a household filled with hormonal teenagers and unending sisterly fights and drama, she never lost her cool. I can't even ever remember her crying or raising her voice. When she was calm, it settled the rest of us down. But she had to have been going nuts on the inside."

Josh stared at her for a moment. "My mother is the same way," he said. "Unless there was arterial blood splattering or bones were obviously broken, she never got upset, never got emotional. That taught me a valuable lesson about keeping your emotions in check during stressful work situations. But"—he pulled his hands from his pockets and leaned them, knuckles down, on the desk in front of her—"what you've been going through isn't simple everyday family drama or normal work stress, Kandy."

Her eyes were wary as she looked up at him.

"I can understand you wanting to show a brave front, but this has to be taking some kind of toll on you, whether you'll admit it or not," he added when it looked like she was about to interrupt him. "I can't imagine the level of pressure you're under. Business aside, you've made yourself responsible for most of your family, and that weight alone is heavy. Add what's been happening to you lately into the mix and I have to wonder how much longer you can carry on the way you have."

She didn't answer him. When she pulled her bottom lip under her top teeth and frowned, he knew he should stop.

Knowing and doing were two different things though, so he pushed back upright and asked, "Doesn't the pressure of being everything to everybody ever get to you?"

"All the time," she said softly.

He could tell she regretted giving voice to her feelings when she immediately blushed and lowered her eyes.

After a moment she lifted them back to him and said, "Sometimes…"

"Sometimes, what?"

She nibbled at her lower lip again and took a full breath. "Sometimes I wish I could go back to when I could just cook and not have to worry about book deadlines and production schedules. No publicity tours or guest appearances. Sometimes…sometimes I wish Grandma was still here and in charge of the family…instead of me."

Her blue-eyed gazed pierced him straight in the heart.

"How awful does that sound? Really, how terrible is that? After all I've accomplished? All I've worked toward? I sound so ungrateful."

"I don't think it's awful at all," he told her, "to feel that way. I think you're entitled to."

She studied her hands, avoiding his gaze again.

"It's a lot for just one person to handle," he said. "Being responsible for yourself. For your family. For all the people who work for the show." She looked up at him, her body perfectly still, her eyes watchful. "Maybe…"

"Maybe?"

In for a penny, he thought. "Maybe it's too much.. Ever think about that?"

He wasn't surprised when her eyes widened.

"Yeah," he said. "I thought so."

They were silent for a moment, then Kandy, her voice barely above a hush, said, "Sometimes I'm just so scared I'm going to do something wrong or make a monumental mistake and it will all fall down around me. Everything I've worked for. Everything I've accomplished. If that happens, where will it leave everyone else?"

Her words, and the meaning behind them, shot straight through him. To have to be so strong, so intractable, so focused all the time must be physically and mentally exhausting.

She shook her head and rolled her shoulders.

One thing he knew he could do for her was find out who was at the bottom of all the torment. At least that would give her some peace of mind.

"I'm pretty sure you and every one would bounce back just fine," he said.

"I wish I was that confident."

With a nod, he said, "All that aside, Kandy, now that you're okay and you're going to be busy filming, I need to leave for a little while."

"Why?"

Concerned when alarm entered her eyes, he came around the desk and gathered her hands in his. When he felt the frigid chill suffusing them, he rubbed her knuckles with his thumbs and tried to give her back some warmth.

"Couple of things I have to do. One, I've gotta get more clothes from my apartment. I brought only the basics with me. Two, I need to get the knife analyzed, see if there are any prints on it."

She shuddered and then composed herself just as fast.

"And last, I need to do some background checks on a few people. It'll be easier to do from my office. Plus, I need to speak with my partner, Rick. He's free at the moment, and can do a lot of the computer research work I can't, since I need to stay close to you. You'll be tied up baking and filming for a while and I'll make sure there's someone with you every second until I get back. Okay?"

When her throat bobbed, he read the apprehension washing through her. He didn't want to leave her, and if there were any way he could, he'd take her with him. But he understood how determined she was to move forward and act normally. He admired her for the way she'd stood her ground with her cousin and sister. It would have been easy just to take the rest of the day off and remove herself from the problem.

Josh knew in his bones it wasn't how Kandy was made. Stacy had described her as stubborn and determined, possessed of a will that at times bordered on the obsessive. Well, right now it was a good thing. Her strength would get her through this. Her determination would give her the fortitude to carry on when a lesser, weaker-willed person would just surrender.

Admiration continued to grow inside him.

"How long do you think you'll be?" she asked.

"Not more than an hour, two at the most. Here, I wanted to give this to you last night."

He pulled a small, flip-top phone from his pocket and opened it. "It's preprogramed to my cell. Just press *one* and you'll get me immediately. I'm the only one who has this number. Just me. Don't give it out to anyone—and I mean anyone, Kandy."

"All right."

"You can call anyone you want from it, it's untraceable. No caller ID shows up. Keep it with you, even on the set."

"What if it rings while I'm filming? Cort will have a heart attack. No one's supposed to have a live phone when we shoot."

Josh handed her the phone. "First of all, you're the boss. You can do whatever you want." He put up his hands when she started to interrupt. "And second, I'm the only one with the number, the only one who'll be calling, and I promise you I won't. This phone is strictly for you to get in touch with me. To feel safe and connected if I'm not around."

She looked down at it for a few seconds and then licked her lips. "Okay."

"Come on. I'll walk you to your dressing room."

She stood and slipped the phone into her pocket.

"Remember it when you change clothes," he said, guiding her from the office, one hand settled on the small of her back.

"Why do you think I'm going to change?" she asked. Nonchalantly he picked up the paper bag and rolled the top down closed.

"You're going from gardening to baking. My guess is the aunts have a charming cooking outfit all picked out for you. One that'll make every woman who watches your program want to look just like you in the kitchen."

He was pleased to see her lips curve into a tiny groove. "I bet you had a crush on Beaver Cleaver's mother when you were a teenager."

His mouth split into a wide grin. "*God,* I loved that she wore pearls when she cleaned. Peg Bundy, too. Always spiffy in a tight, sexy outfit. It was a real turn-on to a thirteen-year-old. God bless Nick at Nite."

"That's sick," she said, gazing up at him. After a second, her eyes grew serious and a faint blush spread across her cheeks. "I'm sorry I was such a basket case before. That…thing…caught me by surprise."

"Totally understandable," he said. "And normal."

"I hate rodents." She shuddered. "Of any kind. My sister has a five-year-old with a pet hamster. I can't even go into Declan's room because he keeps the thing's cage in there. Silly," she added, shaking her head.

Josh stopped, laid his index finger under her chin, gently lifting it so their eyes met again. A pool of swirling emotions stared back at him.

"I don't like snakes," he told her. "Everyone's got something that grosses them out. Don't be so hard on yourself."

Because he liked the feel of her soft skin against his fingers just a tad too much for correctness, Josh pulled his hand away.

Silently, they continued down the corridor.

The aunts, Stacy, and Cort were all present and the room grew abruptly silent when they came through the door.

"That's a classic sign you were all talking about me," Kandy said, eyebrows arched.

In a throng, they grouped around her, firing questions.

"One at a time," she said, with a glance at Josh.

He caught Stacy's eye and motioned for her to follow him.

Out in the corridor he looked down at her concerned face and said, "She's fine and wants to work. Don't hassle her on this."

Stacy ran a hand through her hair and shook her head. "Cooking. Working. It's always been the way she copes. She gets it from Grandma. Okay. What should I do?"

"Stay with her. No matter what. I need to leave for a while and I don't want her left alone for a second. Go with her into the bathroom if you have to. No matter what. Can I trust you?"

"Yeah. No problem."

"Even on set, Stacy. I mean it. Stay with her even if it looks like she doesn't want or need you there."

"I get it. Believe me, I'm good at it. Her sister Belinda used to call me a leech when we were kids. Don't worry."

He gave her a quick nod, and then left the building.

Chapter Eight

While she searched through the clothes in the wardrobe closet, Lucy asked Stacy, "Can anyone hire him?"

"I suppose. Why?" Stacy asked.

"Well, what woman wouldn't want a man like him watching over her, keeping her safe, offering comfort? My goodness, I'd pay through the nose for it."

"Double," Callie said, removing Kandy's light base before applying a thicker one.

"Mama."

"Oh, for goodness' sake, Stacy, the man's a living, breathing god," Lucy said. "You didn't see the way he just scooped Kandy up when she was about to faint, as if she weighed no more than a piece of paper. I almost wanted to faint myself just to see how it felt to be gathered up like that."

"I have to admit, it was like something straight out of a Nora Roberts book," Callie said. "All big and brawny, muscles and heart. Gave me goose bumps just riding down in the elevator."

"You two are unbelievable," Stacy scolded.

"It's a good thing Hannah wasn't there. He'd have had to carry her, too."

Kandy blocked out their banter. She knew firsthand what it was like to be lifted in those tree-trunk arms as if she weighed nothing. She'd felt his warm breath as it pressed into her hair, the soft, deep rumble of his voice consoling her, reassuring her, chasing away the terror. When he'd kissed her temple she'd wanted to turn and take his lips with her own.

He'd made her forget everything but the feel of his body against hers.

Without even really knowing him, Kandy realized she wanted Josh in the most elemental, basic of ways.

When she looked into his eyes she was reassured and calmed by the strength and honor she saw there. Sitting in his lap, his hands rubbing down her back and her arms, she'd felt safer and more secure than she had in years.

Kandy had always been the comforter and the dependable one of her sisters, roles she'd cherished and assumed from the time her father walked out. While her mother had been off working, it was Kandy the younger girls turned to for advice, council, and consoling. She'd been the one to herd the younger ones off to school in the mornings and help them with schoolwork in the evening. She listened when they cried about being bullied at school, kissed skinned knees, and cuddled away bad dreams. She'd never complained, ridiculed, or even blamed her mother for the absence that shunted Kandy into a maternal role. Instead, she gave the girls someone they could always turn to if needed.

But it had felt so damn good to be the one getting the comfort, drawing on the strength, leaning against the solid, steady expanse of a man.

A man she wanted to make love to her.

Never before had she felt such an intense yearning for a man she barely knew. She'd dated Evan for more than a month before sleeping with him. And even then, it hadn't been the life-altering experience she'd hoped it would be. After that first night, they'd had sex only a handful of times, Kandy feeling Evan needed and wanted more than she was giving. He'd never said anything to the contrary, but she knew there were no sparks between then in the bedroom.

And yet, Evan had stuck around.

Sure, and now you know why.

How could she be so smart in business and yet so dumb in her personal affairs?

Her first sexual experience had been at the age of nineteen. She'd purposefully chosen an older man, a chef whose tutelage she was under at Le Cordon Bleu. Kandy felt she wanted to get it over with, see what all the fuss was about. Her partner had been willing and almost thankful she'd chosen him. Their one brief encounter took place on a baking slab after class had been dismissed. Kandy thought it memorable only because she thought of it every time thereafter when she needed to roll out dough.

There had been a smattering of men through the years, men who'd been attracted to her looks and growing celebrity, but who'd quickly tired of her once they realized she was more devoted to her cooking, her career, and her family than she was ever going to be to them. Kandy knew she hadn't been able to put any of them ahead of what she wanted because none had made her feel more than a passing fancy.

Until now.

The nervous way butterflies filled her stomach every time Josh looked at her was becoming a constant occurrence. When they touched, she'd felt a spark each and every time. She'd never experienced that with any other man. And she'd actually been scared when he told her he would be leaving.

In the brief time he'd been with her—*Lord,* was it only two days?—Kandy could admit she'd grown almost dependent on seeing him, having him right there next to her, with her.

For her.

How had he done it? How had he made her so comfortable with his presence that she felt alone when he was gone?

"You're all ready, honey," Callie told her. "Go change."

Kandy rose from the makeup chair and took the clothes Lucy handed her.

In the dressing room, she told herself to concentrate on the work at hand. She had obligations to fulfill. People depended on her. She had to keep going no matter how tired or frightened, and dear God, she was tired. When she'd told Josh she sometimes wished her life could go back to the way it used to be, it was the first time she'd ever admitted it out loud.

Kandy wouldn't change her life for anything, that was certain. Her success had enabled her to fulfill the promise she'd made to her grandmother before the old woman died: to take care of the family. Her drive, abilities, and willingness to work and sacrifice had propelled her to the top of the cooking world.

But sometimes she wondered if she'd ever be able to relinquish the role her grandmother had groomed her for.

Reaching into the pocket of the overalls she grabbed the tiny phone. Flipping it open, she stared at the small console. Just to make sure it really worked, she pressed the number *1*.

"Kandy?" she heard him say a half second later.

"Yeah."

"What's wrong?"

"Nothing," she managed, astonished at the relief hearing his voice washed through her. "I just wanted to make sure the phone worked."

"I told you it would. Don't worry."

"Where are you?"

"My office. Are you all right?"

"Yeah. I'm a little sleepy, but I'm okay."

"Where are you?" he asked.

"In my dressing room. I'm changing for the baking segment."

"Is Stacy with you?"

"She's just outside the door. She told me you ordered her to stay with me no matter what. You'll be happy to know she's being a good little leech."

When she heard the deep rolling timbre of his chuckle, she sat down on the bench in order to quell the trembling in her knees.

"Good." A moment passed. "Are you going to make some pies?"

"Yes. Cort's got it all set up."

"Save me some of the apple. It's my favorite."

Smiling, she said, "I will. A big slice."

"I've got to go. I'll see you soon. Don't worry," he told her again.

"Okay."

She waited until he disconnected before flipping the phone closed.

Putting her head down into her hands she mumbled, "You've got it bad, girl. Really bad."

"Kandy? You okay?" Stacy said from the other side of the door.

"Almost ready."

* * *

Kandy smiled into the camera and said, "Ice-cold vanilla ice cream is one of the world's most perfect toppings for warm apple pie. But why not try a twist? Grind a little nutmeg and cinnamon on top of the ice cream and then sprinkle it with a coating of shaved dark chocolate. Believe me, your taste buds will never be the same."

She held the slice of pie up to the camera, adorned just as she'd instructed, put a small forkful in her mouth, and rolled her eyes. With a lick of her lips she told the camera, "Heaven."

"And…cut!" Cort called.

The crew broke into spontaneous applause as Kandy wiped her mouth and bowed. "You're only clapping because you know you can eat it now."

Stacy moved to her cousin and took the first piece. Kandy removed the two extra pies from the warming oven and began slicing them, offering them to whoever came forward for a slice.

"That was great, Kan," Cort said, throwing an arm around her and squeezing. He bussed her temple and added, "No more for today. That was perfection, pure and simple."

"We won't really know if that's true until we go to editing," she tossed back, handing him a dish and fork.

"I have no doubts." He shoved half the piece into his mouth just as his cell phone rang.

She grinned, looked up, and found Josh staring at her from across the set. Her stomach flipped and, to hide her unnerving emotions, she lifted a dish and one eyebrow.

He nodded and found his way around the camera equipment.

"When did you get back?" she asked, shaking the chocolate shavings onto the ice cream.

"Just before the last take."

"Eat this fast," she said, handing him the plate and a fork. "The lights are melting the ice cream."

He took the dish from her. Once again, when their hands made contact, Kandy felt as if she'd been scorched by a white-hot poker.

"Are you okay?" He leaned in closer, his voice lowered so only she could hear. She stared up at him and her breath caught at the intense, probing depth of his gaze.

"I am now."

"Something's up with Cort," Stacy said, interrupting them.

The director stood off to one side of the set, his back to them, cell phone at his ear. His shoulders were tense, and he was jangling his keys in his pocket with his free hand, his head shaking back and forth as he listened to the caller.

"Who's he talking to?" Kandy asked.

"I don't know."

Just then, Cort's shoulders slumped, and he ended the call.

When he turned back to the set, his face was pale, his mouth drawn downward.

"Alyssa," Kandy and Stacy both said.

"His wife?"

Kandy nodded. "There's been something going on with her. Cort won't talk about it, but it's no secret it's affecting him."

He came back to them, the whiteness encircling his lips prominent. "Kandy, are you ready for editing? I need to get it done and get out of here."

"Problem?" She placed a hand on his sleeve.

"No. No, I just have an appointment I forgot about."

"We can do it tomorrow morning," she offered. "Oh, no, wait. I've got to be out of here by noon."

"Eleanor's party." Stacy nodded.

"So let's get it done now," Cort said, his hand still jiggling his keys. "Then in the morning we can edit everything we've got together. That'll leave just the herb segment."

As soon as he said it, Cort clamped a hand over his mouth, his eyes bugging wide. "Oh God, Kandy, I'm sorry. Why don't we just scrap that one? We don't need it. We can come up with something else."

"No. It'll get done. Tuesday morning," she said, mentally going over her daily calendar in her head. "I'll keep an eye on the weather reports over the weekend."

She turned away from him and called, "Last chance. There are a few pieces left."

Cort grabbed the discs from the four studio cameras and left. When all the pies had been cut, habit had Kandy starting to clean up the kitchen.

"Go edit," Stacy told her, grabbing a dish from her cousin's hand "and let the cleaning crew do this. Josh is back. You don't need me anymore."

Kandy placed her hand over Stacy's and said, "I'll always need you, Stace. Don't ever forget it."

Blushing, the younger woman said, "Go to editing. Cort's waiting."

Chapter Nine

Josh left her sequestered with Cort and a film technician in the editing room with a command to stay put until he returned while he sought out Kandy's mail assistant. After getting directions, he took the elevator to the thirteenth floor.

He introduced himself to a secretary and asked where he could find Tricia.

The large, spacious office he was directed to impressed him. "This certainly isn't the mailroom," he told her, shaking her hand.

"A few steps way above," she answered.

She looked like Callie's daughter. The same chin-length auburn hair, cut stylishly into a wedge. Like all the relatives he'd met so far, except for Stacy, Tricia was at least five-foot-nine.

"Did Stacy tell you about me?" Josh asked and took a seat in front of her desk, which was laden with several huge piles of correspondence and mailing boxes.

"Yeah. I went back a few months in the files to try and see if anything popped on the weirdo radar."

"Did you find anything?"

"No. It almost borders on boring how much positive stuff Kandy gets. No drama at all."

"She gets a lot of mail?"

"Upward of a thousand written correspondences a week. E-mail's double that."

"And you go through it all? By yourself?"

"Don't be impressed. Most of it's standard and short." She pointed to the heaps on her desk. "These are all since Monday. This pile's the flowery, you're-so-wonderful fan letters that Kandy gets by the bushel.

'Thank you for making my dinner party so easy and enjoyable with your new recipe book.' Stuff like that. In this one are invitations and requests for appearances."

"What kind of appearances?"

"Well, take the top one here." She lifted it off the pile. "Came in this morning from the Ladies Garden League in a little town outside Des Moines. They want Kandy to come and cut the ribbon on a new city park the league has sponsored. The one under it is from some new winery in California. The owners, or should I say, *vintners,* want her to be their guest of honor at this year's uncorking."

"Why would they want her for that?"

She shrugged. "Aside from all the free publicity it would bring just by having her there, the winery owners are hoping she'll use their product in some recipe pairings."

Josh nodded. "Then the wines will be mentioned on her show, giving them even more publicity."

"Yup, and generating a public interest."

"How does she decide what to attend from all these requests?"

Tricia leaned back in her chair, legs crossed at the knees. "Stacy and Aunt Trudi usually decide most of them for her because they're the keepers of the sacred schedule."

Josh laughed when she put her hand over her heart and closed her eyes in reverence.

"Kidding aside." Tricia tossed the paper back on top of the pile. "Kandy couldn't possibly honor even one-one-hundredth of these invites. There aren't enough days in a year."

"So what happens to them?"

"I write a nice, polite thank-you for the invitation in Kandy's voice, state that unfortunately, the busy work schedule doesn't permit acceptance, and then I have her sign it, and we send the letter out, usually with a signed copy of her latest book."

"Doesn't that get a little expensive? There must be over a hundred requests on your desk right now."

"The cost is negligible, since it keeps Kandy in the person's good graces. When you consider all the time and trouble the letter writer went to just to extend the invitation, when they know in their heart of hearts she couldn't possibly be everywhere all the time, they're actually happy to receive a nice, well-written letter and a gift as a consolation prize. Kandy's a remarkable hostess and, because of that, she's a great guest. If she can't attend something, she always sends a note of regret and a gift.

People remember that kind of kindness and class."

Josh agreed. "What's the last pile?"

"How-to requests."

"What are those?"

"Are you familiar with the 'Ask Martha' column in her *Living* magazine?"

"My mother's a faithful and devoted fan."

Tricia nodded. "This pile is 'Ask Kandy.' For instance." She picked up the first few from the group. "'Dear Kandy, How do you know when melting chocolate has reached the correct temperature for tempering?' Or, 'Dear Miss Laine, What kind of inexpensive wine can I serve with my Easter ham dinner?' We get truckloads of these every week. The e-mails are mostly 'Ask Kandy's."

"She should have her own magazine."

"Don't laugh. She's been approached to, but she's too busy right now. One of the network's goals for next season is a weekly newsletter. The circulation on that will be insane, especially if she does it as e-mail."

"Impressive. So, nothing sticks out as crazed or threatening, then?"

Shaking her head, she said, "Sorry."

"What about on social media? Anything quirky or weird there?"

"I usually post to Facebook twice a week for her. Give a new recipe or a link to something domestic and Kandy related. But no responses or comments have been threatening or anything."

"Twitter?"

Tricia rolled her eyes again, and then chuckled. "Well, there are always weird things there, because people just love to say negative things, especially since they think they're being anonymous."

"Haters gotta hate?"

Her chuckle grew into a laugh. "Kinda. Twitter is the one place I have seen some not-so-nice comments about Kandy, but I have to tell you, it's usually that she's too perfect, or can't be real. That kind of thing. But again, nothing I'd ever take a second look at because it felt off or menacing."

Josh thought for a moment. "Does she ever get requests for money?"

"Like donations?"

"No, more along the lines of, I'm a big fan of your show, my kid is sick. Can you help me out?"

"I don't think I've seen something like that cross my desk in the year I've been here."

"So you haven't been with her from the beginning?"

"No, just since the television show really took off. Before, I was still in school, and Stacy was the one who dealt with all this"—she swiped her hand over her desk—"in addition to everything else she had to do. It was my mom who suggested Kandy hire a reader."

"And you got the job." He smiled at her.

"I'll tell ya, Mr. Keane, nepotism's a great thing."

Josh had to agree.

He thanked her and went back down to the editing studio. He found Kandy in the same position he'd left her in.

* * *

"Here's Josh," Kandy said when he came into the room. "Let's get his opinion."

"About what?" He took the chair next to hers.

It was Cort who answered. "We disagree about artistic concept."

"It's more that he knows I'm right and can't stand it," she tossed back.

Director and star bantered for a few more moments while Josh listened silently. When it was over, and he'd watched the two shots of contrasting images, he admitted they were both right and wasn't there some way they could use both?

"Whatever you do for a living, you're in the wrong line of work," Cort said, having the editor rewind both pieces and retool them.

"What should I be in? Hostage negotiations?"

With a snort, Kandy replied, "No. Visual arts. You're right about combining them. This looks great."

"It sure does," Cort said, reclining back in his chair. "That's it, then, for today." To the editor he said, "Just add the music playback and you're done."

His cell phone rang and he pulled it out of his back pocket. When he read the number, Josh noticed his good humor dropped a few notches.

"Sorry, all. That's it for me. I'll see you in the morning."

Without looking at anyone, he left, the phone still clutched in his hand.

Kandy sighed as she watched his retreating back.

"Something wrong?" Josh asked.

"I don't know." She looked askance at the editor and asked, "Need me for anything else?"

When she told her she didn't, they left the editing room.

"What's up?" Josh asked when they were in the empty corridor.

"Something's going on with Cort. He's been edgy today, and his cell phone has hardly stopped. He took three calls when you went down to see Tricia."

"Who from?"

"I don't know. Nosiness aside, I'm worried about him."

Josh nodded. "I need to discuss a few things with you about some information I found out today."

"Can it wait until we get home? It's been a long, not-great day and I just want to change and get something to eat."

"I'm surprised you aren't dropping to the floor. You haven't eaten anything all day. Not at the condo, nor the production meeting, and nothing for lunch."

With a shrug she said, "Par for the course most days."

"You need to go back to your office for anything?"

"Just for a few papers. I'll be quick."

Once there, Kandy gathered the items from her desk and tossed them into her briefcase.

"All done?" Stacy asked, knocking and entering at the same time.

"Yup. You need me for anything else?"

"A couple things." She consulted her tablet. "You've got a seven A.M. interview with the *Food & Wine* reviewer tomorrow. He's coming here."

"He knows no recording, right?"

"Yeah. I double-checked. Food?"

"I'll make something from the new book tonight and bring it. It'll be easier."

"Mind a suggestion?"

When Kandy nodded, Stacy said, "Since he'll be here so early, how about the cranberry-apple muffins and Grandma's blend?"

Kandy's smile bloomed full force. "That's why I can't live without you," she said. "A perfect little nosh. Great idea. I'll make a batch tonight. And maybe some bread."

A blush spread from the top of Stacy's ears all the way across her cheeks.

"What else?" Kandy asked.

"Just more plugs. Monday morning you're doing a *Today* spot. Call is four-thirty to prep. Then the radio station interview. After that, Reva's got you at the Barnes & Noble book signing uptown at twelve. You're doing a guest spot on the five o'clock news at ABC Studios and then the mayor's Citizen of the Year reception at Gracie Mansion at eight. Dress is semi."

"That's all in one day?" Josh asked.

"Close your mouth," Kandy said. "That's not even a lot in a day around here. Tuesday's all studio, right?" She turned back to her cousin.

"Wednesday, too. The second show's recipes are all from the new book, like you requested. Just food, no other segments for the episode." She snapped her tablet cover closed. "That's it for now. I'm sure I'll have more in the morning."

"Okay. Call it a night, cuz."

When she turned to leave, Kandy suddenly stopped her by saying, "And thanks…for everything you did today, Stace. I don't know what I would do if you weren't here every day. I really don't. I appreciate it. More than you know."

The younger woman blushed again. With a quick smile, she left the office.

Kandy found Josh's gaze locked on to her, his head cocked to one side. "What?"

He took the briefcase from her hand and said, "You're a good boss."

"She's a great assistant. And cousin. And friend. All that matters."

"Yeah, I can see it does."

Without another word, they rode the elevator down to the waiting limousine.

* * *

The first thing she did when they got back to the condo was change into comfortable jeans and a white pullover, tugging her hair back into a relaxed ponytail. Then she started dinner while Josh excused himself to his room to finish up some computer work.

A half hour later Kandy had poured herself a small glass of red wine while two enormous filets were cooking on the kitchen grill and asparagus was steaming on the stove.

"So, tell me what you found out," she said when he came to join her in the kitchen.

"Couple things," he said. "First, did you know your cousin Daniel is in trouble with some bookies?"

"What? No. How did you find that out?" She chopped a few broccoli florets and tossed them into a large salad bowl with the other vegetables she'd cut for a salad.

"Basic digging. He's into one for over five thousand, seven at another. Bets on sports. Since he's not working, paying them off is a bit of problem."

"To say the least. Does Aunt Lucy know?"

"That I don't know."

She slammed her hand down onto the counter. "Damn it!"

"It explains his erratic behavior," Josh said, taking a pull from a bottle of water. "And the problems at work."

"Yeah, it does." She started to julienne some carrots. "This stinks."

"His wife walked out on him about a month ago, too. Doesn't look like she's filed for divorce yet."

Kandy chopped for a few seconds, tossed the slices into the salad bowl, and then took a large sampling of her wine. "Betsy's a great girl. They've been together since middle school. I wish I'd known about this. I wish someone had told me."

"Your family may not know. From what I've sniffed out, this betting's been a problem for about a year or so. He's always been able to pay off his debts before now, so he's never really been in any trouble. But one thing you don't want to do is owe bookies."

Kandy nodded and drank some more. "What else?"

"Your buddy Evan Chandler."

"Ex-buddy."

"He's hurting for cash, too. Overextended on all his credit cards and has two personal loans coming due at the end of the month. He's facing eviction from his apartment if he doesn't pay within two weeks the three months' back rent he owes."

She took another gulp of wine and turned the steaks. "Serves him right for being such a moron."

"He needs some capital influx immediately or he's going to wind up in litigation, probably even do some jail time."

Kandy's lips pulled upward while she bit into a carrot. "Grandma always said to leave people to themselves. Give them enough rope, the hanging starts at noon. She was right."

"Be that as it may, I can understand why he sniffed around you last night. I bet he was going to hit you up for cash."

She snorted. "Fat chance. I'd sooner pay Daniel's debt than Evan's any day. Daniel's family. Evan's, well, a jerk."

She pulled two dishes from the cupboard, accompanied by salad bowls.

"Reva mentioned your uncle Peter," Josh said. "About what happened."

Kandy chewed on the inside of her lip and then sighed. "That one's my fault."

"Didn't sound like it from Reva."

"You've heard only one side. Uncle Peter thought I offered him the original job as researcher for my book out of some kind of family obligation. He felt I didn't take his writing seriously. I tried to help. I gave Reva his work and asked for an opinion."

"She told me she didn't think it was any good."

"It wasn't. I read it, too. I couldn't understand the plots, or even where he was taking his characters. They all sounded the same. No individual voices. Reva tried to explain—nicely, I might add, which isn't her strong suit—that she wasn't able to help him."

"And he blames you."

She nodded. "The male ego is such a mystery to me."

"Considering you were raised in a female-laden household with an absent father, I can understand that."

"He hasn't spoken to me since. Won't return any of my calls. I even sicced Mom on him. If she couldn't bring him around, I knew it was a hopeless case."

"Any idea what he's been doing?"

"Aunt Lucy does. She keeps an eye on him because they're the closest in age. He's been drinking a lot, not answering his phone, but he's still writing, still trying to prove he's the next Hemingway."

She took the meat from the grill and put a steak on each plate. "Eat your salad first. The meat needs to rest for a few minutes."

"Yes, Mom." He grinned.

When their eyes met across the counter, she grinned back. "I don't mean to be overbearing, but the meat really does need to simmer in its own juices for a while. It'll taste better, be more tender when you cut into it if you let it just sit. *Lord.*" She put her hands across her eyes. "I sound like we're taping the show. Sorry."

"Forget about it."

They ate in silence for a few minutes.

It was Kandy who spoke first. "You're still convinced someone close to me is responsible for everything, aren't you?"

He swallowed. "It makes sense. Only someone close would know your shooting schedule, your private numbers, would have access to the studio in order to stage the light fall, plus today's little present."

Her color paled. "What did you do with it?"

He explained that he'd brought the rat to a friend at the city's crime lab. "If there are any prints on the knife, he'll be able to trace them and get back to me."

"Well, I think Uncle Peter is out of the picture. He doesn't come to the studio, and I'm pretty sure I never gave him my private numbers."

"He could have gotten them from one of your aunts, or from someone else connected to you."

"But if he was at the studio, he'd be stopped. He has no security clearance."

Josh nodded. "But Daniel does. Or did. And Chandler was around you long enough he'd know the ins and outs of the building. Either of them is a possibility."

Kandy cut into her meat and sighed. "Who else is on your list?"

"Pretty much everyone who comes in daily contact with you has the potential to be."

Her fork stopped midair. "Well, that's certainly a depressing thought."

"By the way, I had the rental company in LA fax me a write-up of your accident, along with the official police report."

"Why?"

"Just tying up ends. After going through all the info, I'm beginning to think it might actually have been just an accident. The initial report mentioned a routine vehicle parts check done on the car about three weeks before you rented it. Cited was a weakened axle and brake line with a recommendation that both be replaced before the car went out for usage again. Somehow, no one ever followed through on the advice."

"So nothing mysterious about what happened, then? It really was brake failure?"

"The line may have fatigued to the extent it snapped. But it's unusual for a brake line to tear with such uniform precision. It would be more plausible if it broke apart in irregular pieces. But yours had the appearance of a cut or slice to it, so it was deemed suspicious."

"What you're saying is these weird things might not have started in Los Angeles."

"Maybe. What's the first strange incident you can remember?"

She thought for a few seconds. "The clothes in my closet. I was sure someone went through them, moved them around."

"Anyone aside from the cleaning lady and Stacy have a spare key? Chandler, for instance?"

"No. No one."

"Not even Mom?"

"Oh God, she'd be the last person I'd give one to. She'd be here every day, camped out, waiting for me to come home, like a spider hiding in wait for prey."

Josh sniggered. "Did you ever ask the cleaning lady if she let anyone in while she was here?"

"No, I didn't."

"Okay. I will. But first, I have to tell you, you were right about the steak. This is the best meat I think I've ever eaten."

She smiled, more pleased at the compliment than she'd thought she could be. "It is good, isn't it?"

Together they finished their meal.

When the dishes were done and put away, Kandy turned to him and was about to ask a question when the house phone on the kitchen wall rang.

She stared at it and then up at Josh.

"Go ahead and answer it. I'll grab the cordless from the living room."

When he had the phone in his hand, he motioned to her from the living room. Kandy picked up and he hit the *on* button.

"Hello?" Kandy said.

At first there was silence. Kandy stared across the length of the room at Josh, who nodded.

Then, *"Bitch! Did you like your present today? There will be more, Kandy. Soon."*

The line went dead.

When nothing else came through, Josh waved his hand for Kandy to disconnect. When she did, he attempted to trace the call.

"Must have been a burner," he said, coming back into the kitchen. "Can't be traced."

She was standing at the sink, leaning over it, her head bowed. Her knuckles were bone white where they gripped the porcelain so tightly, she couldn't feel the tips of her fingers.

"Kandy?" He placed a hand on her shoulder.

She turned her head to settle her gaze on his face. Concern and worry stared back at her.

"That's the first time my name's been used," she said, her voice breaking on the last word. "All along, I wanted it to be a mistake. Some crazy person got my number by accident. Didn't really want me, but someone else. All those taunts, those mean things, were for someone else. I guess I can't think that anymore."

His face started to blur as her eyes filled. "I guess it really is me," she said as the first tear spilled down her cheek.

Without a word, Josh pulled her into his arms.

His heart pounded against her cheek, echoing the pulsing of her own blood. His fingers were strong and sturdy and soothing, as they trailed up and down her back. Their height, so similar, allowed their bodies full range of touch as she clung to him.

Kandy felt every hardened sinew, every throbbing muscle pressed against her and shivered.

Josh's hold tightened.

"I feel like an idiot," she said against his shirt. "I never cry like this. Never. And twice today I've lost it."

"I can't fault you for being emotional," he said against her hair. "Anyone in your position would be."

"Why is this happening?" She pulled back to look up at him. She could see the outline of his lashes against his lids, the small, fine lines just beginning in the far corners and branching outward.

"That's what we have to figure out," he said, running his hands up to her shoulders. Gently squeezing them, he asked, "You okay?"

She nodded and swiped at her wet cheeks. "Sorry about all the blubbering. I'd blame the wine, but it would be a lie. Wine has no effect on me."

"Don't worry about it. You deserve a good cry after all that's happened."

Kandy stared at him for a moment, profoundly aware of how cold and empty she now felt out of his hold. "Did you grow up in a house full of women?" she asked. "You do the comforting thing really well, where most men run for the hills when they see tears."

"Sorry." He shook his head, as if trying to clear it. "Male-dominated household. Mom was the only girl. And she never cried in front of us."

"Wailing and sobbing were a daily occurrence in mine. If someone's emotions weren't going off the deep end, we got scared and wondered what was wrong."

She wiped her face with a paper towel and then tossed it in the garbage. When she turned back to him, she'd gotten ahold of her fright.

"I want to know who's doing these things and why," she said.

"I know."

"And," she added, "I want to go see Daniel. Now. I don't believe for a moment he's responsible for any of this, but I agree he does have easy access to the studio, and it doesn't look good for him."

"You're sure you want to go right now? Unannounced?"

"Yes. I don't want to call and give him a chance to avoid us. It's better if he doesn't know we're coming."

"Okay. I'm ready whenever you are," he told her, rolling down his sleeves.

Kandy watched the slow, determined way his fingers folded the cloth back into place. Small tufts of hair peeked out from just below the line of his sleeve and her insides jumped as he fastened each button with steady, controlled movements.

She swallowed, shook her head side to side a few times to try and clear it, and said, "I'll get my car keys."

Chapter Ten

Minutes later they were speeding through the post–rush hour traffic.

"Daniel lives in Queens," Kandy told him, checking the side mirror and easing into the left lane. "But you already know that from your background check."

Josh was thankful he'd secured his seat belt when the Corvette accelerated. Kandy had a habit of shifting around cars and into alternate lanes, gaining speed as she did.

Stacy's portrayal of her cousin's driving skills came back to him: "Like a NASCAR pro."

Dead-on description.

"You might want to stick to the speed limit," he told her.

"I am. I've never gotten a speeding ticket in my life."

The seat belt jerked against his chest when she whipped the car around a tight turn.

"Never mind a ticket, it's a wonder you haven't been killed."

He said a silent prayer they'd live to make it to Queens. To divert his nerves, he played the scene in her kitchen over in his head.

He wasn't certain whether he pulled her to him first, or if she eased into his embrace. Either way, he'd wound his arms around her back and tugged her close, her head falling onto his shoulder. The movement felt natural and oddly familiar. When her arms wrapped around his waist and he felt her shaking, his grip tightened.

Josh's hands continued their journey up and down her back, kneading the flesh beneath her top as they traipsed from neck to waist. Her sweet breath touched his neck as her head stayed cradled on his shoulder, the cloth on his shirt wet from her tears. She was usually so strong that having her fall into his arms needing him, needing his strength, needing his reassurance, made him feel ten feet tall. He knew if he bent his head just a whisper, he could kiss her forehead, the tender skin at her temple, the line of her jaw. He could lift her so effortlessly in his arms and carry her wherever she wanted and take them both away from what was tormenting her.

Kandy Laine was the most puzzling, driven, and desirable woman he'd ever met, but she was a client first. Someone who needed protection, not temptation, security not seduction. No matter how good, how sweet, how just plain *right* she felt in his arms.

He needed to remember that.

* * *

When they arrived at the house, Josh said, "I'm driving us back," as he stepped from the car. "No arguments."

"Bossy," she mumbled and walked up the steps of the old brownstone.

"Nice house."

"It's the one he grew up in," Kandy said. "Aunt Lucy and Uncle Max moved into a smaller one three years ago. They gave the house to Daniel and Betsy, although I think they still own it."

She pressed the doorbell. "The lights are on so he should be home," Kandy said, scraping her hands down her face.

"You sure you're up to this?"

"I'm fine."

The sound of the locks being thrown sounded a moment later.

Josh's first opinion of Daniel Peters was he looked and smelled like a man on a bender. His hair was a mess, the black curls flat on one side, sticking up on the other. He had raccoon circles under his eyes making him look a great deal older than his thirty years. He was unshaven, by Josh's estimate, at least three days' worth. The rank odor of stale beer wafted through the open door.

When he saw his cousin, though, his expression quickly turned to irritation. "What'a'you want?"

"Daniel," she said, staring him down, "let me in. I need to talk about something with you."

"You're not wanted here, Kandy. You or your friend," he added, motioning to Josh with the thrust of his chin.

When it looked like he was going to close the door in their faces, Josh was ready to force his way in.

Kandy beat him to it.

"Please?" she said simply, her eyes trained on her cousin's face.

Josh watched the indecision play across Daniel's weary, strained features. After what seemed like an eternity, he pulled the door fully open, turned, and walked away from them. "Suit yourself."

Kandy threw Josh a quick nod and followed Daniel in.

The house was anything but tidy.

Abandoned clothing hung from the staircase's newel post, the receiving table laden with unopened envelopes and an empty McDonald's bag.

Josh strode behind Kandy as she went deeper into the interior. A brief glance at the living room showed the room in disarray. The couch cushions were thrown to the carpeted floor. Empty beer bottles lined the numerous tables in the room and the fireplace was filled with discarded newspapers. The hallway had a dank, musty, closed-in smell.

Kandy marched straight to the back of the house and into the kitchen, where Daniel leaned a shoulder against the refrigerator, a half-empty beer bottle in his hand.

"Gonna cook something for me, cuz?" A fine trickle of beer dribbled from the corner of his mouth down his chin and he swiped at it with the back of his hand. "Sorry, but I didn't get to the store today. I'm pretty low on food."

Kandy ignored the biting jibes. Instead, she moved one of the kitchen chairs from the table.

"Sit down, Daniel. I want to talk."

"I'll stand in my own home."

"Technically, it belongs to your parents."

He pulled the beer bottle from his lips and snarled at her.

"But," she said, putting up a hand, "stand if you want. I've been on my feet all day. Josh?"

He pulled out a chair and joined her.

"What's this all about?" Daniel asked, his gaze Ping-Ponging between them. "What's going on?"

She took a moment, considering him, before she said, "I know about the gambling. And about Betsy."

His face contorted into a mask of pure, raw pain.

"Why didn't you come to me?" she asked. "I would have helped."

"Yeah, right." He snorted. "The great and powerful Kandace Laine can make all bad things disappear."

He downed the remainder of the bottle and pulled another from the refrigerator.

"Daniel, stop it. We're family."

"As if that means anything." He yanked the top off the bottle.

"It means everything."

He started to take a swig, stopped, and stood, just staring at the bottle. Finally, he put it down, full, into the sink.

"I couldn't ask for help, Kan," he said, avoiding her eyes. "Especially from you."

"Why not?" She stood and crossed to him, placed a hand on his shoulder.

They were the same height, and, standing side by side, Josh could see the physical similarities in their hair color and texture and the curve of their jaws.

"You've helped everyone in the family. Everyone's got a job, a good lifestyle, because of you. Hell, my parents even moved into a swanky new place because of you."

"So? Your mom works hard. As does your dad. You worked hard, too. Always on time, always ready when you were needed. What changed?"

Daniel crossed his arms over his chest and hung his head.

He exhaled deeply and then lifted his gaze to hers. "Betsy wanted kids." He stopped for a moment and rubbed a hand over his heart. "A year went by and nothing was happening. She went to her doctor, who sent her to a specialist."

"A fertility expert?"

"Yeah. Said her tubes were scarred from an infection she had a while back. She could have kids, but it would be hard. And expensive. She went through a bunch of shots for six months. Implantation, everything. Nothing took. We went through all our savings with the first round. The doctor told her to take a few months off before trying again. The hormones were expensive. So were the harvesting and implantation procedures."

"How come I never knew you guys were going through this?"

Daniel shook his head. "No one knew. Betsy didn't want to tell anyone. She was embarrassed she couldn't get pregnant the normal way. Wanted to surprise everyone when it was finally official."

"What happened?" She moved back to her seat, Daniel following suit and pulled out a third chair. Turning it backward, he straddled it and sat.

"We didn't have a lot of money left and she wanted to start the treatments again. I got the idea to bet on the Jets during a home game. They were favored, so I figured I couldn't lose. And I didn't. Made over three grand. That paid for a month's treatments. But they didn't take. I had nothing in savings. I sold my new truck. More treatments. No luck. I kept selling stuff, trying to get ahead. At one point, Betsy gave me her engagement ring. Instead of leaving it at the pawn shop and taking the money to pay for another treatment, I took the cash and bet it all on a Knicks game. I covered the spread and figured if I won, we'd be okay for a few months."

"They lost, didn't they?" Josh asked.

Daniel's laugh had a hollow, bitter bite to it. "Big time. After that, things got pretty bad. I was betting my paycheck before it was even cashed, just trying to get back ahead. Betsy gave up on the treatments because we couldn't pay the regular bills, never mind the doctor fees."

"I still don't understand why you didn't tell me this when I confronted you at the studio. I accused you of slacking off, drinking, being irresponsible. Why didn't you tell me the truth?"

Daniel dropped his head into his hands. "I was drunk, that much was true. But I couldn't tell you why, Kan. I felt horrible about disappointing you. You gave me a great job, a great opportunity. I didn't want you to know what a loser I was."

"I would never have thought that, Daniel." She reached across the table and grabbed one of his hands. "We're family. You and I grew up together. We spent almost every day of our childhood together. I'd do anything I could for you. Anything."

Moisture grew in the corners of his eyes.

Swiping at his face, he said, "I was stupid and arrogant, I know. Grandma always said a man's greatest sin was a sin—"

"Of false pride," Kandy said with him. "She was right then and she's right now. I want to help. Let me, please."

She squeezed his hand.

"Why did you come here tonight?" he asked, his brows pulling in. "How'd you find out about all this?"

Kandy glanced over at Josh and then told her cousin who he was, and why they'd come.

"*Jesus,* Kandy. You could have been killed when the light fell. You and Mason."

"I know. And believe me, I never considered you were behind any of this." She tossed a quick glance at Josh.

Daniel shook his head from side to side several times. "I'd never hurt you, Kandy. Or anyone else. Never. Self-destruction seems to be my strong suit."

"Stop that kind of talk," she said, frowning. "I feel better knowing what's happened. It explains your crazy behavior. Now, let's figure out how to get your life back in order, and get your wife back where she belongs."

* * *

"You really think he'll do everything he said he would?" Josh asked an hour later, when they got back in her car.

He'd lost the driving battle, and Kandy was at the wheel again with a promise to keep her pace to less than the speed of sound.

"I do. He loves and misses his wife. You can see what he's been going through since she left."

"And you really think paying off his gambling debts is the way to go?"

She shrugged and shifted lanes. "Of course. With that worry gone and my offer to return to work, he should be back on firm financial footing within a month or so. Betsy can come home and not have to be concerned about money. Now I just have to find someone good who specializes in in vitro."

"You paying for that, too?"

"Initially."

"What?"

"I'll pay for all the expenses and they can pay me back by naming their firstborn daughter after me. Kandace Sophia Peters. Has a nice ring to it, doesn't it?" She took her eyes off the road and grinned at him.

What felt like a fist slammed into Josh's midsection, knocking all breath and sense out of him. For the first time since getting into the car he was glad he wasn't driving. If he had been, an accident would have been guaranteed.

"And the fact that you're interfering in their lives doesn't bother you just a little?" he asked when he could trust his voice not to betray his thoughts.

"That's not what I'm doing."

Josh's eyes narrowed. "What do you call it, then? Paying off debts, providing jobs, even going so far as getting medical treatment? That's not interfering?"

"No, it's not," she replied in a regal, haughty tone that made his insides vibrate. "It's giving a hand up to a family member when they're down. I'm simply providing them with the means to fulfill their plans and wishes. Daniel does have to come back to work, you know. It's not easy work by any sense. And start going to Gamblers Anonymous meetings. That was one of the conditions. I have faith in him."

"What's changed in the past hour to make you so certain he'll do as he claims?" Josh asked. "His behavior lately hasn't been exemplary."

"He's family, Josh. That's enough for me."

He stared at her in the darkness of the car.

Daniel might be family, but Josh had seen the man as something more. Gamblers and drinkers, in his experience, didn't change their behaviors overnight, no matter who asked them to. Cousin Daniel may be at rock bottom or close to it, but Josh doubted Kandy's edict and intervention was enough to get him back on track. And despite her protestations to the contrary, Josh wasn't ruling him out as a suspect. He'd noted the spiteful glint in the man's eyes when he'd opened the door to his cousin. And he'd heard a voice laced with jealously and scorn of Kandy's success and influence on their family.

Daniel had been in the perfect position to rig the studio light. It might have been a stupid idea if he did do it because suspicion would turn to him almost immediately, but if he'd been drunk when he thought of the plan it would make sense.

The one thing Josh couldn't figure out was why Daniel would want to harm or harass his cousin. Jealousy and destructive behaviors aside, he had no obvious motive. Josh made a mental note to dig a little deeper into Daniel Peters's past.

They traveled along in silence until they arrived back at the condo.

"I have to prepare a few things for tomorrow's interview," Kandy told him, tossing her keys on the foyer reception table. "There's nothing like a well-fed interviewer to ensure a good book review," she added, making her way to the kitchen.

"Can I help?"

She stopped short and turned.

Josh laughed at the surprise on her face. "What? I can't?"

She shook her head. "No, it's not that. Sure you can. I'm just surprised you'd want to."

"Let me check your machine first," he said.

He crossed into her bedroom. No blinking message light met his gaze, a fact he was grateful for. The previous malicious communication had been enough for one day for both of them.

Back in the kitchen, he found her taking out items from the pantry.

"Nothing," he told her.

She nodded.

"What can I do?"

For the next half hour, Josh helped sift, fold, and beat ingredients into what smelled like heaven laced with delicious sin.

Kandy was a good teacher, explaining and clarifying when he needed guidance, without any of the rancor or sarcasm he might have expected from a world-class chef.

And watching her cute butt sashay around the kitchen, bending, bowing, reaching, and stooping wasn't a bad way to pass some time.

They mapped out an easy rhythm between them, coordinating all the effort it took to make the bread and the muffins Stacy had suggested to go along with the interview. When the kitchen began to fill with the incredible aroma of their efforts, Josh sighed.

With a laugh, Kandy said, "I know. That's the best part of this. I could live on just the scent of Grandma's muffins if I had to."

"I have to admit," Josh said, taking a sip of the coffee she'd brewed while the bread rose, "this is more fun than I ever thought it would be."

Kandy's left eyebrow slanted upward and Josh's stomach felt like it was dancing the hula when she looked at him.

"Never helped Mom in the kitchen?"

"God forbid. None of us—my brothers, father, or me—were allowed in it. It was strictly Mom's domain. We were banned for life."

"Why?" she asked, taking a seat at the breakfast bar across from him, her own brew in front of her. She rested her head in her hand, one elbow bent, supporting it, and stared right into his eyes.

For a moment Josh forgot what they were discussing. All he could think about was tugging on her arm and sitting her in his lap, covering that beautiful face with his mouth, caressing the flawless skin, and nibbling at the dimples nipping in her cheeks.

"Josh?"

He saw the concern flit across her creased brow and gave himself a mental shake.

"I think it had something to do with the kitchen fire my younger brother Ian started," he managed to say at last.

"What?"

"He was about five at the time," Josh said, with a twist of his lips. "Mom was making something for dinner, I can't remember what, and Ian wanted to help. She let him put a pot on the unlit stove and turned away to get something. Without asking, Ian lit a match to the stovetop. It was one of those old-fashioned ranges where you had to fire-light the individual coils, you know?"

She nodded and took a sip of coffee. "My grandma had the same kind."

"He'd seen her do it a thousand times, and I guess he figured he could, too. He turned the knob to let the gas come up, just like he'd seen Mom do. Before she could blink, he'd struck a match and put it to the coil."

"Stop," she said, putting up a hand. "Let me guess what happened next."

"Go ahead."

"I'm betting Ian didn't know there were height controls on the knob and he just turned it all the way up, right?"

He pointed his thumb and index finger at her in the form of a gun. "Got it in one. When the match hit the gas, *boom.* The pot shot up to the ceiling and a flame jumped onto a potholder sitting near the stove. Engulfed it in a heartbeat."

"Was your brother hurt?"

"No. Mom turned at just the moment he tossed in the match and grabbed him away from the stove. He was okay. So was she. The kitchen was trashed, though. After that, none of us were ever allowed in there again when she was cooking. We didn't even have basic food prep skills growing up. The first time I ever made toast for myself I was in college."

Kandy laughed. "Did you burn it?"

Josh's mouth split into a grin. "To a crisp."

Chapter Eleven

Her heartbeat accelerated when she saw the childish glee in Josh's eyes and the curve of his full lips. Lips she wanted to feel against her own.

When she'd been in his arms earlier, his powerful hands caressing her back and arms, Kandy knew a peace she hadn't felt in quite some time.

It felt so good, so *blessed* good, to be held by this man. Not many men were physically matched to her height. Josh was a good several inches taller and yet she fit against him as if they were each a piece of a puzzle. She'd felt coddled and protected, secure and safe.

But she felt much more against the hard, solid wall of his chest, his stone-cut, muscular thighs pressed against hers. Feeling safe and secure was one thing. Lust and longing were quite another. Drops of passion drizzled down her insides and puddled into a simmering heat in her pelvis. If Josh had kissed her at that moment she would have exploded all over him, giving into the escalating desire that had been drilling within her.

Kandy was a woman who knew the benefit of the visual. Her cooking show proved it in the way its every shot was conceived to make the food look as good as it tasted.

Because of her discerning eye, she noticed every little nuance about Josh. The way his hair fell across his neck, curling at the ends, that his eyebrows were uneven, one slightly bushier than the other. She'd memorized the line of his cheek as it curved into a jaw that was as firm and dense as an oak. She could see the lines of his chest without a shirt since she'd had a glimpse of it that morning in the gym. Broad and firm, with a smattering of hair traveling all the way down past his waist, the rest of her view hindered by the trousers riding low on his narrow hips, draped down his long legs.

She knew she shouldn't be distracted by such thoughts. She needed to concentrate on her work and her family. She had her plan.

But what good was a plan if it didn't provide for unforeseen contingencies?

And Josh Keane was a very unforeseen contingency. A sexy, unabashedly, all-male one.

"So thanks for letting me prove not all the Keane men are hopeless in the kitchen," he said, pulling her out of her introspection.

"You're not hopeless." She rose when the oven timer dinged. "You just need guidance."

When she pulled the batch of muffins from of the oven, Josh groaned.

"Please tell me you can get extra out of that batch," he said, one hand over his heart.

Smiling, she put the tin down on the cooling rack and ripped off her oven mitt. "Of course I can. I always make more than I need."

"I'm your eternal slave," he said, adding a sigh.

"You're a cliché," she tossed over her shoulder as she checked the second oven for the status of the bread.

"How so?"

She turned to him and saw by the quick way his eyes darted up to her face he'd been checking out her butt while she'd been bent over.

Her insides quaked with pure female delight.

"The fastest way to a man's heart is…"

"Through his stomach," he finished. "It's true. In my case, anyway. A woman gives me food this good and I'll shoot the moon for her."

Kandy laughed and sat back down. Downing her coffee, she stared at him over the cup and asked, "So, is there anyone waiting at home with a hot recipe file?"

She watched his face squint into a puzzled expression. "Are you asking if I'm married?"

She flipped her hand in the air. "Married. Involved. Whatever." Her heart stalled like a flooded car engine while she waited for his answer.

"None of the above."

When she could breathe again, she asked, "Why not? Were you ever married?"

He shrugged. "Came close twice."

"What happened?"

He leaned back in the chair, the coffee mug wrapped in his fingers. "The first, we met in high school, dated through college. Then I got accepted to the police academy. Things were fine initially. But after a few months she realized she didn't like the gun or the danger aspect involved, not knowing if I was going to come home for dinner or be brought home in a box. That's what she told me, anyway. She broke it off. I stayed with the police force. Since then I've been busy. Haven't had time for much dating."

"Why did you quit the force?" she asked. "I've been wanting to ask you since we met. I mean, you're still young enough to be on it."

She watched some unreadable emotion pass over his face as he took another hit of the coffee.

"I'm thirty-four, for the record," he told her. "I was on the force for seven years. And it's not such an interesting story about why I left," he told her. "I was forced out."

"What?!"

Josh scratched absently at his chin. "Five years ago, my partner and I were involved in a shooting. We were chasing a rape suspect down an alley. The guy pulled a gun and I didn't see it. My partner was in front of me. He took a bullet in the neck and I got shot in the shoulder. Luckily I managed to shoot the guy in the leg. He couldn't get far after that."

"What happened to your partner?"

Josh pitched forward, put his elbows on the table, his hands out in front of him on the counter, clasped. "He's in a nursing home in Queens, pretty much brain dead. His only family, his sister, won't give up on him. She's a devout Catholic and prays every day for a miracle."

Without thinking, Kandy reached forward and wrapped her hands around his. "I've heard they do happen."

His smile was sad and she wanted to comfort.

"Why do I get the idea there's more to this story?"

When he lifted his gaze and nailed her with it, the heat she felt rise throughout her system was overpowering.

"You're very perceptive," he said with a sigh.

"That's one word for it. Grandma used to call it just being plain nosey."

She was happy when his mouth tilted upward. In the next instant he was all seriousness again.

"At the time of the shooting, I was…involved with my partner's sister. We were pretty much living together and had talked about getting married. A lot, actually."

He stopped and Kandy stayed silent.

"After the shooting, things changed. She…blamed me."

"That's ridiculous."

"Not to her. She thought—still thinks—I should have anticipated the perp would have a gun. I should have been faster to get my own gun out, should have pushed her brother out of the way. You name it, she's thought of it. The end result is she feels I was responsible."

"I think she's wrong."

Josh shook his head. "I've been over that night so many times in my head, trying to figure out a way it could have been different, and I've never been able to see it ending any other way than how it did."

"So why were you forced to leave?"

His gaze dropped to their joined hands. "Disability. I got shot on my dominant side, my shooting arm. I was out for more than three months recuperating. I failed my first two firearm checks after that, so the department decided I couldn't be trusted with a weapon, even though I'd shot the guy after being shot in the arm myself. They wanted to give me desk duty. I said no. I didn't join the force to sit at a desk. I'd wanted to be a cop since I was six. It was all I ever wanted to be. Get the bad guys. Sitting at a desk wasn't being a cop to me. So they gave me the option of an early out and I took it."

Kandy could see the pain his decision had caused written in the flatness in his eyes as he spoke. She had no doubt he'd been good at his job. To be retired to a desk at such an early point in his career must have hurt.

"You turned it around though, didn't you?" she said. "Started your own business. Utilized your skills and knowledge of law enforcement. That's something to be proud of."

He chuckled and continued staring down at their hands. "My family said pretty much the same thing."

Kandy realized she'd been rubbing his hands with her thumbs, comforting him much the way he had her earlier.

"Funny thing was, after I left, I spent a ton of time getting my shooting arm back in shape. I was at the range every day for almost six months. I could pass that firearms test now with a perfect score. And with my eyes closed."

"Would you consider going back?"

He didn't hesitate before replying. "No. I'm done with it. I've got a good business, I'm my own boss. I'm cool with the choice."

"Your family's right, you know. Stacy told me her dad hired you a few months ago to look into something having to do with his business. She wouldn't tell me what it was, just that Uncle Max was impressed by how professional and thorough you were. High praise from him. You should be proud of what you've done with your life."

He didn't answer for a few moments, just continued staring at their hands. All of a sudden, his head shot up and he pierced her with an intense gaze that caused her lungs to stop expanding.

"So how come you're not married?" he asked. "I'd think someone who values family and home as much as you do would be."

She wanted to tell him the plain truth. No one had ever asked her. Pride kept the words unspoken. "I've been busy, too," she said, instead, "building my business, my brand. As you've seen in the short time you've been around, it's an all-consuming entity. I don't really have time to devote to a relationship. It's a full time job just being in one, and men don't like coming in second. They tend to like being number one in your universe."

"What about moron-boy?" Josh asked. "You made time for him."

She laughed with a tinge of bitterness and removed her hands from his when the second oven timer dinged. Rising to remove the bread, she pulled on her oven mitts again. "And look where that got me. I didn't even realize I was being played. Pretty pathetic loser radar, if you ask me."

She took the two loaves from the oven and placed them on the cooling rack. "You want one of these muffins? They're cool enough now."

She turned to ask him the question and was caught off guard when she found him right behind her, barely a hair's width away. She stumbled back, falling into the counter. Josh grabbed her by the upper arms to steady her.

"Careful," he said.

She could feel the heat from his fingers searing through her thin shirt. All he had to do was tilt his head down a tiny bit, or she could raise hers, and their lips would come together. For a moment Kandy wondered who would feel the need to move first.

"For the record," he said, his hands still holding her, "I think you're wrong."

She swallowed. Hard. "About what?"

"Most guys respect a woman with career aspirations and goals. If the relationship is worth it, if the woman is, we're willing to compromise time together. It makes the time spent as a couple all the more satisfying."

Kandy couldn't think of a response. In all honesty, she couldn't think of anything but the feel of his fingers wrapped around her arms, the gentle warmth of his breath floating down across her face. Her heart was hammering against her chest and she knew he could sense the drumming since their bodies were so close. She stared up into the forest color of his eyes and lost herself in the reflection. Rising, just slightly, on her unshod toes, she arched, ready and wanting his lips on hers.

His head bent toward hers at the same time. In the next instant their bodies were jarred apart by the shrill shriek of the wall phone.

When Josh stepped back he said, "Wait until I get to the other line."

He jogged from the room while she took a deep breath and placed a hand on her quaking stomach.

"Go ahead and pick it up," he called.

"Hello?" She held her breath. "Oh. Hi, Mom. No, I was just baking."

Chapter Twelve

Josh replaced the receiver to give her some privacy.

He needed some air.

Hell, he needed to have his head examined.

What had that scene been all about?

He moved into the guest room, tore open the sliding doors, and went out to the balcony off his room. The warm night air slapped him in the face and he was thankful for the jolt.

If the phone hadn't rung he'd have had Kandy on her back, spread naked across the kitchen counter, pounding into her without a moment's thought.

What the hell was going on with him?

He'd never talked about leaving the force. With anyone. Not even the police-appointed shrink he'd been forced to see. He'd dealt with the demons and disappointments alone. His own family didn't know about the weeks he'd spent sequestered in his apartment, drinking himself into semi-consciousness night after night in an attempt to purge his mind of the nightmare. If he'd only been a split second quicker, as his partner's sister had accused, the perp would never have gotten a shot off. If he'd ducked or turned when he saw the gun, the bullet would have missed him.

His career, all his dreams of a life in uniform, of marriage to a woman he thought he loved, ended in a millisecond.

It wasn't fair.

With time, though, he'd come to accept what he couldn't change.

Kandy had been correct when she'd said he'd taken his skills and made a new career for himself. He was proud of that.

But why was he still yearning for something more? And just why did the touch of her hands covering his make every bad feeling in him slip away into nothingness? What was it about her that made him want to protect and comfort while craving to be treated the same?

It didn't make any sense. She was a job…a client.

He kept repeating it, but it still wouldn't sink in. Not when she looked at him with those warm, soulful eyes, or when she licked those full and luscious lips nature had blessed her with.

And certainly not when she was standing before him, desire pouring off her, begging to be kissed.

After he cleared his head he returned to the kitchen to find it empty, a note perched atop the counter.

Josh—I'm beat. A long day tomorrow, so I'm off to snoozeville. Have a few muffins while they're still warm. Butter's in the fridge.

With a deep, tired sigh, he pulled the butter out and slathered three muffins, all the while thankful he was alone.

His reaction to Kandy Laine was perplexing. More than just the physical desire he had for her—and that was strong enough—it was the person she was who intrigued him, pulled him in, made him want to be around her. She was one of the most single-minded women he'd ever met when it came to family, something he admired her for. She hadn't batted an eyelash while giving Daniel her ultimatums, yet she'd been gentle with him. And her excuse for her actions was simply because he was family.

Nepotism was the name of her game. She had the means and opportunity to supply her family with well-paying jobs and secure positions, and yet he hadn't seen her lord it over any of them, something she could easily do since it was her money, her earnings, her hard work and sacrifice paying for their wages and lifestyles. If anything, she felt responsible for them all instead of them feeling beholden to her.

The fact that she was so career-driven didn't faze him in the least. It added to her fascination. At an age where she should have been going to proms, making out with boys, and trying on clothes, she'd been focused on a goal. A goal was the last thing to enter the minds of most teenagers. Kandy had put her career choice at the forefront. She'd worked hard for her achievements and could, by rights, sit back now and start to relax, having attained the kind of notoriety and success of a much more seasoned woman. Instead, she was forging ahead with new projects and plans.

He'd discovered she was a brilliant businesswoman when he'd done a financial background check prior to accepting the job offer. Astute, brave, and savvy, she'd propelled herself, her personal image, and brand, to the top of the culinary elite, all the while giving full credit to her grandmother's tutelage.

Grandma Sophie may have been a great cook, but it was her granddaughter who was the clever and savvy megastar in the family tree. With every second he spent in her company, Josh was coming to enjoy being around her more and more.

But he was here to find out who was tormenting her, not to be tormented by the sheer want of her. He had a job to do, and do it he would. He'd find out who was responsible for harassing her and when he did, when it was all behind them, he'd walk away.

He had to. He couldn't risk caring for someone again, no matter how much he wanted to. It hurt too damn much when it didn't work out.

For now, he'd concentrate on the task at hand.

Do what he'd pledged to do.

* * *

They met in the gym at the appointed morning hour, both beginning their run at the same time. Kandy's iPod was in place and Josh turned the television to the news. After forty minutes, he heard her machine switch to the cooldown mode. It didn't take his investigative skills to recognize she was averting her gaze.

Realizing she might be upset about what had almost happened in the kitchen, he wanted to explain, to apologize, but she didn't give him the chance. When the machine stopped, she hopped off and said over her shoulder, "We have to leave in a half hour."

"I'll be ready."

All thoughts of her being upset with him vanished when she smiled straight at his face and said, "No surprise there," before tossing a towel over her shoulder and leaving him alone to finish his run.

Relief washed through his system as her cute butt strutted out the door. Either she hadn't realized what his intention had been, or she'd put it from her mind, choosing to ignore it. Whatever way she'd decided to play it, Josh was grateful she wasn't angry.

* * *

"Kandy, these are the best muffins I've ever eaten," the reviewer said, rolling his eyes and smacking his lips together.

"I'm so glad you like them." Kandy smiled.

So far he'd consumed half the loaf of bread she'd buttered, in addition to the muffins. The pot of Sophie's blend was almost empty as well.

"If he keeps this up, he'll explode before the interview is over," Stacy whispered to Josh as they stood off to one side of the set.

Stacy had suggested the studio kitchen for the setting of the magazine interview, thinking it might give a homey air to the food critic's mind-set when he wrote his article and book review.

Kandy effortlessly answered all the questions posed to her while refilling the reviewer's coffee cup frequently and catering to all his gustatory needs.

"He *looks* like a food reviewer," Josh said, taking in the man's ample girth.

Stacy bit back a giggle. After a moment she looked up at him and asked, "How was she last night? Was she okay after…everything?"

He didn't tell her about the phone call or the visit to Daniel.

"Fine. She started baking the second we got back to her place. It kept her occupied for most of the evening. Then her mom called. I went to do some work and Kandy went to bed."

Stacy's sigh was heavy. "Good. Cooking and baking are Kandy's therapy. At least it took her mind off all this for a while."

Josh nodded. "Like clockwork, she was in the gym this morning."

A smile traipsed across Stacy's face, full of mirth. "You get up at that ridiculous hour, too? What is it, four thirty?"

Josh winced, remembering how little sleep he'd actually gotten. "Yeah. Right on time."

"Like I told you, she's a creature of habit. But it works for her."

Kandy and the reviewer rose at the same time, the man's hand outstretched. She clasped it and pulled him forward to plant a chaste kiss on his cheek. The man, flustered and caught off guard, nonetheless beamed like a lit Christmas tree as he pumped the hand he still held. Stacy took this as her cue and came forward to escort him from the set.

When they were out of hearing, Kandy came over to him and laughed. "I was worried I didn't make enough food."

Josh chuckled while his eyes raked over her.

She appeared relaxed and worry-free, as if the horror of the past few days had been erased from her mind.

"Oh well, at least I know he'll write a good review of the book, so it was worth it."

Josh followed her as she made her way to her dressing room.

"I've got just one segment to film before we leave," she told him in the elevator. "I want to be at the house by two at the latest to start Ellie's cake."

"The way you drive we'll be there by one," he mumbled.

"I heard that. Do you have beach clothes with you?"

"What, like bathing trunks?"

She nodded. "Shorts, sandals. Beachwear. We'll be there until Sunday morning."

"No, but it's okay. I'm not big on swimming. I'll be okay with slacks and shoes."

She shrugged and said, "Suit yourself."

He walked her into the makeup room, enjoyed the flirting of the aunts for a few minutes, and then listened as they all began talking about the birthday bash.

More than a hundred people were descending on Kandy's hospitality this weekend and she was responsible for the entire menu. Games were planned for the kids, and a bonfire idea was tossed around for Saturday night.

As Kandy was made-up, primped, and fluffed, Josh excused himself to make a few phone calls. He didn't go far, just retreating to the empty hallway outside the makeup room.

The first call was to his friend at the city's CSU lab.

"Got anything on that knife for me, Paul?"

"Nothing useful," Paul said. "I lifted a clear set of prints but I couldn't find a computer match, so your guy's never been in the system. Knife's a standard kitchen issue, probably from a steak set."

"So, not really traceable."

"No. One interesting thing, though, with the rodent."

"What?"

"It didn't die from the stab wound or the decapitation. It was poisoned first. Routine rat poison. Stab and slice was made postmortem."

"Anything else?"

"Not now."

"Okay. Thanks. I appreciate it."

"Don't mention it. Just buy me a couple beers sometime when you're free. It's been a while."

"You got it."

After breaking the connection, Josh called his office. He'd made several calls the day before, doing background checks on a few of Kandy's associates, and was awaiting results.

Rick answered on the first ring.

"Got anything for me?"

"Yup," his partner said. "First, this Mason guy?"

"Yeah?"

"He's got a long acting history in his background. Did some Broadway, a couple films, before the switch to directing."

"So what does that give me?"

"Nothing, but he went to an all-boy's school straight up until college. Was the lead in a bunch of plays and musicals. The *female* lead in a few."

Josh's ears perked up.

"The reviews I could find in the local papers said he made an excellent Maria in the *Sound of Music* and a pretty good Emma. Know what I'm thinking?"

"Yeah. He can sound like a woman if he wants to. Interesting."

"I thought so. I've still got some feelers out on the others you asked for. Should have them by later this afternoon."

"I'll check back then."

After he put his cell back in his pants' pocket, Stacy got off the elevator and made her way toward him.

"I can guarantee she's going to get a four-star review," she told him with a big smile. "He couldn't stop talking about how great everything tasted. He asked me twice if Kandy would divulge the secret blend of her coffee."

"What did you tell him?"

"The truth. It's a secret from everyone except Kandy, and she's not about to tell. Not in this lifetime, anyway."

Josh nodded. "I wanted to ask you something and I'd prefer not to do it in front of an audience."

Her happy face grew serious at his tone. "What's the matter?"

"Nothing. I just wanted to get a bead on some of the people who'll be at the party this weekend. I heard your mom and aunt say there's about a hundred guests."

She nodded. "The whole family's invited and most of them are coming."

"Uncle Peter, too?"

Her eyebrows rose at the question. "I don't really know. Aunt Hannah was in charge of talking to him about the party."

Josh nodded. "Anyone not family invited?"

"The Masons, although I don't know if they'll make it. According to Cort, Alyssa doesn't like the beach. I know Reva's coming, and she's bringing her live-in. Some of the crew. Kandy gave Ellie the option of inviting some of her friends, and I think there's about twenty of them coming. But they're all college kids. They're not connected in any way to Kandy, other than she's Ellie's sister."

"Anyone else?"

Stacey shook her head. "Kandy doesn't really have any girlfriends outside of her sisters and cousins."

"No college roommate? No cooking school buddies?"

"No. Look, you've seen for yourself how her life is. When does she have time for friends? When does she even have time for herself?"

It was a question he'd asked as well. In the brief time he'd been with her, Kandy had basically gone to work and then home, with the book bash a brief stop along the way. Other than himself, Daniel, and her chauffeur, she'd seen no one else except her working crew and family. She'd spent long hours at the studio and then gone home. No dinner engagements, no trips to the movies, or shopping.

It was a hard, lonely life, to his mind, for such a young, vibrant woman.

Speaking to Stacy made him realize his life was much the same. All work and nothing much else.

Kandy emerged from the makeup room a moment later.

"What are you two conspiring about?"

Once again he was taken by how beautiful she was, even under the heavy studio makeup. Her lustrous, healthy skin shone right through it, the dramatic lining of her eyes to accentuate them on screen made the blue color more intense, more striking, like winking crystals.

Lucy had chosen a floral short-sleeved shirt for her to wear over a slim-fitting pale blue skirt. White sandals graced her feet and Josh noticed for the first time the ruby-red nail polish accenting her toes. Her thick, curly hair was pulled back at the sides, secured in the back with a pink rose barrette.

She looked like a teenager and a society maven all rolled into one.

"Nothing," Stacy said. "You ready?"

"Yup."

"I just spoke with Cort. He's got the kitchen all lit and ready to go. It'll just be the premiere intro for today. He wants to shoot the finale when everything else is done and edited together."

"Okay. That's what we discussed yesterday.You coming?" she asked him.

He nodded. "Joined at the hip."

Chapter Thirteen

They'd finished earlier than expected and she'd taken the opportunity to cut out for the weekend. After telling the crew to take the rest of the day off, she'd washed away Aunt Callie's makeup, changed into jeans and a T-shirt with a cashmere sweater tossed over her shoulders, and pulled her hair into a ponytail.

Her chauffeur had driven the Corvette over from her garage and was waiting downstairs to hand over the keys.

"I'm driving," Kandy declared once they were in the elevator.

"I'd like to get there alive," Josh told her, his overnight bag in one hand, her small one in the other.

"You will," she said. "Anyway, I know exactly where my house is. You don't. The turnoff to my lane is very tricky and you can easily miss it, so it just makes sense for me to drive."

"You can navigate," he said. "I'm very good at taking direction."

"Oh really?" she countered. "I haven't seen you do anything but give orders for the past few days."

He stared at her lovely face, now free of everything but moisturizer. Her lips were delicately curved upward at the corners and he could see the playfulness mixed with steel in her eyes.

"Then you'll be relieved to know I'm not stopping now. I'm driving. No arguments."

It was her turn to stare at him. The small smile vanished and a mote of anger blossomed in its place.

"You can be very overbearing, you know that? It's not an attractive trait."

"Part of the job, Kandy. You can rest for a while. I know my way out there. I'll just need you for the final detour."

"Let me make myself clear, Josh."

He saw the warmth in her eyes drop several degrees and felt his insides flash hot at her ire.

Since when did anger turn him on?

"My car. My house. I'm driving. No arguments."

With his own words thrust back at him, he tried valiantly to stifle the grin threatening to erupt across his face. The elevator doors opened and she sprinted out on those long legs into the lobby without another word.

Josh knew she wasn't a woman used to being challenged. She threw her purse over her shoulder and he watched, engrossed, the haughty sway of her hips as she galloped out of the elevator. Without a moment's hesitation he got hard as a stone at the look of her cute butt in those tight jeans.

He'd probably lost the driving fight, but it had been worth it to see the temper surface on her. He hadn't thought she could be lovelier than she already was, but the heat in her eyes and fire on her cheeks proved him wrong.

He alighted from the elevator in time to catch Evan Chandler jog up to Kandy, startle her, and grab her upper arm.

All carnal thoughts vanished. She was a good twenty feet ahead of him, and the lobby was busy due to the hour, but, like a rocket firing, he covered the space in seconds.

Chandler seemed to be pleading with her, his hand still on her upper arm. Kandy tried to pull away but as she yanked backward, he tugged her forward, never stopping his speech.

Josh took it all in as he bolted toward them. The one goal in his mind was protecting Kandy. Getting Chandler to release her was the main objective in that goal and he had the advantage of surprise on his side. Seizing Chandler's arm, he spun her ex-lover around. The astonishment on the man's face would have been humorous if Josh had been in the mood for comedy.

He wasn't.

The only thing on his mind as he dragged Chandler off was to hurt him. In a nanosecond his fist connected with the man's face.

Sprawled on his back, blood shooting from his nose, Chandler screamed and cursed.

Ignoring him, Josh turned to Kandy. "Are you okay? Did he hurt you?"

She stared at him with such intensity, such severity, he thought she might faint as she had on the roof. Her color had turned to chalk and her pupils were so constricted, all he could see was blue ice.

"Kandy?" He reached for her and, when she recoiled, snapping her arm out of his reach, he flinched.

"No. Don't touch me." Her voice was deathly low and raw.

Two security guards ran up to them and began helping Chandler to his feet.

"You asshole," he screamed, clutching his hand to his obviously broken nose. "Look what you did to my face. I'll sue your fat ass."

"Go ahead," Josh told him. "And while you're filing the police report, I'll be filing one for the harassment and stalking of Miss Laine."

"I wasn't stalking her, you dumb fuck. I was talking to her about something and you cold-cocked me. You attacked me for no good reason. I have witnesses."

"Calm down, sir. Want us to call the police, Miss Laine?" one of the guards asked.

A small flock of onlookers had gathered around them, whispering and pointing. Several cell phones were pointed at them, their built-in cameras recording everything.

Still stunned, Kandy took a moment before she answered. She was still staring up at Josh, her mouth a silent *O*.

"Miss Laine?"

"What? No—no. No police. I don't want them called. Just…just make sure he gets out of here."

Her voice trembled with nerves.

"Kandy, please." Chandler's annoying whine would put a three-year-old to shame. "Please. I need to talk to you."

Ignoring him, Josh bent and retrieved her dropped, forgotten purse and the bags he'd let go of. "Come on," he told her, a hand at her back to propel her away from Chandler.

He shouldn't touch her. Her reaction when he'd tried to take her arm proved it. She didn't want his hands on her, pawing her as Chandler had.

Kandy glanced once over her shoulder as the security guards began walking Chandler to the opposite doors. No one had bothered to give him a handkerchief and his nose was still spouting blood like an open faucet. He was ranting about being attacked, but the guards were paying him no heed.

Outside, the Corvette waited at the bottom of the steps, Kandy's driver, David, leaning against it.

His wide, open smile vanished the moment he caught sight of them.

"What's up?" he asked Josh.

Without embellishing, he related the scene in the lobby as he stored the overnight bags in the trunk.

"Between you and me, I never liked that guy," David said, closing the hatch.

"That's the general consensus." Josh took the proffered car keys.

Kandy stood on the passenger side, her back against the closed door, arms crossed in front of her chest.

"Do you still want to drive?" Josh asked.

Turning to face him, the wind came up and whipped her ponytail into her face. She looked exhausted and beaten down since seeing Chandler, and Josh's heart turned over as he came to stand next to her.

"I trust you to get us there alive," he said, dangling the keys in front of her.

"I don't," was her small reply. She opened her door and got in.

"You need a ride anywhere?" Josh asked the chauffeur before doing the same.

"Nah. I'm meeting someone for lunch around the corner. Have a good weekend, guys."

Both were silent for the first few minutes as Josh maneuvered them through heavy midtown traffic and out of the city. When they were through the tunnel and aimed for the Long Island Expressway, he looked over at her. "Why don't you close your eyes? I'll wake you when we get off at the exit."

She didn't speak, just continued to stare out the front windshield.

"Kandy?"

"I can't believe you hit him."

Josh took a deep breath. He'd figured that's what had been bothering her. Trying to explain, he said, "The way he grabbed your arm, it looked like he was hurting you. I only thought about getting him off you. Of protecting you."

"Of protecting me?"

"Yeah," he said, flicking his gaze toward her for a second. "Remember why I'm here? To protect you?"

When she didn't respond, he turned again and found her staring at him.

"What's wrong?"

Her color had returned and she didn't have the haunted, fearful glaze across her eyes any longer, but Josh could tell there was still something not quite right.

"When I was a teenager," she began, her voice small but starting to regain its body, "after my father walked out, we got teased a lot about it in school. There were some girls who knew about my mother. How she went a little…crazy after he left. They'd yell things at me in the halls, whisper taunts on the bus. Nasty things about her, about my family."

When she stopped, he said, "I think girls can be way crueler than boys. Just plain mean."

"Yes. Mean." She nodded. "That's what they were. One day a small group of them followed me into the bathroom at school. They circled around me, chanting, teasing. Saying terrible things about my mom. I couldn't get away. One of them started poking me in the ribs. Another one grabbed my books and stuffed them in the trash bin. One of them pulled at my hair while another kicked me. I wasn't this height yet. They were taller and bigger. And older."

"What did you do?"

"Nothing. Absolutely nothing. Grandma told us it was wrong to fight. Wrong to get physical. We had to take the high road. She told me so many times growing up that girls were jealous of me, of all of us, because we were smart and pretty and loved. She tried to make us see it didn't matter what people said. We had one another. So I just stood there, taking it. Finally, they got bored because I wasn't fighting back, and left. I got my stuff together, cut the rest of my classes, and went home in tears. Grandma was furious about the ditching school part."

She laughed joylessly. "I always felt cheated because I didn't have anyone to stand with me against them. No one who had my back."

Josh stole another glance at her. "I wonder why you weren't upset with your mother for putting you in that position in the first place."

She shook her head. "I've never blamed Mom for what she did with her life. I was the oldest. I saw everything my poor excuse for a father did to her. She deserved to live however she wanted to."

Silence filled the car.

"What I'm trying to say," Kandy continued after a few minutes, "is…well…thank you. Thank you for standing up for me, for defending me. For being on my side. I've always had to fight my own battles—or not fight, as the case may be," she added. "It felt good to have you there when Evan jumped at me."

He flicked his eyes toward her and then turned back to the traffic in front of them.

"I thought you were angry," he said. "When I tried to take your arm, you pulled back, like you were terrified of me."

She shook her head. "I don't know why I reacted that way. I know you'd never hurt me. I know it. It sounds crazy since I've known you only a few days, but I trust you. Completely. With my life. I really do."

It was his turn to nod. "What did Chandler want?"

Her laugh had a caustic bite to it. "Money. He needs cash. Fast. He sounded desperate."

"He is. Maybe you should reconsider and get a restraining order against him. It would keep him out of your hair."

"No. I don't want the police involved."

"Why not?"

"The publicity, mostly. I can't afford anything negative right now with the season premiere looming and the book just out. If I had him arrested and charged, it would hit the media in a millisecond. Reva would kill me for the bad press."

"First of all," he said after a few seconds, "Reva is one of the people who want to find out who's been making your life miserable, so she's not going to be mad at you. She's concerned for your safety and well-being. Second, I always thought when you were in the public eye any publicity was good publicity."

She shook her head. "Maybe if you're an actor or a rock star. But in my line of work, anything that creates a pall on the domestic tranquillity image is a big fat, no-no."

"Seems like a double standard."

Her sigh was heavy. "It is. But regardless, I don't want the police brought in. You're enough. Now that you've hit him, bloodied his pretty face and not just tossed him out of an event, Evan will back off."

Experience told him not to be convinced.

"You'll see." She nodded. "I'm right."

* * *

For the next few hours they talked little as Josh navigated through the crowded summer weekend beach traffic.

Kandy sat and stared out the window, replaying the scene in the lobby over and over in her head.

Evan Chandler had scared her to the bone when he'd grabbed her arm. What scared her more, though, was her reaction when Josh pulled him off and bashed him to the ground.

He thought she'd been mad at him when she recoiled from his touch. Kandy knew it was just the opposite.

She'd been filled with such a powerful, overwhelming sense of primal bloodlust at seeing Evan sprawled on the lobby floor, that she grew frightened of her response. When Josh reached out to touch her, she *was* terrified, but not of what he would do to her. It was more what *she* would to do *him*.

Kandy knew the minute he touched her she'd have thrown herself into his arms and let loose all the contained emotions running through her.

Basic bloodlust, that's all it was. Blood had been spilled over her, for her, and in her defense. Caveman safeguarding his mate. The only problem with that image was Josh wasn't a caveman and she wasn't his mate.

But it felt awfully good to know he was on her side.

* * *

"I need directions from here," he said a half hour later.

He turned where she instructed him to and they drove down a long and winding sandy road surrounded on both sides by shoulder-high beach grass. After a few more minutes the top of the house come into view.

"Nice," he said, when he stopped the car in her seashell-strewn driveway.

"It's a good getaway spot. The beach is private." She alighted from the car and, arms stretched above her head, closed her eyes and took a deep, full breath. "Heaven," she said, a few seconds later. When she opened her eyes, she smiled at him.

They took the bags inside after Kandy disarmed the security alarm.

"Who knows the code?" Josh asked, watching her do it.

"Greta, me, Gemma, Stacy."

"No one else?"

"No. I don't loan the house out when I'm not here. Stacy and Gemma have it because they're out here a lot of weekends with me and I don't want them to feel they have to spend every minute at my side. It gives them some freedom to come and go as they please."

"How many phone lines do you have?"

"Just my cell out here."

"No landline?"

With a shrug, she said, "No."

"Good. One less worry. Enough people can get in touch with you as it is."

He followed her into the house, both their bags in one of his hands. "You didn't bring much."

"This is my second home. I have a complete set of clothes and toiletries here. I come out most weekends in the summer. The fall, too."

Josh looked around.

Kandy wondered, as she had that first day in her office, what he saw when he viewed her surroundings.

This house truly was her sanctuary. She loved being out here, alone, to relax and forget about everything.

The foyer was a giant open atrium ascending up to the second level, a winding staircase its only access. Off to the right sat a spacious sunken living room, complete with a fully functional brick fireplace. French terrace doors opened out to a finished, three-level deck with a magnificent, unobstructed beach view. The house was about thirty yards from the shoreline.

"My bedroom's up there." Kandy pointed. "Originally it was a loft, but I had the room enlarged and a full bath installed last year. It runs the length of the back of the house now."

"How much square footage?"

"Seventy-five hundred. It's small compared to most of the other houses along this strip of beach. This is the first big party I've ever hosted here, so pray the weather holds and it's a beautiful sunny day tomorrow. Otherwise, we'll be cramped. Guest bedrooms are through there." She nodded toward a long hallway. "You can take any one. They all have connecting private baths. I'll give you a quick tour if you want."

Josh nodded. "Let me put my bag down first."

Kandy went into the kitchen while he did.

"Greta took in my food delivery," she told him when he came in a few minutes later. "Everything's here. I can start the prep work immediately."

"How about that tour?"

She smiled. "Quick one. I've got a lot to do."

"I'll help."

She showed him the entire bottom-floor layout and the security system installed in the laundry room.

"Good program," he told her. "This is quality high-tech equipment."

"It came with the house."

They walked out to the beach from the kitchen access.

"Where's the nearest house?" he asked, staring off into the distance.

"The Haskells, about a half mile up that way," she said, pointing.

"Who's the other way?"

"The Cardellinos. Three-quarters of a mile."

"I can't see their houses."

"The same goes for them. They can't see mine. It's called privacy, Josh. We pay a lot for it in these parts."

"Just getting the lay of the land." After a few seconds, he added, "It's private. Secluded. Makes the logistics of guarding you a little difficult."

"How so?"

"There are lots of places for someone to hide. In the tall beach grass, for instance. You wouldn't see them coming until it was too late. The driveway is long and secluded. With the roll of the surf you wouldn't hear someone approaching or walking up the path. Even the beach access is attainable. If you're inside the house, there are at least six rooms downstairs where someone could just walk right in. It's a bit of a defensive problem."

Kandy frowned and folded her arms across her chest. "Thanks for that bit of depressing info. You know, I've never *not* felt safe here. Ever. It's been my retreat, my one escape. Five minutes with you and the feeling's spoiled. Thanks a lot."

He reached out and snatched her hand when she whirled around to go back into the house.

"Kandy, wait. I'm sorry."

She turned back to him, slowly, capturing his gaze with her own.

"I look at everything from a security viewpoint. It's my job. It's why I'm here, remember? But I'm sorry. I wasn't looking at your house as a house but as an impetus to keeping you safe. *I do* see it, though, and it's magnificent. Everything about it, including the fact it's a refuge for you. I don't mean to spoil that. I really don't."

She digested his words, the apology steeping into her. "I understand why you need to think the way you do. It's your job, like you said. I guess you wouldn't be so good at it if you didn't."

Her gaze traveled down to where his hand still held hers. He removed it and said, "I'm sorry," again.

Her lips flattened and she took a few beats to calm down. "So am I," she said at length. "About this whole situation. Digging into my friends' and my family's personal lives. Making them admit things they'd rather keep silent and private. I want it to be over. Now."

He nodded. "I'm working on it."

They stood on the deck for a few moments, each silent, the sound of the surf crashing in the background.

It was Kandy who finally broke through the quiet. "I need to get started on the cake."

* * *

"You're a good chopper," she said, glancing over at him as he worked on the carrots.

"It's easy to follow instructions when you're told precisely what to do."

She raised an eyebrow and countered, "I need them to be a certain length and width for the salad. If they're not done correctly, they whole package won't look good."

"Kandy, in all honesty, I'm beginning to believe there's nothing you can whip up that won't look good and taste even better."

She smiled at the compliment and swiped her hand across her cheek to move an errant curl back into place.

Josh's tongue went sandpaper dry. A small speck of flour traced across her face, leaving a white powdery trail along her cheek. All he wanted to do was lick it off.

They'd been working nonstop for hours.

The four-tiered birthday cake was currently cooling on the table and half the hors d'oeuvres were wrapped and in the storage refrigerator.

Josh's nose and taste buds had been assaulted by the various concoctions she'd mixed up. Everything from caviar-filled pastry puffs, toasted almonds over a cracked crab spread, bacon-wrapped baked water chestnuts with brown sugar, to a Mediterranean salad complete with goat cheese. She was rolling phyllo dough for baklava as she supervised his vegetable-chopping technique.

"How much more are you going to do?" he asked, transferring the last batch of cut carrots to a bowl.

"I just need to clean and de-vein the shrimp, shuck the corn, make the ice cream, and put the first two layers of frosting on the cake. Tomorrow morning, we can go down to the docks and get the lobsters."

Josh shook his head, marveling at how much they still had left. "What do you mean by first two layers? How many layers do you put on a cake?"

"Three," she said, swiping at her hair again. "After the first, the cake goes in the fridge to harden up a little. It's like primer. The second layer goes on about an hour later and then sits overnight. In the morning I do one more thin layer to make sure everything is even and then I decorate it."

Josh stared at her, his mouth open.

"What?"

"Is that normal?" he asked, then shook his head. "I mean, not *normal,* but is that how it's usually done?"

"No. One or two layers is the norm for most professional bakers. Why?"

"I can't believe how much work you do just to make a cake. The last one I had was covered with a thin layer of tub frosting. It wasn't bad, either."

"This isn't any cake, Josh, and I never use commercial products," she said, pouting. "Everything's made from scratch. It's my sister's birthday. Her *twenty-first* birthday. I want it to be perfect."

"Believe me, it will be." He moved to the sink to rinse his hands. "Three layers of frosting," he said to himself. "Sounds like overkill to me."

"Stop mumbling." She started the mixer to beat the frosting. "It isn't overkill by any sense of the word."

"Fine." He turned back to her. "Where's the corn? I'll get started on that."

"On the deck. I saw the bags when we were out there earlier. There's a garbage can on the side of the grill you can use. I'll put the husks in the compost later."

He nodded and dried his hands on a tea towel.

When he saw the fifteen bags of freshly picked farm corn, he shook his head again and sighed. "Figures." He called into the house, "How much did you order?"

"A hundred and fifty ears. Why?"

"Looks like they're all here."

"I'll be out in a few minutes to help. I want to get the first layer on," she called over the whir of the mixer.

Josh pulled a deck chair to the bags and began tackling the shucking.

The quiet, hypnotic sound of the surf captured his attention as he did The sun was lower in the sky, about two or three hours of daylight left. A pair of seagulls swooped down and stormed into the sea, disappearing into the waves in search of food. In the far distance a speedboat hurriedly made its way across the waves, a thick, white frothy foam in its wake.

In all, it was life he could easily get used to. Relaxing and enjoying the peace and quiet, the undulating sway of the waves breaking on the shoreline.

Only he hadn't relaxed for a single second since arriving. Kandy put him to work the moment they'd come back into the house. Watching how she tirelessly cooked and baked, it bothered him that she didn't have anyone from her family helping or even someone hired to assist her. Two of her sisters were arriving early in the morning to help decorate the house, but it was something that could be done quickly and without a great deal of thought. Kandy was chained to the kitchen, not in the mood to leave it until every last duty was performed. She was solely responsible for feeding more than one hundred people in less than twenty-four hours, and after she'd worked a full, complete week. Add in the terrorizing incidents, and he couldn't imagine anyone he knew holding up as well as she was.

It didn't seem fair she was doing it all by herself. If he hadn't been there, he knew she'd be up most of the night finishing the preparations.

"Forget about that," he said aloud.

"Forget about what?" She pulled a chair beside him, materializing from inside the house.

Embarrassed, his neck heated. "Nothing."

"What?" she persisted, taking an ear of corn from one of the bags and shucking it in one brisk move.

"How'd you do that?" he asked, stunned. "I can't get it off in less than three, four moves."

"It's easy." She held an ear up for his inspection. "Just grab the biggest part of the husk, twist, and yank. The rest of the covering comes without any excess effort. Try it."

He did and was amazed when the husk came off in one piece.

"Now, what were you talking to yourself about when I came out here?" she asked, shucking another ear.

He winked an eye against the still-bright sun and said, "I was just thinking you're doing everything for this party and you don't have any help."

"I do so," she said, her brow wrinkling. "I have you."

His mouth twisted into a scowl. "If I wasn't here, would you have help with all the food prep?"

A heartbeat passed. "No. Why does it matter?"

"It matters because you've already put in about a hundred hours this week with your real job, not to mention being frightened once or twice, Kandy. I think it's only fair someone in your family should have volunteered to help out."

"I like working alone." She shrugged one shoulder. "I do it all the time. I know you find this hard to believe, but cooking, baking, devising new recipes, all helps me relax. You could say it's a very cheap form of therapy."

"I get that," he said, staring at her, while she deftly removed another husk in a way he envied. "I get you're actually one of those rare people who absolutely loves what they do. It's not just a career for you, but a way of life. But honestly, you work entirely too hard and too much."

"I disagree," she said, tossing another husk into the bag. "It isn't work for me, not really. Oh, the show is, for sure. I can't deny that. Long, sometimes boring hours; a full schedule almost every day. It does get a bit much. But for the rest, well." She shrugged again. "I can only say I love it. I'd never be happy if I couldn't cook."

"And yet, I haven't seen you eat more than two full meals since I've been with you."

A wide, impish grin split her face. "That's because it's so much more fun cooking for other people than cooking for just me."

He shook his head, not understanding her in the least.

It was at that moment his stomach growled.

Loudly. Enough to be heard over the roar of the surf.

Kandy's giggle carried on the breeze billowing around them. She stood. “I’m a horrible hostess. Just because I don’t take time to eat doesn’t mean you have to starve. I’ll go get dinner started.”

He stopped her in her tracks when his hand shot up and pulled her back down into her seat.

“You will not,” he said, the steel in his voice unmistakable.

Frowning, she asked, “What?”

“We’re going out to eat,” he declared, leaving no room for discussion by his tone.

“Josh, that isn’t necessary. I can whip up something fast—”

“No, Kandy. We’re going out. As soon as this bag is finished, you’re taking a break and we’re going into town.”

“But I have so much left to do.”

“It’ll still be here when you get back, don’t worry.” He tossed his last husk into the garbage bag and stood. “You deserve a break.”

She stared up at him and he could tell by the firm tilt of her chin she was all set to argue.

He was amazed when she didn’t. Instead, she tossed her last husk into the garbage and stood with him.

“Do I get to choose where we go?” she asked, wiping her hands together.

“It’s your neighborhood.”

“Okay. Give me five minutes to freshen up.”

“Take ten.”

She smiled. “Five’s more than enough.”

As she walked back into the house he let out the breath he’d been holding since making his announcement.

That hadn’t been as hard as he’d thought it would.

Chapter Fourteen

Kandy knew of a place frequented only by the year-round residents and they'd driven to the small, secluded, off-the-beaten-path Italian restaurant for dinner.

After greeting Kandy like a prodigal daughter, Mario Cuttone led them to a table in the back of the restaurant next to a window overlooking the ocean.

"This is private. You won't be bothered here," he'd told them in his thick, Brooklyn accent.

They ordered fresh salmon and a radicchio salad, plus a bottle of the establishment's best white wine.

"I haven't been here in a while," Kandy said, sipping her drink. "I've missed Mario."

"He an old friend?"

She nodded. "His parents were friends with Grandma and Grandpa. They lived down the street. He was eating dinner at Sophie's table with Uncle Peter before I was born."

"What about this place?" Josh cocked his head. "Sophie have something to do with it?"

"No. Actually, Mario's dad was a chef in Italy before they emigrated. The rumor I grew up hearing was he'd cooked for Mussolini, but I always thought it was a made-up story. Mario Senior opened this place when Junior was in college. He left it to him when he died."

Josh surveyed the room and nodded. "Old-world charm," he said, taking a sip of his water. "I like places like this. The food is always great, always fresh, always plentiful."

Kandy smiled.

When she followed it with a sigh, Josh asked, "What are you thinking about?" He rested his arms on the table in front of him.

She shook her head. "You'll think it's silly."

"Try me," he said, leaning in closer, his hands just a fraction from hers.

In the subdued, soft—dare she think *romantic*—lighting, Kandy could see the circle of dark green surrounding the outer, lighter color of Josh's eyes. For a second she wished beyond hope he'd lean forward, take her face in his hands, and kiss her.

"Promise you won't laugh?"

"I'd never laugh at you, Kandy." His voice was filled with kindness.

She glanced down at their hands, so close, yet so far away, wanting nothing more than to grab them and place them all over her body.

"I've got this plan."

When she didn't elaborate, he tapped a finger on her clasped hands. "And?"

She ran her tongue over her teeth and stared across the table at him.

"I've never told anyone this. Not even Gemma."

He waited.

"Like I said, I've got this plan. In two years, when my television contract expires, I'm not going to renew it. I want to open a restaurant," she said all in one breath. "A bunch of them, really. Specializing in comfort foods. I want to use Sophie's recipes from when we were kids. Baked macaroni and cheese, grilled ham and cheese, the best tomato soup ever. Chicken potpie to die for."

"Why would you think I'd laugh at that?" he asked.

She lifted her shoulders. "Not you maybe, but people in general. Opening a restaurant seems like such an inconsequential thing, considering all I've done with my life."

"Like a consolation prize?"

Her head whipped up and she met his eyes. "I can't believe you said that. It's what I've been thinking all along, ever since I came up with the idea. I've thought people wouldn't understand why I would want to go from the limelight of a national cooking show to the relative obscurity of owning and running a small, boring restaurant."

Josh laughed. "Believe me, when you open it, it won't be small or boring. We all have comfort foods in our memories. Foods that make us feel good, feel loved like we were as kids. Whenever I get home, my mom always makes me her meat loaf. Sends me back with enough to last a week. I love it."

"You should taste mine sometime," she said with a huge grin.

"Glad to. Your restaurant will be a big hit, Kandy. In fact, I'll make a reservation right now if you'll take it."

In that moment she knew without doubt he was the kind of man she could lose her heart to if she allowed herself that freedom. The realization pierced through her like an arrow. To fall for Josh was definitely not in her plans.

But how could she help it? How could she steel herself against it? He was sweet and kind, yet totally masculine and male. He was man enough to beat the living daylights out of Evan for her, and yet he'd helped her chop and prepare the food for the party without blinking or complaining.

He was everything a man should be. Everything she'd always dreamed of finding and never had.

Her father's defection from their family had traumatized her more than she'd ever admit. As the oldest, she'd watched her parents' marriage unravel from a young age, knew the pain and hurt her mother had endured from his philandering and spiteful ways, and had vowed never to let a man treat her in the same fashion. When the divorce was finalized, Kandy's emotions had warred between giving thanks, spewing anger, and feeling abandoned.

As strong-willed as she was about ever letting a man get close enough to hurt her, she'd still found herself picking men similar to her father through all her short-lived relationships.

Womanizers, narcissists, and shallow men, one and all. Evan Chandler had been the only one whom she'd thought was different. He'd never seemed to mind her tunnel vision where her work was concerned, never once argued with her when she had to choose it over time to spend with him. Kandy had thought she'd finally found a man evolved enough in his own right and secure enough in his own ego to start getting serious about.

The thought had flown once she'd found out his true motives.

Josh Keane was as different from every other man she'd ever been with—as different as chalk was from cheese.

And he'd told her more than once he was with her because he was doing his job. That's all she was to him. Nothing more.

Looking out over the water while the sun settled low on the horizon, Kandy admitted to herself she really wanted there to be something more.

They ate with a slow and leisurely ease, enjoying the quiet atmosphere and delicious food. When it came time to settle the bill, Mario called her an idiot in Italian and kissed her on the mouth.

"You don't pay," he said, his firm voice brokering no debate. "You make me one of Grandma's cheesecakes."

Kandy laughed, hugged him, and promised she'd deliver it before heading back to the city.

* * *

"I have to admit," she said, when they walked back through the front door of the beach house two hours later, "that was a nice break. But I still have a ton of things to do."

She turned on the lights in the foyer and both of them immediately saw the blinking light on the dock station where she'd left her cell phone to charge.

"Go ahead and listen to it," Josh said, coming to stand beside her, sensing her unease. Her spine had stiffened the moment she'd spotted the flashing blue light.

She took a deep breath and hit the voice mail and speaker icons.

"You have four new messages," the mechanical voice recorder told them.

The first was a frantic call from Gemma saying she would be late arriving in the morning because a filling had come out and she had an early appointment with her dentist.

"But Abby'll be there. Plus, I imagine you've got the hunk with you, so you won't have to do everything by yourself."

Josh's left eyebrow rose at Gemma's descriptive phrasing.

Kandy grinned.

The second message was from Hannah Laine.

"I'll be a little late to the party, honey. I'm having my highlights redone at one, so I'd say four at the earliest. Carlo couldn't get me in earlier and I do want to look good for my youngest one's happy day. Hope this isn't a problem."

Kandy turned to Josh and shrugged. "You'll understand when you meet her."

The third call was a hangup.

Kandy stared up at Josh and he could see the pulse pounding at her neck. After the fourth beep, they both heard a familiar voice.

"Think you're smart by running away, Kandy? Well, we'll see who's smart, bitch. *Whore!*"

The last word was shouted.

Kandy's hand slammed the message function off.

Her breathing grew erratic and labored as she turned to face Josh.

"Let me see if I can trace it," he said calmly as he picked the cell phone up and punched in an access code. "No," he said a moment later. "I'm sorry."

She ran her hands up and down her arms. "I need some tea," she said, moving toward the kitchen. "And I need to finish up the food."

"Kandy."

She turned, heat and anger in her eyes. "I need to finish," she repeated, her hands still hugging her upper arms. "I need to work. I won't let anything, or anyone, stop me."

Her face, just a few minutes before so happy and carefree, was now ashen and drawn. But Josh saw the determination in the hard set of her lips.

He nodded. "I'll help."

For the next three hours Kandy was in constant motion, not standing still once. Josh marveled at her focus and concentration. Every movement was deliberate and precise as she rolled, floured, spread, and baked herself into what he knew had to be exhaustion. He was tired just watching her.

He let her do it, though, understanding her need for the distraction.

When the last tidbit had been taken from the oven and placed in the storage refrigerator, she pulled a mop and bucket from the cleaning closet.

"You're gonna wash the floor? *Now?*" He glanced down at his watch.

It was almost midnight.

"I never leave off cleaning my kitchen after a big prep," she said, filling the bucket with hot water from the sink.

"Here, let me do it," he said, taking over. "You've been going since four thirty this morning. It's time for bed, Kandy. Go get ready. You've had a full, exhausting a day."

She wouldn't give him the mop. "I'm doing this, Josh. It won't take more than five, ten minutes, tops."

"Your work ethic astounds me. I can't decide if you're just plain stubborn or obstinate, but you'll be no good tomorrow if you're overtired and have a house full of company to entertain. And you still have stuff to do in the morning."

She didn't budge.

"Kandy, it's midnight. You need sleep. Rest. Now let me have the mop."

He put out his hand. She glared at it for a few beats and then ignored it, turning back to the sink to lift the bucket.

"No. *You* go to bed. I'm finishing this."

"Look, I'm not playing around."

"Of course you're not. You're just naturally bossy and domineering. Well, here's a news flash, Joshua Keane," she said, dropping the bucket back into the sink, water sloshing out the sides. "I'm a grown-up. I do want I want, when I want. And I want to wash my floor. Now. *You* go to bed."

He couldn't believe she was arguing with him over something so stupid. For that matter, he couldn't believe he was contending with her. But something in her tone rattled him and, even though he knew it was childish, he refused to back down.

Arms crossed, legs braced in a stance of defiance, he said, "You know, I weigh double what you do. I can just take that mop out of your hands. It wouldn't be hard at all."

She turned back to him, the blue in her light eyes deepening. "Go ahead and try," she challenged, one hand on her hip in a stance of rebellion, the other gripping the mop handle.

They were standing toe to toe, each unwilling to bend.

Josh's hand snaked out to grab the mop and Kandy effortlessly slapped it away. Without missing a beat, his other hand wound around her back, yanking her full force against his chest, the mop between them.

Kandy's cry of surprise spit from her as she stared, wide-eyed, up into his face.

They were so close he could see the pulse beating at her temple as he stared down at her.

"Don't challenge me if you're not prepared to meet the consequences," he said, his voice low and blunt.

She stared up at him, a sneer just beginning to form on her lips. "You don't scare me."

In the span of a heartbeat his head came down to hers, while she craned her neck toward him.

When their lips met the argument died.

Damn it.

He knew she'd feel like this, taste like this.

Heaven. Pure and total heaven.

Josh snaked his hands down her back, delighting in every curve and crevice he touched, to settle on her sweet ass. He swallowed her gasp against his mouth and gripped her butt, grinding her against his immediate, rock-hard erection.

When he felt her, soft, warm, and plastered against his body, he echoed her groan with one of his own.

He'd dreamed it would feel like this with her. Hot and spicy, delectable and scrumptious, just like her cooking. Her mouth was made for kissing, full and lush, swollen with need and desire.

Josh wanted nothing more than to eat her whole.

Clenching her even tighter, his lips left the mouthwatering taste of hers to wander across her cheeks, down to her chin. His tongue tasted the hollow behind her ear, his lips gliding across the silky skin of her neck.

Like a man starved for a lifetime, he devoured her.

Kandy arched backward, giving him free access to all those regions, while clutching fistfuls of his hair in her strong hands.

His tongue laved at the exposed skin of her collarbone, trailed back up to the corner of her ear, and when he captured the small lobe in his mouth and sucked, felt Kandy shudder with such erotic violence against him, he almost dropped to his knees.

"Josh."

He pulled back and stared down at her flushed and glowing face. Her eyes were closed, her lips parted, waiting for him to kiss her again.

She was, without doubt, the most beautiful, most desirable woman he'd ever seen.

She felt so good, so right, against him. As if they'd been created and carved for each other.

And he wanted her like he'd wanted nothing else in his life.

But he knew he couldn't have her.

A cold fist of reality punched through his desire-drenched body. She needed him to protect her, not seduce her. The notion that she wanted him as much as he did her didn't change that fact.

"Kandy. Open your eyes."

When she did he almost lost the small amount of sanity he still possessed and took her right there, braced against the sink.

Her beautiful blue irises were transparent crystals filled with heat and longing. Josh swore he could see to her very core; he could have melted into them without thought. Her gaze raked down his face to his lips, and she pulled a hand from his hair and traced a delicate line in the dimple under his bottom lip, just above his jawline.

Josh's abdominal muscles contracted. He grabbed her hand, placed a chaste kiss on the open palm, and watched her expression change from captivated to confused.

"Josh—?"

"Shhh." He placed his own finger against her lips. When he shook his head, she pulled back.

"You don't want—?" Her brow creased, a frown forming on her lips.

His hands rubbed her upper arms. "We can't."

"Why not?" she asked, trying to pull away. He kept her prisoner, the sink ledge behind her. "We're both adults. Single. Free to do what we want. And I want you, Josh. So much I can taste it," she added, a nervous laugh trickling from between her lips. She brought her hand up to his hair to try and pull his mouth back to hers, but he stopped her.

His hand went to her lips and he gently rubbed them back and forth. When she sucked one finger into his mouth, her gaze never leaving his face, Josh groaned and tugged his hand away.

"Don't."

"Josh, I want you. Now. Isn't that all that matters? Both of us, here and now?"

He shook his head. "I was hired to protect you, Kandy. To keep you safe. Not to sleep with you."

He saw the lust in her eyes turn from sultry heat to artic frost in a heartbeat and guilt flooded through him.

"Let go of me." Her voice was barely a whisper.

"Kandy, please—"

"I said, let go of me."

The curtailed fury in her voice gave him no room for discussion. When his hands came down to his sides, Kandy pulled away, turned, and quickly quit the room.

Josh stared down at the mop lying on the floor in front of him. Exhaling, he picked it up and pulled the bucket from the sink.

* * *

Idiot, her mind screamed as she bolted up to her bedroom.

Why don't you just wear a sign around your neck that reads DESPERATE.

She threw herself down onto the bed and scraped her hands over her face.

More than embarrassed by her wanton behavior, Kandy was disgusted for having no control.

One kiss. That's all it had taken. Just one kiss and she'd begged him for more.

The second his tongue wound with hers, sucking and tugging it ravenously, her mind stopped functioning. The challenge for domination of the mop was over the moment their lips met.

She'd released her grip on the handle, vaguely hearing it slam to the floor between them, and snaked her hands up and around Josh's neck, massaging the prickly hairs at the nape of his collar. Twining her fingers into his thick, coarse hair, she pulled him down and deepened the kiss further, her galloping heart almost leaping out of her. As his hands floated down her back to circle her waist and pull in her tighter, she felt her legs start to give out from under her. When he gripped her butt a heartbeat later and pressed their bodies closer, imprinting and molding himself to her, Kandy thought she could die from pleasure.

He felt so damn good. So unbelievably good.

Better than anything she'd ever felt before.

She wanted more, much more, than just a stolen kiss in the kitchen. Kandy wanted to be under him, staring up at him, calling his name when he made her come.

The very thought as it passed through her mind made her blush scarlet.

She pulled a pillow from under the covers, punched it, and threw it behind her neck.

How many times had he told her over the past few days he was with her for one reason and one reason alone? To find out who was harassing her.

He's here to help, that's all. When he's done, he'll leave.

How ironic is that?

She'd spent her whole life concentrating on building her career, never wanting to be bothered having to choose between a man and her goals, knowing the goals were always the prime objective, never wanting to have to make a choice between her head and her heart. Now, when she'd finally found a man who might be worth sacrificing for, worth letting in, she was nothing more to him than a responsibility.

Oh, he desired her, all right. The proof hit her squarely in her midsection when she was in his arms. But, apparently desire wasn't enough. No, he wasn't going to do anything—including her—but the job he'd been hired to do.

Karma really was a bitch to bring a man she could be comfortable with, one she could laugh with, who appreciated her skills and career choices, and, more important, a man she could trust in her private sphere, only to have him deny both of them the pleasure of a physical relationship because his job came first.

She rose and crossed to the bathroom. To the reflection in the mirror she said aloud, "He's right about one thing. You need sleep."

Face washed, teeth brushed, she changed into pajamas.

Kandy wanted to hear the lonely roll and call of the surf as it broke on the shore so she left her lanai doors open. Rhythmic and hypnotic, she hoped the sound would lull her to sleep without any further thoughts of the man downstairs. The man who, she knew without doubt, was rapidly becoming something much more than just her bodyguard.

An hour later when she was still wide awake, remembering the fiery taste of him, the firm and forceful feel of him against her, the craving his body had so blatantly shown to her, Kandy knew sleep, if it ever did come, would be troubled.

* * *

At four-thirty her eyes peeked open and she turned to the clock on her bedside table.

She'd slept a total of half an hour. A forty-minute run was the last thing on her mind. Turning to her side, she pulled the blankets up and drifted back to sleep.

The next time she opened her eyes it was after ten.

"Oh. My. *God.*"

Kandy sprinted from the bed, wrenched her pajamas off, and jumped into the shower. She didn't even give the water a chance to warm, but stepped into the stall while it was still regulating.

Teeth chattering against the chill, she denounced the wasted hours lying in bed when she still had so many things to do before her guests began arriving.

Hair sopping, she pulled it into a high ponytail and threw herself into jeans and a T-shirt, her body still glistening from the shower spray.

How could he let her oversleep, she railed, running down the spiral stairs? Because, of course it was Josh's fault she had. She rolled to an abrupt stop at the bottom of the stairs when she saw some of the decorations hanging in the foyer and heard laughter coming from the kitchen.

Kandy recognized one voice in particular, and her eyes widened as she guardedly approached the room.

Through the pass-through window connecting the dining room with the kitchen, Josh, a coffee mug in one hand, a filled balloon in the other, smiled as he listened to the voice of a woman.

And not just any woman.

"So I simply said to myself, Hannah, don't be so selfish. Your youngest only has one twenty-first birthday. You should be there when she arrives. So I forfeited my appointment with Carlo and drove out early with Abby to help Kandace decorate. If I'd known you were going to be here, I'd have come last night."

Kandy winced at the forward coquettishness in her mother's voice and was shocked to her core when Josh threw back his head and laughed, a full-bodied belly shaker.

"Hannah, I have to tell you, your reputation precedes you *and* doesn't do you any justice at all." He smiled across the breakfast bar at her.

"I think there's a compliment in there," she replied. "Or if there isn't, I'll take it as one."

Hannah turned when Kandy came through the doorway.

"Honey, there you are." Hannah Laine sauntered to her oldest daughter and pulled her into her gym-toned arms.

"Mom." Kandy inhaled the familiar fragrance of Chanel N°5 as her mother's arms snaked around her waist. "I didn't expect you until this afternoon."

"I know, dear. Josh told me you got my message last night when you returned from Mario's." Hannah pulled back and scrutinized her eldest. "How is he, by the way? Still cooking his sinful shrimp bolognaise?"

Kandy stared at her mother's beautifully made-up face.

At forty-eight, Hannah looked ten years younger in any lighting. The hard and emotion-laden years she'd spent with her inept husband had done nothing to mar her basic God-blessed beauty. The crystal blue of her eyes, so similar to that of all her daughters, was as vibrant and clear as ever. Her original jet-black hair had been softened with time and a colorist's brush to fall in soft auburn waves down to her shoulders. Skin, still relatively unlined, glowed with health and radiance. She was dressed casually in linen cropped pants and a silk baby blue–colored shirt, which, on her toned and tanned body looked like couture.

"Mom, you look great," Kandy said, pulling her in for an exuberant hug.

"Oh, how sweet you are." Hannah smiled and patted her daughter's back with affection.

"Did I hear you say Abby was here?"

"She's at the dock getting the lobsters," Hannah said. "We've already decorated the deck, and Josh set up the volleyball net and croquet kit for the kids. He and I were just going to finish with the rest of the house when you finally decided to join the living."

It was said with warmth and love, but Kandy blushed anyway. "I can't believe I overslept." She crossed to the refrigerator and pulled out the cake tiers. "I haven't done that since the sixth grade."

"Well, with all you've been going through it probably did you a world of good to get some extra rest." Hannah took one of the trays from her and placed it on the counter. "Oh goodie. Mama's vanilla cake," she said, taking a whiff. "Ellie will be so pleased. She's always loved this cake."

Kandy slammed the refrigerator door and threw an accusatory glare at Josh.

He held up his hands in surrender. "Not me."

Kandy turned to her mother. "What do you mean all I've been going through?"

Hannah wiped her hands on a dishrag and stared at her daughter. "Gemma called me last night and told me what's been going on. I called

Lucy and Callie for confirmation."

Kandy closed her eyes and inhaled deeply. "I now know how it feels to want to commit murder. How could they? I asked them to keep it a secret from you."

"But, honey, why? I'm your mother. I should know if someone's trying to hurt you."

"I didn't want you to worry," she said, gathering Crisco, sugar, vanilla, egg whites, and butter for the frosting. "I knew you'd be upset by the news."

"Of course I'm upset, Kandace Sophia. This is your life we're talking about." Her voice had risen and lost some of its soothing tone.

Kandy rolled her eyes and stared at her mother. "This is what I was worried about, Mom. I don't want you upset about all this."

"Too late." Her mother fisted her hands on her slim hips. "I don't know what makes me madder: you being stalked or you not telling me about it."

Kandy plugged in the mixer and began creaming the butter and the shortening.

"I don't know I'd call what's happened stalking," she said over the machine's whir.

"What then? You've been harassed by phone, had a potentially fatal car accident, you think someone broke into your apartment, and I hear a dead rat was left for you at the studio. Not to mention narrowly being injured by a falling light. What do you call all that?"

"Bad luck?" Kandy asked, grimacing.

"Kandace Sophia Bernadette Laine, I know you're trying to make light of this for my sake, but I don't like it one bit."

"Oh boy. When you call me by my whole name I know I'm in for it."

Over the sound of the mixer Josh said, "Hannah, you can understand Kandy's reluctance to tell you, especially when only very few people knew. She didn't want to concern anyone."

"I'm her mother," Hannah said. Her expression was firm and resolute. "It's my lot in life to be concerned. I live for my children."

Kandy burst out laughing at the theatrical, deadpan tone in her mother's voice, and the tension of the moment passed. "Oh Mom. You're too much," she said, and gathered her in for another hug.

With what looked like confusion, Hannah patted Kandy's back again and said, "Well, I guess I am if you say so. But I'm still worried about you. You may be an adult, honey, but you'll always be one of my babies."

Pulling back, Kandy smiled and said, "I'm a little tall for a baby. But look, you don't have to worry about any of this. Josh is handling it. That's what he's here for," she added, trying to keep the bitter edge from her words.

Hannah stared at her daughter for a second, her eyebrows rising in an expression Kandy couldn't read.

"Hey, I've got ten crates of squirming, snapping crustaceans out here and I'd appreciate a little help."

"Abby," Kandy yelped, springing to the door.

For the next few minutes, the sisters and Josh were engaged with the unloading and storing of the live lobsters in Kandy's large, walk-in storage refrigerator in the garage, while Hannah watched from the kitchen.

Chapter Fifteen

"How do you plan on cooking these?" Josh asked as he stowed the last crate.

"Well, that's where I hope you come in."

Josh's left eyebrow rose almost to his hairline. "I don't know nothin' 'bout cooking lobsters."

Kandy's easy grin split from ear to ear. "Cute. But I really need your help."

"What can I do?"

"Dig a pit in the sand. About two feet deep, six wide. I have five lobster pots and four corn pots that will fit perfectly in that footage. There's firewood on the back of the deck and a metal grating I can use to balance the pots. If you could put it all together for me, it'll be a big help when it's time to cook."

Josh nodded. "Want me to do it now, or help decorate?"

"Let Mom and Abby decorate. You've already done the sports stuff, and I need to finish the cake, so now's a good time. Do you mind?"

"Not at all."

She stared at him for a moment longer, looked like she wanted to say something else, but at the last minute decided not to.

While she walked back into the house, he went in search of a shovel.

After she'd fled the kitchen, he'd been consumed with guilt at what he'd let happen between them. Her emotions were right on the edge, deny it though she did, but the second he'd pulled her into his arms, all reason and thought left his head, replaced by longing and the simple craving to just love all her concerns away.

He'd never been with a woman who was such a dichotomy of strength and need before. It not only intrigued him, it captivated him.

Josh was well past thinking of Kandy as just a client or a job. From the moment her lips met his he knew it. He'd opened himself to her as he had to no other woman. He'd never even told his brothers about the incidents after the shooting, but he'd confessed it to this woman he'd known for such a brief time, and felt so comfortable doing so. It seemed right to him. Balanced.

They would have ended up first on the kitchen floor and then in Kandy's bed if Josh hadn't put an end to their actions. That she'd desired him as well made it all the more difficult to stop.

But he had, and in so doing he knew he'd hurt her, something he'd never planned on. As savvy and smart as she was in business, Josh knew in the area of romance Kandy was almost an innocent.

It was his job to be responsible for her safety, but the feeling swirling around in the center of his chest whenever he looked at her, thought of her, was near her, had nothing to do with work, or the lust he'd first thought it to be. No, Josh realized Kandy was becoming important to him in a way he wasn't sure was good for either of them.

After his first broken engagement and then the shooting, Josh had sworn to never again mix work and a relationship. He could live with the reason his first fiancée had broken off with him. In hindsight he knew they'd both been too young and immature to make a lifetime commitment when she'd been so worried about his safety.

But after the shooting, when the woman he'd thought he was in love with had summarily thrown him out of her life, Josh swore he'd never make the same mistake again. He vowed to keep his work life separate from his personal life. Always.

Until now he'd succeeded. He'd dated, but it never lasted longer than a few casual months. He kept all women at a very long arm's length. Numerous protection jobs had placed him directly in contact with women who had told him in no uncertain terms they were interested in pursuing something more with him. Beautiful, successful, and powerful women. Women most men wouldn't have thought twice about becoming involved with.

Josh had resisted up until now and had been satisfied with his decision.

His mother had assured him one day he'd find an everlasting love just like his parents had. He would know the woman he was meant to spend the rest of his life with when he saw her.

And he was starting to think Kandy might be *that* woman.

Now, if only he could discover who was tormenting her.

Josh slammed the shovel into the soft sand and went over everything he knew about the people closest to her again.

He needed to find the answer.

He needed to find it fast.

* * *

“Can anyone hire him?” Abby asked. She stood on a ladder, a birthday streamer in one hand, as she gazed out the window at Josh.

“Aunt Lucy asked the same question,” Kandy said.

“Well?”

Kandy stared up at her sister. “What, exactly, do you need a bodyguard for? *I’m* the one being harassed.”

Abby took the pushpin from her sister and secured the streamer into the ceiling beam. She shimmied down the ladder and said, “Sorry. I forgot. How *are* you with all this? It must be weird.”

Kandy snorted. “Weird doesn’t begin to describe it.” She went up the ladder next and secured her side of the streamer. “I’m still having a hard time believing I actually need protection.”

“Gem told me everything.”

“Remind me to cut out her tongue when she gets here.”

“Okay, I can tell you don’t want to talk about it. Let’s talk about gorgeous out there instead. Is he married?”

Kandy rolled her eyes.

“*With* anyone?”

Kandy went back up the ladder.

“Sis, come on. This is the first truly godlike man you’ve ever been involved with. I want to know all about it. About him. What have the two of you been doing together? I mean, he’s around all the time, right? Goes where you go, sleeps where you sleep?”

“*Lord.* You’re as bad as the aunts. Mom hasn’t even asked me questions like that.”

“Because I haven’t had a moment alone with you, honey,” Hannah said, coming into the foyer, a huge smile on her face. “But since he’s outside,” she added, glancing out the deck doors, “and looks absolutely fabulous from this angle, why don’t we just watch him for a few minutes and you can tell us all about your relationship.”

Kandy came down the ladder, stood in front of her mother and sister, arms akimbo, and said, “First of all, our *relationship* is a professional one. I’m not involved with him. There’s nothing going on between us in any way your lascivious little minds can come up with. He was hired by Stacy to find out who's been annoying me. End of story. All I am to him is a problem to be solved. A job. Nothing else."

"You can't be serious?" Her sister gawked at her. "A man who looks like that and you don't even try to tempt him? I can't believe it. I can't honestly believe there isn't an attraction."

"Oh, there's an attraction," Hannah said.

Kandy's eyes narrowed.

"All you have to do is look at the man when you're in the room to know he's interested, honey. It's as plain as day."

"You're crazy," Kandy said, swiping a dismissive hand at her. "I have a cake to decorate."

As she left the room, her mother said, "He's not married, never has been. Lives alone. He started his own business about four years…"

Leave it to Mom to worm out all his basic info within five seconds of meeting him. Kandy pulled her decorating bags out of a drawer and got to work.

* * *

The guests began arriving at one, and but for a brief fifteen minutes for Kandy to get ready, she'd been without a break, cooking, serving, and acting as a hostess. Josh had stuck by her side for most of it, acting as waiter, drink-getter, and overall kitchen factotum. He'd been introduced to the remainder of her sisters, and in an attempt to keep them all straight, began categorizing and filing them away in his head.

Abby, the one closest in age to Kandy, was twenty-seven, unmarried and worked as a receptionist in a law firm in Brooklyn. Belinda, twenty-six, was married and had two children—Declan who was five and MaryBeth who was six months. Her husband, Brian, was a welder, and from Josh's viewpoint a heck of a volleyball player. Gemma he knew, and grinned when she arrived and greeted him with a bewitching kiss full on the lips and a "hiya Hunk!" greeting. Next came Fallon who was twenty-four and a newlywed. She and her husband, Hal, had been married for a little over a year. Twenty-two year old Daisy came next, complete with a starting quarterback for an NFL team boyfriend. She told him she was one of the team's professional cheerleaders. Her beaux was as competitive at volleyball as Brian. Lastly was the birthday girl, Eleanor, or Ellie as the family called her. At twenty-one she was the shortest of all the Laine women, standing at only five foot five.

"She the only one who got our father's height genes," Gemma said when she introduced them.

Ellie had arrived with twenty college friends in tow who were now scattered around the beach, enjoying and lazing in the sun.

In addition to the sisters and their families, Josh met the remainder of the aunts and their families. The exception was Uncle Peter, who, Hannah informed him, had pleaded a prior engagement. Josh made a mental note to pay the man a personal visit as soon as he could when they arrived back in the city.

Reva Lowenstein and her partner, Cherry Jones, were lounging in deck chairs, conferring with Harvey Little and his partner, Paul.

When Daniel arrived with his estranged wife, Betsy, Kandy headed straight for the couple and gathered them both into her arms. Her vigorous embrace was returned in full measure.

In all, he counted eighty adults and fifteen children of varying ages at the beach house.

* * *

"Heck of a day for party," he commented a few hours later.

"I'm so glad the weather held," Kandy said. She rested her elbows on the deck rail. "It would have been a disaster if it rained."

"Maybe not a disaster," he told her, "but it would have been tight with all of us inside, that's for sure."

She nodded and watched her brother-in-law Hal spike a ball over the net. Gemma instantly volleyed it back, the opposing team missing it on the rebound.

Laughing, Kandy said, "I've always said she's the most competitive of us all."

Josh grinned and glanced over his shoulder at her. "How come you're not playing?"

"I could ask the same of you."

"That's an easy one."

"Joined at the hip," she said with a small sigh.

He nodded. "Feel up to it?"

"Not especially. I like to watch more than play."

"Fine with me. Your food, by the way, has been a tremendous hit. Especially the shrimp. I don't think there's any left."

"Don't bet on it. I always have reserves." She glanced down at her watch. "Think you could give me a hand with the lobsters and the corn? The water's just about ready."

"Sure."

They made their way out toward the garage, Kandy getting rave reviews along the way from her relatives for the food, the party, even the weather.

Several pair of eyes followed them, gossiping as Kandy and Josh passed.

"Your relatives are talking," he told her.

She sighed. "I know. Mom told me almost everyone in my family knows about it now." She shook her head and frowned. "They're like a new communication device."

"What?"

"Telephone. Telegram. Tell-a-Laine."

He laughed.

"I don't know how I feel about everyone knowing. How 'bout you?"

"In a crazy way, it might help."

"How?"

He shrugged. "Someone might have seen or heard something that didn't make any sense to them at the time. Since your secret is out and they all know what you've been going through, it might jive and someone will let me know. Or you."

"Tell me honestly, now that you've met everyone, you still think it's someone close to me?"

"You know the answer, Kandy. As much as you'd like to deny it, it just makes sense."

"I still think it stinks," she said as they came around to the garage.

Josh opened the door for her.

They entered, the sudden shift from bright sunshine to black blinding them.

"Just give your eyes a sec," Josh said. "They'll adjust."

"I know where the light switch is," she told him and reached out to the wood panel.

When her hand came up against a brick wall of flesh and muscle, she yelped.

"That's not the wall, Kandy." There was laughter in his voice.

She wanted to remove her hand, she really did, but it felt too good where it was. Kandy opened her palm and laid it flat against the wide, hard expanse of his chest. She could feel his heart beating, rapid and strong, the tempo tantalizing and inviting as it played under his shirt.

"Kandy." There was a warning in his voice, when his own hand snaked up to sit on top of hers.

Her eyes hadn't begun to adjust, but she could feel how close their bodies were from the heat he perpetually threw off. Wanting to feel his firmness next to her again, Kandy took a small step forward. When her knees knocked with his and she heard his swift intake of air, she let the desire she'd been forced to squelch the night before break free without any thought she shouldn't.

Josh's hand closed tightly over hers, preventing her from moving away. Taking this as a sign to get even closer, she shifted her stance.

When she could feel his warm, fast breath on her face, she threw all reservations of rejection aside, forgot all the self-recriminating railing she'd done the night before, and rose on the balls of her feet to find his mouth with her own.

An instant of touch was all it took for her to forget about everything else. There was no party raging outside on the beach, she didn't have a hundred guests waiting for her to cook for them, no one was harassing her.

All she knew, all she felt, was this moment with this man.

His body stiffened at first, firm and resolute, but in a heartbeat it changed. His shoulders relaxed, a deep sigh drifted over her skin, and his lips pressed against hers in a determined, mind-blowing embrace.

Kandy parted her lips, inviting Josh's slow and thorough possession of her mouth, an invitation he accepted without any further hesitation. Her head swam with the sensations his touch drew from her. All she wanted to do was jump into his arms, wrap her legs around his waist, and let both of them consume each other.

When Josh's hand skimmed under her blouse and boldly closed over one breast, the instantaneous hardening of her nipple was a reward to them both. His hands were huge and firm when they kneaded her skin and pushed away the small silk bra cup to take her fully into his grasp. Her thin silk shirt whispered against his hands as he moved it out of his way.

Kandy threw her head back and moaned, while his lips trailed down her neck and torso to capture the swollen nub between his teeth. When he drew it into his mouth and began to suck, Kandy's insides clenched, and a sweltering lava flow of heat spread throughout her core, turning her legs to water.

"Josh." Her voice, choked with raw need and fever, echoed in the dark garage.

Wanting to know the feel of him, she slipped one hand from her grip on his shoulders and traipsed down his chest, passed the waistband of his pants, to rest on the solid, rock-hard bulge beneath his trousers. When her fingers outlined the length and width of him, the sound that came from the back of his throat was part moan and all growl.

Flattening her palm against him, she moved it up and down, and absorbed his shudder, spurred on by the power of her touch.

"Kandy, we can't do this," he whispered, taking her earlobe into his mouth and biting down on it.

"Why not?" She tightened her grip on him and rubbed her lips across the exposed section of his neck.

He tasted good. *Really good.*

Josh tossed his head back allowing her better passage. "You have a beach full of company for one thing," he managed to say.

When her teeth scraped across his shoulder, his knees shook against hers. He yanked on her shirt, completely pulling it out of her shorts, then his hands sailed up her sides to cup both breasts. He squeezed just enough to make her jump with longing.

"People saw us come out here, for another," he said, licking the sweet spot under her ear. "Someone will come looking for us if we don't get back."

Kandy molded herself to his body, running her hands up and down his arms and back, loving the rigid feel of him. When his mouth closed over her nipple again, a hot shot of lust bolted through her groin.

"Oh *God.* Tell me again why we can't do this, because I'm not real clear on why not just now."

She pulled his head back to hers before he could answer and devoured his mouth. With her hands fisted in his hair, she hiked one leg up to his hip. Josh grabbed both her thighs, lifting her full against him, his hands nestled in the swell of her butt as she wrapped her legs around his waist and hung on for dear life.

"You feel so good," he whispered, lifting and rubbing her against his erection. "So damn good."

"You do, too."

Their lips came together again.

Kandy felt as if she'd been starved for a lifetime and was only now learning what real food, real sustenance, was. She wanted to swallow him whole and go back for seconds.

Thirds.

No concoction, no food, no delicious dessert had ever tasted as appetizing, as delectable, or as satisfying as Josh did. She could live off of his taste for the rest of her life and never know hunger.

When he twined his tongue around hers, nursing off of it as if he couldn't get enough of her, Kandy knew for the first time in her life what it meant to be completely and totally consumed.

In one fluid move Josh pivoted and braced her against the garage wall. With one hand harboring her against him, the other slaked up one of her thighs, wove inside her shorts, and pushed the thin silk of her panties to the side.

"*Christ.* You're saturated."

He began rubbing back and forth across the small bullet of skin he found pulsing beneath his touch.

Kandy lost her mind.

"Oh. My. *God,*" she cried, hanging on to his shoulders for dear life. The rhythm his long, strong fingers strumming against her flesh quickened.

He slipped two of those firm fingers inside her, pressing into her core, almost to her soul. Kandy knew she could die right here and now of pure undiluted pleasure. Her insides cramped around him at the same time his thumb scraped against her, his fingers continuing to slide in and out with a breath-shaking rhythm.

She couldn't breathe, couldn't see, couldn't hear. All she could do, did do, was feel.

"Don't stop," she pleaded. "Please don't stop." She didn't recognize the complete and utter hunger in her own voice.

Josh did as he was bid. While his fingers kept up their ever-increasing pulsing inside her, his thumb continued its rhythmic rubbing to and fro against her clitoris. The heat from his breath scalded her as he gently bit down on a corner of her collarbone and feasted on her skin.

Her mouth skimmed his jaw, his cheek, his temple, her breathing erratic and quick. She whispered his name on a sigh.

The scream of satisfaction she felt bubbling up from deep down inside her was devoured as Josh captured her mouth with his own. Against her lips, he whispered, "Come for me, Kandy. Come for me. Now."

And she did.

Harder, faster, and wilder than she could ever remember. Josh's grip tightened as wave upon wave broke from within her. His lips anchored against hers, swallowing her cry when she finally let go.

Panting, barely able to scrape together a full breath, Kandy went limp against him.

Never in her entire life had she felt such an utter release. No man had ever made her come apart so quickly, so totally, as Josh just had.

Pinioned against the wall on one side, Josh's stonelike chest on the other, Kandy laid her forehead across his and noticed his breathing was as erratic and irregular as hers.

"That was…" She couldn't find the words.

Josh's sigh was long and deep, the feel of his breath as it washed over her face making her excited all over again.

"Yeah," he said.

His kissed her forehead with such tenderness she wanted to cry.

"Josh—"

"For God's sake, Alyssa, give it a rest."

The sound of Cort's irritated voice boomed into the garage and turned the two of them into statues.

A half second later the bang of a car door slamming shot to their ears.

"I will not, and don't you walk away from me, Cort Mason. I'm speaking to you."

"Shrilling is more like it," he said. "Just give it a rest and try not to embarrass yourself, or me, for the next few hours, will you? Please?"

"Why you had to drag me out here to some stupid party for a chit I don't even know—"

"You didn't have to come."

"As if," she countered. "Like I'd let you drive all the way here without me. Not bloody likely."

The voices trailed off as the warring duo made their way toward the beach.

Kandy could see the outline of Josh's face, just inches from her own, her eyes finally accustomed to the darkness. His fingers were still buried deep inside her, the aftermath of her orgasm continuing to clench and roll around them.

Without speaking, their gazes still locked, Josh slowly pulled his hand from within her.

A small wheeze squeaked from the back of her throat as his fingers slid away.

In one slow glide, Kandy slithered from his clasp to stand upright again, Josh's hands holding on to her waist until she was surefooted.

She stared up at him for a second and then backed away, banging against the garage wall she'd just been held against. Josh's hands fell to his sides while she tucked her breasts back into the cups of her bra, her shirt back into her shorts.

"Kandy, I...we need to talk." Josh said. He shook his head and blew out an exasperated breath. "What just happened…*Jesus.*" He raked his hands down his face and just stared at her.

"Corn and lobsters," she answered, in a voice she didn't recognize. She heard the tremor in it and steeled herself to calm it. "That's what we came out here for. Everyone's waiting." She grabbed three bags of corn at once.

Not wanting to meet his eyes, she shifted, intending to go around him.

Josh put a hand on her arm. “We need to talk about this.”

She knew every emotion she was going through was probably written in her eyes, but could do nothing to prevent it. Embarrassed beyond belief at how she’d thrown herself at him again; terrified of how her raging desire had overcome her, overcome them both.

Mixed with the humiliation was an equal part of absolute conviction that what had just happened was the most exciting, most erotic, and satisfying experience she’d ever had. Never in her life had she felt so totally wanted and so completely desired.

And she wanted more of it. A lot more.

But she couldn’t have it. Not here and certainly not now.

That thought alone was what finally prompted her to move again. With a shake of her head and, through a jagged breath, she said, “Not now. Please.”

She could tell from Josh’s continued grip he wasn’t finished. After a few moments, though, he dropped his hand.

The need to escape was profound, so she darted toward the door.

“We’re going to talk about this, Kandy,” he said to her back. “We have to. Sooner or later.”

Without turning to him, she nodded.

Chapter Sixteen

Josh's gaze followed her while she bantered with her guests as they lined up around the pit, hungry for the lobsters and corn.

For the moment, the scene in the garage was forgotten.

For the moment.

But they were going to come back to it. They had to. Something had changed between them during those few amazing minutes. Josh remembered every vivid detail of the encounter, including the unabashedly free way Kandy had come apart in his hands. When he'd kissed her flawless, silky skin, he'd tasted sunshine, while the exotic fragrance of the small dab of perfume at her neck reminded him of piquant hothouse flowers.

He'd absorbed her scream not wanting anyone to hear and discover their intimate moment together, but in truth, he'd been desperate to prevent his own frenzied groan from being heard.

If they'd been alone, and not surrounded by a crowd of guests and relations, Josh would have allowed her free access to scream her head off, and he'd have followed her lead. There, right there against the wooden garage wall, Josh would have made sure both had the release they so desperately craved and would have pounded into her until they were both satiated.

To clear his head and remind himself of the real reason he was with her, he surveyed the guests.

Hannah sat in the lap of a man at least half her age, her arm woven around his neck, surrounded by Eleanor and her friends. No one appeared to think it odd the mother of the birthday girl was holding court with a crowd a quarter-century younger.

Kandy's mother was, without doubt, beautiful. All her daughters resembled her in some physical way and, except for the height difference in Ellie, any stranger would have known who they belonged to in an instant of meeting Hannah.

He'd sensed her flagrant flirtatiousness was harmless the moment they'd met. The sudden widening of her blue-violet eyes when he let her and Abby into the beach house while Kandy got some much-needed sleep, and the slow raking she'd covered him with, combined with the natural, playful light he saw in her smile, made him realize her daughter's descriptions of her were accurate, if somewhat tainted. She was a woman who'd come into fruition like a rose waiting for the sunshine to bring it to bloom.

And she was as harmless as a puppy.

Josh's gaze swept to the far side of the deck, where Cort Mason and his wife were standing with Stacy. The director was listening with what Josh assumed was only half an ear because he seemed more focused on his wife than on Kandy's cousin, often turning his gaze to Alyssa. She ignored him, studying the crowd instead. Mason had one hand behind her, resting against the deck rail, almost in contact with her back.

Almost.

Alyssa Mason was a complete surprise. When he'd heard the shrewish tête-à-tête between them, Josh pictured an older woman, past the first phase of life, overweight and graying.

The shock of his inaccurate presumption floored him. Alyssa Mason was no fiftyish, bland, and boring housewife. British, if he could place her accent, she couldn't be older than twenty-three or -four, was at least six feet tall, and had the blondest, longest hair he'd ever seen, in addition to being cadaver thin. Her hard collarbones stood out from the A-line linen sheath she wore, and there was nothing but skin covering her exposed upper arms. No muscle tone, no underpad of fat. At present, she was taking a huge drag of a long cigarette, and appeared bored with her surroundings.

Stacy broke away from Cort and headed back into the house. Josh stole a quick glance at Kandy, saw she was laughing with one of her brothers-in-law as she pulled a lobster from the pot, and decided to follow Stacy.

He found her in the foyer, hunting through her purse.

"You okay?" She had a bottle of aspirin in her hands.

"Killer headache. Allergy time, you know? Being out here with this beautiful fresh ocean air is almost toxic to me." She tossed the bottle back into her bag. "I'm much better in the city, where there's lots of pollution to block the allergens."

Josh grinned. “Do you have a few minutes?”

She nodded.

“Let’s go for a quick walk.”

When they started out along the driveway, Stacy asked, “What’s up?”

“Couple questions about the Masons.”

Surprise jumped in her eyes.

“There seems to be some tension between then,” he began. “How long have they been together?”

Stacy sighed. “About a year or so. They met when Cort was directing a music video for Caged when we were on hiatus. Alyssa met the lead singer at one of her shows and they started dating.”

“Shows?”

She nodded. “Alyssa’s a model.”

“Her face isn’t familiar.”

“According to Cort, she doesn’t like print work because it’s boring, so you won’t see her on any covers. Anyway, they met on the shoot and Alyssa dumped Tavish DeCloud, the lead singer, immediately for Cort.”

“And he’s, what? Twenty-five, thirty years older than she is?”

Stacy thought for a moment. “Closer to thirty, I think.”

“What’s the attraction? I don’t mean to sound like a jerk, but they don’t exactly look like Barbie and Ken.”

“Understatement.” She crossed her arms in front of her as they kept walking. “I know Kandy’s tried to talk to him about her, but he always clams up. From what I’ve gathered, Alyssa wants to be an actress. It’s why she agreed to the original video. Saw it as a way to make connections in the industry.”

“Like Cort.”

“Yeah. My take is she thinks Cort should be helping her. Full-time. Devoting himself to making her a star. Obviously, he can’t. His contract with the show goes another two years.”

“Alyssa can’t be happy about it.”

“I don’t think she’s happy about life in general. In fact, I’m shocked she’s even here today. She usually avoids stuff like this.”

“Why?”

Stacy shook her head and said, “I wish I knew. I’ve tried to talk to her, but she always ignores me. I used to think it was just me she disliked, but it’s not.”

“She’s like that with everyone?”

“Everyone except Cort. She hangs on to him like a tick.”

Josh slipped his hands into his pockets.

"During working hours she calls him almost hourly, never caring if he's shooting or involved with something. It's almost like she's checking up on him, but really, that's ridiculous."

"Why?"

"Where else would he be but at the studio? You've been there a few days now; you've seen how everything works. No room for error, no room for breaks, especially when we're doing an outside shoot. It can get crazy."

Josh suggested they turn back, not wanting to leave Kandy for too long.

They were almost at the house when Stacy asked, "Have you found out anything useful yet?"

"A few things."

When he didn't elaborate, she said, "Not commenting, huh?"

He considered how much to tell her. "Have you spoken to your brother Daniel recently?"

Stacy's expression softened. "He called last night. Spoke to Mom and Dad, too. He told us everything." Her smile saddened just a little. "It's hard to think we missed what was happening with him. I feel a little responsible and a whole lot guilty."

"For what it's worth, I don't think you're the only one," he said. He debated with himself about whether to tell her Kandy's involvement.

Before he could come to a decision, Stacy said, "He told us what Kandy's doing for him and Betsy. Hiring him back, looking for infertility docs. She can't know how much he—we all—appreciate it. She could just have easily turned her back on him, let him figure out how to muddle through on his own."

"You don't really believe that, do you? I mean, you're the one who told me she values family above all else."

She looked over at him and nodded. "You're right. If Kandy had known what they were going through, Daniel never would have felt the need to gamble in the first place. She would have paid for everything, done all the research. Heck, she would have gone to the doctor visits and implantations with them."

They walked for a few moments, silent.

"There's no one I know who loves her family more," Stacy said. "She'd do anything for them."

"I've seen the proof with my own eyes."

Stacy stopped as they approached the house. Turning to him, she asked, "You're going to find out who's doing all these things to her, right?"

"I promised I would. I'm getting close, Stacy. That's about all I can tell you. But soon you'll have an answer as to who and why."

When she stared up at him, just as he had the first day in her office, Josh felt as if he were being silently appraised.

Without another word, she walked into the house.

Josh took the circuitous route around the garage instead of the shortcut through it. The memory of what recently transpired there was still so fresh in his mind he wanted to avoid the area.

Kandy was sitting in the sand near the fire pit, a small black-haired boy glued to her lap. A few of her sisters were seated around them, plates in their laps laden with food. Gemma's camera hung from a strap around her neck and she lifted it to snap away at the pair.

He took his time moving to their little group, observing Kandy as she cuddled her nephew. He could have been her own child, their coloring was almost identical. Jet-black hair, pale skin, and magnificent large, light blue eyes. Josh marveled at the twin dimples that played at the corners of the boy's mouth, just as Kandy's did, and the way his nose turned up at the tip when he smiled, a twin to his aunt's, as well.

Declan said something to her and threw his arms around her neck, planting a ferocious kiss on her cheek. Josh's heart turned over and filled when she fell backward to the sand, planting kiss after wet kiss on the boy's face, making him squeal with glee.

Since she was wrapped by the security of her family, Josh decided to approach the Masons, his discussion with Stacy leaving him with more questions than answers.

He found the couple in the same spot as earlier, Cort now speaking with Mark Begman as Alyssa stared off at the ocean.

Josh surveyed her before moving toward the couple.

Alyssa Mason had one of the most beautiful faces he'd ever laid eyes on. Her skin, even from this distance, was flawless. She'd encircled her eyes dramatically with kohl, making the outer edge tilt seductively upwards.

She held a new cigarette in her hand and was puffing with a great deal of concentration and vigor. Even though she took a stance of boredom, every few seconds she'd lean in closer to Cort, brush an arm or a hand across his upper body, forcing his attention to her.

Why so lovely a woman needed constant affirmation of her position in her husband's world puzzled Josh.

"Keane," Cort said as he approached the trio.

"Cort. Mark," Josh said, nodding at the men.

"Meet my wife," the director said.

Josh put out his hand and said, "Josh Keane."

"Alyssa," she said, raking her eyes across his face, ignoring the proffered hand. “How do you know my husband?”

“We met at the studio, sweetheart,” Cort said, swiping a hand at his brow.

It was then Josh noticed the man was sweating despite the cool ocean breeze.

Alyssa’s eyes brightened and her body came to attention. “Are you in the business?” she asked, her gaze penetrating right through him.

“The business?”

“Production. Direction. Development,” she clarified, swiping the cigarette in the air.

“Oh, I’m not in the entertainment field,” Josh replied, watching her attention immediately wane.

“Oh.” She took a puff and stared off again, Josh now forgotten.

“Josh is a friend of Kandy’s,” Cort said.

Alyssa managed a bland uplifting of her lips. “How lovely.” With a quick, last drag of her cigarette, she dropped it to the deck and smashed it with the toe of her shoe. “Darling, can I drag you away for a sec? You don’t mind,” she added to Mark and Josh with a fake smile plastered across her face.

Cort was pulled to privacy down the deck stairs and onto the beach.

“It’s a shame all that beauty is wasted in all that bitch,” Mark said, hands in his pockets, staring after the couple.

Josh nodded. “She’s not the friendliest person I’ve ever met.”

“You ain’t lying. I don’t know what Cort sees in her. I mean, despite the obvious. Why he puts up with all her crap.”

“What do you mean?”

Mark propped back against the rail and faced him. “They’ve been married like, what? Just a little over a year? You’d think by now she’d be used to his schedule. But no. She calls him ten, fifteen times a day wanting to know where is he, what he’s doing. She even managed to get my cell phone number. Calls me when she can’t get through to him. I mean, come on. The guy’s the director of the hottest food show on cable television. Where does she think he is?”

“Good question,” Josh said.

“She’s just crazy, if you ask me. I mean, look at her. She’s drop-dead gorgeous. Could be on the cover of any magazine in the world, but she doesn’t like print work.”

“I’d heard that.”

“Dumb, if you ask me. A face like that, she could be making millions of dollars in endorsements. Could have any guy she wanted just by wagging a finger his way. Cort adores her, but she’s the most insecure woman

I've ever met. Complains all the time about him being away. What does she think he's doing, for cripes' sake? The guy's a workaholic. Just like Kandy." He stopped, his mouth bending into a grin. "Now there's my kind of woman. Give me a Laine girl any day. They're all confident, self-assured, and have sex appeal to the max."

Josh agreed with the apt description. Glancing off at the Masons, Josh saw Alyssa stabbing a finger into Cort's chest, their discussion heated and one-sided. Hers.

"Look at her," Mark said, disgust heating his voice. "She's not a happy camper. I'll bet you twenty bucks they leave in the next five minutes."

"I won't take that bet," Josh said, "because I think you're right."

Alyssa turned from her husband and stomped off toward the front of the house. Cort, head and shoulders sagging, trudged his way across the sand to Kandy.

From his facial and body expressions, Josh realized Cort was making the couple's excuses. Kandy, still holding Declan in her lap, nodded.

A moment later, the director left without a word to anyone else at the party.

"Predictable," Mark said, shaking his head. "Glad I don't have to drive back to the city with her. Had any lobster yet?" he asked, dismissing the Masons.

"No, and I was thinking I should, since I lugged them all out here."

"Man, it's the best. Kandy does something to the water, makes the meat taste like ambrosia. Go get yourself one before they're all gone."

Josh made his way over to the food after being stopped first by Callie and then by the Peters, senior.

Both parties asked if he was making progress with finding out who Kandy's tormentor was.

To both of them, he gave the same line he'd given Stacy earlier.

By the time he made it over to the pit, Kandy had disappeared into the house. In the next moment, the lobster forgotten, he heard the shouts and chorus to "Happy Birthday."

Kandy was surrounded by her sisters on the deck, the huge four tiered cake atop a table, loaded with twenty-two lit candles. Eleanor, beaming from ear to ear, stood next to her oldest sister, both with their arms about each other's waists.

Kandy sang, pleasure on her face and smile, but he knew fatigue and worry were hidden in her eyes and the back of her mind.

The clapping and cheering brought him back to the birthday girl. Ellie gave her sister a full-body hug and thanked her for all the work and effort she'd put into the party, the food, and especially the cake.

"Since she made it," Ellie announced, "Kandy should be the one to cut it. That way we'll all get perfect pieces."

Kandy blushed at the compliment and began to slice the cake, Ellie getting the first piece. After a few minutes, he made his way through the line to her side.

"Want some?" she asked, smiling up at him. "You did help make it."

Josh nodded, and leaned in closer. Lowering his voice for her ears alone, he asked, "How you holding up?"

Her smile wavered just a tad, but enough for him to glimpse the weariness camouflaged beneath it. "Okay. I've been busy. Anything happening I should know about?"

With a subtle shake of his head, he took the offered cake and fork, and said, "Nothing unusual or out of the ordinary. Everyone seems to be having a great time."

She smiled and put down the cake server.

"Aren't you having any?" he asked.

"Later. I know what it tastes like."

"Heaven," he said simply, his mouth filled with the delicious confection. "Pure heaven."

She grinned up at him. All of a sudden the noise around them ceased. They could have been alone and isolated on the deck for all the attention they paid to their surroundings.

"Magnificent as usual, honey," Hannah said, coming up to them with an empty plate in her hand.

Kandy blinked rapidly a few times.

"Thanks, Mom. Want more?"

"Oh, good gracious, no. I'll explode."

Josh and Kandy both laughed as Hannah patted her flat stomach. "Would you mind if I kidnapped Josh for a bit?"

Kandy turned to him, her eyebrows rising. "Is everything okay?"

"Fine," her mother assured her, wrapping her arm through Josh's. "I just want to get to know him better. That's all."

Kandy's grin held an evil, playful glee in it. "Sure. But Mom?" She lowered her voice, turning serious. She placed a hand on Hannah's arm and said, "Be gentle, please. I need him around for a little while more. In one piece."

With the skilled finesse years of coquetry had instilled in her, Hannah maneuvered Josh away from Kandy and down the deck stairs.

"I thought we might take a little stroll down to the water's edge," she said, her arm still entwined in the crook of his elbow.

They began at a slow amble.

"Was there something you wanted to talk to me about, Hannah?"

She squeezed his arm and charmed him with her dimpled smile. "Can't a girl just want to spend some time with a handsome guy on a lovely day?"

Josh smiled and relaxed. "Sure. I'll buy that."

Her laugh sounded like crystal chandelier drops blowing and twinkling against one another on a gentle breeze. "My sister said you were smart. And gorgeous. A pretty lethal combination in a man."

"Your reputation precedes you, too."

"Yes, well, we've all had our moments in life, but I didn't ask you to walk with me to discuss my past."

"I didn't think so."

Her blue eyes impaled him. "Lethal." She sighed heavily and said, "I want to know what's going on. Gemma and the others have peppered everything they've told me with drama. But I want to know the facts—without the drama—about what's been going on with my daughter. Will you tell me?"

He nodded and did. She was Kandy's mother and he felt she was entitled. Revealing everything, including the phone calls, he finished by asking, "Do you have any idea who could be behind this?"

She gazed off at the ocean for a few moments, silent and pensive.

"Unfortunately, I don't. I can't see my brother doing any of these things. Oh, I know he was upset about the whole agent thing, but deep down he knows it wasn't Kandy's doing. Peter is, and always has been, a middle child. Having two girls in front of him and two girls behind wasn't easy when we were growing up. And Dad was more interested in flirting with the neighborhood women than in playing baseball or doing other father/son things with him. It had to have an effect on Peter."

"Kandy mentioned Mario was a good friend when they were kids."

"They were best friends. But then they grew up. Went their separate ways. Peter has always just, well, *floundered* is the best word. He's single-minded when it comes to his writing. He wants to be the next Hemingway."

Josh stayed silent.

She stared up at him and cocked a crooked smile. "You're being polite by your silence, but if you know about Peter, then you know he's not the world's next literary laureate."

With a nod, Josh said, "I got that impression. So you don't think he could have had anything to do with it?"

"No."

They stood for several seconds, the cool water lapping at their bare feet. "What about the man Kandy was seeing for a few months?" Hannah asked.

"Evan Chandler?"

"Yes. I heard through the family grapevine he didn't go quietly."

Josh told her what he knew, including the incident that had occurred as he and Kandy were leaving the city.

"Gemma said he was an idiot."

"You never met him?" he asked, surprised.

"No, and I'm glad I didn't after hearing about him and how he hurt Kandy. Do you think he could be behind all this?"

"He's definitely up there on the list. Although, she doesn't think he's smart enough to have done it. Stacy agrees with that."

"Well, where does that leave you in your investigation?"

He wanted to say "at a wall."

"Things are progressing. I've had a few new thoughts and tidbits of info today I need to look into. I'm hopeful this will end soon. She's holding up well, but who knows how long she can last without breaking."

"Oh, don't sell my daughter short, Josh. Kandy is nothing if not a fighter and survivor."

"I agree. But sooner or later all this tension and worry is going to take its toll. She is, after all, human."

"That she is." Hannah nodded. "And when you do find out who's responsible for making her life so miserable, what happens then?"

"Whoever's doing this will be arrested and prosecuted. It's Kandy's right."

"Yes, I know, but I mean what happens with the two of you?"

"I'm sorry?"

Hannah's broad smile twinkled and lit up her eyes. "You're not that good an actor, Josh. Take it from one who is."

Stunned, he said, "Hannah, what are you talking about?"

She smiled and patted his cheek with her free hand. "You're just like Kandy," she said. "You wear your heart on your sleeve."

When he remained silent, she continued. "I saw it the moment she walked into the kitchen this morning. The look in your eyes, the way your breathing increased. Your entire face came to life when she joined us. I'd say you have some feelings, other than just professional ones, for my daughter."

Because it wasn't a question, he didn't answer.

"Not going to confirm or deny, huh?" She laughed. "I imagine you're very good at what you do. But your feelings toward Kandy are what they are. I'm sure."

"How can you be?"

Her grin grew wicked and dazzling. For a second, Josh mistook her for Kandy, their smiles almost identical. "From one who's seen that look tossed her way a few times and recognizes it for what it is."

He could only stare at her, not trusting his voice.

"Do you know how she feels about you?"

"In all honesty, no. I think this situation has been hard for her. I've been thrust into her life without warning, and without being prepared for it. I can't expect she's happy about it."

Hannah looked up at him, a strange expression in her eyes.

"Whatever happens later, I can't let anything cloud my judgment right now. I was hired to find out who's been making threats and to protect her from further harm. I can't do that if I'm preoccupied. I need to focus on her safety. Uppermost in my mind right now is that and that alone."

Hannah considered him. "I can see why Max thinks you're the best. All right then, what about when this is over? What do you intend to do?"

"I haven't let myself think that far ahead yet. I can't."

"I understand, I really do. But for what it's worth, I think you're wrong about Kandy."

"How so?"

She turned away from him and stared out at the ocean. "When they were growing up, all my other girls would go to sleepovers, spend time with friends when they could. Do normal girl things." She turned back to him. "Kandy never did. She was always focused on cooking. It was her passion and her life. Even as a child. After my husband left, she became even more focused. Driven, if you like. Nothing was going to get in the way of doing what she loved best."

"She's the most goal-oriented person I've ever met."

Hannah smiled. "It's more, though. It's almost as if she needs to prove to everyone, including herself, she's self-sufficient and self-reliant. That she can do it all by herself and never feel dependent on someone else. She doesn't need another person to feel complete. Do you understand what I mean?"

"I think so. From what I've experienced so far, she likes being in control of her world."

"Kandy to a *T*. But in addition to her world, her emotions, even her very being. I'm sure my divorce affected her much more than she realizes. She's never once slipped off that pedestal of self-reliance."

She looked up at him and put a hand on his arm. "Just as I saw how you looked at her this morning, I saw how she looked at you."

Josh was afraid to hear what her next words would be.

"I also happened to notice the two of you when you came out of the garage."

"What do you mean?"

"Don't be coy, Josh. That's my job. I saw how flustered and disheveled the two of you were."

Josh couldn't help it, his face got red.

Hannah laughed. "Now that's the most charming thing I've seen a man do in quite some time."

"Hannah—"

Interrupting him with a wave of her hand, she continued. "I think Kandy's beginning to slip, Josh, and I think you're the reason."

"I don't understand what you mean."

"Don't you?" She smiled and looked back toward the house. "Well, maybe you don't. Just be there for her when she stumbles off that platform. She could use a man like you to catch her."

Josh didn't know how to respond, so he stayed silent.

Hannah solved the problem when she twined her arm back into his and said, "Well, I've had enough of the water. What say we go back?"

Chapter Seventeen

"What's going on with you and the hunk?" Gemma asked as she helped Kandy carry the leftover cake back into the kitchen.

"What are you talking about?"

"The two of you have been walking around each other on eggshells all day. I noticed it the second I got here. What happened?"

"Why do you think anything's happened?"

"Stop answering me with questions, Kandace Sophia, and tell me what's going on. I know you like I know the lighting stops on my camera. Have the two of you slept together?"

"No." The explosion echoed in the kitchen. "For goodness' sake, Gem, what do you take me for?"

She shot her sister a cool, smug smirk. "A fool if you haven't. I'd fall into bed with him in a heartbeat if he asked me." When her sister's mouth fell open, Gemma added, "Don't be mad at me for the truth."

She took Kandy's hand in hers and rubbed it. The sisterly show of affection made Kandy sigh. "I'm not mad at you."

"Then tell me. What's going on with you two?"

Kandy sat on a breakfast bar stool and rested her hands on the counter. "I don't know." A second later she added, "No, that's not true. I think I know, but I'm not sure."

When she sighed again, Gemma took a seat next to her. "Tell me."

Kandy looked into her sister's eyes, identical in every way to her own, and saw concern wash through them.

With a great deal of reluctance, she related the scene in the kitchen the night before. Supreme embarrassment prevented her from telling Gemma what had transpired in the garage earlier.

"I've never acted like that before," she said, dropping her head into her hands. “So needy, so totally off the wall sexually. It was scary.”

“It sounds exciting as all get out.”

Kandy shook her head and gave her sister a small smile. “Beyond exciting. I can’t describe how good it felt to be kissed like that. I can’t believe it was me.” She threw her head down into her hands again.

“It’s about damn time,” Gemma said, yanking her sister up by her hair, her gaze slicing into her. “All you do is work. You never have any fun, Kan.”

“Cooking *is* fun for me.”

“Yeah, well, we all know you’re not normal.”

“That’s mean.”

“No, it’s the truth. I can’t imagine a better diversion for you than having a hot, torrid, sexfest with this guy. It’s absolutely perfect. Go for it.”

“Gemma, I can’t have an affair with him.”

“Why not?”

“Well, for one thing, he doesn’t want me.”

Gemma’s eyes widened, making her brow groove in disbelief. “I don’t believe it for a second. I saw the way he looked at you in your office the other day. There was enough longing in his eyes to comfort a small, underdeveloped nation.”

“Then why is he the one who keeps pulling the plug every time we get in a clutch?”

Gemma shrugged. “Some weird sense of duty, maybe?”

“Right.” She shot a finger at her. “He keeps telling me I’m a client. That’s all I am to him, Gem. A job.”

Kandy’s heart ached when she said the words out loud. Admitting them to herself was one thing. Telling them to her sister, giving a real voice to them, was quite another. And it hurt.

It hurt like hell.

“Did he kiss you back?” Gemma asked.

Oh, baby, did he ever! “Yes.”

“Peck-on-the-cheek kiss, or I’ll-die-if-I don’t-wrap-myself-around-your-tonsils kiss?”

Kandy snorted. “The latter.”

“There you go.” She sat back, a smug smile wiggling across her mouth. “What more proof do you need? The guy wants you, Kan. I say go for it with all you’ve got. Enjoy the heck out of him.”

“And then what?”

“What do you mean?”

“What happens next? When this whole thing is over and he leaves? What am I supposed to do then, Gemma? Just go on as if it never happened?"

Gemma shrugged and rose. She opened the refrigerator and took out a pitcher of ice tea. "I don't know. Why think about it now?"

"Because I think I may be falling in love with him."

Gemma stopped pouring midstream and leveled a frown at her sister. "You can't be serious."

"I am. I've never felt like this about a guy before. It's more than just the physical attraction. I *like* being with him, having him around. When we went out to dinner last night, for the first time in a really long time I was relaxed and comfortable. I can talk about anything with him. He *listens.* He hears and understands. I get a safe and warm feeling in the pit of my stomach every time I think about him. I can *see* the two of us together, sitting in the kitchen, drinking coffee, discussing the kids. I've never let myself think about children and carpools and starring in my own happily-ever-after before. Never. It's never been an option for me."

Gemma cocked her head. "Because of Daddy and what he did?"

Kandy nodded. "I don't want to love someone as much as Mom did and then have it all turn to crap. I've done everything I could to protect myself from ever being that vulnerable."

Gemma's sigh was forceful. "And you all say I'm the one who's screwed up the most in this family."

"Gem, no one says that. Truthfully."

"But you all think it. I know you do."

The sisters stared at each other for a moment.

"Look." Kandy finally broke the silence. "I don't know what to do about this, how to handle it. Whenever we're in the same room, all I want to do is have him hold me. When he's not around, I'm thinking about him." She told Gemma how he'd left her for an hour after the rat incident. "All my mind could focus on was how long it was taking him to get back."

Gemma sat next to her sister and took her hand. "You sound like you're in love with him already, no maybes about it."

Kandy swallowed.

"Can't you ever do anything halfhearted?" Gemma said, a lopsided grin tripping over her face.

"What?"

"Why'd you go and fall in love with the guy?"

"It's not like I could help it. Don't you remember what Grandpa used to tell us?"

Brow furrowing, she answered, "The thing about lightning?"

"Yeah. One day you're walking along without a care in the world, and then *bang,* like lightning, you get struck through the heart for good."

Gemma grinned again. "Grandma used to get all teary-eyed when he'd say that."

"Because it's what happened to him the day he met her."

"And you feel this way about Josh?"

Her head moved up and down, slowly, a few times. "Believe me, if I could have prevented it, I would have. I don't need this right now in my life, you know I don't."

On a sigh she said, "Yeah. I do." Gemma took a sip of her tea. "So, what are you going to do? Pursue it and get your heart potentially stomped on, or let it go and wonder what could have been?"

"Oh, don't be so melodramatic," Kandy said. "This isn't some Jane Austen novel. I have more choices than just those two."

"Like what? Aside from using him for sex or marrying the guy, I don't see a lot of options looming on the horizon."

Kandy shook her head and hugged her sister. "You're an idiot. I love you dearly, but you're an idiot."

* * *

Kandy squeezed Declan's little body in a hug and kissed his cheek before she settled him in his car seat.

The sun was low across the ocean and the majority of the birthday guests had departed.

Gemma, Abby, and Hannah had decided to spend the night, while the rest of the family said their good-byes and thanks to Kandy.

Mother and sisters were in the kitchen cleaning up and talking.

"Come on, Kan," Abby said. "Come out with us. It'll be fun. There's a great jazz band at the Wagontrain tonight."

"I really need to clean up and get some sleep," Kandy said. "You guys go, though. Take Mom. She loves jazz."

"She's already on board," Gemma said. "Come on. Come with us. You haven't been out in ages."

"I'll remind you I was out twice this week."

"Those times don't count," Gemma said, flipping an impatient hand at her. "They were both for business. You need to get out for fun."

Josh came into the kitchen.

"Josh," Abby said, crossing to take the lobster pot from him, "convince Kandy to come out with us. She deserves a break after all the hard work she did today."

Kandy didn't—couldn't—look at him.

"You saving that?" he asked, pointing to the corn.

"I'm freezing it so I can make corn chowder next time I'm out here."

"That's my baby," Hannah said, wiping her dripping hands with a towel. "Waste not, want not. I should have named you 'Recycle.' It's much more fitting."

Kandy smiled at her. "*Sugar-Coated Recycle* isn't the greatest name for a cook book."

"Neither is *Cooking with Recycle*," Josh added, grabbing an ear of corn from her hand and biting into it with a ravenous gusto.

"Are you hungry?"

"Starving."

"Didn't you eat anything at the party?" she asked.

"Nope. Just the piece of cake you gave me. I was too busy working and being grilled by your relatives," he said, raising an eyebrow at Hannah.

"I don't grill," Hannah said, a Madonna-like smile on her face. "I merely elicit information in the most effective way I know how."

"Yeah," Gemma said, "by grilling."

"You didn't even have any lobster?!"

"Nope. Got any left?"

"That's like asking if the Good Humor man has ice cream in his truck." Gemma opened the refrigerator. "Here, she's already cracked it."

She handed him a large glass container laden with lobster meat.

Kandy reached into the cupboard to grab a dish at the same time he did.

"I can get it," he told her, batting her hand away.

Blushing and hating herself for it, Kandy turned and asked, "Want me to heat it up?"

"Nope. It's fine as is."

He sat down at the breakfast bar and forked over a helping onto his dish. "What were you all talking about when I came in?"

"We're going out," Abby said, watching him eat. "We want Kandy to come, but she's being obstinate."

"Do you want to go?" he asked her.

"Not really."

"Can't you convince her?" Abby asked, perilously close to a whine. "Use your testosterone wiles or something? It'll be fun. We'll all go. We haven't all been out together in decades."

Josh swallowed and looked at each of the four women in the room, three of whom were staring at him while he ate, and then back to Kandy. "Your call," he told her.

"I'd really rather just clean up and go to bed."

Josh nodded. To her sisters and mother he lifted a shoulder. "Sorry."

"You didn't even try." Abby crossed her arms in front of her and pouted.

He cocked his head to one side and asked, "How old are you?"

When she blushed, Hannah laughed. "Come on, you two," she said, throwing an arm around Abby, who was closest to her. "Give your sister a break. She worked her butt off today."

"Which is why she should come out with us and blow off some steam. Have some fun," Gemma said, glaring at her sister.

Hannah threw Josh a quick look. "Oh, don't worry about her. She'll be fine."

As they went to prepare for the evening ahead, Josh and Kandy remained in the kitchen.

The silence echoed like a bomb detonating.

Kandy maneuvered in a nervous whirl about the room, putting away extra food, drying the lobster pots, doing anything she could to avoid looking in his direction.

"Mark Begman told me your lobster was unbelievable," Josh said. "He wasn't kidding."

Kandy glanced quickly over at him and then back to the sink. "Thanks."

"He said you add something to the water."

"Just some spices and a little sugar to cut the acid. Plus a few beers."

"Sophie's recipe?"

"No. Mine."

She stacked the pots together by the back door.

"I'll take those out for you."

"Oh thanks. They go in the garage," she said, automatically.

A wildfire of heat blazed up her neck and face and she couldn't look at him for fear he'd say something about what had happened just a few short hours ago between them.

She said a silent prayer of thanks when he kept silent, grabbed the pots, and went to store them in the garage.

* * *

Josh had just put the last pot away when he heard the scream.

Bolting back into the house, he collided with Kandy in the foyer.

"Who was that?" he asked.

"I don't know. I think it was Abby," she said, looking up the stairs to the loft.

"Kandy, come up here," Hannah called.

The urgency in her voice was hard to miss.

Josh took the stairs two at a time, Kandy right at his heels.

They found Hannah holding a shaking, crying, and clinging Abby, Gemma rubbing her back.

"What happened?" Josh aimed his question at all three of them as they huddled together in the hallway.

"Look on the bed," Hannah said, her arms tightly woven around her daughter.

He moved into the room and toward the head of the white-washed brass canopy. On one lace pillow sham lay a typewritten note. The paper, once plain white, was tainted and dripping with a watery, scarlet substance, saturating the sham it was attached to, as well as the comforter and sheet beneath it. The liquid originated from an object over the letter: a snakehead.

Behind him he heard Kandy muffle a scream. When he turned, she clamped a hand over her mouth and dashed into the bathroom, Gemma right behind her. In the next instant the sound of retching filled the room.

* * *

"Tell me what happened," Josh said to Abby as he handed her a tall glass of scotch, straight.

He'd moved them down to the living room after Kandy finished vomiting. Gemma was seated next to her oldest sister, a protective arm tossed over her shoulder, Abby still wrapped in her mother's embrace, opposite them. Hannah and Gemma had both declined drinks. Josh hadn't even asked Kandy if she wanted one, knowing she'd heave it up. Abby was the only one who needed something to calm her nerves.

After draining the glass and handing it back to him for a refill, she took a deep breath, and said, "I forgot my mascara and knew Kandy had some in her vanity. When I went into the bedroom, I didn't notice…that…thing at first." She swallowed hard, her mouth twisting in revulsion. "I got the mascara and then saw the note on the pillow. When I got closer to the bed, I saw the blood…the head…and screamed."

"Abby's always hated the sight of blood," Gemma said.

"Anything that bleeds," Hannah offered, cuddling her daughter. "Ever since you saw Grandma decapitate a chicken when you were three."

Abby groaned.

Hannah glanced over at Kandy and then at Josh. "What did the note say?"

He'd made them all leave the room before any of them could read it.

"Was it a death threat?" Gemma asked.

Josh looked from sister to sister, finally settling on Kandy. "Not a death threat, no. There was no mention of any detailed intent to harm Kandy."

"But a threat of some kind, right?" she asked.

Her eyes were misty and unfocused as she looked up at him.

"Yeah."

"What did it say?" Hannah asked again.

Josh debated what to tell them. In truth, Kandy was the only one who should be told. But he knew none of the four women were going to give up without knowing.

"'Stay away from the studio. If you go back, people will get hurt. Can you live with that, Kandy?'"

Her quick inhalation was deafening.

"Pretty clear meaning." Hannah stared at her oldest daughter.

"What's the significance of the snakehead and all the blood?" Gemma asked. "Assuming it was blood and not some weird food coloring or something. Just for effect? It doesn't seem to make any sense."

"Nothing, so far, in this whole situation, makes any sense," Kandy said, rising. "I'm making tea. Any takers?"

Hannah expressed a desire for a cup, as did Gemma.

Josh watched her exit the room. Her shoulders were slumped, her movements robotic, her torso and legs stiff. He knew it was taking every ounce of willpower she had not to fall apart.

"Who could have done this?" Hannah asked when Kandy was out of earshot.

"The obvious answer is someone who was here today," Josh said, rising from the couch. "Excuse me."

She was leaning against the counter, her back hunched, shoulders slumped. A teapot sat on the porcelain bottom of the sink, the running water overflowing out of it.

Josh reached around her, noted her knuckles were bone-white from the death grip she had on the ledge, and turned off the tap. Placing a gentle hand at her back, he asked, "You okay?"

She turned and his heart cleaved in two.

Two fat, silent tears streaked down her pale cheeks from eyes that were too large and haunted. Her mouth quivered, the corners turned downward. He was surprised she'd been able to hold on to her emotions as long as she had.

"It was somebody who was here today," she said. Her voice raw from earlier. "In my house. It's true, isn't it? I invited this person here."

He wanted to lie and ease some of her pain. The heartache so in evidence when she looked at him made his own heart break. He wanted to calm and comfort her, eliminate her cares and concerns, take her in his arms and love the worry away. Do anything he could to make her feel better.

That's what he wanted to do.

Instead, he did what he had to do.

Josh lifted the filled teapot from the sink, secured the whistletop, and placed it on the stove. After making sure he'd turned the burner on correctly, he faced her again.

She was still staring at him, her eyes a tad more focused and clearer than they'd been a few moments before.

"Yeah," he said. "It was someone who was here. Someone who came with the specific purpose of leaving you that little present."

Shaking her head, she moved away from the sink and swiped the back of her hands at her eyes. She took two deep breaths as she stood, rock still, her palms digging into the sockets. When she removed her hands, she gave her shoulders a shake. Eyes clearing, her face getting back some color, her lips had stopped trembling. Once again he was amazed at her ability to take control of herself. In that instant, watching her regain her composure and knowing the supreme effort it took, he was more intent than ever on finding out who was harassing her.

"I want this over," she said, breaking the silence in the room. Her voice was regaining its full body and strength. Reaching into one of the cabinets, she began taking out teacups and saucers. She placed them on the counter and added, "It's not just about me anymore. The game has changed. Whoever did this threatened people I care about. People I love with all my heart. I won't allow it. Tell me what we have to do to find out who's responsible. I'll do anything you tell me to."

"Anything?"

Standing at her full height, shoulders back and strong, she looked him straight in the eye and said, "Anything that will help you get this bastard."

Josh nodded. He hated what he was about to say, but had no choice. "You realize now, Kandy, one of the people you care about, maybe even love, is the one responsible, don't you? There's really no other explanation after this incident. Can you handle that? Handle knowing it?"

"I have to, don't I?" she answered, slamming her hand down flat on the counter. "It's obvious now. There were no strangers here."

He shook his head, kept his voice calm.

"No. It was all family, people who work with you, and your sister's friends."

She waved a dismissive hand in the air. "Who can be eliminated. No, I know it's someone close to *me.* I accept that. We have to figure out who as quick as we can."

Josh understood her intent. "There's no way you're going to stay away from the studio, is there?"

Again, her eyes pierced him with a hard, determined, glare. "Not a chance in hell. I refuse to be intimidated by anyone."

"That's my baby."

They both turned to see Hannah standing at the threshold, smiling. "Sophie's backbone to a *T.*" She moved toward her daughter and embraced her. "You're the strongest, bravest person I know, Kandace Sophia. I'm proud you're my daughter."

"Mom."

Kandy wrapped her arms around her mother's waist and closed her eyes. They stood for a moment, just holding each other.

"I came out to help with the tea. I didn't mean to eavesdrop," Hannah said, pulling away. She stared at her daughter's face and laughed. "Well, that's a fib," she said with a chuckle. "Of course I did."

"Of course you did," Kandy repeated, hugging her mother again. "You wouldn't be you if you didn't."

"The three of us came to the same conclusion you have," Hannah said, glancing across the room at Josh. "It has to be someone who was invited here today. We've been racking our brains to try and figure out who."

"That's my job," Josh said, turning the burner off when the whistle sounded. "Let me do it."

Kandy placed four tea bags into the boiling pot of water. Letting them steep, she said, "I think we should pool our resources."

"What do you mean?" he asked, taking the cream from the refrigerator and handing it to her.

"Let's sit down and try to figure out if we noticed anyone acting strange or weird today. I bet we can come up with something one of us saw that struck us as odd."

"It's not that easy," Josh said, lifting the tray she'd placed the cups on, along with cream, sugar, and spoons.

"I'm sure it isn't, but it doesn't hurt to try." She led him out of the room, Hannah in tow.

For the next hour the five of them sat in the living room, drinking and talking. When Abby complained of being cold, Josh lit a fire. He let them hash out their thoughts, listening, making comments once or twice.

He knew they needed this, needed to introduce some kind of control and order back into the day.

Especially Kandy.

While they spoke and hedged back and forth with their various theories, Josh surreptitiously watched her. She sipped her tea, wiping her tongue across her lips after each swallow, and obviously relishing every last taste of it.

At one point, Josh had to shift in his seat because just watching her drink got him hard. The memory of her taste on his lips and in his mouth washed over him, sending a tidal wave of desire tsunami-ing throughout his system.

With half an ear to their musings, Josh let his mind drift to what it would feel like to have Kandy under him, writhing and bucking to their own rhythm. To feel that skin, that soft-as-a-whisper skin next to his, warming him, feeding him, was something he realized he craved, like water to a dehydrated, desert-stranded man. From the moment she put her hand on his chest in the garage there had been no going back for either of them. His heart had vaulted when he'd found her equally aroused, and when she came apart in his hands, he promised himself it was only for the first time.

Right now, he wanted to tangle his fingers in her sexy curls and hold on for dear life as he kissed her senseless. Wanted to run his mouth over every naked inch of her body, sucking, tasting, and feasting on her like a man who'd always known hunger.

He wanted to fall asleep with her in his arms and wake with her spooned against him.

He wanted her. Pure and simple.

"Well, I think she's an absolute bitch," Hannah said, thumping her empty cup back on the tray. "How she manages to keep Cort is beyond me. I'd divorce her in a minute if I were him."

Josh blinked, his reverie broken by Hannah's words.

"You're not being fair, Mom," Kandy said from the sofa. "You don't know anything about their marriage."

"Yeah," Gemma said. "Alyssa may be a royal pain in the ass, but Cort adores her. I don't think you know what you're talking about."

Hannah graced her daughter with a focused and shrewd glower. "Gemma, I've been around men like Cort Mason for a long time. Much longer than any of you. I've seen enough to realize when a man is cheating."

"Mom."

"Oh, come on, Kandy." With a swipe of her well-manicured hand, she added, "Don't tell me he isn't. The signs are as clear as a bell."

"Maybe you'd like to share those signs with us," Josh said, at once on investigative alert.

Hannah cocked her head at him, a flirty smile on her lips. "You've been very quiet up until now," she said. "What have you been thinking about, sitting there all big and brooding?"

Josh shook his head. "Sorry, Hannah, it won't work on me." He grinned and added, "But thanks."

When she laughed out loud, her eyes dancing from the light of the fire, Josh could imagine any red-blooded male making a fool of himself for this woman.

"You're too darling for words," Hannah told him. "It's not many a man who can rebuke and compliment at the same time."

"Would you two quit the lovefest?" Gemma said, disgust in her tone. "Mom, tell us why you think Cort's playing around."

Hannah met her daughter's heated glare and said, "It's really so obvious, I'm ashamed none of you see it." She blew out a breath. "Okay. First, whenever I've seen him recently, Cort has been racked by nerves."

"That's because we're shooting on deadline," Kandy said. "He's just rattled we won't finish on time. He hates going over budget."

"Money has nothing to do with his mental state," Hannah declared. "The few times I've been in the studio he's been on his cell phone nonstop when you weren't filming."

"Well, that's true," Gemma said, grudgingly. "Stacy even said something about it the other day, remember?" she asked Kandy.

She nodded. "I assumed he was talking to Alyssa. He always looks so beat up after the conversation ends."

"True," Hannah said. "But those calls aren't from Alyssa."

"How do you know?" Josh asked.

There was a moment of silence before Kandy gasped. "You didn't? Please tell me you didn't, Mom."

Hannah waved a hand in the air again. "It wasn't my fault. It just happened."

Scratching his ear, Josh asked, "Someone want to fill me in?"

It was Gemma who did. "You should realize by now my mother is a world-class eavesdropper."

"That's not a very flattering thing to call someone, Gemma Anne," Hannah said, lips pouting and voice stern.

"What would you prefer to be called? Snoop? Spy? Nosey-Parker?"

Josh hid his grin behind his hand when he saw Hannah blush scarlet at her daughter's description.

"Gemma, you're being rude," Hannah said. She turned her attention to Josh. "It was very innocent on my part. Really. I was in the elevator on my way up to Kandy's office a few weeks ago. It stopped on one of the floors and Cort was standing there, his back to the elevator, speaking on his cell. He spoke a woman's name, turned, and stopped dead in his tracks when he saw me."

"What name?" Josh asked.

"Patty. He said, 'Look Patty, I can't go into this right now.' That's when he turned and saw me."

"What did he do then?"

Lifting her hands outward, she shrugged. "Got in the elevator, threw me a lame smile, and whispered into the phone, *I'll call you back.* Then he shoved his cell into his pocket."

Her gaze ran across all their faces. "It rang almost immediately after that, but he ignored it. Tried to make small talk until he got off a few floors later."

"So, from one encounter you think he's cheating on Alyssa?" Kandy said.

"Not much proof," Gemma added, arms crossed in front of her, a sour expression on her face.

Abby, silent for most of the hour, piped in, "It is pretty lame for an accusation of cheating."

"But it wasn't the only time," Hannah said. Josh knew she regretted giving voice to the statement, because she blushed again and put her hand over her mouth.

"I knew it," Kandy said, rising and grabbing the tea tray. "Mom, you're just too much sometimes."

"Kandy, sit down," Josh told her, his voice hard and stern. "We're not done."

She turned, the tray still in her hands. He could tell she was surprised at his tone. She stared at him, mouth open in a silent moue of shock. "Please," he added, pointing to the sofa.

Josh was as astounded as the rest of her family when she complied.

"Thank you," Josh said. "Hannah, maybe you'd better tell us what you overheard."

When it looked as if she were going to protest his choice of words, he put a restraining hand up and said, "All by chance, of course. I understand that. *We* understand that," he added, swiping his hand to indicate her daughters.

When Gemma snorted, Josh threw her a glare that had her squirming in her seat.

"Well, again," Hannah said, "this wasn't my fault. But it was at your book party, Kandy. You'd already left by the time I arrived. Reva wasn't thrilled, by the way," she added.

"We already know about Reva, Hannah," Josh said. "Tell us about Cort."

She pouted for a second. "I was speaking with Kandy's publisher when I saw Cort reach for his cell. He answered it and began behaving in a strange way. Secretive. Looking all around as he made his way to the back of the ballroom. He put his hand over the mouthpiece, and when he passed by me I heard him say 'Patty' again. He didn't look happy."

"I remember that," Gemma broke in. "I saw it happen. I was standing at the bar with Reva. Cort's cell went off, and when he answered it, I remember thinking the same thing. It was like he was upset. He shot straight for the men's room, the phone glued to his ear."

"I know I heard him say 'Patty,'" Hannah said with conviction. "I'm not wrong."

"Is that it? Is that why you think he's cheating on his wife?" Kandy asked. "Because Patty could be anyone from his accountant to his dental hygienist."

"True," Hannah said. "But if there's one thing I know, girls, and you can't deny this—any of you—it's men. I just know he's being unfaithful to Alyssa. I can feel it. Not that I blame him. She gives the term *bitch* a whole new meaning."

"What do you think?" Gemma asked, turning to Josh.

He glanced from her to Kandy and then back to Hannah. "I think your mother may know a little more about these things than you do. I'll run a more in-depth check on both of the Masons."

"Both? You can't think Cort is behind any of this?" Kandy shouted, jumping up from the sofa again. "He's one of my best friends, Josh. He loves me. He wouldn't hurt me."

"Kandy, calm down." Josh rose as well and took her arm.

She snatched it back, recoiling. "Don't tell me to calm down. Not when you're accusing one of the best men I've ever known of trying to harm me."

"I haven't accused anyone. And remember, you told me you'd do anything to find out who's behind these things. Anything."

She glared at him, her eyes scalding with burning rage. Without another word, she turned and bolted from the room, through the foyer, and out the kitchen door. When they heard it slam shut, Josh and Gemma both moved to follow her.

"Haven't you done enough?" Gemma threw at him.

“Gemma, sit down,” Hannah ordered from the chair.

Ignoring both of them, Josh sprinted from the room.

“Mother, I’m a little old to be told what to do,” Gemma said, her top lip curling back in a sneer.

“I. Said. Sit. Down.”

The two women stared at each other for a few moments before Gemma relented. “Damn it!” She plopped back on the sofa, her arms twisted in front of her. “He upset her.”

“Then let him fix it.”

Chapter Eighteen

Kandy ran outside, fighting the urge to scream at the top of her lungs, and headed straight down to the sand. Hands fisted so tight her short nails stabbed into the flesh of her palms, she fought for air.

It was all too much.

Too many questions, too many thoughts, too many feelings.

When had this become her life? When had her life—the one she'd planned and sacrificed for—become a confused mix of distrust, fear, and suspicion? Of raging, uncontrollable reactions? Of being forced to admit the life she'd always dreamed of wasn't quite what she'd expected or wanted?

Kandy closed her eyes, squeezing back tears. She wouldn't be weak, wouldn't be the cliché of the overwhelmed woman succumbing to her overwrought emotions. She had her grandmother's tough and stubborn DNA woven through her. Sophie would have given her a stern shake of her head with a lecture attached if she'd discovered her granddaughter falling into an emotional heap.

She sensed Josh come up behind her. Wordlessly, he turned her around to face him.

"Go away," she said, fighting to break free of his hold.

He wouldn't release her.

He wove his hands around her upper arms, pulling her into his own. She knew his intent was to give comfort, but Kandy wouldn't be comforted, her anger still hot and burning. She lifted her fists and beat at his chest, her arms conduits for the fury and frustration swirling within her as she unleashed it all on him.

"I hate this!" She pushed against him so hard that she stumbled backward, almost losing her footing in the soft sand, and wobbled to remain upright as she glared at him. “I hate all this supposition and gossip. Poking into people’s confidential business, speculating on their marriages, their behavior, their finances. And I hate you for forcing me to question people I trust. People I consider friends. People I love.”

“Kandy—”

“No!” she roared.

His lips clamped down.

“This is *your* life, Josh, not mine. You have to distrust people, question every move, every motive, everything they say and do. I’m not made that way.” Her hand pounded her chest. “I’ve built my career on entrusting the people around me to do their best, to support me, to help me. I hate that you’re making me doubt them. They’re good people. Honest. *Loyal.*”

Under the bright moonlight, his face was a mask of calm.

“They don’t expect to have their private lives combed through like someone burrowing through garbage. They have a right to their privacy, as do I. As do you. It’s a basic right.”

“I agree with you.” He nodded. “On principle, if nothing else.”

“On principle?” She took a step toward him, her hands fisted on her hips. “How can you stand to do what you do? How can you go on day after day, digging up dirty little secrets, being suspicious of everyone you come in contact with? Never trusting anyone?”

“I trust people, Kandy. But this is my job.” He said it so simply, with such acceptance, she wanted to scream.

“Well, forgive me,” she spat, “but it’s a lousy job.”

He stared at her a moment, then cocked his head. “Answer one question for me.”

“Just one?” She folded her arms across her chest. “Why not ten thousand? It’s what you do, isn’t it? Question everything and everyone?”

He wouldn’t be baited, instead asking, “What are you really mad at, Kandy? Me, for forcing you to consider someone close to you could be responsible for all these incidents? Or that you think I’m invading their privacy—”

“You are.”

“—Or are you mad at yourself because you’re beginning to realize you don’t know the people around you as well as you think you do?”

Her brows pulled together. “What does that mean? Of course I do. They’re all family and friends.”

“You’ve told me they all work *with* you, but the reality is these people work *for* you. You’re the boss. It’s your name on the banner. Friends, family, all of them, it makes no difference. You’re in charge. You make the decisions, and you decide what's best. For everyone."

"It's *my* career." She slapped her fists against her thighs. "It's my name. Of course I'm in charge."

"Did you ever consider that maybe, just maybe, someone close to you is sick of that, sick of being, for lack of a better word, one of your minions? That maybe someone doesn't want to drink the Kandy Kool-Aid anymore?"

Kandy froze. "That's a despicable thing to say."

"Is it? When you're filming and the take is as perfect as it can be and you demand another one, everyone falls in line, even knowing the first one was fabulous and can't possibly get any better."

"But—"

Now he took a step closer to her, his own hands balled on his hips. "Or when the incident on the roof happened and everyone felt it was better to call it a day—everyone but you—production commenced despite what they wanted."

"We have contracts to honor, budgets to comply with—"

"You can wrap it up in any excuse you want, Kandy, the simple fact is you wanted to go on, so no one fought you about it. Your word is law. You never stopped to consider how the crew felt about finding something as unpleasant as a speared rat at their place of work. How they might need a break, mentally and physically, from something so gruesome and threatening. Or even how worried your aunts and Stacy were about the whole thing. No. You wanted to continue, so, like soldiers following orders, everyone fell in line, despite their own feelings and misgivings."

"But you said you understood," she cried. "That whole speech you gave me about being the captain of the ship and what it meant."

Josh nodded. "I do understand, and believe me, I admire your dedication and sense of commitment. But I don't work for you. I'm not one of the people forced to comply with what you demand of them every day."

Confusion mixed with hurt, leaving a sour taste in her mouth.

"What I *demand* of them? What am I asking for that's so horrible? That people do their job? That they honor the commitments they've made? Strive to put out the best, the highest-quality product they're capable of? Why is that so wrong? You're making me sound like a dictator."

"Am I?"

"Yes!"

"You don't think someone could be tired of trying to live up to your high standards? That maybe they've had enough and this is their way of cutting ties with you, of getting out?"

She threw up her hands, turned and, stalked toward the water's edge. "I don't understand a thing you're saying. Enough of what?"

He followed her to where she'd stopped. "Your quest for perfection."

Kandy closed her eyes and swallowed, a giant ball of uneasiness lodging in the back of her throat. Her voice shook when she said, "I'm not a perfectionist."

I'm not.

But wasn't she? Really? At her core, didn't she strive to make every recipe, every project, every piece of her life, perfect and ideal?

Of course I do, but I demand perfection from myself, not anyone else.

Don't I?

"Call it whatever you want, but the result is the same. The people around you know you accept nothing less from yourself and from them. And you don't broker any arguments or discussion when you've made up your mind."

Kandy opened her eyes and stared at the inky black darkness in front of her. The ocean tide lapping against her bare feet was cold, her toes beginning to tingle from its chilly temperature.

Had she really put that kind of pressure on the people around her, the people she claimed to love and trust? Pressure to be the best at all costs? Forcing them to strive for a perfection that was unattainable? Was she really that person? Had she pushed someone so far to the brink they were now lashing out against her?

She'd steamrolled through her career, moving from one project to the next at full speed, never stopping, never resting, always focused on her ultimate goal. In doing so, had she alienated someone close to her? Stacy and the aunts had never once complained, never once confronted her about her grueling schedules, about how she pushed herself—and, apparently—the people around her. Neither had Cort.

Had she missed clues to how they were feeling, what they might be going through because of the constant stress? She certainly had with Daniel. She'd never questioned why his behavior had become so erratic or why'd he taken to drinking during work. He wasn't doing his job to the best of his ability, so she'd summarily fired him without ever asking him about the cause of his behavior.

With Cort, she'd dismissed the secrecy he'd cloaked himself in of late, and never gave a thought to why he'd had such a sudden desire for quick flights from work at the end of day. Until this season's filming began, Cort had made a habit of sticking around the studio after everyone had left, preparing for the next day, or making notes on editing changes he wanted. Now he was just as eager as everyone else on staff to leave once shooting was completed. She'd ignored this change in his behavior as long as the work was finished and perfect—*that word again!*

Thinking back, she realized even Stacy, usually as unflappable and calm as a statue, had been snapping at coworkers. She'd taken to wearing her glasses more and more instead of her contact lenses, and Kandy realized now it was probably to shield the purple smudges under eyes that had sprung up, caused, no doubt, by lack of sleep.

Hard work had been drilled into her as a child by Sophie, and, in truth, Kandy thrived on it. She'd never considered until this moment, though, that someone around her might not feel the same way, might not have the same dedication, the same drive, maybe not even want the same things, she did, and was fed up.

Had her strive for success and dedication to perfection forced someone she knew to lash out to the point of tormenting her? She hadn't looked at it from that perspective before, and when she did now, she shuddered at the thought. While she wasn't the dictator Josh made her sound like, she admitted she certainly wasn't the easiest person to work with.

For the first time in, well, *forever,* Kandy took a good hard look at herself and questioned the person she truly was. She shivered, retreated a step back from the frigid water, and knocked up against the solid wall of Josh's chest. His hands rose to clasp her elbows.

When she turned to face him, his quiet look of concern and acceptance humbled her.

"It kills me to admit this," she said, a sob strangling her voice, "but you could be right. Today proved it's someone I know, someone who can"—she swallowed, tasting bile—"get close to me. And while I hope I haven't done anything to or hurt someone enough to cause all this, I can't deny what you're saying could be true."

Every fiber in her being was drained. To know she'd pushed herself to exhaustion only added to the guilt she felt, realizing she'd done the same to those around her.

It was an eye-opening discovery.

Without another word between them, Josh folded her into his arms. This time she clung to him as if he were a lifeline, drawing the strength and calm she needed from his gentle touch. He lowered them to their knees in the sand.

The moonlight above shone brilliant from the cloudless night sky. The thunderous waves breaking against the shoreline roared around them, their rhythmic roll and pitch a quieting and soothing serenade.

For several minutes Kandy held on to Josh, soaking in the solid warmth he gave her.

After her breathing and mind calmed, and she could trust her emotions not to betray her again, she looked up at his face.

Every plane and angle of his jaw and cheekbones were silhouetted by the brilliance of the moon. The hard line of his nose as it tapered down into the full mouth she wanted against her own, the cut-from-stone chin she'd dreamed of sliding her tongue along, the drumming of his heart beneath her hands. She knew the second it kicked up its pace, deepened its rhythm: when her gaze drifted from his eyes down to his lips and stayed there. The beat of his pulse accelerated when her gaze dragged from one corner of his full mouth to the other. Without thought, her fingers dug into his shirt and fisted in the fabric.

His hands, which, moments before had given comfort, changed in an instant. His grip tightened and the fingers splayed across the small expanse of her back pushed her closer. Her mouth was level with his as she snaked her hands up and around the back of his neck and molded her torso to his, barely a whisper of space between them.

She didn't think about how angry she was with him for forcing her to doubt and spy on her friends.

She didn't think about the fact that someone close to her wasn't what they seemed.

She didn't think about her mother and sisters, probably watching them right now from the living-room window.

She didn't think about anything at all, but being here, in this moment, with this man. Under the shimmer of the moon's light. Under the stars.

Kandy didn't think about a thing but how amazing Josh's lips felt against her own when she leaned in and pressed against them as if it were the most natural and familiar thing in the world to do.

The kiss was slow and sweet at first. Just a brief touch. She could feel him trying to control his response, not let what she was doing become too much, allowing it only to be an extension of the comfort he'd given her moments before.

But Kandy didn't want consoling. Not now and not from him.

Grabbing the back of his neck with one firm hand, she tugged him closer, leaving no confusion about her intent. When their lips fused together, she made certain he knew what she wanted; what she craved.

Him.

Hungrily, ravenously, and with more passion than she'd ever devoted to her cooking, Kandy feasted on his mouth. She raked her teeth over his swollen lips and parted them open with one brush of her tongue. When she got the effect she wanted, she almost cried out in joy.

His body yielded to hers, his grip tightening almost to the brink of being painful.

But it wasn't. It was ecstasy.

Pure and simple.

His hands cupped her bottom, grinding her pelvis into his, as his mouth devoured hers, equally as famished and voracious.

Somehow the buttons of her blouse came undone and Josh's lips and tongue dragged a wet string of desire from her shoulder down to her bra. Freeing one hand, he moved the soft material out of his way and gently kissed her smooth breast.

Shards of light burst from behind Kandy's closed eyes when she felt his hot breath billow against her skin. Fisting his hair as an anchor, she arched, allowing him the freedom to explore. Her spine tingled all the way up her back when his tongue laved over her bra, right over her puckered nipple. Falling backward, she flattened both of them down to the sand, Josh on top. The feel of his body, forged in granite, warm, and full of want, was almost too much.

Through the fabric of his pants she reached for him and her insides turned to liquid when she found him pulsing, hot, hard, and huge beneath her grasp.

Josh ground out a feral moan against her breast and draped a hand between the triangle of her legs, pressing his fingers into the cotton shorts.

With slow, determined movements, he traced two fingers up and down her length, over her panties, back and forth in a rhythm that drove her mad. Opening her legs wide to give him free range, Kandy began stroking him in a similar manner.

When she heard him hiss against her neck, a sensation of power vaulted through her. Never thinking of the consequences, never imagining what would happen afterward, Kandy gave voice to the one thing she wanted more than anything else.

"Josh, please. Please. I want you so much."

His lips crushed hers again, as Kandy's long legs wound around his waist, crossing in back, imprisoning them both. His hands trailed and tracked the skin up and down her arms, at her waist, finally scooping and settling on her butt and forging her upward and into him.

Arching, Kandy turned her head to give him access to her throat and inhaled a huge whiff of sand.

The grains wound their way through her mouth and nose, lodging in the back of her throat, forcing her to gag and hack to expel them.

In a flash, Josh jumped up and pulled her with him.

“Sand?” he asked, wiping her back free of it.

She nodded, continuing to cough and spew it from her mouth.

After a few moments and one very un-ladylike spit, Kandy stopped.

“Okay?” Josh asked. Undisguised mirth danced close to the edge of his mouth.

“Don’t you dare laugh,” she chided, collapsing into another choking paroxysm, and pointed an accusatory finger at him.

“I’m not.” His lips spasmed.

“It’s not funny.” She swiped at leaking tears and tried hard to keep her own grin in check. “It’s not.”

“I didn’t say it was.”

Her hand balled and she punched him in the chest. He must have seen the movement because, quick as a lightning flash, he pulled back, the hit landing with no force.

They stared at each other for a heartbeat and then burst into peals of laughter. Kandy placed a hand across her mouth, resulting in another round of coughs from inhaling sand still on it. Gagging and laughing at the same time, she doubled over, bracing her hands against her sides.

“Stop. Please. It hurts too much,” she begged.

Josh took her arm and pulled her upright. Wiping away small traces of sand from her face, his fingers lingered on her chin as he stared down at her, his eyes dark and hooded in the moonlight.

“Are you okay now?” he asked after a moment.

Kandy knew he wasn’t referring to her hacking episode.

She nodded. “I’m sorry for running out like that. For shouting at you and acting like a two-year-old. I really don’t hate you, I’m sorry I said that. It just got all…too much.”

He pulled her back into his arms, settling her head against his shoulder. Rubbing her back, he said, “I’m sorry, too, Kandy. Sorry you have to go through this whole ordeal. Sorry I have to make you question and doubt everything and everyone around you.”

She nodded against his shoulder.

It was Josh who finally broke the spell.

His hands still encircling her upper arms, he said, “We’d better get back in. It’s late. I need to do a few things.”

Kandy kept her eyes cast down, knowing that if she looked at him, he would see the disappointment and confusion on her face.

If the mishap with the sand hadn’t occurred, she knew in her heart they would have made love right there on the beach, with the sea surging behind them and the stars shining above them.

He'd wanted her as much as she did him.

She crossed her arms over her chest, turned, and began walking back toward the deck, silent and thoughtful, Josh following behind, his hands folded into his pockets.

* * *

Before retiring for the night, Josh spent more than two hours on his laptop, tracking down information about Cort and Alyssa Mason. The information, though useful, didn't send up any red flags.

Cort Mason pulled an excellent salary as Kandy's director, well able to sustain the couple in their pricey lifestyle. Alyssa, although she appeared to be a mild shopaholic—evidenced by her monthly credit charges—made more than enough to support herself. They had no crippling outstanding debts, nothing strange in their bank account balances.

So far, except for Daniel and Chandler, everyone around Kandy was financially solvent and having no apparent money problems. With Daniel's gambling debts paid, that let him out of the picture as well.

"It's got to be something personal, then," Josh said aloud, leaning back on the bed, the laptop across his legs. "Something where I can't see the gain outright."

Before going to sleep, he jotted down a few questions he needed to ask Kandy and Stacy.

In the dark, the gentle, salty breeze from the ocean drifting into his room, he tried to sleep.

It wasn't easy.

Every time he closed his eyes, graphic memories of what he'd done with Kandy played across his vision. Josh's most intense memory was how she'd looked with Declan sitting in her lap as she bent to kiss and cuddle him.

Running a hand across the sensation burning in his chest, Josh realized how much he wanted that; how much he wanted to see Kandy with a child of her own—his child—dancing and bouncing in her lap.

Crazy. It was just crazy to be feeling like this after such a short amount of time. His mother had been right all those years ago about the thunderbolt.

The first time Josh's lips had claimed Kandy's, he'd felt it charge right through his body to his very core, joining him for life to this one woman.

He and Kandy were so alike when it came to their careers and life choices. He'd gone the job route, sacrificing love and relationships, for the higher need within him. The need to serve and protect. When those needs changed, he had as well, going private and utilizing his knowledge and skills in a different way.

She'd followed her dream all the way to fruition. Successful, celebrated, and happy in what she did, she'd fulfilled her goals. Along the way, she hadn't forgotten about the most important part of her dream, and hadn't let anything stand in her way of achieving it.

It was strange, almost providential, that they'd been brought together. Kandy at her peak careerwise, but relationship poor, and he settled comfortably into the next phase of his life, but also lacking in a personally fulfilling relationship.

Sleep, when it finally came, was because of mental and physical exhaustion. Josh woke the next morning to the sound of the tide pounding through his window.

Glancing at the clock, and thinking Kandy might want an early-morning run, he threw on an old sweatshirt and shorts, brushed his teeth, and was in the kitchen in less than five minutes.

He wasn't surprised when he saw her there, taking something from the oven.

"What are you making?" he asked, deliberately keeping his voice low and soft.

She gasped and almost dropped the cake pan. "*God.* Don't sneak up on a person like that. You scared me."

"Sorry."

"I'm not used to anyone being up at this hour out here," she said, closing the oven and shutting it off. "They all tend to sleep in. I think it's the sea air."

"Is that Grandma's blend?" he asked, pointing to the coffee urn.

She nodded while placing a cake tin on the counter. "Of course it is. Want a cup?"

"I can get it," he said when he saw her move to the cabinet. "You don't have to wait on me."

Blushing, she turned back to the cake.

While Josh poured a cup of coffee, he asked again, "What are you making?"

"Mario asked for a cheesecake. I want to deliver it before we head back today."

Josh remembered the chef's request. "Sophie's cheesecake, right?"

"The best you'll ever have."

"Does he offer it at the restaurant?"

"No. Mario would never *sell* this. It's strictly for his own enjoyment. This has been his favorite cake since he was a kid sitting at Grandma's table. She never gave the recipe to anyone."

"Except you."

"Well, yeah. Except me." She wiped her hands on a towel and rested a hip against the counter. "I'll make the topping later. Are you hungry?"

When those violet blue eyes met his, Josh's one thought was, *Yeah. I'd like to eat you whole.* He refrained from saying it out loud, instead opting to ask her if she wanted to go for a run.

Kandy glanced at the clock. "That's a good idea. I won't get a workout tomorrow because I have to be at NBC Studios by four thirty. And this crew won't be up for another two hours at least. Mom even later. They'll all be up, though, to make eleven A.M. Mass. I can deliver the cake before we head back to the city."

Josh drained his coffee. "How long do you need to get ready?"

"Two minutes. My running clothes are in the closet upstairs."

Her color paled the moment she said it.

"I can get them for you."

"That's a sweet offer," she said at last, a hint of wistfulness in her words. "Thank you, but I'll be okay. Gemma stripped the bed last night and tossed everything into the laundry. I'll be quick," she added, making her way out of the kitchen.

Josh let her go, impressed once again by her determination and fortitude.

He went back to his room, tied on his sneakers, and checked his laptop to see if he'd gotten any e-mails from his partner, Rick. By the time he came back out to the foyer, she was waiting for him, hair pulled back into a high ponytail, a bright blue sweatshirt and track shorts in place. The same brand of expensive running shoes he'd seen her wear in the city were on her feet.

"How many pair of those do you have?" he asked, pointing to her feet.

Glancing down, she wiggled her toes and said, "Six. I catered the yearly stockholder's meeting for the company and the CEO was so grateful she sent me a box filled with their most popular colors."

"Nice perk."

"They got a great meal out of it. Ready?"

They exited through the deck door, Josh careful to re-alarm the house from the outside.

"With everyone still asleep," he told her, "I don't want to take any chances."

Kandy's hard gaze drilled him. "It's never far from your mind, is it?"

"Safety? No, it isn't. You should know that by now."

She turned away and stared off at the ocean. "Yeah, I do. Let's go."

Without another word, they jogged down to the water's edge and headed east.

* * *

The day was starting crisp and clear, and, evidenced by the cloudless sky, it promised to turn into a hot one. The beach was empty save for a few other early morning runners, who nodded and greeted them as they ran by.

After thirty minutes, Kandy slowed and said, "Can we head back?"

"Whatever you want."

She was a little irritated he was neither winded nor appeared to be sweating.

"You have to stay in shape, I guess, to do what you do," she said as they turned and retraced their route.

"Yeah. I don't do it only for the job, though. It makes me feel good when I've had a hard run or a good weight workout. I feel better overall."

"Kind of like a natural high."

"Yup. Don't you enjoy it? You're in the gym most every day."

"I guess I feel the same. Working out gives me an edge. More of a mental focus. The hours at the studio can get long, especially if we're behind schedule. Although lately, we haven't been. In fact, this is the first show we've ever been in front of. The only scene left to film for the premiere episode is the one in the herb garden. Cort and I have been able to arrange things in a more manageable way for this season. Working out is just another thing I have to do, so I budget the time and adjust for it."

Their feet pummeled the hardened sand at the water's edge.

"Speaking of Cort, I have a few questions I need to ask you."

Even though they were running, Kandy's spine turned to steel.

"About Cort?"

"Among other things. But I can start with him."

She mentally braced and said, "Go ahead."

"I was thinking last night about what your mother told us. It's obvious you don't think he's cheating on his wife."

"I don't."

"But you do admit things have changed around the studio lately?"

"Yes."

"How? What's different?"

She thought about it for a few seconds. “Usually Cort, the editing chief, and I, work down to the wire getting the show ready. For this episode, Cort suggested editing as we went along.”

“How come you didn’t work that way before?”

She shrugged. “It seemed better to begin editing when we were all done with principal production. We could splice the show together knowing the entirety beforehand.”

“Do you like it better this way?”

“I don’t really know. We’ll see what the final product looks like. Up to now it seems like everything is flowing well. You never really know until you see it all the way through, though, beginning to end.”

Josh stared off into the ocean. “You mentioned Cort’s been leaving earlier than he has in the past.”

“Yeah. He’s never fallen into the category of wanting out by a certain time. He never minded staying late if he and I had to.”

“But he hasn’t stayed late since you two changed the editing process?”

“No, he hasn’t. I guess it’s a good thing because he can spend more time with Alyssa.”

“Or whomever,” Josh said.

Kandy ran for a few moments without replying. Finally, she said, “Or whomever. But wanting to leave at a normal hour doesn’t mean he’s the one doing all these things to me.”

“No, it doesn’t. But it’s changed behavior. Something to be explored.”

They were silent again for a while, each running at a relaxed pace as the sun began its slow and steady climb toward the center of the cloudless blue sky.

“How well do you know Alyssa?” Josh asked.

“I don’t really *know* her. She hates coming to events. When she does show up, she’s usually not in the mood to talk to anyone unless they can get her in a commercial or a movie or something. Why all these questions about the Masons?”

Ignoring the annoyance in her tone, Josh said, “Because they left before anyone else yesterday, while the party was roaring along.”

“So?”

“Everyone was outside on the beach. No one would have seen them go up to your loft. One of them had plenty of time to leave the note for you.”

“You really think it’s one of them doing this?”

“Strongest probability so far.”

Kandy thought for a second. “I’d bet on Alyssa.”

“Why?”

"Mostly because the calls I've been getting sound like a woman."

"Any other reason, aside from the fact that you just don't want it to be Cort?"

She threw him a look and said, "If I'm being honest, no. I just can't see him doing it."

"Fair enough. It's my job to find out who it is, not yours."

Her irritation grew at the mention, one more time, of his job. "Anything else?" she asked, not bothering to hide the displeasure in her voice.

"Mark Begman. Ever have any problems or concerns with him?"

"None. He's been with me since the beginning, too. Why? Did you find out some nasty little secret about him?"

Josh stopped midstride, and planted his feet in the sand.

Turning back to him, she stopped and saw him, hands fisted on his hips, glaring at her.

"I thought you were over this, Kandy. I thought you were going to help me, not fight me, at every turn," he said.

Ashamed, she felt twin stains of heat leap out on her cheeks as she looked down at the sand. "I'm sorry." Raising her head to meet his eyes, she added, "I did agree to help. I want to. Sorry for being so bitchy."

Josh let her stand there for a few, penitent moments. "*Bitchy* is a word I would never use to describe you," he said, walking to where she stood. When he was close enough for her to tip her head back to maintain eye contact, he stopped. "Determined, stubborn, and loyal to a fault are more appropriate."

She could feel the color spread down her neck.

"I ask about Mark because he's in a position close to you and has access to the studio. Plus, another network wants him to direct a sitcom for the replacement season."

This was news to her. "How did you find that out?"

He shook his head. "Professional sources is all I'll tell you. But it's true. He hasn't said anything about it to you? Or Cort?"

"To Cort, I don't know. He certainly hasn't said anything to me. You should ask Stacy."

His brows pulled together. "Why would Stacy know?"

"They were dating up until a few weeks ago. Just casual. Nothing serious."

"Why'd they break it off?"

"I don't know if there was anything to break off. Like I said, it was casual. A drink now and then. Maybe a movie and dinner."

"I wonder why she never mentioned it."

Lifting her shoulders and glancing out at the sea, Kandy said, “I’d guess she didn’t see it as important.”

“Maybe. How tight is Mark’s contract?”

“He has the same one everyone else does. Run of the show, guaranteed.”

“Are there any out clauses?”

She squinted, thinking.

“Probably. I mean, don’t there have to be for legal reasons? You’ll have to ask someone in the legal department because I honestly don’t know.”

“Cort has the same contract?”

“Yes, because I remember the day he signed it, Stacy and I took him to lunch. He was thrilled to be working at a steady job in television. He’d been dry for a while, opportunitywise.”

Josh nodded. With a quick glance at his watch he said, “It’s getting late.”

They ran the rest of the way in silence, and were met by three very tired, still waking women, gathered around the coffee urn.

Chapter Nineteen

After attending Mass as a family and dropping off the cheesecake to a grateful Mario, Josh had acquiesced and allowed Kandy to drive them back to the city. Gemma drove herself, while Abby and Hannah carpooled.

Due to the heavy end-of-the-weekend traffic, Kandy had to keep her speed to a delicate rush and wasn't able to weave in and out of lanes. She was as acutely aware of the man seated next to her, typing away on his laptop, as she was of the bumper-to-bumper traffic they were stuck in.

A torrent of thoughts washed through her while she inched forward a few feet per minute.

She'd finally admitted and agreed the person responsible for tormenting her had to be someone within her realm. That simple fact hurt more than she could give a voice to. She'd always tried—in business and in dealing with her family—to be fair, appreciative, and available. To know someone she trusted, someone she'd probably helped, was determined to cause trouble and potentially harm her was upsetting at the very least. Kandy knew she was considered hard and intractable by some people she'd had business dealings with. As she'd told Josh, she'd risen fast and stepped on a few professional toes along the way. But she'd never intentionally or purposefully hurt anyone—not that she knew of. When she'd had to take a hard line with someone she usually felt guilt more than anything else afterward.

Kandy's generosity to her family was something she also knew many in the business world looked down on and questioned her for. But again, every person she employed, whether related to her or not, was tops at what they did. She truthfully would never have hired them if they weren't.

Someone she knew wanted her to suffer emotionally and physically. The incidents like her closet being disturbed, the misplaced wallet, and the harassing phone calls all seemed malicious and determined to annoy her. The light falling at the studio and the rental car mishap could have killed her.

Who hated her so much?

When the traffic finally edged its way onto the expressway, Kandy sped up and concentrated on driving, wishing she never had to know the answer.

* * *

"This is a ridiculous hour to be awake and working." Stacy stifled a yawn and readjusted her glasses.

Josh agreed.

They stood off to one side of the studio set as Kandy put together a simple three-course brunch for the *Today Show,* while at the same time conferring with the segment director about the best shot angles and how she was going to present the food. Josh glanced down at his watch.

"What time did you get here?" he asked.

"Four. I had all the ingredients shipped over from the studio on Friday, but I wanted to make sure everything arrived and was ready. Live shows like this leave no leeway for problems. Kandy's got to have everything timed and paced to perfection. They're doing a full sit-down interview in the seven-thirty hour and then this demo during the eight o'clock segment."

"Three hours from now. Why did she have to be here so early?"

"Logistics."

When he just stared at her, she explained. "Like her show, Kandy has to prepare at least two separate meals. One as the finished product for the end of the segment, ready to show and serve, and one for during the preparation stage. She's so obsessive she makes two finished products just in case one doesn't come out exactly the way she wants."

"What are the chances of that happening?"

"Nil. But she does it anyway. And she never wants help. Wants to do it all herself." She turned to stare up at him. "Remember I told you she borders on obsessive-compulsive?"

He turned back to the set to watch Kandy roll out pastry dough, confer with the director, and evaluate the lighting all at the same time. "Yeah, but it pays off."

"No argument there."

She lowered her eyes for a moment and took a breath. Facing him, she said, "Aunt Hannah called me last night."

Josh put his hands in his pockets and turned his attention back to

Kandy's cousin.

"She thought we might want to halt production until you find out who's doing this."

"Knowing your cousin, do you think that's a possibility?"

Stacy yawned into her hand. "No. I said as much to Aunt Hannah. I didn't even have to call Kandy for confirmation. There's no way she'll stop working."

Josh looked down at the clipboard she held, which outlined the schedule for the day.

"Are you any closer to figuring this out?"

He nodded. "A few new things have come up, but I can't do much about them today since Kandy's going to be all over the map. I need to stick close."

"Just knowing this may be over soon is a relief."

He put a hand on Stacy's shoulder. "I need to ask you something. Personal."

Hesitation grew in her eyes and her unlined brow rose above her glasses.

"It's about Mark Begman."

Her cheeks turned a hot pink before his eyes. "What about him?"

"Kandy told me the two of you were dating."

"Not dating. Not really. Why?"

"You never mentioned it."

She shrugged. "It was nothing serious. He invited me out for drinks twice, dinner once. That was it."

"No breakup, then?"

"No. I haven't been out with him for about a month or so."

"Any specific reason?"

"No. Why is this important?"

"Two reasons." He leaned in closer to make sure no one around them could overhear. He'd have preferred to have this conversation in private, but he wasn't leaving Kandy's side for any reason. "First, Mark isn't listed as a person who has her private numbers."

"He doesn't need them."

"I realize that, but I have to look at every possibility in this matter and it may be that he obtained them from you."

"I never gave them to him."

"Lower your voice." A few of the setup crew threw glances their way. "I didn't accuse you of doing so. He might have gotten them without your knowing, say, from your purse or even your tablet."

He could see the moment the realization hit her.

"Are you saying he only went out with me to gain access in some way to Kandy?" Hurt danced across her expression and he hated himself for putting the doubt in her mind.

"No, Stacy, I'm not. But I have to look at everyone and everything related to her from every angle and perspective. This is just one of those angles."

She stared at her clipboard for a few seconds. He could see her knuckles turning white from the intensity of the grip. Eyes narrowing behind her glasses, she aimed a cold, deadly glare at him. "You said two reasons. What's the other?"

He'd debated with himself about letting Mark's secret out of the bag. But Kandy's safety was uppermost, not the career machinations of an assistant director.

Josh told her about the offer to direct the sitcom.

"I had no idea," she said. "Does Kandy know?"

He nodded.

"But why would you suspect him of doing these things? He has no grudge against her."

"Not an obvious one, but Kandy told me you all have run-of-the-show clauses built into your contracts. Is that true?"

She nodded. "Who wants to leave a hit show? They were put in for all the production staff to protect both management and workers."

"How hard is it to break the contract?"

She bit her lower lip and scratched a spot under her chin. "I don't know. You'd need to talk to the legal department. Do you really think Mark's behind all this because he wants to break his contract?"

Shaking his head, Josh said, "I have no proof one way or the other. But it's an interesting point to look into, simply because he's never mentioned it to anyone. I wonder why, and wondering why makes me think there's an ulterior motive behind it."

Stacy adjusted her glasses once again and stared up at him. "Pretty big leap to even consider," she said. "Are you very suspicious by nature, or is it just something you have to do in your job?"

The question floored him, because he had no response for it.

"Never mind. I don't think I want to know the answer."

On the set, Kandy spooned fresh berries into a tart.

"You know," she said, rubbing her chin again, "Kandy's wallet was missing for a week."

Josh nodded again.

"Whoever took it could have gotten some of her personal information that way and not necessarily from anything connected with me. Have you seen her wallet?"

"No."

She rolled her eyes. "It weighs about a pound and it's filled with scraps of paper with everything from phone numbers of friends and business people to passwords for some of her accounts. I've been telling her for years she needs to transfer information as soon as she gets it to her cell phone or computer, but she never does."

He felt bad he'd put the idea into her head, but in the next minute he thought she might be protesting just a hair too much.

"Regardless," he said. "I need to look at everything, every bit of info, no matter how small, as it relates to Kandy."

Stacy nodded. "I'm going to get some coffee. Want some?"

He declined.

For the next three hours he stood watch. With a comfortable ease, Kandy sailed through the interview with the cohost, trading light and humorous banter, and then just as effortlessly moved to the cooking segment. As he'd been before, Josh was amazed at how simple she made everything seem, while he knew the real truth behind the hours of preparation it took to bring the meal to delicious fruition.

When the segment was completed and they were ready to leave, Kandy asked her cousin, "They know where to send it?"

"Yup. I gave the delivery service a time and approval to pick up the food."

"What am I missing?" Josh asked as they settled into the limo.

"Everything I just cooked is being sent to a women's shelter in Harlem."

He stared at her, speechless.

"What?" she asked.

"Nothing," he said. "I'm just continually surprised by you."

A crooked smile coupled with twin commas of confusion lit her brow. "I think that's a compliment."

Without stopping for a break, she went from the television interview to the radio station, and then on to Barnes & Noble for the book signing. Josh couldn't believe the throng of people lined up and around the two-block-square area. When she alighted from the limo, waving and smiling at the crowd, Josh said to Stacy, "She's like a rock star."

"Yeah." A huge grin split her face. "She is."

Reva met them inside the bookstore, beaming like a beacon when she saw the swarm.

"I called the local news stations when I got here and saw all this," she told them, reaching up to kiss her client's cheek. "The manager says there haven't been this many people waiting for an author since that kid wizard's last book. You're a hit again."

Kandy smiled, and shook the bookstore manager's hand.

As he stood behind her for the next few hours, Josh was again impressed by Kandy's graciousness. She never hurried a fan along, or interrupted a story about cooking or baking thrown at her. She was courteous, pleasant, and considerate to all who asked for an autograph or to take a picture. Several times Josh moved in closer when a fan got a little too close or became a little too ardent for his taste. As many times as he did, Kandy shooed him away with a flick of her hand. At two o'clock, the beaming store manager thanked her and kissed her cheeks.

Laughing, Kandy followed Reva and Stacey out the back door to the waiting limo.

"All three local networks showed." Reva was unable to keep the glee from her face or voice. "Babe, you can't buy this kind of publicity."

"I'm starving," Stacy announced as they climbed into the limo.

"You coming?" Kandy asked Reva, who stood outside.

"No. I have things to do. But I'll meet you at the television studio at four thirty. Don't change. That color looks great on tape."

"I wasn't planning to," Kandy told her, bussing her agent's cheek.

"Where to, Kandy?" David asked from the driver's seat.

"What do you want?" she asked her cousin.

"I'm craving pork dumplings."

"Call Wong Fat's and tell them we're on the way. Did you hear that, David?"

"You got it. ETA, fifteen, twenty minutes."

"You like Chinese food?" Kandy asked Josh.

"It's a food group."

She laughed. "Then you'll love Wong Fat's. Best lo mein in the state."

For the remainder of the ride to Chinatown, the cousins worked out the scheduling for the following three days of studio production.

Josh was amazed at how fresh and unfettered Kandy looked. She'd been up for almost twelve hours, cooked two full brunches, and been asked more questions than he'd been asked in all of his professional career. And she still smiled, laughed, and appeared in general to be having a good time.

"No cooking for the five o'clock news, right?" she asked Stacy.

"Nope. Pure book promo."

Josh felt his gut twist when she sighed and closed her eyes.

How anyone could keep a pace like this and not drop to their knees with exhaustion intrigued and baffled him.

But then, the gorgeous woman seated across from him intrigued and baffled him as well.

* * *

Directly after the late lunch, the trio was back in the limo and on their way back uptown for her next television spotlight piece.

Once again Kandy sailed through the interviewer's questions about her cookbook, charming both her and the television audience. It was almost six thirty by the time they were dropped off at the condo.

A quick check on the answering machine showed, thankfully, no messages.

Kicking her shoes off in the foyer, she stretched. "I'm taking a shower," she told him. "We have to leave at seven forty-five for Gracie Mansion."

Nodding, he asked, "No tux for this event, right?"

"No. Jacket and tie is fine."

She disappeared into her bedroom, leaving Josh to do the same.

The nervous energy he'd stored up all day following her around and not being able to gather any new information needed immediate attention.

He went into the guest room and called Rick.

"What have you got for me?"

"A couple of interesting things about Mason."

"Go ahead." Josh grabbed a notepad and pen from his briefcase.

"In addition to having a background as an actor, it seems he's been trying to get out of his contract just like the other guy, Begman, has."

"You're kidding."

"Nope. Hired a hotshot Hollywood litigator by the name of Patricia Grimble. Ever heard of her?"

Patty. "No. She any good?"

Rick snorted. "Evil is a better word. She's all shark. Anyway, she's been burning up her cell phone with calls and texts to Mason for the past month."

"How did you find out it was about the contract and not something else?"

He could hear Rick's smile through the phone. "The old Bannerman charm."

Josh pinched the bridge of his nose. "Just tell me whatever you did was legal," he said.

"How long have you known me? Or course it was legal. But I may have to fly out to California next week to make good on a dinner invitation. Anyway," he added, "my *source* said Mason wants out and he wants out ASAP. No reason given."

"I wonder if getting out of his contract would become a moot point if production was halted."

"What put that thought in your head?" Rich asked.

Josh told him about the note on Kandy's pillow.

Rick whistled and then said, "Yeah, makes sense. Threaten the safety of the cast and crew, production would stop, and maybe the show would be canceled because of it."

"That's a pretty big stretch to cancellation," Josh said. "From everything I've seen and heard about this show, the network isn't going to do anything to jeopardize it being on air. It's a cash cow for the sponsors."

"Does Kandy have the authority to pull the plug?"

"Actually," Josh said, frowning, "I don't know. Whoever wrote the note thinks she does, because everyone knows how loyal she is to her crew."

"So making a threat against them might influence her to cease production."

"Yeah." Josh nodded. "Makes the most sense so far. I'll find out if she has final say. Anything else?"

"Yes," he said. "Alyssa Mason was in rehab about six months ago. Very hush-hush. The press never got wind of it."

"For what?"

"Booze. She's a bit of a nasty drunk, too. Went in kicking and screaming, but completed the program. She was discharged thirty days later."

"Interesting."

They signed off a minute later with Rick promising to keep digging. Josh booted up his laptop to get some more work done before they had to leave.

* * *

For the third time Kandy searched her jewelry cabinet but couldn't find the pieces she wanted to complement her outfit. The same uneasy feeling she'd had when she'd arrived home from California and thought her clothes had been rearranged blew through her head. These were the times she felt her borderline OCD was a good thing, because she knew without doubt she'd been robbed.

She bolted from her bedroom wearing just her robe and called out Josh's name.

He materialized from his side of the condo in an instant.

"What's wrong?"

He moved so quickly, she barely blinked before his hands were wound around her upper arms. Like her, he hadn't finished dressing yet, his feet and torso bare.

Kandy had to mentally force herself to look up at his face and not the broad, chiseled, expanse of his chest.

His naked chest.

"I've been robbed," she told him, swallowing hard. "There's some jewelry missing I know I saw just the other day in my cabinet."

"Show me."

Kandy described the pieces she'd intended to wear: two diamond bracelets with a matching drop-slide necklace, the diamond teardrop, three carats.

"You're sure these pieces were in here? You didn't put them someplace else so they'd be easily accessible, planning for when you'd wear them tonight?"

"No. They were in here Friday morning. I checked before we left for the studio because I knew how tight my schedule was going to be today."

Josh ran a hand threw his still-damp hair. "How come you don't keep them in a safe, or at the bank?"

"Because I like easy access. If I kept them at the bank I'd be making trips to it almost weekly. And I never had a safe installed in here because, well, I *felt* safe."

Josh shook his head. "Are you sure nothing else is missing? It's just those three pieces?"

"I don't know," she admitted. "I was focused on those."

"Go look while I call the police. A theft like this needs to be reported."

With a sigh, she frowned. "Josh—"

"I know, Kandy." He gripped her upper arms again and through the robe she felt his warm fingers soothe. "But I can't handle a theft like this. The police need to be the ones to investigate it."

Resigned, she nodded.

While she searched through the jewelry cabinet tucked inside her walk-in closet, she heard Josh speaking on the phone.

Within fifteen minutes two uniformed police officers were shown into her condo.

In addition to the bracelets and necklace, Kandy couldn't find a ring that had belonged to Grandma Sophie and a pair of pearl earrings that were a present from Gemma.

"Your insurance company have pictures of the pieces?" one of the uniforms asked.

It was Josh who answered. "I've already called them and reported the theft. They're faxing the photographs over to my office and I'll have my partner run them over to the precinct."

"Any idea of the value of the jewelry, Miss Laine?" the other officer asked.

Kandy stole a quick look at Josh and then said, "In total, they're worth about two hundred and fifty thousand."

The police asked to speak privately with Josh, so Kandy took the opportunity to call Stacy and relay the events of the evening so far.

"Are you going to come to the event?" Stacy asked. "I can give your regrets to the mayor."

"No, we'll be there. Just get everyone settled at the table. I don't want to miss this."

"Kandy, it's perfectly understandable if you cancel."

"I know, but we'll be there. Let everyone know we'll be late."

Stacy's sigh was long. "Okay. You know best. I'll see you when you get here."

Kandy pressed the End icon on her phone. When she turned, Josh was standing in her bedroom doorway, his hands folded into his pants pockets.

"Are they gone?" she asked.

He came into the room and nodded. "Since there was no evidence of forced entry and you live in a doorman-protected condo, there's not much they can do except file a report and put the word out to local pawnshops and such."

"They're not even going to dust for fingerprints or anything?"

His lips lifted a little at the corners. "I doubt it. Unless whoever took the jewelry tries to sell it, their hands are pretty much tied."

"This just sucks."

"I agree." He stared at her for a moment. "I heard you talking to Stacy. You really feel up to going to this shindig?"

"No, not really." She sat down on a corner of her bed. "But I feel like I have to. Do you think this is related to…you know?" She bit the edge of her bottom lip. For some strange reason she couldn't bring herself to say it.

"I actually do." He leaned a hip against her dresser. "And I think you do, too."

She nodded and dropped her gaze down to her phone. "It feels the same way it did when I got back from California. Like someone was in here, going through my things."

"Only this time they took something."

The sadness that had soaked into her system when she'd discovered the theft gave way to anger. She nailed Josh with a determined glare. "I want to know who's doing this. And I want to hurt them."

"I know, Kandy. I want that, too. I promise you I'll make whoever it is pay for all this."

In that moment she knew one very real and total truth about the man she was rapidly losing her heart to: he kept his promises.

"Come on," he said, pushing off the dresser. "Let the police do their job. Get ready."

She nodded again and rose from the bed with a sigh. "I need about ten minutes."

* * *

When he met Kandy in the foyer, he was clean and fresh in a deep blue suit and matching tie.

"You look nice," she said, tossing her keys into her purse. "Very professional."

When he saw the midnight-blue strapless dress she was garbed in, he wanted to say, "You look good enough to eat," but didn't. Instead, his gaze raked from tumbled-coiffed head to four-inch-heeled toes, his stomach doing flips at the length of leg in front of him, and said, "So do you." He hoped the heat burning inside of him didn't show in the gravel in his voice.

She dazzled him with a broad smile and Josh realized she knew exactly how damn good she looked. In lieu of the jewelry she'd planned on wearing, she'd opted now for simple and sparse, just a gold chain with a small sapphire at the base, a pair of matching earrings, and a thin, gold wristwatch on her left arm.

In the elevator she explained the evening ahead of them. "Every year the mayor hosts his Citizen of the Year banquet. I always buy a table."

"It's a fund-raiser?"

Nodding, she fiddled with the stone at her neck.

"Proceeds go to summer programs for inner-city kids. It's a good cause. Most of the people who get this award have helped the public in some major way. Last year the award went to Captain Brad Stefans. Have you heard about him?"

Josh told her he hadn't, realizing he'd been caught staring at the low-slung bodice of her dress.

With a smile he could describe only as sly, letting him know he'd been caught, she continued. "He was a chaplain stationed in Afghanistan and was wounded during one of the air strikes. Came home in a wheelchair and started teaching English to non-English-speaking Latinos and Asians in the community, free of charge."

"Impressive," he said, shifting his gaze to the doors when they opened. He left first, glancing around the area, and then stepped aside for Kandy to exit.

"The only down part is the food. It's usually not very good."

Josh grinned. "Are you saying that because you're not catering it, or because it really isn't?"

Tossing her hair over her shoulder with a quick flick of her wrist, she pierced him with an ice-cold gaze and said, "You can judge for yourself when it's served, but one thing you should realize by now is I'm not catty when it comes to food. I cook well. That's just fact, not hubris. The food at this affair is donated by various restaurants in the city so all the money raised can go toward the charity. There's no set fare, just small samplings off their menus. Usually it's either overcooked, undercooked, or cold. Last year Reva had a piece of fish that was raw on the inside —and it wasn't supposed to be. Plus, there's no set theme, so spicy is mixed in with bland and you never really know what you're getting. I hope you have a strong stomach."

The haughty tone, meant to put him in his place, failed. As Josh watched the cavalier way she walked away from him, balancing perfectly on shoes any other woman would have cringed in pain to wear, he felt a live wire shock him with a megavolt of power.

He wanted those legs wrapped around his waist, holding tight while he disappeared into her.

He wanted to yank that barely-there-dress off her body and brand her, letting everyone know she was his and his alone.

He wanted more than anything to tell her how much he desired her, craved her, hungered for her, as no man ever had before.

He wanted to do all that and more.

But what he wound up doing was following her through the lobby. A sudden thought blew into his head and he put out a hand to hold Kandy still and turned back to the porter's desk to the doorman, whose name he'd learned was *Andy*.

Before he could ask a question, Andy said, "Miss Laine, I'm so sorry about what happened."

"It's not your fault," she told him.

"Did the police ask you anything? Anything about suspicious visitors, or people you didn't recognize?" Josh asked.

"Yes, sir. I told them no one unusual came by, and I've been here all weekend."

"No one came with, say, a delivery for Miss Laine?"

"No, no one, just—"

Josh's ears perked up. "What?"

His brown eyes looked sheepishly from Kandy then to Josh and back to Kandy again. "Well, Mr. Chandler stopped by on Friday evening, asking if you were home."

"Evan?" Kandy's risen voice echoed in the entranceway. "Evan was here?"

"Yes, miss. He arrived, oh, about, ten-ish on Friday. Told me to let him up to see you. I remembered you'd taken his name off the visitor list, so I told him no and asked him to leave."

"How'd he react?" Josh asked.

The doorman's lips thinned, his eyes narrowing. "Not well. He called me a few nasty names. I told him I was going to call the police, and after a few harsh descriptions about my mother, he left."

"Moron," Kandy muttered.

"Did he come back?" Josh asked.

"No, and like I said, I've been on duty all weekend because Sanderval's wife is sick."

Josh pulled at this bottom lip and asked, "Would it be possible for me to get a look at the security footage for the building?"

"Right now? I can't leave my post until I'm relieved at eleven."

He turned to Kandy, "We should be back by then, right?"

"We should. But even if the program goes long, we can just leave whenever we want."

"Okay," Josh told Andy. "Wait for us to get back. Don't leave, okay?"

"You got it. Anything for you, Miss Laine."

Josh understood the sheepish devotion dancing across the man's face. He put a hand to Kandy's back and said, "Let's go."

Chapter Twenty

"Food's lousy as usual," Reva declared, tossing her fork down.

Kandy looked over at Josh and lifted an eyebrow.

He smiled into his water glass.

"You should volunteer to do this shindig next year, sis," Gemma said. "At least we'd get a decent meal."

Josh put down his glass and surveyed his dinner companions.

Reva was seated next to her client and across from him. When they'd taken their seats after being shown into the spacious ballroom, Kandy had purposely placed herself opposite Josh, squeezed in between her agent and Stacy. To Stacy's right was Harvey Little. Next to him, Gemma—without her camera for once. Alyssa Mason was seated to Josh's right, next to her husband, who rounded out the table of eight.

When they'd arrived almost an hour late, everyone began asking Kandy questions at once about the robbery. She attempted to downplay the incident, saying the police were on the case and that she was lucky she was insured. Reva had pierced Josh with a penetrating stare, but she'd backed down when he gave her a small shake of his head.

"You know," Gemma said, "I had to cancel my date tonight so you could have a seat with us."

Turning his attention to her, Josh tried to discern by her expression if she was mad about it.

She smiled at him. "Thanks. The guy was a real bozo. You did me a favor."

Josh grinned. "I aim to please."

"Have you found out anything about…you know?" Her eyebrows rose as she finished her sentence.

"Moving along."

Thinking of what his partner had discovered, Josh turned his attention to Alyssa. She'd been drinking heavily since they'd arrived and hadn't touched any of the food offered to her. Neither had Kandy, but she wasn't guzzling Cosmopolitans by the cocktail glassful.

Josh studied the model for a few moments, concerned when he saw her eyes trained on Kandy. Her gaze never wavered from its piercing scrutiny, and the expression on her face turned sour when Kandy laughed at something Cort said.

For his part, the director appeared more nervous than usual. He frequently snuck glances at his wife and to the drink in her hand. Several times Josh heard him whisper for her to eat something, but she flipped her hand at each entreaty, dismissing him.

Wanting to draw her attention away from Kandy, Josh leaned over and said, "You're not a fan of the food either, I see."

Amber-colored eyes, slightly bloodshot and glassy, tried to focus on him when she turned.

"I wouldn't eat this bloody crap if you paid me," she said, in a voice that didn't care if it was heard.

All heads at the table turned toward her. Cort slid his chair closer and said, "Babe, not so loud. One of the chefs is at the next table."

"I don't care." Her voice remained shrill. She polished off her drink and commanded her husband get her a refill.

"Don't you think you've had enough?" he asked.

"No."

"Come with me to the bar, then."

"No. I want to sit here. Go on. *Go.*"

Josh was embarrassed for the man when he saw Cort's shoulders sag as he rose to do as he was told.

Next to him, Gemma whispered, "What a bitch."

As soon as Cort was gone, Alyssa slithered into his seat and said, "I'd like to speak with you, Kandy."

Kandy's bland smile was in total contrast to the vibrant one she'd had on her face just moments before.

"It's about you and my husband." Alyssa's words were slow and slurred as they stumbled from her fuchsia-colored lips. Reaching across and draping herself over an annoyed Reva, her voice remained loud and piercing. "I know what's going on."

Confusion on her face, Kandy asked, "What are you talking about."

"I know about the two of you. About the late hours together, just you and him. He's always at the studio with you. *Working,* he says. You can't fool me. Everything's 'Kandy this' and 'Kandy that.' I know you're having an affair with my husband."

The last sentence was shouted. Several inquiring gazes turned toward their table.

"Alyssa," Kandy said. "Lower your voice."

"I will not." She tried to straighten in her seat, her spine falling flat against the chair back. "Everyone should know what a whore you are."

"Oh, *Christ,*" Reva exclaimed, rising. "Here comes Baker from the *Post*, pen flying. You don't need this. Come on. We're out of here."

Kandy rose, as did Gemma and Stacy.

"Wait just a second, you," Alyssa said, pointing at Kandy. "I'm not finished."

Gemma sidled up along the drunken model and grabbed one of her emaciated arms, while her sister took the other. "We can talk about this more outside. Ladies' room. Now," Gemma ordered.

Kandy nodded, and together, they pulled Alyssa along with them, Stacy following. Josh thought it looked like an easy task, since all three women were roughly the same height, and Kandy and her sister weren't drunk.

When he rose from his chair to follow them, Kandy caught his gaze and shook her head.

Alyssa continued to sputter and spew as they made their way from the room, all eyes glued to them. Reva strode up to the *Post* reporter and barred him from following them. Slinking her arm in his, she propelled him to the other side of the room, smiling her killer grin and promising him who knew what, just to divert his attention from the evolving scene.

Josh told Harvey, "I'll go get Cort."

He found the director at the cash bar, a half-full glass of beer in front of him.

"They all out of Cosmos?" Josh asked.

Cort jumped. "Sorry."

When Cort looked up at him, he related the scene at the table, saying, "Alyssa thinks you and Kandy are having an affair." His eyes gauged the director's expression.

Cort gaped at him. "Well, it isn't true. *You* know that."

"Yup. *I* do. Your wife is another matter."

Cort took a large gulp of his beer. Shaking his head, he said, "She's been like this for weeks. Crazy. Accusing me of cheating on her, of not loving her anymore." He clicked his tongue and added, "I love her so much it hurts."

"Why does she think you're straying? What have you done to make her think that?"

He got the reaction he wanted. All the color drained from Cort's face. "N-nothing."

Josh shook his head. "You can lie to your wife, Mason, but not to me."

"What are you talking about?" He took a handkerchief from his pocket and swiped at his brow and upper lip.

Josh waited until Cort had returned it to his pocket before replying. "I'm a private investigator."

Silence met his declaration. The sweat on Cort's brow multiplied and the handkerchief was once again pulled free.

Josh regarded the movement. "And I know you've been meeting with a lawyer to try and get out of your contract."

If it were possible, Mason's color paled more, his skin turning an ashen, waxy hue.

"How—?"

"It doesn't matter."

"Does Kandy know?" he asked, his voice small and scared.

"Not yet. But don't you think it would be better if you told her, instead of having her find it out from someone else?"

Cort downed the last of his beer and signaled to the bartender for another. "I can't," he said, head hanging, eyes closed for a moment. "I just can't. She's been so good to me, so unbelievably fair and kind. I know she'd hate me for trying to jump ship when the show is number one."

"I think you're being unfair to her," Josh said, shaking his head when the bartender asked if he wanted anything. "If she's been so good to you, why have you been sneaking around behind her back? What kind of payback is that?"

Exhaling deeply, Cort dropped his head into his hands. "The worst kind, I realize now. But you don't know what it's like at home."

"Try me."

Cort's eyes were beginning to cloud over. He downed more of his drink, then said, "Alyssa wants a film career, and she wants me to help her. She's a good actress, she really is, but she's just so demanding and picky. She wants me to direct her because she thinks I'll give everything to her, do anything for her. She's right, too. But day after day she harps at me about it. She's threatened to leave if things don't change. I can't let that happen. I love her so much. But she hates Kandy. She thinks she has this huge, impenetrable hold on me."

"Alyssa doesn't know you've been trying to get out of your contract, does she?" Josh asked.

"No. I wanted to surprise her when it was all done. I knew there would be bad feelings with Kandy and the network. But I love Alyssa. I want to help her. I can't do that *and* direct the show."

Josh nodded and waited for a second, debating with himself. The investigator in him had the final say.

"Did you know Kandy's been receiving harassing phone calls, in addition to some other incidents, including the dead rat in the herb garden?"

Cort's head shot up. "What kind of calls?"

Ignoring the question, Josh said instead, "Your wife called her a whore in front of everyone inside."

Cort's eyes, just a few seconds ago beginning to look glassy from the alcohol, instantly cleared.

"That's been the general tone of the phone calls," Josh said, waiting for his reaction.

The moment Cort's eyes froze in fear, Josh knew he'd made the connection.

"You don't think Alyssa..." Shaking his head, he said, "No. She couldn't. She wouldn't. Can't you have the calls traced or something? You said you're a private investigator. Isn't that what you do?"

"They're always from disposable cells. Untraceable."

"I don't think Alyssa even knows about those kinds of phones. She's not the one doing this. I know it."

At that moment, Josh spotted Gemma making her way toward them.

"Alyssa wants to leave, Cort. She's over by the ladies' room."

"Is she...how is she?"

"Drunk but cooperating. Kandy had a good, long talk with her."

"What did she say?"

Gemma's gaze went from the director to Josh and back again. "She'll tell you on the way home."

Cort chugged the remainder of his beer and slapped a few bills down on the counter. He fled without another word.

Gemma moved into his vacant spot and sighed. "I don't want to have to go through a scene like that again in my lifetime."

"What happened?"

"Kandy will fill you in. She took most of the hit. I just stayed by the door to make sure no reporters snuck in. She wants to leave, too. I told her I'd come get you."

Josh turned to go.

"One thing I will tell you," Gemma said, pulling at his sleeve. When he stopped, she said, "I think Alyssa may be the one tormenting Kandy."

"Because?"

"Alyssa called her some very descriptive names. They sound like the gist of what's been said in the phone calls, according to what Kandy told me. What are you going to do?"

"Take Kandy home."

He could tell his response annoyed her, but he didn't care. What he did care about was seeing if Kandy was okay.

He spotted her when he came out of the bar. She was talking with the mayor, or rather, the mayor was talking. Kandy had a tight smile plastered on her face as she listened. Anyone else would have thought she was engrossed in what the man was saying, but Josh could see from the flat, distant look in her eyes she wasn't.

For the first time since he'd known her she looked tired and worn-out. Beautiful as always, but weariness had finally surfaced.

He cut a quick path across the spacious lobby.

When she saw him coming toward her, she visibly relaxed under his gaze.

* * *

"All the recording equipment for the security system's in here," Andy said once they'd returned to Kandy's apartment building. He'd led them to a room the size of a large utility closet down the hall from the visitors' desk.

"It's on a continual loop," he said, taking a seat behind a small desk.

"Can you call up Friday and Saturday night?" Josh asked.

"No problem." He fiddled with the computer keyboard connected to a series of flat screens in front of them.

"There's Evan." Kandy pointed to one of the screens.

"This is Friday," Andy said. "You can see here is where he started getting nasty."

Kandy's gaze flicked over the monitor as Evan became increasingly agitated. He'd balled his hands into fists and they hung, suspended from his sides, as if poised to strike. The hallway camera was situated above and behind him so they were able to see his face only in profile, but Kandy could almost feel the rage flying across it. After a moment he spun around to storm out and they had a full view of his face.

"It looks like you really did break his nose," Kandy said, slanting a look at Josh.

"And he never came back?" he asked Andy.

"Nope. Not the next night, either. I was here. I'd know."

"Scan the cameras on Kandy's floor, anyway, please. Friday and Saturday."

Andy nodded. "Here's the one outside the elevator on her floor."

He sped through the playback and Kandy watched several of her neighbors getting on and off the elevator. Her mind began to drift, exhaustion both physical, and emotional, starting to seep into her bones.

The scene with Alyssa had been unnerving, the venom the young model released at her, vicious and potent. She gave example after example of the times Cort and she were supposedly together while Alyssa waited expectantly at home for her husband. Through the booze-filled torrent, Kandy started to feel sorry for the girl, but knew she wasn't the one responsible for Cort's late nights away from home.

Her mother's words drifted back, and for the first time Kandy considered Cort *could* be cheating on his wife. How else to explain his absences?

She was pulled out of her musings by Josh's voice.

"That's Saturday night. The time stamp reads two A.M."

A figure stepped from the elevator on her floor.

"Who is that?" she asked. "Is that…Evan?"

It was hard to tell from the clothing. The man—if it was a man—had a black, nondescript hoodie pulled up over his head, the brim jutting out to conceal most of the face.

"The height's right," Josh told her. "Stop it there," he said to Andy. He continued to stare at the screen, his eyes darting back and forth across the silhouette. "Is there any way you can clean this up, get better definition?"

"No. Blowing up the image'll just distort it more."

"Okay. Can you follow where he's going?"

"Yeah. There are cameras at the end of each hallway."

He typed in a few keystrokes and the images came up on the screen. "I'll put them in columns so you can see them side by side."

"That's my door he's stopping at," Kandy said, moving closer to the screen.

The trio watched as the hooded figure removed something from his pocket. In the next second he disappeared into the apartment.

"He's got a key. I never gave him one," Kandy said. She whirled around to face the doorman. "How did he get by the security desk?"

Andy's face reddened and his gaze dropped to the floor. "I honestly don't know, Miss Laine. I usually make my rounds at about that hour. Maybe he was just waiting until I left the desk."

"Don't you lock the front doors when you leave the desk unattended?" Josh asked, cutting Kandy off from asking the same question.

"Yes, and I did. I'm sure of it. I don't know how he got in."

"Well, it's apparent he has a key to my apartment," Kandy stated, anger pushing through her exhaustion. "He probably has one to the front entrance as well."

"I wish we had a better view of his face," Josh said, his eyes on the monitor again, "to prove it really is Chandler."

"Who else would it be?"

Josh ignored her and told Andy to fast-forward a few minutes.

"Here. He comes out of the apartment at two twenty. Enough time to take the jewelry."

"He's not going back to the elevator, though," Kandy said, pointing. "Looks like he's heading down by the stairway."

"That leads down to the parking garage," Andy said, typing in another series of keystrokes. "Let me line up the time stamps."

"There." Josh pointed now. The hooded figure exited through the garage stairway door. "You still can't see his face. And his hands are shoved in his pockets, so you can't tell if he's holding the jewelry."

"There's no doubt he's got it," Kandy declared. "Everything fits. The time, the fact that I was gone for a few days. If this is Evan, he's the one who stole it."

And the fact that he had not only infuriated her, it saddened her as well. Evan Chandler was just one more man who'd been a disappointment to her.

For someone so smart and business shrewd, Kandy recognized how naïve she was when it came to judging men. She'd loved her father unconditionally until he'd destroyed her trust by leaving the family and never looking back. That she'd chosen men throughout her life who were more like her father than not was worrisome.

Josh took a moment to flip through his phone and, while he called the officers who'd been assigned to the case, Kandy crossed her arms over her chest and closed her eyes.

Chapter Twenty-One

They rode the elevator in silence, Josh sensing she didn't want to talk about what had happened, and he allowed her the quiet time, knowing they'd get to it eventually.

"I'm starving." Kandy tossed her keys on the foyer table and toed off her shoes when they got back to her apartment. "You hungry?"

"I could eat." He followed her into the kitchen.

"Is an omelet okay?" she asked, reaching into the refrigerator.

"Kandy, I think you could make shoe leather okay."

Tired amusement flickered in her eyes.

"An omelet is fine," he told her, taking off his jacket and laying it across the back of a chair. "Can I do anything?"

"No. Just sit."

Kandy set about making the omelets without a word between them. She chopped scallions and grated cheese as the eggs set in the pan. There was something almost mesmerizing and hypnotic about the way she prepared a simple meal. All her movements were as precise and coordinated as the most arduous and exacting ballet choreography.

When she tossed the ingredients into the pan then swirled them up in the air, flipping and mixing them together, an unconscious sense of accomplishment and pride crossed her face. She poured them each orange juice in cut-crystal glasses, and set the filled plates before them.

Sitting across from each other at the breakfast bar, Josh's stomach muscles contracted when her eyes rolled and her lips curled in delight at her first taste.

"You know." He swiped his mouth with the linen napkin she'd given him. "I think I finally get it about cooking. About the way *you* cook, anyway."

"What do you mean?" she asked, forking in another bite.

"Watching you put together a full meal or just cook something simple like this, you get an incredible rush from it, don't you? From the prep work to the actual cooking to the eating. It calms you. Consoles you. Makes you feel better no matter what kind of a day you've had."

Kandy lowered her fork to her plate, all the while staring at him.

"It also," he added, "lets you be in total in control. The way the food comes out is dependent on you, on how you prepare it, cook it, and serve it. You're in absolute control from beginning to end. Comfort and control." He took a sip of orange juice and met her gaze. "Two very powerful emotions."

Kandy's hand continued to grip the fork. "How do you do that?" she asked. "How do you break something so complex down into something so easy? It's amazing."

Josh finished off the omelet. "No, it's not, not really. I'm a good observer. Most people aren't."

"More than good. You pegged my mother from the moment you met her. I've never seen another man do that."

Josh's grin split across his lips. "Your mother is priceless and harmless. My guess is most people don't look past her blatant flirtatiousness to see the actual woman beneath."

"You did. From the second you met her, you knew what she really was."

"Of course I did, Kandy," he said, refilling his juice glass. "Don't forget, I'd already met you and Gemma. I figured the rest of your sisters were pretty much like you two, personality-wise. None of you could be the way you are without a strong female in your lives to have influenced you so positively."

Kandy frowned. "But what about Grandma? She was one of the strongest women I've ever known, and she never flirted with anyone. Grandpa was the big tease there."

With a nod, Josh said, "And a lot of *what* you are is based on her influence. *Who* you are is another story."

"I don't understand," she said, finishing off her omelet.

Josh took a breath and then finished his juice. He rose and crossed to the sink, glass and plate in hand. "Sophie gave you a love for cooking. All the aspects of it, including the sense of accomplishment it brought."

"That's obvious."

"Hannah, on the other hand, taught you how to be a survivor."

Scratching her head, Kandy asked, "Explain that."

"You were thirteen when your dad left?"

She nodded and took her own dish to the sink, rinsed both sets and put them in the dishwasher while Josh continued.

"Old enough to understand the implications. Old enough to see how it affected your mom. And old enough to appreciate how difficult it must have been to keep you all together."

Resting back against the counter, Kandy crossed her arms in front of her, making her breasts swell across the top of her skimpy, tantalizing dress.

Josh's heartbeat galloped when he saw the beautiful flesh pop up into his view.

"Right. I remember some discussion about the younger ones going to live with Aunt Lucy or Aunt Trudi for a while. Mom refused to split us up."

"And worked two full-time jobs and a part-time weekend one to make sure you could all live together."

She nodded. "Mom was a sticker. She could have run out on us just as easily as Dad. Seven kids—and all girls—was a big responsibility. But she didn't."

"No. She stayed and tried to make it as easy as she could on all of you.."

They were silent for a moment as Kandy digested that. When her eyes found his again, she said, "So you think seeing how she stood her ground and went on with her life is what makes me the way I am?"

"Pretty much. Gemma's the one who still has some anger issues with your mother. Displaced anger, I think. But when I've seen you together with your mother, or heard you on the phone with her, I only hear and see love. And acceptance."

Kandy made her way back to her chair. Folding her hands in front of her on the table, she said, "Simple Psych 101 profile, aren't I?"

Josh sat down across from her, leaned his elbows on the counter, and said, "You're anything but simple, Kandy."

"I feel simple lately. Simpleminded, anyway. I never saw Evan for who he was, how he was just using me." She shook her head and sighed. "I actually thought he understood how important my career is to me. He acted like he did. When I found out he'd used me, I thought it was over once I kicked him out of my life. I never thought he'd steal from me."

"First of all, we don't know for sure it is him in that video."

"Who else could it be? He'd already come by once. Maybe he really didn't want to see me, just make sure I wasn't home so he could slither back and rob me. You've told me how hard-up for cash he is."

"Those are valid points, but you had nothing to do with his behavior, so don't think you're simpleminded when it concerns him. Chandler, from everything I've found out about him, has always been a user and a loser. Everything about him is phony, every action, every word he ever said to you was done so you'd fall for him, trust him."

"He played me."

The sadness in her voice touched his heart. "You're not the first, Kandy. You won't be the last unless he's stopped. Don't think less of yourself because you thought his feelings for you were real. My bet is the only person he's ever cared about is himself."

"Do you still think he could be behind all the things that have been happening to me?"

"To tell you the truth, I'm not sure."

"He wasn't invited to the birthday party," she said, her smooth brow furrowing. "He knew about it because I'd been planning it for a few months. I'm not sure he could have snuck in without someone seeing him, though. The house was packed. Somebody was bound to have noticed him coming in, don't you think?"

"Possibly. But you had a lot of guests. Not everyone knew one another. Chandler might have been able to sneak in and then sneak out."

"I hear a 'but' in that sentence."

He nodded. "But…why would he? If he'd already planned on robbing you—and we still don't know it was him—why would he drive three hours out and back to put that threat on your pillow? He could have just as easily left it here."

"I didn't think of that. It's doesn't make sense, does it?"

He shook his head. "Not much, like you've said, about any of this, does."

Her frown deepened and he had to physically restrain himself from reaching over to smooth the line between her eyes.

She stared across the table at him for a moment. "You haven't asked me about Alyssa."

"I figured you'd talk about it when you were ready."

"Did Gemma tell you anything?"

He shook his head. "She wanted to let you do the honors, since she spent most of the time at the door, blocking anyone from entering."

Her mouth pulled into a wistful grin. "Like Cerberus guarding the entrance to hell."

Josh chuckled. "Ready to talk now?"

"I guess so."

She gazed down at her hands, still folded and resting on the table. "You heard her accusation?"

Josh nodded.

"She honestly believes I've been having an affair with Cort. *Cort!* Quoted me chapter, book, and verse about how many times we've been together after hours at the studio. She even said she heard me call out to him to hang up once when he was on the phone with her. It's ridiculous."

"Did you tell her that?"

"Of course I did. Numerous times. Didn't do a bit of good. She's convinced I'm trying to steal him away. That I want to be the only woman in his life. She must have said ten times how he'd promised he'd help with her acting career but I was in the way. That everything was 'Kandy this' and 'Kandy that' at home."

She stopped and looked across at him. He could read the hurt and ache on her tired features from Alyssa's allegations.

"None of it's true. Cort is a friend. One of the closest, most dependable, trustworthy people I've ever known. I've never even looked at him as anything but that. Certainly never as a lover. How come she can't believe it? How needy can she be? And how can he put up with her?"

"Did she say anything other than just her suspicions? Give you any facts?"

"How can she have facts? I'm not having an affair with him."

"Calm down, I know you're not. I was just wondering if she had anything tangible to back it up."

Taking a deep breath, she unfolded her hands and ran them down her arms. "I'm sorry for yelling, but I just can't understand any of this. She said he's been meeting with me after work hours almost every night. I told her it wasn't true. Cort has been leaving around the same time as everyone else since we started production this season."

He debated whether or not to tell her. To find out Cort had been keeping something so monumental a secret would hurt. And Josh knew she'd been hurt almost more than she could stand of late.

"Oh," she said, "there's something I wanted to tell you."

He waited.

"Gemma believes Alyssa's behind the phone calls."

Josh nodded. "She told me before we left the banquet. Said Alyssa called you the names you've been hearing on your answering machine."

Frowning again, Kandy said, "Yeah, she did. And we've both thought all along the voice was a woman's. Also," she said, sitting upright in the chair, "she was at the beach house this weekend. She could have easily left the note for me."

"I thought about it after I heard her at dinner. But would she really know how to rig a light so that it would fall on you? And she was nowhere near LA when you had your accident."

"How do you know?"

When he started to tell her, she put her hand up and said, “No, don’t. I already know. Background research.”

He nodded.

She thought for a moment. “So she didn’t rig the car to crash. She still could have had a hand in the lighting accident, or the rat in the herb garden. She has access to the studio.”

“How?”

“Through Cort. She could have swiped his passkey at any time to set those things up, don’t you think?”

“It’s a possibility, yes.”

“I can tell by the look on your face you don’t think she’s the one, do you?”

“I’m not ruling anyone out. I’ve told you that before.”

“Well, for what it’s worth, I’ve changed my mind about Evan.”

“How so?”

“I fully believe he could be behind all this now. Jumping out at me the other day, stealing my jewelry—”

“We don’t know for sure it was him, Kandy.”

“*I’m* sure. He needs money and knows I keep my jewelry here. It makes sense.”

“I’m not ruling anyone out,” he repeated.

“Well, you can’t think it’s Cort. I mean, he’s being persecuted by his wife, for pity’s sake. It can’t be him. There’s no reason for it.”

The inner debate about whether or not to tell her finally came to a head. “There’s something you don’t know,” Carefully, he told her about Cort’s desire to leave the show.

Her expression changed from disbelief to sorrow and then to anger as his words washed over her.

Before he was done, she shot up from the table and bolted out of the room before he could tell her why.

* * *

She ran into her bedroom and came to a full stop in front of the windows, physically barred from going any farther. The drapes were open, the nighttime Manhattan skyline lit and shining into the room.

“Why?” she asked the empty room, her body rigid and taut. *Why, when everything is going so well? Why does he want to leave?*

She stared at the glass, imagining Cort’s face reflected back at her. His kind eyes and poet’s mouth pulled into the chronic grin she hadn’t see him wear for a while. When had it disappeared?

She'd thought they had a great working relationship, thought they were friends. She'd trusted him, had put her professional faith and judgment in him.

They'd clicked from day one, and now he wanted out and hadn't given her the courtesy of telling her. Had he even considered her feelings or how his leaving would impact the show?

Kandy closed her eyes.

When Josh had told her about Mark Begman's desire to leave the production, she'd been surprised, but had understood his longing to branch out, move up in the industry. She even silently applauded him. In her mind, it was a strategic career move and when the day eventually arrived, knew she'd wish him good luck and much future success.

But Mark wasn't a friend. Cort was. Or at least she'd thought he was.

Heated anger ran through her system.

Some friend. Friends don't sneak around behind your back, betray your trust for their own gain, and dismiss your loyalty.

Betrayal. It was, apparently, a running theme in her relationships with men. Kandy shook her head and scrubbed at her eyes with the palms of her hands.

First, her father had claimed to love his wife and his daughters—*his girls,* he'd called them, always with a bright smile. After he'd left, she'd remembered noticing how his smile didn't quite make it to his eyes when he asserted that love. She hadn't understood why at the time. Looking back at her childhood, her father had never done things with them like take them to the park, play, or read with them, leaving the bulk of the parenting to Hannah. There wasn't a time in her memory that she could recall her parents not yelling and arguing, despite her father's words that he loved them all. Too young to recognize this dichotomy, she'd nonetheless learned a valuable lesson when he decamped. Namely, words and actions don't always go hand in hand. Her father had claimed to love them but had never really demonstrated it.

His defection from their family was her first experience with betrayal and pain caused by a man.

Evan Chandler had been the second big one.

Clicking her tongue in disgust at the thought of him, she crossed her bedroom rug and flung open her closet door. She'd told Josh there was no doubt in her mind Chandler was the one who had stolen from her, and there wasn't. She knew he was fully capable of it. She'd dropped her guard, let him into her protected heart, and, once again had been deceived by untrue words. If she'd looked at him with open and assessing eyes as she did now, she would have seen a carbon copy of her father. A smile a little too tense around the edges, laughter a tad too forced, even a way of looking at her when she was speaking, giving the impression he was totally engaged, but a subtle glassy shift in his gaze telling her he wasn't, that his attention had been wandering.

Evan Chandler was a phony through and through, and even though she now knew him for the man he was, his deception still stung. With hindsight, though, she realized it was her pride and not her heart that had taken the brunt of the damage.

Two men who'd been important to her at different times in her life, and both of them had betrayed her.

And now she could add Cort Mason to the list.

Yanking at the chain around her neck, she gave vent to all the resentment boiling in her while she wrestled the clasp open.

How could she have been so stupid? So naïve? He'd pretended to be her partner, and then conspired with a lawyer, attempting to slither out of his contract.

She stopped, the unclasped necklace dangling from her fingers.

Again, why? Why did he want out? He'd always seemed so happy at work, so eager to be there. Well, until recently. She tried to think back to when she'd started noticing his nervous tic of jiggling his keys. It appeared when they'd started filming the new season, she was sure of it. She'd thought the unconscious movement had been related to problems with Alyssa. Lord knew the woman was a bitch in stilettos and the most emotionally needy woman she'd ever met.

Stacy agreed with her that Alyssa's continual interruptions during the day were annoying, but she was Cort's problem, not theirs.

Was that the reason he wanted to leave? To appease Alyssa in some way?

Kandy played with the chain, running it through her fingers. It couldn't be about money, could it? As the director of such a popular show, he must have been making more than enough to support his lifestyle. And even if he did want more, all he had to do was ask. The network made a bundle from her show through their sponsors. There wouldn't have been an issue in raising his salary.

If not money, then…what?

Had he, like Mark, been approached to do something else? Another show? Possibly a movie? Cort had mentioned at the beginning of their working relationship that his ultimate goal was to direct a major film. Maybe he'd been given the opportunity to do so and was too worried about how she'd react if he wanted to leave.

Her old insecurities suddenly reared up. *Or is it me? Am I the reason he wants to leave?*

What had she done or said, or even *not* said, to force him to stab her in the back this way?

Scenes of the two of them in editing, easily bantering back and forth a point about a shot, or the way something was lit sprang into her mind. The scene morphed into a verbal showdown about a recent camera angle and how she'd forced her opinion on him, making him edit out the part she didn't want, even though he'd wanted it left in.

Several times during filming she'd demanded more than one take during a scene, even though Cort had assured her the first was perfect. She'd fought him every time, and every time he'd given in.

At the beach house, Josh had accused her of being demanding, of assuming total control in every aspect of her life, especially her show.

She closed her eyes again.

He's right. *Good God,* he's right.

She'd acted like a dictator. All her talk about the staff working with her not for her, all of them being a well-connected team, was nothing more than pompous chatter. It meant nothing.

Had Cort finally had enough?

Okay, so his ego was probably sore, but he still could have told her he wanted out.

Kandy sighed, loud and deep. Men and their egos were such a mystery.

Cort's betrayal cut to the bone. He was one of the few people she felt she could trust implicitly, and now that trust was shattered.

He should have come to her, told her what he wanted. She would have understood.

Kandy bit down on her lip. But would she have? Really? Could she understand why he wanted to leave? Given him her blessing and sent him on his way?

No. She wouldn't have. She would have been as mad and as hurt as when Josh told her, no argument there.

She tossed the necklace into the cabinet, took the earrings from her ears, and dropped them carelessly into a drawer.

She concentrated on opening the clasp on her watch, but for some reason couldn't quite undo it.

After several failed attempts, she grew frustrated, shook her hand back and forth, and then punched the top of the jewelry cabinet a few times with the flat of her hand.

A stream of curses exploded from her, and like a chained animal she scratched at her wrist in a vain attempt to remove the annoying piece of jewelry.

"Kandy?" Josh appeared behind her. "What are you doing? What's wrong?"

His voice was low and calm and all she wanted to do was scream.

"Nothing."

He glanced down at her wrist. She did as well, realizing she'd scratched herself raw. Jagged red lines had sprouted up her forearm and around her wrist.

"Here, let me help," he said and reached for her hand.

"I don't need any help." She snatched her wrist back.

He didn't respond, just simply waited her out. After a few tense moments, all the fight oozed out of her.

"Oh okay. Fine. Here." She thrust her hand back at him. "It's stuck. Probably broken, like everything else in my life," she muttered.

Before she ended the sentence Josh had the watch open and was handing it back to her.

"You don't have to look so smug about it, you know." She tossed it into one of the cabinet's drawers, then slammed it shut.

When she turned around to face him again, he'd moved back to her bedroom and was leaning against the dresser.

"That was some pretty colorful language," he said, trying to suppress a grin.

Her face heated and she crossed her arms in front of her chest. "I'm sure you've heard worse."

He let the grin break free. A moment later his face went serious again. "You okay?"

"I'm hurt, more than anything."

"Mason?"

She nodded. "I get he wants to leave. I really do. But I wish he'd been honest about it and had come to me, discussed it. Talked it over. It hurts that he felt he had to go behind my back. But." She stopped and took a ragged breath. Biting down on her bottom lip, she glanced away from his face and added, "I realize that's probably as much my fault as his."

"Oh?" His own face could have been a blank piece of paper for all the expression—or lack of it—she saw looking back at her.

Her eyes narrowed to slits, her lips creasing at the edges. "Yes, *oh.* You're the one who made me see how overbearing and domineering I could seem—"

"I never said that, Kandy."

"—to others." She shook her head. "Maybe not in those precise words, but the thought is the same, so I take some of the blame for him being so secretive. What I can't understand is why he wants out. The show is number one. Nobody leaves a hit show. It's like professional suicide."

"You ran out of the kitchen before I got a chance to finish." Josh told her about the conversation he'd had with Cort at the reception bar.

When he was done, she sighed. "I should have realized it had something to do with Alyssa. That woman is a soul-sucker."

His soft chuckle warmed the air around her.

With the pads of her fingers she rubbed her eyes, and blew out a breath. "I'm so tired of all of this. Every bit of it, from nasty phone calls to thieving ex-boyfriends. I want this over. I want my life back, Josh."

"I know."

What propelled him to reach out for her she'd never know, but when he pulled her into his arms—arms she folded into easily and willingly—and whispered against her hair, "It'll all be over soon, Kandy, I promise. It'll all be okay. Soon."

She closed her eyes and drank in the comforting, solid, and steadfast feel of him. "When?" she asked, her face burrowed in his shirt. "I want it over now."

With one hand around her waist to keep her secure, Josh trailed the other up and down her back, gently rubbing, while his lips pressed against her temple. "Shhh."

In a heartbeat she went from tired and angry to aroused, as his fingers danced up and down her spine. She knew he meant to comfort her, but his actions had entirely the opposite effect.

She stilled, and when his grip loosened, her hands wound up around his neck and she brought herself fully against him, clinging with all her strength. She tilted her head and skimmed her lips across his jaw.

"Kandy—"

She ignored the warning plea in his voice and brought her mouth to his.

At first, the kiss was slow and thoughtful. His mouth was gentle and full of tender solace as it pressed against hers.

But Kandy didn't want gentle, and she certainly didn't want solace. She laved at his bottom lip with her tongue, pushed his lips apart and dived in.

In a snap, the kiss changed.

What was unhurried and caring, became urgent and wanting, sending spirals of delight up and down her spine, making her feel as if she'd burst into flames.

Her mind went into a tailspin at the velvet warmth pressed against her. Her nails raked at his neck, slunk down the collar of his shirt to tease the skin at his back. When his mouth moved to her neck, sucking at the soft spot just under her ear, Kandy's nipples hardened to hot, throbbing pebbles.

Cupping his face in her hands, she forced his lips back to hers and with a boldness she was coming to accept from herself, plunged her tongue back into the delectable caverns of his mouth, and feasted. His heart pounded under her fingers as she wove them into the front of his shirt, snaking a hand around the buttons and popping them open. His chest was stone-solid and molten-hot. When her nail scratched across one flat nipple and felt it pucker in a twinkle of time, power surged to her very soul. She moved her lips down the angle of his jaw, over the rapid heartbeat at his neck to rest in the soft mat of hair on his chest. Trailing wet, open kisses across the firm pack of his pecks, Kandy heard him moan, and felt his shudder of need burst underneath her hands.

In one swift and effortless motion, he lifted her and carried her to the bed.

Staring up at him, a myriad of emotions blazed like gamboling flames in his moss-colored eyes.

"Kandy?"

She laid her palm across his mouth and her stomach muscles tightened when his tongue licked across it.

"Don't say anything," she whispered. "Please."

He took her hand with his own and kissed it with such utter tenderness, Kandy melted from the inside out.

Stretched out fully on his side, Josh rested on an elbow; Kandy was spread on her back next to him.

Without another word, he brought his mouth back to hers.

As they drank from each other, Kandy sensed how right being with him felt. Nothing was as right, as certain, as this was.

Their kisses grew frenzied, bolder. The dull ache in her heart at Cort's betrayal disappeared as if it had never existed when Josh sighed against her neck.

She rolled on top of him, her dress hiked all the way up her thighs, and straddled him, her hands tethered around his neck so she could kiss him again.

His erection pulsed against her, held in check only by the fabric of his pants.

Josh reached behind her and dragged the dress zipper down her back, slipped the material from her shoulders and down, freeing her breasts into his hands. She knew no other man, at no other time, would ever make her feel this good, this cherished, or this adored.

The couture dress was reduced to a huddled slip at her waist as he dragged it down the length of her torso, his wicked mouth following in its wake.

As his tongue tantalized and teased her sensitive nipples, rolling around their hardened peaks, she arched to give him free range to all of her. When his tongue dipped into the tiny opening of her navel, she lifted her hips and Josh switched their positions, holding her as he spun them around.

Flat on her back now, Kandy laid back on the pillows as Josh moved lower, his mouth never leaving her skin, marking her as his own with each and every touch. He pulled her dress off and carelessly tossed it to the floor. His teeth scraped along the outer edge of her lace thong, grabbing it between them and drawing it down. Kandy lifted her hips as he slid it down and off with mind-numbing slowness. Every inch of skin it skimmed across, his lips and tongue followed.

All kinds of sensations danced on Kandy's body as he sucked the hollow at the back of her knee, the indentation where her ankle began, the spot just below the arch of her foot.

At last, he tossed the thong on top of the dress and parted her legs with a gentle nudge of his nose. When he put his mouth on her and drew his tongue across the length of her heat, she fisted his hair in shaking hands. His tongue danced and dipped around her, pulling the swollen nub deep into his mouth, sucking as if its existence was nourishment he desperately needed. Wave after rolling wave of pleasure shot out from his touch.

He glided two fingers inside her, his thumb continuing its rhythmic dance across her heat.

"Josh."

She wasn't sure she'd said his name or even why until she felt his warm breath against her and heard him say, "Right here, Kandy. I'm right here with you."

His fingers continued their tantalizing torment, moving in and out, stretching her sensitive skin. She clenched around him with each soft thrust, his fingers slick with her moisture.

The crest began to peak and she grew helpless against it. When the deep, rolling spasms engulfed her a moment later, all her senses were centered on the pleasure pitching through her.

Her insides were still quaking when Josh placed a sweet kiss to her thighs. Slowly, slowly, he removed his fingers from inside her. Kandy watched him stand and shed his own clothes, carelessly tossing them on top of hers.

Raised in a house almost entirely of women, the Laine girls had spent countless hours as teenagers wondering about the male body and imagining what it looked like, how it felt, how it functioned.

Naked before her now was a man so magnificent, nothing in her imagination had come close to the reality of Joshua Keane.

He bent to her and claimed her mouth again, his hands exploring every inch of her body.

Kandy's hands began a none-too-subtle exploration of their own.

She trailed her fingertips across his torso, raking the skin with a featherlike scrape. She smiled when she felt how rapid his breathing was, his chest rising and falling as she moved in his arms. She pinched his biceps, charmed when he flexed against her fingers.

His stomach muscles were defined and toned, and the glimpse she'd seen of them when he'd gotten into bed reminded her of a marble statue, carved and cut to exquisite perfection. The thick mat of hair trailing down his abdomen, down farther, had her fingers itching with need. She circled her hand along his shaft, felt it jump and pulse as she wrapped her fingers tightly around it. Kandy swore Josh stopped breathing. His mouth, his glorious, hot mouth, went still on her neck, as she moved up and down the length of him, deliberately, tortuously.

"Kandy."

"Right here." She smiled, giving him back his words. "I'm right here with you, Josh."

He pulled up to look at her. Kandy's own breathing ceased at the shocking, mindboggling level of intensity and heat in his eyes. She couldn't see any green at all; his black, dilated pupils had obliterated all color.

"Sweetheart," he said, softly. "I don't have anything to protect you."

Without a word, she reached over to the nightstand. In a heartbeat she had a condom foil in her hands, ripped, opened, and on him in less time than it took him to draw a jagged breath from her touch.

He shifted and parted her thighs with his knee when she fell back again. Kandy opened for him, lifting her legs up high over his hips to rest, crossed at the ankles, on his back. She could feel the coiled tension across it, the muscles flexing and extending. Josh, stared down at her face again, a question in his eyes and across his brow.

For a silent answer, she snaked her hand around his neck and pulled his mouth back to hers.

In the next instant, she felt him, stiff and fiery, at her entryway. She dragged a hand down his back, rested it on one exceptionally fine, firm butt cheek and pressed him fully into her.

Heat met scalding heat.

He fit perfectly, sliding along her walls, not a fraction of space to spare between them. With a slow and languid rhythm, Josh moved within her, filling her all the way up to her soul with each small thrust.

That extended beat promptly changed, as he quickened the pace, Kandy keeping up with the tempo, movement for movement.

This was the only man for her, now and forever. She knew it in her heart, in her very being.

Blinding lights exploded behind her eyes when Josh moved one final time, emptying into her and draining them both. On a broken sigh, Kandy whispered his name and with it, her love.

Chapter Twenty-Two

It was difficult to believe he could still breathe. It was unfathomable to think he could experience such pleasure and live. He had to have died and shot straight to paradise, because that's where he was.

Heaven. Pure and simple.

When her nails scratched gently at his back, Josh knew even heaven didn't feel this good.

Rising on an elbow, he stared down at her lovely face.

The lazy smile traipsing from corner to corner of her mouth made the hairs on the back of his neck stand at attention. They hadn't even moved apart and already he wanted her again.

She was so beautiful. Her face, calm and peaceful for the first time in hours, was devoid of all the heartache she'd been put through.

To say he was pleased to have put a smile on her face was an understatement.

To feel his life and their relationship had changed forever in the span of an hour was the absolute heart-stopping truth.

To know he loved her with all his being and yet he still had a job to do for her was torture.

Complete and gut-wrenching torture.

He hadn't meant for this to happen now. He'd wanted the person tormenting her locked away and out of her life before he told her what she meant to him.

Seeing her so despondent, so saddened by her disappointment in Cort had cut right through his heart. When he'd taken her in his arms, his only goal had been to reassure. The moment he felt her lips on his, that objective had shifted to need.

His.

He'd heard those small words, gasped, just as she came that final time with him buried deep inside. Words that changed everything, not only because he felt the same, but because he knew she would never have given them a voice unless they were true.

He needed to tell her what she meant to him, what he wanted with her, for her.

For them.

But still, his deep sense of honor to see her problem through came first.

"Kandy?" he whispered.

"Mmmm?"

Her satisfied, sexy smile made his insides clench.

When she opened her eyes, and he saw every emotion she possessed swimming in them, he hated himself.

"Are you okay?"

Her mouth spread into a huge grin, as her eyes laughed at him. "I am now."

He rested his forehead down on hers and sighed. His own ears heard it wasn't the sound of contentment it should have been after what they'd just shared. She shifted and stared up at him, her unlined brow furrowing.

"What's wrong?"

His heart broke when he heard the doubt seeping in the simple question.

"Kandy…I don't know what to say to you." He sat up and threw his legs over the side of the bed, head hung in his hands.

"About what just happened?" she asked, sitting up as well, pulling the sheet over her exposed body.

"Yeah." He swiped his hands through his hair and sighed again. He moved to the bathroom, discarded the condom, and came back to her. "It shouldn't have. Not like this. Not now," he said, unable to meet her eyes. "You were upset. You needed to be comforted and I, well, I let it go further than I should have."

When he finally looked at her, his heart broke in two.

Ravaged was the only word to describe the way she glowered at him. Eyes wide and constricted, moisture forming at the corners, trembling lips now white, almost matching the chalk in her cheeks.

He'd hurt her. Hopefully, not beyond repair.

"Kandy, I'm sorry—"

"No." She shot up from the bed, yanking the sheet as a shield. "Don't you dare say that. *I'm* the one who's sorry. More than I can ever tell you."

"Kandy, please—"

"Get out!"

On that order, she fled into the bathroom and slammed the door.

Her sobs broke free immediately. Knowing he was the cause of such heartache was devastating. Torn between duty and love, he had to choose duty. Rising, he reached for his pants, gathered up the rest of his clothes, and went back to his room.

* * *

Kandy cried herself dry.

He's sorry. Sorry! God, what a thing to say after...she sat down on the edge of the tub, still cocooned in the sheet.

It was more than just sex. *It was.*

There'd been a connection, a melding of more than just bodies. She'd felt it the moment his lips responded to hers. Total surrender on both their parts to what was happening between them.

She was no fool, no naive little girl. She knew the mechanics of sex, the hows and whys. She hadn't known what true lovemaking was, though; that was the truth. To give yourself—your total self, your control, and all that came with it—over to someone, was amazing. She'd never done that before, never allowed herself to be so unconcerned, so uncontrolled in her actions. She'd relinquished every ounce of herself, her body and her spirit, to him. Kandy knew what they'd shared had been unique. She could feel it in her bones. Josh had wanted her with a desperation and desire only she could quench.

And she'd felt the same.

He was everything she'd never let herself dream of, wrapped into one beautiful and able-bodied package.

"And," she said aloud, turning on the shower, "he's *sorry* for what happened."

While the steaming water sluiced over her, she could feel small tremors shuddering through her insides, where Josh had been just minutes before.

She wasn't sorry for what they shared, that was certain.

Stepping from the shower, she wrapped a towel around her body and sighed as she towel-dried her hair.

Mechanically, she slathered lotion on her face and ran a comb through her hair, pulling it up into a high ponytail.

Men.

A look of disgust fanned her face as her reflection mirrored back at her.

Angry, hurt, confused, and knowing she'd never get any sleep, Kandy tossed on a pair of jeans, a T-shirt, and her running sneakers.

Work was the only thing to help her forget all the unpleasant things she'd heard tonight. From Alyssa's accusations, to Cort's secret, and finally to Josh's hurtful apology, all Kandy wanted to do was run away from it all.

So she sought refuge in the one place she knew no one would be around to bother her.

* * *

Josh finished his shower and wrapped a towel around his waist. He thought he heard a noise in the foyer, opened his bedroom door, and peeked out.

Nothing. No sound, no light, no movement.

Thinking Kandy might be in the kitchen, he walked across the hallway.

Again, he found nothing.

The apartment was quiet. Uneasily so. Stealthily, he moved down to her bedroom. The door was ajar, the light still on, the bed unoccupied. He crossed the carpeted floor with as little noise as possible and went into the bathroom.

It, too, was empty. He noticed the towel, folded on the rack, and felt it.

Damp. The shower, as well.

He moved back into her room and looked around. Her purse was gone, as was her cell phone, and the one he'd given her.

He jogged back to his room and dialed the number. When the metallic-sounding message came on, Josh cursed and tossed his phone on the bed. Without wasting a moment, he dressed, took his gun out of his briefcase, checked it, and slid it into the waistband of his pants.

In the parking garage the space her Corvette occupied was empty.

Cursing, he ran out onto Park Avenue and tried to hail a cab.

He knew at once that she'd gone to the studio, knowing how work was her salve for everything.

And he was royally pissed she'd gone alone.

Chapter Twenty-Three

Kandy tossed her purse on her desk and glanced over the day's filming schedule Stacy had left for her. They'd be shooting two segments patterned on recipes in her new cookbook, so she decided to get the prep work started.

Taking the elevator to the studio kitchen, she thought of Josh.

By all rights, as her bodyguard, he should be with her. Because she'd been angry, she hadn't told him she was leaving. When he found her gone, he'd be mad.

And right now she didn't care.

In the functioning kitchen she preheated two ovens to the desired temperatures. There were six professional stand mixers in a rainbow of colors along one countertop and she pulled two of them to sit next to the ovens, then gathered all the ingredients she needed to prepare the cream cheese–coffee and pineapple-blueberry upside-down cakes on the schedule.

When both mixtures were placed into buttered and floured tins, she put them in the ovens and set the timers. She wanted to make sure the studio was prepped appropriately, but when she went down the hallway something struck her as off. When she crossed to the set, the studio lights were on. The last thing her crew did every night was shut off the stage lights. To find them blazing bright at two A.M. was odd. The second thing she noticed was the toolbox, opened and sitting atop a counter. It was then she heard a noise coming from behind it.

"Hello?" she said, startled when her own voice echoed back. "Is someone here?"

The noise ceased. When no one answered her call, Kandy's stomach clenched.

"Hello?" She moved behind the counter and her heart all but stopped. "Mark? What are you doing here so early?"

"I could ask you the same thing." He rose from his crouched position, a wrench in one hand.

The calm, quiet tone of his voice sent a shivery thread of worry down her spine. She glanced at the wrench and then back to his face.

"Is something wrong with the oven?"

Taking a step toward her he said, "Not yet." His eyes were bright and focused, his gaze glued to her face. Smacking the wrench against one palm, he asked, "Why are you here so early, Kandy?"

"I—I had some work to do before filming."

"That's too bad. I'd hoped to finally end this today."

"End what?" But as soon as the words were out of her mouth, she knew.

"You."

Tossing his hands up in a "What can I say?" gesture, Mark shrugged.

"Why? Why would you do this to me?"

"It's not about you, Kandy." With a shake of his head and a frown, he added, "It's those damn iron-clad contracts of the network's. They can't be broken."

"Any contract can be broken, Mark."

"Yours can't."

Squinting, the bright set lights haloing him from behind, she asked, "Is this why you've been tormenting me? Just to get out of your contract?"

He nodded again. "It was the only way I could think of. Try to rattle you, maybe get you to take a leave. I figured I could get production stopped, the show would be put on hiatus, or better yet, canceled." He shook his head, his gaze trained on her face. "You should have stayed away from the studio, like I warned you to. I've got no choice now. This has to look like an accident."

Adrenaline shot through her system. In the time it took to decide what she should do, she sprinted across the studio, aiming for the hallway. Running as fast as her legs would take her, Kandy felt herself tackled from behind just as she reached the closed set door.

Mark shoved her up against it, the force of his body flattening her face across the steel portal. He ground the sharp edge of the wrench against the small of her back, pinioning her to the door.

"This show's killing me," he growled into her ear. "Killing my career. I've got opportunities. Now. Not in two years, when the contracts expire. I'm sorry, but I've got no choice."

He grabbed her ponytail and yanked her away from the door.

Kandy saw lights explode behind her eyes when he hauled her in front of him. She tried to smack at him with her hands and nails.

When he brought the wrench down hard on her shoulder, Kandy felt the blow, sharp and cutting, and then the room dissolved into blackness.

* * *

"Can't you go any faster?" Josh asked the cabbie.

"There's laws against speeding, mister."

Josh pushed back into the seat, disgusted.

It had taken him ten minutes of running around Kandy's neighborhood before he found a cab with its light on. It was just his luck the cabbie had to be an honest, law-abiding citizen.

"We're almost there," the driver said.

Josh saw the building looming close ahead. Before the cab came to a complete stop, he tossed a twenty-dollar bill at the driver and bolted.

"You want your change?" the cabbie called.

Josh ignored him and tore up the front steps.

One of the night watchmen rose from his seat as soon as Josh burst through the revolving door.

"Where do you think you're going?" the man asked, a hand dangling above his weapon belt.

Josh tore his license from his wallet and shoved it in the man's face. "Is Kandy Laine here?"

Gazing from the picture on the license to Josh several times, the man finally asked, "Why do you want to know?"

With every ounce of reserve he could muster, Josh blew out a breath and said, "I'm her bodyguard. She left without telling me where she was going. Now, is she here?"

Nodding, the man snorted. "Gave you the slip, huh? Yeah, she's here. Came in about a half hour ago. Said she had work to do."

Without thanking him, Josh ran to the elevator and pushed the button for her office floor.

What was I thinking?

Leaning the back of his head against the ice-cold metal, Josh realized he hadn't been thinking at all. He'd been reacting, pure and simple.

To the way Kandy looked when she reached out to him.

To the way she smelled—sweet and tangy like warm apricots—when he cradled her close.

To the delicious way she tasted.

No thoughts were needed when it came to figuring out why he'd broken every rule he'd made for himself and given them both an hour of relief, of pleasure.

Of love.

Jumping out of the elevator when the door opened, he bolted to her office.

"Kandy?"

When he found it empty, he searched her desk. Seeing the day's shooting schedule, he quickly guessed she was in the studio.

Forgoing the elevator, he shot to the stairwell and thought about how he'd left her, the harsh words between them, and the way he'd hurt her.

His only thought was how he could make it up to her.

The bitter odor of gas assaulted him when he pushed through the studio doors. Alarmed, he ran down the corridor to the set, the smell becoming more intense the closer he got.

The scene he found stopped him dead.

Kandy was sprawled on the floor in front of an open oven, not moving. Mark Begman stood over her, a propane torch in one hand, a cigarette lighter in the other. The hiss of gas releasing from the oven was loud and Josh's nostrils burned at the acrid stench.

"I'm sorry about this, Kandy, I really am," Mark said. He coughed and swiped a hand at his eyes. "It's my only way out."

Mark cocked the lighter open. Without thinking, Josh called out, "Mark, *no.*"

The assistant director turned, the lighter and unlit torch still suspended in his grasp.

"Keane."

Josh ran toward him, the powerful smell choking him.

"No! Stop," Mark called out. "Don't come any closer."

Josh halted. "What are you doing, Mark? Don't light that torch. This whole room'll blow."

"That's the plan."

Josh inched closer. "Think about what you're doing. You'll kill yourself along with Kandy and me."

"No, I won't. I've got it timed. Stop right there, Keane. Stop."

Josh pulled up short.

"You won't get away with this," he said. "You know you won't."

"You're wrong."

"Is it worth committing murder just to get out of a contract?" Josh asked.

Mark's face registered his surprise. "You know?"

"About the contract and your chance to direct."

"It's all I've ever wanted to do. I can't let that damn contract stop me. Not now. Not when I'm so close." Mark lifted the lighter.

Josh needed to get closer. His gun was tucked into the back of his pants, and he knew he could stop Mark if he could get off a good shot.

Mark flicked open the lighter, moved his thumb to the crank position.

"Mark, don't!"

As the words came from him, Kandy moaned and rolled to her side, her hands bracing her head.

Distracted, Mark glanced at her and Josh took his chance.

In three steps he had his gun out, poised and cocked at the AD. "Drop them, Mark. Drop them! Now."

Josh knew he was on dangerous ground. One spark from either the lighter or his gun would set the place ablaze.

"Mark?" Kandy rubbed her neck. "What are you doing?"

"Kandy! Get up. Run."

She looked over at him.

"Drop them, Mark," Josh repeated, his eyes never wavering from the man.

With one swift glance at Kandy, Mark tossed both items directly at Josh and bounded from the set. Josh deflected them, ran to Kandy and asked, "Are you okay?"

Helping her stand, his arms tight around her, Josh saw the dark, ugly bruise forming on her neck.

"Y-yes."

He reached over to the oven and turned the knob to shut the gas off.

"Come on." He hauled her from the room, through the double doors and into the hallway. Gently, he slid her to the ground. "Stay here." He shoved his cell phone into her hand. "Call 911."

"Where are you going?" she cried, trying to hang on to him.

"Call."

He ran in the direction Begman had.

* * *

The heavy sound of feet running on metal was all the information Josh needed to know where Mark was headed.

The roof garden.

Gun still poised and ready, he took the stairs three at a time until he came to the entrance. The access door was thrown wide open.

Josh went through it.

During the daytime, sunlight engulfed the huge terrarium, warming it, bathing it in natural, brilliant light.

Now, in the dark dead of night, the large, rectangular structure threw shadows and confusing curves at the naked eye. The day's warmth was gone, replaced by an eerie, dank chill.

Josh bumped into a table, stifled a curse, and slunk along the edge of it for a reference point.

"Mark, I know you're in here."

Silence.

Creeping, Josh moved around the perimeter of the table, his eyes trying to adjust in the faint glow seeping in from the moon.

Through the wall-to-wall glass he could see night was fast ending and being replaced by the inky blackness that evolves before dawn eventually creeps over the horizon. In a moment there would be barely any illumination in the garden.

"Come on, Mark. It's over. Don't make this any harder on yourself. Give up now before the police get here."

A soft noise to his left made Josh turn. He never saw the clay pot that pounded down on his trigger arm.

He cried out as the gun shot from his hand, skittering across the floor and out of his reach.

Mark flew after it. In considerable pain, Josh bounded to it as well.

Striking him from behind, Josh landed a blow to the side of the AD's head. Mark countered it by shifting and knocking Josh to the ground. Rolling, each vied for dominance. Mark's fist connected with Josh's throat as his own hand rammed into the AD's midsection.

A shaft of light illuminated Josh's gun and both men saw it at the same time. Mark, who'd been on top, sprinted up and crab-crawled to it, Josh at his heels.

The elevator arrival chime pinged in the distance.

Both reached the gun at the same moment.

Josh thought he had a good grip, but just as he tried to fully wrap his hand around the butt, Mark elbowed him in the throat again, knocking him backward.

Recovering, Josh rose up on the balls of his feet and pushed Mark forward, the gun tight in his grasp.

A moment later, as the struggle for the gun continued, the elevator door opened and the room was thrown into a stark stretch of fluorescent light.

The gun discharged, the blast loud and echoing.

The last sound Josh heard was Kandy's scream.

Chapter Twenty-Four

"Drink this," Kandy said, handing him a filled-to-the-brim coffee mug.

"Grandma's blend?" His voice was dry and gravelly, an aftereffect of being punched twice in the throat.

With a nod, she said, "It'll help."

"I don't think a cup of coffee is going to help heal a bullet wound or make him feel better, Kandy," Gemma said, looking at her sister over the kitchen counter, her eyebrows creased in twin commas of irritation.

"You'd be surprised," Josh said, taking a long, blissful draught of it. Staring across the counter at Gemma, he repeated, "You'd be surprised."

It had been a long, tedious few hours.

Just as Kandy arrived in the herb garden, two armed security guards with her, Josh's finger gripped the barrel of the gun, Mark's finger its trigger. In an instant Josh made a decision to roll right and would think later about how fortuitous the action had been. Mark pressed the trigger at the same time Josh yanked on the AD's hand. The result had been the bullet's deflection off Josh's flank instead of straight into his torso. It was obvious Mark wasn't used to firearms, because he fell backward from the recoil, which gave Josh the edge. He planted his balled fist squarely into Mark's nose, causing a knockout that left both of them sprawled on the floor.

A second later, when Kandy threw the lights on and saw Josh's fallen and bleeding body, she screamed again and flew to his side, while the security guards restrained an unconscious Mark.

All his protestations that he was fine, just bullet grazed, fell on Kandy's deaf ears. She became an oracle of command, issuing orders left and right to the security guards, and then the police and paramedics, who arrived soon after.

She rode in the ambulance to the hospital with him, gripping his hand in a vise clutch. When the paramedic guided an intravenous needle into Josh's arm, her face paled and her lips blanched.

They were met at the hospital by a frantic Stacy, Gemma, and Hannah, who had been notified by the police, at Kandy's request. Reva arrived as Josh was being wheeled into the emergency room bay. Kandy was prepared to march right in with him, but an intractable nurse instructed her to wait outside. When she'd begun to loudly and vehemently protest, it was Hannah who was able to pull her daughter away before they were asked to leave altogether. The moment Hannah saw the growing bruise on the back of her daughter's neck, she'd then started shouting her own orders, demanding someone examine Kandy. While Josh had been tended to, Kandy had been as well. A very quick exam and then a trip to X-ray confirmed she was bruised and battered, but had not suffered any more serious injuries.

Ten stitches, an official visit from two responding officers, and five hours later, Josh was discharged into his own care.

"Is this nightmare really over now?" Reva asked.

"Yeah," he said, draining his coffee mug. Before the ceramic hit the table, Kandy was refilling it.

"Thanks."

"I still can't believe it was Mark," Gemma said, wrapping her fingers around her upper arms. "Why didn't he just ask to be let out of his contract?"

"I know why," Stacy told them.

With all their attention settled on her, she took a deep breath. "After speaking with you, I called the legal department," she said, looking at Josh. "The way the network set up the out clauses, it monetarily penalizes anyone who wants to leave before the contract ends. Heavily."

"How heavily?" Josh asked.

"Depending on the position, anywhere from half to three-quarters of a year's salary per year left on the contract."

"As an AD, Mark must make what? Sixty, seventy thousand a year?" Gemma asked.

"Ninety-five," Stacey said. "I had personnel pull his salary records."

"That's quite a chunk of change," Josh said, "to level all at once."

"I can understand how he rigged the light," Gemma said, "and left the disgusting present at the Hamptons house. But I still think Alyssa was responsible for all those calls."

"She wasn't," he said.

"How do you know?" Hannah asked, finishing her second cup of coffee.

"The uniforms who came to see me told me they found several disposable phones in Mark's car. They backlogged the calls and traced three of them made to Kandy in the past few days."

"Why did he do it?" Gemma asked, tossing an arm around her sister's shoulders.

"My guess is he wanted it to look like Alyssa," Josh said. "He made sure to casually mention Alyssa called Cort numerous times every day, and pegged her as a jealous bitch."

"He did," Stacy said. "One night when we were out to dinner, I don't know how it came up, but he said he thought she was insanely jealous of Cort."

"He said something about it to me in the Hamptons, too," Josh said. "He planted that seed of doubt in many minds."

Kandy shook her head and then looked back over at him.

"One other thing you need to know," he told her. "Mark was in LA when you were. I had my partner check. He arrived the day before you did, left the day after the crash."

Kandy swallowed. "Then he did do something to our car."

Josh nodded.

"We could have been killed," Kandy cried.

"Could have, sweetheart," Hannah said. "But you're all here, safe and sound."

"He sure had me fooled," Gemma said. "I thought he was a nice guy."

"Me, too," Stacy said, her lower lip trembling. "I feel like a jerk, Kandy. And I feel responsible. He probably got your private numbers from me somehow, just like Josh suspected."

Kandy broke free of her sister's arms, and went to hug her cousin. "Don't say that, Stacy. Don't even think it. He fooled all of us."

"Still," Stacy said.

"Was he behind my wallet going missing?" Kandy asked.

"Yup," Josh answered. "The cops think it's how he got some info he needed about you, not the least of which is a spare key you keep in it to this place. Something you neglected to tell me."

Kandy's cheeks turned red. "I forgot it was in there."

Josh nodded and sipped from the mug. "He made a copy of it. It's how he was able to get in and riffle through your clothes."

"Why would he do that?" Stacy asked, her brows scrunched together under the top rim of her glasses. "It's…weird."

"A campaign of annoyance is the best bet. He wanted to rattle you, make you nervous, make you doubt yourself."

"It worked," Kandy said.

The kitchen grew silent for a moment.

"Obviously," Stacy said, taking off her glasses and rubbing the tears from her cheeks, "we're not filming today."

Kandy smiled for the first time in hours. "Really? Who made you boss?"

"Me. It was a bloodless coup," she replied, hugging her cousin again. "I've already let everyone know. Even Cort."

Kandy's smile died at the mention of the director's name.

"He wanted to talk to you but I told him he couldn't," Stacy continued. "I said you needed to rest and relax for a day or two."

"How'd he take it?" Gemma asked, glancing at her older sister.

"He said to take all the time you needed. He'd be ready to go again as soon as you gave the word."

"Really?" Kandy said. "I'm sure Alyssa loved that."

"Don't worry about it, Kandy. After all this, I don't think Cort is going anywhere anytime soon," Stacy told her.

"What aren't you telling me?"

Stacy shook her head and stared straight into her cousin's eyes. "Nothing. Don't worry."

Kandy stared back. Finally, her shoulders dropped and she let out a sigh. "I'll deal with him tomorrow," she said. "Maybe."

Stacy grinned and put her glasses back in place.

When Kandy's cell rang a moment later, she answered it and the room quieted while she listened.

"From the gist of what I heard," Josh said when she disconnected, "that was the police."

She nodded. "They found my jewelry."

"Already?" Hannah asked.

Kandy snaked a glance at Josh. "It seems they knew where to look."

Gemma's gaze Ping-Ponged from her sister to Josh. "Well? Are you going to tell us, or make us guess?"

Kandy took a bottled water from the refrigerator, opened it, and before taking a pull, said, "Evan Chandler's apartment."

Gemma made a sound remarkably like a snort. "Asshole."

"That's one word for him," Kandy said. She turned her gaze to Josh. "You told them where to look."

He shook his head. "I just mentioned to the uniforms who were here last night that Chandler had been showing up places, bothering you. From the security recording, the guy who we saw could have been him. Same general description. I mentioned they might want to speak to him. Rule him in or out."

"Well, he's ruled in and, right now, he's in custody for theft. When the police got to his place, they noticed my jewelry sitting on his coffee table from the front doorway. Because it was in plain sight, they were legally able to enter his apartment."

"So a stupid asshole, to boot," Gemma said.

"They want me to come down later and identify everything, but the cop assured me it's my stuff."

"I can't believe all that's happened in the past twenty-four hours," Gemma said, through a yawn. "It feels like a lifetime ago we were in the Hamptons."

Hannah put her coffee mug into the sink and said, "Come on, girls. Let's let these two get some rest. They've had a pretty horrible few days."

Each woman, in turn, bent and kissed Josh's cheek or gave him a hug, thanking him for saving Kandy.

Gemma's hug was the longest. "You're okay. For a hunk," she told him, kissing him full on the lips. With a brilliant smile, she hugged him again.

"Walk us out," she told her sister, grabbing her arm.

Hannah bent down to Josh, took his face between her well-manicured hands and, after kissing his forehead, said, "All this madness is over now." She slanted her head to one side, smiled, and added, "Time to face the music."

With that, she left him alone in the kitchen.

When Kandy returned a few moments later, he could feel her nerves palpitating from across the room. She didn't look at him as she asked, "Want more coffee?"

"No. I've had my fill, thanks."

She nodded and began loading the dishwasher.

Her silence was killing him.

Since coming back from the hospital, she'd kept her distance, playing hostess and catering to everyone present.

And she looked ready to keel over from the strain.

"Kandy."

She didn't turn or stop her actions, just said, "Yes?" as she put another mug into the machine.

"Stop."

She closed the dishwasher door, grabbed a paper towel, and began drying the sink.

"I need to get this done. The porcelain tends to stain if you don't wipe it down right away. I don't want to have to use any harsh chemicals on it if that happens, because it degrades the stone—"

Josh gently yanked on her upper arm, turned her, pulled her into his arms, and silenced her with a kiss.

A sob choked against his mouth.

"Oh, God, Josh!" She threw her arms around his neck. "I was so scared you were going to die. When I heard the gun go off, I knew it was you who'd been shot. I don't know what I would have done if—"

"Shhh," he cooed, rubbing her back. "It's okay. I'm okay. It's all over now. Mark's been arrested. Chandler's out of circulation. Nothing else is going to happen. I promise."

She hugged him tighter and then pulled back when he winced.

"I'm sorry," she said, her eyes trailing to the spot under his shirt that was bandaged. "Does it hurt?"

"It's tolerable," he said with a half wince. "The first time I got shot was worse. Believe me, this is nothing."

She continued staring up at him. Her eyes were wet, her nose was running, and she had purple blotches forming under her lids from lack of sleep and stress.

She was the most beautiful woman he'd ever seen.

And he wanted her to know it.

"Since this is now over," he said, keeping his hands folded behind her back, forcing her to stay close, "we need to talk."

Apprehension shook through her gaze and she tried to pull away.

He tightened his grip.

"Josh, I know what you're going to say. It's okay. I understand."

His eyes became slits. "What, exactly, is it you understand?"

Her shaking started up again and he knew she was having difficulty keeping her nerves at bay.

She swallowed. Twice.

"About…well…about last night. What happened. Between us," she said, clarifying. "You *know,*" she added when he didn't answer.

"You mean when we made love?"

The crimson blush that galloped up her neck to her face almost did him in.

"Well, yes. When we…when we had sex," she said, trying to avert her eyes.

Josh wouldn't let her. "Look at me."

When she finally did he said, "We didn't just have sex, Kandy, and you know it. It was more than that. Much more."

Her eyes widened. When she wet her lips with the tip of her tongue,

Josh clamped down on the little control he had left.

"Much more," he repeated.

"I don't…I mean…"

"I love you, Kandy," he said, rubbing her back, trying to soothe all the nerves and fears away. "I know it sounds crazy since we've only known each other a short time. But believe me when I tell you, I love you."

"What? You…you can't. I mean…what?"

He grinned at her, loving the confused Kandy almost as much as the in-control Kandy.

"I said I love you. I'm in love with you. However you want me to say it, the truth is the same. It's like a lightning bolt struck me, right in the heart, and it had your name on it."

Her eyes widened more, her beautiful mouth parting as her jaw, quite literally, dropped open.

"What did you say?"

"I said, Kandace Sophia Laine, I love you."

"No." She began shaking her head. "No, I mean, what was that about lightning?"

His lips pulled up at the corners. "Something my mother used to tell me and my brothers about falling in love. We'd know it was the real thing because we'd feel like we were hit by a bolt from the sky. Like a—"

"Thunderbolt! Oh my God! I can't believe this. Grandpa used to tell us the same thing. He said the first time he saw Grandma he knew he was destined to spend the rest of his life with her because he felt like a bolt of lightning shot right through him."

Josh's smile grew. "That about describes it."

She continued looking up at him. After a moment she said, "I thought you regretted what happened."

He shook his head. "Not *what* happened, Kandy. Never that. The timing. You needed protection and someone to find out who was terrorizing you. You didn't need everything you were going through clouded. I wanted to wait until I found out who it was. Then I was going to tell you how I felt." He sighed and rubbed her cheek with the pad of his thumb. "Things have a way of getting complicated, though."

"I thought all I was to you was a job."

Through a caustic and melancholy laugh, he pulled her head back to nestle it against his chest. "You stopped being a job the first day. Hell, the first five minutes into it."

They stood, holding each other for a few moments.

A sudden thought sparked through him. Pushing back from her, he raised one eyebrow and said, “I seem to be the only one confessing here.”

It took her a second. The wicked grin that erupted across her face was pure childish glee. “The male ego has always been such a mystery to me.”

“You told me that once before.”

Her grin widened.

“Come on, Kandy. I’m hanging by a thread here.”

She lowered her lashes coquettishly, and he was suddenly reminded of her mother.

“Kandace Sophia Laine.”

Her laugh was free and wild and filled with joy. She threw her arms around his neck, planting kiss after kiss on his face, as she said, “I love you, Josh. I love you, I love you, I love you.”

“Okay, I get the picture,” he said, yanking her back and grinning. He gazed down at her lovely face, and said, “I know this is a lot. Maybe it’s too fast. I know you have plans for your future. Big plans. But do you think those plans could include me?”

Her blue eyes widened again and she cocked her head to one side. “What do you have in mind?” she asked in all sincerity.

He knew she was playing with him. She wouldn’t be her mother’s daughter if she didn’t have some delightful devilry in her. She knew damn well what he was asking, but he said it anyway, wanting and needing to hear her reply.

“Marry me?”

Brows drawn, she appeared to be giving it serious thought.

Playing was one thing. Killing him was quite another.

“Kandy?”

“Tell me one thing first,” she said.

“Anything.” Her pulled her close, inhaled the sweet scent of her hair, and planned on never letting her go.

“You’re not just asking me to marry you because I can cook, right?”

He pulled back and gaped at her. After a moment’s thought, he said, “No, but it sure is a great perk now that you mention it.”

With that, he laid claim to her mouth and her very soul.

ABOUT THE AUTHOR

Peggy Jaeger is a contemporary romance author who writes about strong women, the families who support them, and the men who can't live without them.

Peggy holds a master's degree in nursing administration and geriatric psychology and first found publication with several articles she authored on Alzheimer's disease during her time running an Alzheimer's in-patient care unit during the 1990s.

A lifelong and avid romance reader and writer, she is a member of RWA and her local New Hampshire RWA Chapter, where she is the 2016 Chapter Secretary. Visit her at www.peggyjaeger.com.

Keep reading for recipes from Kandy's Kitchen.

Grandma Sophie's Cran-Apple Muffins

Makes 12 cupcake-size muffins or 6 jumbo muffins

Muffins
1¾ cups all-purpose flour
¾ cup sugar
2 teaspoons baking powder
¼ teaspoon salt
½ teaspoon cinnamon
¾ cup Craisins
1 cup peeled, diced apples
1 large egg
1 cup milk
¼ cup vegetable oil

Glaze
1 cup confectioners' sugar
2 tablespoons cold water

For the Muffins

- Preheat the oven to 375 degrees.
- Coat a muffin pan with nonstick cooking spray.
- In a large bowl combine all the dry ingredients, including the Craisins.
- In another bowl combine the wet ingredients, including the diced apples.
- Add the wet ingredients to the dry, mixing just until a batter forms.
- Fill each muffin cup three-quarters full.
- Bake for 15 to 18 minutes, until a toothpick inserted in the centers comes out clean. The tops of the muffins will appear dry—this is okay.
- Remove from oven and let cool for approximately 1 hour before glazing.

For the Glaze

- Slowly mix the confectioners' sugar with the cold water until a watery paste forms.
- Drizzle the glaze evenly over the muffins using a fork or a pastry bag with a #2 tip, to coat the muffin tops in swirls and streaks.
- Place in refrigerator to cool, or serve slightly warm—the glaze will be gooey!

Kandy's Lobster Mac and Cheese

The ultimate comfort food!
Makes 6 servings (4 if you're really hungry!)

Ingredients
2 slices whole wheat bread
1 tablespoon Italian seasoning
1 pound elbow pasta
6 tablespoons butter, unsalted
1 small onion, chopped
½ cup all-purpose flour
5 cups milk (whole is best)
¾ cup shredded cheddar cheese
¾ cup shredded mozzarella
¾ cup shredded Parmesan cheese
½ cup shredded Swiss cheese
1 teaspoon regular iodized salt
Pinch freshly ground black pepper
8 ounces cooked lobster meat, cubed

Directions

- Preheat the oven to 375 degrees.
- In a food processor, tear the bread and pulse until coarse bread crumbs form. Mix in the Italian seasoning and set aside.
- Bring a 6-quart stockpot of salted water to a boil. Cook the elbow macaroni according to package directions until al dente. Drain and set aside.
- In another 6-quart stockpot, melt the butter over medium-low to medium heat. Add the onion and cook until soft, about 4 minutes. Whisk in the flour, stirring to coat the onion.
- Add the milk slowly, whisking continually so that no lumps form and the flour doesn't cook.
- Whisk for 7 to 9 minutes, until the mixture is thick and bubbly.

- Add the cheeses and stir until the mixture is thickened and the cheeses have melted fully.
- Add the salt and pepper.
- Add the pasta back to the stockpot with the cheese mixture. Add the lobster meat and stir to distribute.
- Coat a 9x13 baking dish with cooking spray covering the bottom and all the way up each of the four sides (glass is best).
- Transfer to the baking dish.
- Spoon the bread crumbs evenly over the top of the macaroni. If desired, add an extra handful of any of the cheeses to the bread crumb topping.
- Cover and bake on center oven rack for 20 minutes.
- Uncover, and bake for an additional 15 to 20 minutes. Do not let the bread crumbs scorch.

Variations:

- Use 8 slices (1 pound) cooked and crumbled bacon instead of the lobster.
- Add an 8-ounce can of peas, drained, to the macaroni mixture.

Keep an eye out for the next in the Will Cook for Love series Coming soon from Peggy Jaeger and Lyrical Shine

Special Agent Kyros Pappandreous scanned the midtown Manhattan street in front of him and swore.

"I want to see the cops who were first on scene *right* now," he demanded of the uniformed NYPD officer next to him. Ky turned to his partner. "How did this happen?"

"It looks like a blitz attack." Jon Winters squinted an eye at the midday sun. "They'd finished lunch, were walking back to the car."

"We didn't have eyes or ears on them?" Ky asked, surveying the gory scene. Two of his best agents were dead, and his witness lay with his face kissing the curb, pooling blood drenching his inert form, arms bent back at his sides in unnatural angles.

"Neither," Winters said. "They were out of touch for an hour, tops. Our guys had their cell phones, but no communication since they left the hotel."

"This is unbelievable." Ky squeezed the bridge of his nose between his thumb and index finger and let out a heavy breath. Three years of work shot to hell in a matter of seconds.

"Agent Pappandreous? You wanted to speak with me?"

Ky turned to the metro officer who approached him, noting the name badge over the left breast pocket of his blue uniform shirt. "Officer Johnson, you got here first?"

"Yes, sir. My partner and I responded to a *shots fired* at one fifteen."

"I want details. Where were you when the call came?"

"Outside a deli between Madison and Fifth, two blocks over. Dispatch alerted us, we raced down, saw the victims on the sidewalk. Whole thing was done by the time we got here."

"Any ID on the shooters? Witnesses? Did anyone see anything?"

"It was pretty chaotic when we arrived. The area's packed this time of day with lunch business. Lotta banks and professional offices are headquartered around here. People heard shots, ran for cover." He referred to his notepad. "I got a few statements about a black van, dark blue, maybe. No one got a license or has been able to give an accurate description of the vehicle. It pulled up, shots were fired, it sped off. Matter of seconds, it was all over and your three vics were on the ground."

"Johnson, I've got a witness," another metro uniform called as he sprinted up to the trio. Ky turned in the direction of the voice.

"This is my partner," Johnson said.

"Where's this witness?" Ky asked.

"I've got her isolated by my squad car." He shot his thumb in the direction behind him. "Says she saw everything, and—get this—she's a professional photographer. Filmed it all as it went down."

"Take me to her," Ky said. "Jon?"

"Yeah, Papps, I know. Go interview this witness. I'll coordinate from here."

"Let's go," Ky commanded the officer.

"That's her." A moment later, the officer pointed to a police vehicle blocking traffic in the middle of the street. "Name's Gemma Laine."

A woman stood next to the vehicle, a cell phone at her ear, her back to him. Tall, maybe as tall as him, and slender, her back tapered down to a minuscule waist, her legs clad in tight, faded jeans. When she turned, Ky almost stopped midstride, the questions he intended to grill her with jumping out of his head. His breath caught as he simply stared at the loveliest woman he'd ever seen.

Hair the color of midnight, straight as a board, fell to just below her shoulders, blowing back from her face in the gentle afternoon breeze. Blunt, chopped bangs, fringed a pair of large, bright blue eyes. Plump, coral-colored lips moved as she spoke into the phone and for a brief, hot second, Ky wondered if they'd taste as delicious as they looked.

Her gaze stayed on him as she spoke.

"I've gotta go," she said into the phone. "Yeah. I'll call when I'm done. Love you, too."

"Miss Laine?"

She tucked her cell phone into her back pocket.

"I'm Special Agent Pappandreous. I need to speak with you about what you saw."

"Special Agent?" Those delicate brows furrowed under her bangs. "Like, FBI?"

Jesus, where does a woman get a voice like that? Whiskey laced with honey and rolled into one smooth pitch.

"Yes. I understand you witnessed the shooting? You photographed it?"

She nodded. "I was working when it all started. I took a series of shots while it was happening."

His gaze flicked to the camera she held in one hand.

"I need to see those pictures."

His first impression of her height had been correct. She was maybe three or four inches shorter than his six foot one frame. As she moved closer, the hairs on the back of his neck stood straight at attention. She smelled as good as she looked and his nostrils flared.

"It all went down so fast," she said. "But I got some good shots." Handing him the camera, she added, "Press this button to advance."

The first few pictures showed his witness ambling along the sidewalk, hands in his pockets. There was a smug, satisfied smile on his face as he was flanked by the two agents assigned to protect him. Ky pressed the button a few times. The next series of pictures showed the impact of the bullets as they pierced one of his agents, the next detailing the second man as a single shot impaled the center of his forehead. Shock, horror, and stark fear replaced the smile on his witness's face as he bent forward and appeared to run from the bullets. The next few photos showed him struck and then felled by several shots, all clustered in his back. Ky depressed the Advance button again. The photographer had moved to view a black van with no windows on the sides or any identifiable markings on the body. He wanted to curse when he saw it, thinking the van would be a dead end, when he flipped the Advance button again to see she'd zoomed in on the license plate.

Elated, he glanced up and found her eyes trained on him.

"I need you to come with me." He grabbed her arm.

"Where?" She stretched across him and tried to take back her camera. Ky held it up and away from her reach.

"My office. I need a written statement from you about what you saw. It's better to do it now, right away, so you don't forget any details, anything of importance."

"I never forget details," she said, reaching across him again. "Can I please have my camera? I don't like anyone carrying it but me."

"This piece of equipment is the only link to finding out who killed my men. It's not leaving my hands."

She stopped and tried to pull her arm out of his grip. Ky tightened his grasp.

"Look, Agent Pappajohn—"

"Pappandreous," he corrected. It was a common mistake, one he'd heard a number of times in his career, but having her say it, wrapping the syllables around those pouty lips with that husky voice, for some reason, charmed him.

"Whatever." She swiped her free hand in the air. "I want my camera."

"You'll get it back, I assure you." He started walking, giving her no choice but to follow.

Before she could protest again, he stopped. "Jon?" His partner turned from the interview he was conducting with a restaurant waiter. "Can you have someone escort Miss Laine back to the office? She needs to have her statement written up."

"Sure, Papps."

"Wait a second," Gemma said, wrenching her arm from his grip. The smooth, natural warmth in her voice had turned to frosted ice. “I know my rights. I’ll be happy to give you a statement, but I want my camera. *Now.*”

“I won’t break it, Miss Laine, if that’s what you’re worried about.”

“Then stop holding it like it’s a cheap piece of tin! Give it back to me. I’ll hold it.”

“This is digital, right?” Jon Winters stepped between them and asked her.

“Yes, and it’s very expensive,” Gemma said, still trying to yank it from Ky’s hand.

“We really only need the SD card then, Papps, not the camera.”

“True.” Ky examined the device, found the button to expel the memory card and depressed it. He took the card and slipped it into his pocket. “Here.” He handed the camera back to her.

“Wait a minute.” She clutched it to her chest as if she were protecting a child from a threat. “You can’t keep the card. All my work is on it.”

“We won’t erase anything you need,” Ky told her. “Or let anything happen to it.”

“This is ridiculous.” Gemma blew at her bangs. “How do I know you won’t keep it as some kind of evidence? I haven’t uploaded the pictures I took today. I need those shots.”

“I told you you’d get the card back,” Ky said, his patience wavering. “Now, we’re wasting time. Jon?” Dismissing them, he walked away and over to the scene of the shooting.

* * *

Gemma paced the small room for the hundredth time, her arms folded across her chest, desperately wanting to hit something.

No, not something. *Someone.* Agent Pappa-pain, or whatever the heck his name was.

For more than two hours she’d been confined to this cramped and drab room. During the first, she’d written, in full detail, everything she’d witnessed on the street corner. Agent Winters had guided her through the questions while she wrote the answers in her smooth, precise script. When they were finished, he’d left her, promising to return shortly.

His definition of *shortly* was exceedingly different from hers.

With a heavy sigh, she plopped back down into a metal chair, arms still crossed. Agent Moron. Reconsidering, she added, *a hunky moron*, but one nonetheless.

She’d been speaking on the phone when she’d first turned and seen him approaching her. Her first thought had been *serious eye candy.*

Clad in a supremely well-fitted dark blue suit, he simply tore up the pavement on his way to her, those long legs striding with purpose and determination in each step. His face was a contradiction in origins. Deep, milk chocolate–colored hair, cut just a bit too short for her liking, had soft, gold flecks framing his temples and the top of his head. His skin was a light golden brown, giving the impression he spent a great deal of time in the sun. Eyes the color of the sea at sunrise, so light green they almost appeared crystal with the sun hitting them, were surrounded by jet-black eyelashes Gemma admitted she was jealous of. His face was angular, the jaw tapering into a rock solid *V* at its tip, a small crevice winking out right below his lower lip.

All in all, it was face she wanted to photograph, knowing just the way she'd capture it. The fact he'd yanked her along after him like an errant child got her dander up. Coupled with the way he'd carelessly held her camera made her want to kick some sense into him.

God, what a day.

All she'd planned on doing was spending a few hours walking along the city streets, shooting interesting faces. She was almost done when the dapper-looking gentleman alighted from the restaurant, a self-satisfied smile on his lips. Gemma recognized that smile. It was the same one she always had after treating herself to some well-deserved Cherry Garcia after a tough, demanding day. She knew without a doubt the man had just eaten a pleasant meal. Satisfaction like that came only from two things: good food or great sex. Since he was walking along with two testosterone hulks in conservative suits, she figured it was the food part of the equation dancing on his face.

In the blink of her camera shutter's eye, the scene had changed to one of horror. Professional instinct made her continue shooting the events as they unfolded, capturing the slaying of the three men. She turned her camera when she realized the direction the shots were coming from, and through her viewfinder found the van speeding off. Pointing her lens at its retreating back, she zoomed in on the license plate. Without even thinking about the composition of the shot, she snapped as fast as she could, trying to get as much information as possible.

After the van escaped, she ran to the victims to see if she could help in any way. It was too late for all three of them. The sound of sirens glued her to the spot. She'd located the first officers to arrive, told one of them she had footage of the incident, and then had been led away from the scene to wait. A quick call to her brother-in-law Josh was interrupted by the arrival of the FBI agent.

* * *

Ky watched her pace the length of the room from the video camera mounted on the wall in the corner. "What do we know about her?"

"Aside from the obvious?" Jon's grin was quick. "She's awfully easy on the eyes."

"Aside from the obvious," Ky said, his own gaze never leaving the monitor.

"Twenty-eight, single, lives alone. Her professional rep is pretty impressive."

"How so?"

"Ever heard of chef Kandy Laine?"

His eyes widened. "My mom and YiaYia love her. They have all her books, used to watch her show every time it was on. Laine? Any relation?"

"Sister. One of seven. Owns her own photography business called GAL Photos. Pretty famous in her own right. She shot three magazine covers last month alone. She's what's called in the entertainment biz the 'go-to' when you need a great headshot."

"So what was she doing in midtown today when our witness bought it?"

"Seems she's doing a coffee table book of faces. Today she was walking around, looking for interesting ones, spotted Calafano, and thought he'd make a good subject. She started snapping away and then the proverbial shit hit the fan."

Ky nodded.

"Here." Jon handed him a copy of her typed statement. "Read it for yourself."

Ky took it and within a few minutes had it committed to memory.

"You don't think there's anything more to this, do you?" Jon asked. "I mean, she was just in the wrong place at the wrong time, right?"

"Appears that way," Ky answered. "I have a few more questions before we let her go, though."

"She's still asking about the SD card. Wants it back, undamaged and unaltered. Now."

"She'll get it back when we're done with it," Ky said, buttoning his jacket.

When he entered the conference room a moment later, he thought he was prepared for the jolt that seeing her in the flesh would cause again. He was wrong. The second he opened the door and saw her eyes tracking him like a caged animal, he realized just how wrong. A subtle, unmistakable, pang of unease sliced right into his midsection, cutting off all circulation except to his groin. With a mental and physical shake, he approached her.

Anger percolated through her from across the room.

"Miss Laine—"

"Why am I still here? I gave my statement. I want my memory card and I want to go home. I have a ton of work to do."

Ky reached down deep to curb his temper. "I need to clarify a few things first."

"What things?" She stood and leaned against the wall, leveling him with a hard stare. "I told your partner everything I remember. In vivid detail."

"Yes, I read your statement. Please." He motioned to the chair she'd vacated. "Have a seat."

"I'd rather stand."

He couldn't tell if she was being purposefully obnoxious when her chin tilted defiantly up at him or if it was a character trait. Regardless, he pulled the facing chair from the table and sat.

"You mentioned in your statement you were out walking when you noticed the shooting."

"No, that's not correct." She must have forgotten her reason for standing because she moved back to the chair and sat. "I said I was out working and noticed the trio of men coming out of the restaurant."

Ky knew that. He wanted to see if she'd change any of the details with time.

"The older man had an attention-grabbing face," she continued, resting her arms on the table. "I'm on the lookout for interesting faces."

"So you notice him, see his face, and decide, what? To take his picture? Just like that?"

She nodded. "It's what I do. I'm working on a book called *Faces of New York.*"

"What was so fascinating about his?"

"It wasn't so much his face as the expression on it," she said. "He'd just come out of Sam's. I figured he'd eaten lunch because he was patting his stomach and had a contented, gratified smile on his lips. So I took his picture. A series of them, in fact, as he continued walking."

"Why did you continue snapping away? You had your shot. Why take more?"

Gemma blew out a breath and leaned back in the chair, arms crossed over her chest again. "Do you know anything about photography?"

"No, not really."

Gemma sliced a fingers through the sides of her hair and tucked the strands behind her ears. It refused to settle, though, and fell back across her cheeks the moment she removed her hand.

"There's more to getting the shot you want than merely pressing a button. You have to consider the lighting and the motion—or absence of it. A million different things go into capturing the perfect image. A person's face changes in a millisecond. You can go from an expression of rapture to the simple turning up of the lips in the time it takes for a heart to beat just once. I wanted to make sure I got the look I wanted to convey. Taking several shots in a continuum ensures I will."

Ky nodded. "So the only thing you knew about the older man was you liked the expression on his face?"

"Yes."

"You had no idea who he was?"

"No. I still don't. All I know is he and two other men were gunned down on a New York City street. And because of some quirk of nature, I was there when it happened."

Ky waited a beat. "What made you continue taking pictures after the shooting started? Most people ran for cover, got out of harm's way. You stayed where you were and continued to photograph what was happening. I have to ask myself why."

Gemma's eyes narrowed. "What do you mean?"

"You're not a news reporter or a photojournalist. You don't work for any national news publications. You own your own business, work for yourself. What were you hoping to gain from continuing to shoot?"

Gemma shot up, the chair falling to the floor behind her with a resounding thwack. "Your implication is insulting. You think I continued filming for some dark ulterior motive, don't you? Like I wanted to sell the pictures or in some way benefit from them. That's not only insulting, it's disgusting."

"I don't think I said anything along those lines."

"Your veiled wording implies otherwise. For your bigoted information, my brother-in-law is in private security. I've assisted him a few times with surveillance photography, even helped his partner in various filming techniques when he's gone undercover. I'm not a paparazzo, Agent"—she flipped her hand in the air in lieu of addressing him by name—"looking for my next big photographic score. I'm a professional photographer, and I reacted as one today. I kept shooting because I could. I didn't think I was in any danger. The van was speeding away from me, not toward me."

Ky looked across the table at her, weighing her words. "For the record, again, it's Pappandreous, and I never assumed you were anything other than what you've stated, Miss Laine. I simply need to make sure you had no prior knowledge of the men who were gunned down today."

"I don't know them from Adam." Her voice dropped a notch as her gaze bore into his.

Ky wanted to believe her, but a cautious regard for human nature had always served him well.

"Do you recognize the name Mario Calafano?"

Her eyes narrowed again, her gaze never leaving his. "It sounds familiar, but I'm not sure. Why?"

Instead of answering he asked, "How about Jackson Hunter or Paul Ingersall?"

She shook her head. "No."

Ky nodded. Rising, he told her, "I think we're finished for now, Miss Laine. We have your contact information. We'll call when we're done with the memory card."

"I can't have it now?"

The childlike whine in her husky voice reminded him of his nieces and nephews when they didn't get their way or something they wanted.

"We haven't finished with it yet. But I assure you, I'll get it back to you."

"When?"

"As I said, when we're finished with it."

"This blows." She frowned and crossed her arms in front of her again, and this time her hands were fisted.

It wouldn't have surprised him if she stomped her foot next. Reaching into his pocket, he pulled out his card. "These are my contact numbers. If you don't hear from me in a few days, feel free to get in touch."

"A few days?" she cried. "That's a lifetime to someone on a publishing deadline. I have a lot of work on that card and it needs to be uploaded and edited."

"A few days are all we need."

She mumbled something he couldn't hear and didn't think he wanted to, figuring it was something derogatory about himself. Ky made arrangements for an agent to drive her home and then watched as she was escorted out of the office.

"Hell hath no fury." Jon chuckled.

"The quote pertains to a woman scorned."

"Scorned or not, she's one seriously pissed, but fine-looking, female."

Ky agreed, on both counts. "Come on. We've got work to do."

* * *

Gemma let herself into her condo, threw her keys down on the entrance table, toed off her shoes, and then plopped down onto her couch.

"Jerk." She rubbed her tired eyes with the palms of her hands and dropped her chin to her chest. "Special Agent Jerk."

Seething, she thought about all the great shots she'd gotten before the shooting. Pictures she now couldn't work on. An entire day's filming, shot. *Literally*. Shot to hell.

And there were some great images in the batch, too. The toddler twins running down the street with their parents laughingly chasing after them; the tiny, elderly lady carrying her equally frail Pomeranian; the Asian shopkeeper sweeping outside her grocery store, the e-cigarette dangling from the corner of her mouth.

All pictures she knew would be perfect for the book. Only now she had to wait for them to be returned. And if there was one thing Gemma Laine hated, it was waiting.

That, and arrogant Special Agents.

She blew out a breath, making her bangs dance up off her forehead. Since seven a.m., she'd been walking around Manhattan, looking for inspiration. She hadn't stopped to eat or drink before the shooting, and waiting at FBI headquarters had chewed up another few hours with nothing in her system. A loud growl snarled up from her empty stomach and echoed in the apartment.

A quick inventory of the refrigerator reminded her she'd wanted to stop at the local grocery today when she'd finished working. All that stared back at her from the cool interior was a pint of skim milk, a few bottles of beer from the last time her sister and brother-in-law visited, and three eggs.

"Oh, well. An omelet it is."

She put the frying pan her sister had given her for Christmas on the stovetop and turned the coil to medium heat. She'd never be the chef Kandy was, but she knew the basics for making a great breakfast. After whisking the eggs with some of the milk, she added a sprinkling of black pepper and nutmeg to the mix.

When the pan was the perfect temperature and she was about to pour in the eggs, the doorbell rang.

Since she lived in a doorman-controlled condo and all her family were well-known to the man on duty, she assumed it was one of them. Without looking through the peephole, she opened the door. Her smile died in an instant when a gun flashed in front of her face.

"Scream and I'll shoot," the man holding the gun said.

Gemma's first instinct was to slam the door. She pulled back, using the door as armor and pushed. Her intruder pushed right back, knocking her to the floor when the force of the door smashed into her. Flat on her butt, she crab-crawled backward and tried to stand while the man flew into the apartment, banged the door shut, and was on her in a second.

He grabbed a fistful of her hair and pulled her up by it.

Tears of pain sprang into her eyes. She ignored them, slipping into full defense mode. She flattened one of her hands over the one he had on her hair, pushed down, and twisted, turning to face him as she'd been taught to do. She knew if she stood she'd be taller than he was, so she stayed stooped. He was attempting to yank on her hair again, but Gemma pulled her other hand back and, opening the web between her thumb and index finger wide, shot her hand out like a snake, striking him with the *V* straight in the throat.

The hit had its intended effect. He let go of her hair and fell backward, one of his hands automatically going to his gullet. Gemma took a split second to stand tall, stepped one foot back, and then, raising her opposite leg, kicked him full force straight in the chest with the ball of her foot, knocking him back. The gun dropped from his hand and she ran to it, but he reached out and grabbed her leg, jerking her down hard to the floor. Gemma felt her knee splinter into the hardwood and she recoiled into a fetal position from the impact. With his advantage, the intruder jumped over her, grabbed the gun, and pointed it straight at her face again.

"Bitch! I should kill you now." His breathing was labored, his neck bright red and raw from her strike, his voice raspy and raw like sandpaper gliding over fresh wood.

"What do you want?" The gun bobbed up and down in his hand as she stared down its barrel.

"Where is it?"

"What?"

"The camera you were using today." His eyes flicked around the living room and then back to her, the gun still pointed straight at her face. "Where is it?" he repeated.

"I don't have it. The police took it." She rubbed her knee, gauging if she'd be able to stand. It wasn't broken, but she'd landed hard.

"Try again. I watched you leave the FBI building. You had it in your hands. Now stop wasting my time and give it to me."

Gemma quickly ran through all her options in her head. Her knee was pounding, he had a lethal weapon pointed at her face, and she was on the floor, on her butt. A very bad position to deal from. Her gaze swept from the gun to the man's face, memorizing it, detail by detail.

"It's in the kitchen," she told him, rolling over and trying to rise up on her non-injured leg.

"Get it. Now."

"My knee is blown," she told him, standing upright on her good foot. "I can't move fast."

To prove her point she tried to walk and hobbled, almost going down to the floor again.

Her intruder swore. "Forget it. I'll get it." He turned his head, the gun still directed at her. "In here?"

"It's on the table."

He never moved from her sight as he went into the kitchen. Gemma took the few moments to think what to do.

With the camera in his hand, he popped the back open and asked, "Where's the memory card?"

"The FBI took it."

He swore again and threw the camera against the wall, smashing it. The anger on his face was murderous as he came toward her.

"You stupid bitch. You could have told me that instead of wasting my time."

He lifted the gun to her eye level and, just as he pulled back on the trigger, Gemma went into action. Sidestepping backward on her uninjured leg, she brought the other one up to her chest and in one fluid, swift move, knocked the gun from his hand with the front of her foot. Pain recoiled all the way up her leg, but she ignored it. While the gun bounced across the floor, she spun and, using her injured leg again, struck three swift kicks to his temple, knocking him to the floor. The effect of the single-footed spin unbalanced her and made her fall flat on her backside again. Her recovery was swifter than his, though, and she shot up, jumped to the door on her good leg, and, throwing it open, screamed as loud as she could.

She fell into the hall. It was early evening, thankfully, and doors around her opened, quizzical heads popping out from the commotion of her shouting.

The intruder didn't waste a second. He shot up and ran from the apartment, sprinting down the hallway, and toward the stairs.

Gemma, breathing hard and in serious pain, collapsed against the wall as her neighbors gathered around her.

CPSIA information can be obtained
at www.ICGtesting.com
Printed in the USA
FSOW01n1459280217
31247FS

9 781516 1